IF I Die in Juárez

Camino del Sol

A Latina and Latino Literary Series

IF I Die in Juárez

Stella Pope Duarte

THE UNIVERSITY OF ARIZONA PRESS / TUCSON

Dedicated to the hundreds of
young women who have disappeared,
las desaparecidas,
brutally murdered in Ciudad Juárez,
Chihuahua, Mexico.

The University of Arizona Press
© 2008 Stella Pope Duarte

Library of Congress Cataloging-in-Publication Data
appear on the last printed page of this book.

Publication of this book is made possible in part by
the proceeds of a permanent endowment created with
the assistance of a Challenge Grant from the National
Endowment for the Humanities, a federal agency.

Manufactured in the United States of America on acid-free,
archival-quality paper.

13   12   11   10   09   08   6   5   4   3   2   1

The poem "Kéti Ono A'li Rawéwali" (The Creator and a
New Day) was written in Rarámuri and Spanish by Martín
"Makawi" Chávez Ramirez, and translated into English by
the author.

Acknowledgments

When Francisca Montoya heard that I needed to travel to Ciudad Juárez, she immediately volunteered to go with me. Francisca, thank you for your enthusiasm and for introducing me to my beautiful Juárez family: Piedad Huerta and her husband Javier Saucedo, and their children Sergio, Melissa, and Iván. Gracias to all for your help and hospitality. Emmy Pérez and her husband Peter Viola, and Dora Villa and her wonderful parents Gabriel and Irene Villa, were the perfect hosts in El Paso as I continued my trips into Juárez—thank you. Professor David Foster, thank you for your support of my work and for introducing me to Ramona Ortiz, former reporter for *El Diario*, who gave me insights into the criminal investigations. Esther Chávez Cano, founder of the Casa Amiga Crisis Center in Juárez, and Charles Bowden, fellow writer, thank you for the wealth of information you shared about the crimes and day-to-day life along the border. Patti Hartmann of the University of Arizona Press, cheers to you for your confidence in the merit and importance of this project, and John Mulvihill, thank you for the work done in editing the manuscript. With my deepest respect and gratitude, I commend las mujeres, the women who told me the stories of their precious daughters—with all my heart, gracias. May justice and God's blessings abound.

Zona del Canal, Ciudad Juárez, 1995

1 Evita dreamed of peace, once, as a child. It appeared to her as a huge gust of wind, rushing in through an open door, surprising her with its urgency and power. Peace was a miracle compared to her real life, and in her dream it touched her and made her feel as if she was a speck of dust protected by God's almighty hand. Within a few days, the dream of peace had faded for Evita, and she resumed her real life—troubled and uncertain—on the streets of Juárez. Yet she kept a little space hidden in her memory for the hope of peace.

Evita had never accomplished anything in the school she had attended, Academia de Los Niños Héroes, which was dedicated to the brave young soldiers who had fought to their death during the Mexican-American War. She spent two years at a time in most grades because her teachers said it didn't matter anyway, as she was small for her age and no one would know the difference. There were places in Evita's brain where words stuck together like mismatched beads. Numbers were easier to learn, not complicated by the dips, curves, circles, and diagonal lines of the alphabet. Numbers stood in neat little rows, or one on top of another, like the tight stitches of her mother's needlepoint. She could keep track of numbers in the same way she followed a colored thread in a pattern of tiny stitches until she could see the whole image inside her head. Even before her mother completed an intricate piece of work, Evita could sketch out the final product on a piece of paper, adding fancy curlicues for stems and leaves on flower patterns. People said it was almost magical what Evita could do and asked her to explain how she was able to follow complicated patterns, considering she couldn't even read. Evita

1

couldn't give an answer. Things appeared to her in her mind—she had no way of knowing how they got there.

At school, children said Evita was like the dot at the end of a sentence, little and stupid. Evita didn't want to be the dot at the end of a sentence; so one day she drew a big butterfly and named it after herself. With broken bits of crayon, Evita drew huge colorful wings that were so big she needed two pieces of paper instead of one. She took her time to color each wing, filling in the space with different colors, carefully staying inside the lines. Then she glued the two pieces of paper together and pretended to flap the butterfly wings up and down.

Finally, Evita was satisfied that the butterfly would be able to fly happily away, higher and higher over the tattered school building of Academia de Los Niños Héroes, with its three cramped classrooms, cracked windows, and leaky roof. Higher and higher the butterfly would flutter, making its escape, until the colors of the Mexican flag waving listlessly on a wooden pole outside the front entrance would fade away. Already Evita felt the wind rushing through her hair, and felt light as a feather as she flew higher and higher into the clouds, her bright wings outstretched and shimmering in the sun. She proudly took the picture to her teacher, expecting to be told how lovely it was. Instead her teacher frowned at her.

"Why did you draw wings that big?"

"So the butterfly can fly away."

When Evita saw her teacher's frown turn into a scowl, she was sorry for what she had said. She shrugged her skinny shoulders, small bony handlebars outlined under her white blouse.

"That's ridiculous! Draw small wings, like this."

Then her teacher drew two shapes that looked like tiny earlobes. As children nearby laughed at her, Evita looked down at her shoes. She was good at looking down at her shoes, which were actually her sister Lety's ragged tennis shoes, two sizes too big for her. Evita had to lace the tennis shoes extra tight so they wouldn't slip off her feet when she walked. She took the picture of the butterfly in her hands and stumbled away on Lety's big shoes, feeling herself falling from the sky with a thud and landing on the desolate patch of sandy ground that made up the school playground. Now she would never escape.

The teacher was angry at Evita for wasting paper. She considered herself industrious and ahead of the game in planning for her classroom, which had students who, in her mind, would be hard pressed to amount to anything at all, considering most of their parents didn't even know how to read or write. It had taken her months to gather enough scrap paper for her classroom from a printing company that advertised itself as supporting the education of the poor in Juárez—and now Evita had taken advantage of her good will by wasting paper. The teacher told Evita that under no circumstances should she ever draw butterfly wings that big; so Evita never drew the butterfly again.

Some people said Evita had problems in her head because her mother, Brisa, drank and didn't tend to herself like she should have when she was pregnant. Others said she was from a family of freaks, all deformed in some way. Evita thought people were right—she *was* from a family of freaks. Her older brother, Reynaldo, had burned his arms, chest, and neck as a child, playing with firecrackers that had exploded in a dump site filled with chemical wastes from an American factory, and bore the scars from the accident for the rest of his life. Her sister, Lety, limped on her left side because she had been born with one leg shorter than the other. Later, a doctor examined Lety closely and told Brisa that her daughter's legs were the same size; it was her hip that was deformed. In her mind, Brisa compiled a list of all her relatives who had ever been born with deformed hips, but found none. From then on, she blamed her husband, Hermilio, for Lety's deformity.

Relatives said Evita was a living bone, pale and anemic, and that someday she would fade away and no one would remember what she looked like. Evita's lips, eyebrows, and eyelashes blended into her skin like watercolors that lingered on her face, threatening to disappear entirely the next time she scrubbed her face. Evita looked into the mirror, worried, imagining she was already disappearing.

To make matters worse, her baby brother, Fidel, was born an albino in 1989, when Evita was only seven years old. She had waited for him for nine months, expecting to hold a healthy baby brother in her arms and to show him off to her friends. When she saw him, she was shocked and gave up any hope of ever having a normal family. Every day, Evita prayed for Fidel to turn brown like the rest of the family, but it never happened. She looked into his eyes, which were sometimes blue and at other times green or orange or yellow, and she tossed and turned at night trying to figure out why her brother had eyes that changed colors. Her mother told her Fidel was born an albino because she had witnessed a murder on the streets of Juárez when she was pregnant with him. She got so scared, her skin had turned white, and her blood pressure had gone down to zero. It was a wonder her heart hadn't stopped altogether. The fear, el susto, went to Fidel in the womb, and that was why he was born with no pigment in his skin. The fear also froze her womb in a deadly grip, she said, making it impossible for her to conceive another child. After her mother's story, Evita walked around for a long time afraid of being afraid and storing up el susto inside her, an energy that could disfigure her and make her infertile for the rest of her life.

Fidel was one of the very few albinos ever born in Juárez, and reporters from *El Diario* were curious and asked to come by to write up his story. The reporters were used to children with strange diseases caused by contaminated air, water, and dirt, but they had never seen an albino up close and wanted to be the first to examine the phenomenon. After the newspaper printed Fidel's picture and his story, people stopped by the house and stood around watching him in his cradle as if he was a rare breed of insect. After a week of this, Brisa got mad and said her son wasn't a sideshow in a circus, and if they wanted to enjoy freaks, they should look in the mirror. At school, children started calling Evita "el Albino's sister," as if she had never had another name. It made her mad because she loved her brother, and their taunts made her feel ashamed of him.

Fidel didn't last long. One day, when he was only two and a half years old, he slipped into a pail of water, headfirst, and drowned before anyone could pull him out. Evita's mother suspected he had been looking at his own reflection in the water and had been frightened. Evita remembered kissing Fidel's small face in his coffin and putting a red rose in his hands that looked elegant against his white clothes and skin. Fidel had loved bright colors, and Evita suspected he would be happy as he made his way to Heaven with a bright red rose in his hands.

After Fidel's death, hope became a circle of light for Evita that faded away in the distance, invisible and illusive. Huge dark spikes appeared inside her, sharp as knives, and pushed up to the surface of her skin, making painful red blotches appear. Her mother said she was suffering from an allergic reaction and bought an herbal tea for her to drink. The blotches disappeared after a few days, only to return to Evita in times of great pain for the rest of her life. Her brother's death led Evita to believe that someone as strange and beautiful as Fidel was like the butterfly she had drawn in school—too beautiful to live for very long.

Ricardo was the only one of her mother's boyfriends who had ever been good to Evita. He was gentle and handsome, dignified in appearance and soft-spoken. Compared to the other men in her mother's life, he looked like a prince. Truly, Evita didn't know why he spent so much time with her mother, except out of pity, or maybe because her mother was older and he needed a woman to take care of him. Brisa worked at needlepoint and made beautiful covers for beds and fancy lace doilies, pillows, and tablecloths embroidered with flowers, birds, and hearts. They were sold to tourists who made their way into Ciudad Juárez, and sometimes they were taken to other cities and sold for more profits than Brisa would ever see.

One day, Ricardo took Evita with him to deliver her mother's embroidered goods at stores he did business with because Brisa was sick in bed and couldn't accompany him. Brisa told Ricardo to make only a few stops and to hurry home. Then she looked sternly at Evita and told her to act like a respectful young lady and not like una escuincla, a brat, who didn't know her right foot from her left. Evita saw suspicion rise on her mother's face in the form of a frown that started between her eyebrows and spread like a shadow over her face. Her mother's frown made Evita nervous, and she tied Lety's shoes on her feet tighter than ever.

Evita and Ricardo traveled in his car from la colonia Quinto Sol to the marketplace in the center of town, a distance of several kilometers. There wasn't much to talk about except the weather and the latest movies showing at the cinema at Cuauhtémoc Square. In those days, Evita wasn't sure what men liked to talk about, so she spent her time staring out the car window to avoid looking at Ricardo. At every stop, Evita went through the embroidered goods, some stored in clear plastic bags, others wrapped in colorful tissue paper, making sure the orders were correct. She checked off each item on a pad of paper, very businesslike, making neat little arrows for checks, then she wrote down addresses and where the goods were going. She was glad she didn't have to do much thinking or reading, only checking off addresses and recording numbers. Ricardo collected the money and found out how many had been sold and how many more were needed. Evita didn't see much money made in spite of her mother's hard work, but it was obvious that her mother was happier than ever. Evita's older brother, Reynaldo, had a job in El Paso; her sister, Lety, in spite of her bad leg, was married and living with her husband; and her mother had a boyfriend that other women envied—women who gossiped, chismosas, who licked their lips when they had another tale to tell.

Ricardo asked Evita if she wanted to stop by una taquería and get something to eat, since they had finished for the day with time to spare. Evita thought of her mother and her huge shadowy frown, and said she wasn't hungry, but Ricardo convinced her that they would order something small and it wouldn't take long at all. He put his arm around Evita's shoulder, and she felt sorry for him because he said he was starving.

They went to a place called Taquito Sabroso, off la boulevard Diez y Seis de Septiembre, which had a taco in red lights flashing in the window. It wasn't much, but Evita felt proud walking in with Ricardo and waiting for him to choose a table for them, as she had seen her mother do. Ricardo bought her two tacos al pastor, her favorite, meat spiced with chile and pineapple juice, packed into a soft warm corn tortilla. He got himself tacos de carne asada, grilled meat with pico de gallo, a mixture of jalapeños, tomato, cabbage, onions, and spices. They sat together at a small table, and Ricardo took a pen and pad of paper and started going over the accounts. Evita had never spent any time alone with Ricardo, and she took the opportunity to study his face closely. She noticed his neatly trimmed moustache, the small mole over his left eyebrow, and the way he bit his lower lip as he wrote down numbers in vertical columns. She inhaled the scent of his body—a sweet smell. Everything about Ricardo was hard and solid, and Evita liked it because it was opposite of her own pale disappearing form.

As they ate their tacos, they shared the pad of paper and pen between them, correcting their figures. They had filled at least five orders, and three new orders had been placed. It had been a good day, considering that some days didn't bring any sales at all. Then Ricardo took a sip of Evita's Coke. Although he did it in a casual manner, it surprised Evita, because he often did the same thing with her mother, eating from her plate or drinking from her glass. When Evita took a sip through the same straw, it was as if she had kissed Ricardo. Her face got red, and she shifted uncomfortably in her chair as she thought of her mother with her arms wound tightly around Ricardo when they sat together on the couch watching TV. She curled her fingers over the taco she was eating, suddenly ashamed of her ragged fingernails and the tiny white blotches on her thumbnails that girls at school told her represented the number of boyfriends she would have in her lifetime. She looked out the window nervously, feeling guilty about thinking Ricardo was handsome. People were coming and going into la taquería, and that made her feel better, since her mother wouldn't be able to say she had been alone with him. Inside the place, people relaxed at tables, husbands with their wives and children, some of them watching a TV on the counter while they ate their food.

"You're bright, Evita," Ricardo told her. "I swear you could manage your own business and make a fortune. What do you think of that? Then I'd be working for you!"

Ricardo smiled at her, and she realized she had never seen him smile that way at her mother. Then she giggled at the thought of Ricardo working for her. Her dark eyes sparkled with amusement. She swept a few strands of hair from her forehead and leaned toward him.

"No, that would never happen! I've never been smart. I never finished school. There's not much I can do."

"Nonsense, ni lo pienses, you can do all you decide." Then he pointed to his heart. "It begins in here—the things we can do. Anybody can be smart, but not many can follow their hearts and realize who they truly are."

Ricardo's words moved Evita. A power she had never known sparked in her mind, and something else—fear. Wasn't her mother his business partner? She got so confused her fingers trembled, and she dropped the pad of paper she was writing on. Ricardo picked it up before she did, and he smiled and patted her hand. Evita felt the warmth of his hand on hers and wanted him to keep his hand there. No man had ever touched her so gently, so lovingly, and it made her feel dizzy just thinking about it. She couldn't remember the touch of her father's hand, or even what her father had looked like, and suddenly she longed to reach over and hold Ricardo's hand. He seemed unaware of all she was feeling and instead called the waitress over to give him the check.

The waitress put down a tray of dishes she was carrying and walked to their table wiping her hands on her apron. She was a dark round woman, her neck creased with sweaty bands of flesh. She smiled sweetly at Ricardo, as if she was ready to flirt with him.

"Your daughter?"

"No, my business partner." Evita watched the woman's smile turn to a frown.

"We're selling things her mother makes," Ricardo assured her. "It's nothing more than that. In fact, if you'd like, I can show you what we have for sale."

"Save them for someone else," she said. "Really, we have all we need here." Then she looked sideways at Ricardo. He told her to keep the change, and she went off with the money. He looked at Evita and shook his head, as if the waitress had just made a big mistake.

Nothing more than that. Ricardo's words held fast in Evita's mind. He said the words with great conviction. She was only someone helping him sell her mother's goods on the streets of Juárez. They were two people of thousands, like ants, who roamed endlessly up and down the bustling streets selling something—anything—rather than starve. His words made her want to mean something to him, if only for a few minutes at lunch. The woman returned to clear the table. She looked closely at Evita. Her eyes narrowed.

"Aren't you Brisa Reynosa's daughter?"

"Yes, she's my mother."

"I remember when your brother, el Albino, died. Poor little thing."

The woman sighed out loud. Then she looked at Ricardo with a sense of knowing that left Evita uncomfortable. Ricardo ignored the woman and took up the pad and pen and said they had to move on. But within minutes the waitress had called Brisa and reported to her that Evita was flirting with Ricardo, coquetiando, and that he was seducing her, and God only knew if anything had already happened—maybe Evita wasn't even a virgin anymore. Men were good at secrecy and lies and could corral a disobedient daughter into doing anything they wanted. She said if she was Evita's mother, she would tell Ricardo what she thought about men who made passes at thirteen-year-old girls, and what harm could come to them, even death by a woman who found out and exploded in a jealous rage.

So when Evita got home, her mother had her clothes waiting for her in two big paper bags, everything scrambled and poking out the tops every which way. Brisa's face was red with anger, her eyes bloodshot. The veins stuck out from her neck as she yelled.

"Get out, you shameless whore! You have no respect for the mother who has been here for you all your life—so get out!"

Evita couldn't say a thing to defend herself, as by now her mother had worked herself up into a frenzy. Evita stood before her mother shivering, even though it was July in Juárez and the heat was unbearable. She was sweating so much her hair looked like a sponge around her head. This time she wasn't running away like she had before, five times at least throughout her childhood. This time her mother was kicking her out.

The last she saw of her mother, she was fighting with Ricardo, telling him that she had trusted him for one day, and he had failed her. Ricardo yelled back at Brisa, defending himself, telling her that Evita was like his own daughter. Evita knew her mother's frenzy wouldn't stop for hours, but it made her feel good that Ricardo was defending her.

In her mind, Evita saw the dark streets of Juárez, the shapes of men at night, the hiding, the alleys, the houses she might, or might not, be welcomed in. Dusk was falling over the city, and streetlights blinked on. Evita picked up the two paper bags stuffed with her belongings, folded down the tops of the bags to form makeshift handles, and left with her face toward the setting sun.

Brisa thought Evita would go to Lety's house. She planned to call her older daughter later and explain what had happened. But Evita had no intention of going to Lety's house and putting up with her husband, Julio. Instead, she went to Isidora's, a woman she had met once in la Plaza who had told her that if she was ever kicked out on the streets, she could come to her house.

2 Evita met Isidora when she ran away from home at the age of ten. Isidora was in la Plaza sitting on a stone ledge, and she asked Evita to help her get up. Evita was flattered when Isidora spoke to her, as she had spent hours in la Plaza with no one seeming to notice her. She looked at Isidora and wondered how she would help her get up, as the woman was big and lumpy, and her legs looked like two dark stumps

under her skirt. Isidora balanced herself on Evita's skinny shoulder, the only place on her body she could hold onto. Then she asked Evita what she was doing there all alone, and Evita told her that her mother was fighting with one of her boyfriends, and she had to wait until it was all over. Isidora put her arm around her and said she felt bad for her, a tiny girl with big problems.

They walked together to Isidora's house in la Zona del Canal, not far from el Centro and la Catedral. As they walked by la Catedral, with its white walls gleaming in the sun, Evita made the sign of the cross over herself, as she didn't want God mad at her for ignoring His presence. She didn't know what God would do to her if He got mad, and she didn't want to take any chances. Isidora watched her and crossed herself half-heartedly. "Yes, I guess God is inside and deserves respect, even though He's stubborn and doesn't answer my prayers."

Isidora hung onto Evita's shoulder for support as she made her slow trek across the busy streets of Juárez. All around them, traffic whizzed by, frenzied and noisy. Motorists honked incessantly, often making threats to each other from open car windows as the traffic backed up. Although Evita's legs were skinny and her steps didn't carry her very far, she could walk faster than Isidora and found it difficult to cross the streets with Isidora at her side and drivers waiting impatiently.

Isidora's old house was one of hundreds lined up row after row all around las zonas. The front door opened into the street, the back door into a narrow alley. The walls of Isidora's house were discolored and the plaster badly chipped and all but gone in some spots, exposing splintered wooden beams. The house was shrouded in darkness, with sunlight filtering in sluggishly from one window in the kitchen and a tiny one in the bathroom. As they walked in, Isidora switched on a lopsided lamp that made a white halo appear on the ceiling overhead. She told Evita she was planning to paint the place bright orange as soon as she got the money together, which might take her months. She was raised on a farm, she said, and missed the bright colors of the sun coming in through the open windows and door.

"We were so poor when I was a child," she told Evita, "we might as well have lived outdoors, but there was a pack of wolves living nearby, and my father, may he rest in peace, told us they would eat us up if they had the chance. Imagine that! Every night, I went to sleep afraid that a wolf would tear me to bits. And look where I ended up—in a place where people tear each other to bits. But never mind all that, we have each other."

Then she reached over and held Evita in a warm embrace, saying she reminded her of one of her daughters, a baby born prematurely with a tiny purple face. Evita rested comfortably in Isidora's huge arms, suddenly weary from waiting all day in la Plaza for her mother to stop fighting with her new man. Isidora's dark house and her embrace made Evita feel drowsy, as if she had suddenly fallen into a cradle and needed to take a nap. Isidora told her she had some errands to run and had to leave, and this roused Evita, making her flex her thin tired legs and smooth her hair down for the trip back home. Already, her head had begun to throb, as she thought of locking herself up in her dreary room.

Before long, Isidora gave Evita money to get on la rutera, the huge, lumbering bus that would take her back home again. And she gave her tacos to eat along the way, wrapped in aluminum foil so they would stay warm longer. Evita was grateful for the tacos, as she had been starving all day. Isidora told her not to forget where she lived and to come back if she needed to.

Isidora was older than Brisa, and fat, with legs striped blue and veins that formed tight knots down to her ankles. Her hair was dyed red, and her eyes were green. She had been a beautiful woman once, when she was young, but now she was a hag. She told Evita to call her by her first name, and never mind her last name—she kept her life private. We'll be friends, amigas, she told Evita as they walked into her dark house, Evita holding the two paper bags filled with her belongings. In fact, Isidora said, they would become relatives, and if anyone asked her, she should say she was her aunt, su tía.

Isidora told Evita to sit down on an old flowered couch while she got her something to drink. She walked slowly, painfully, to the kitchen that was only a few feet away and poured Evita a glass of orange juice. She told Evita her legs weren't any use to her anymore. And to think men used to whistle at her legs when she wore nylons and tacones altos, spiked heels with narrow tips. Evita couldn't imagine Isidora's legs sleek and shapely, with feet held in spiked heels. So she changed the subject, asking her if she had any children. Isidora said yes, of course she did—women can't escape having children unless there's something wrong with them. But her children grew up and abandoned her, even the baby born prematurely with the tiny purple face. She never imagined they would leave her, as everybody needs a mother. Then she looked over at Evita to see if she was one of the children who needed a mother.

"How old are you now, Evita?"

"Thirteen—but I'll be fourteen next month." Evita didn't want Isidora to think she had invited a baby into her house who would make trouble for her.

"Still young. Pobre! Did your mother beat you?"

"Well, yes. When she got mad or drunk, or when she worried about money." Evita nervously creased down the wrinkles on her skirt, clasping her hands in her lap. She felt as if she was gossiping about her own mother.

"Aren't you in school?"

"Not anymore. My mother couldn't afford the books and uniform." Evita didn't tell Isidora about being the dot at the end of a sentence at school, little and stupid.

"What's your mother's name?"

Evita hesitated, thinking that if Isidora heard her mother's name, she might remember her baby brother, Fidel, el Albino. Then she'd look at her, like everybody else did, with curiosity, and wonder what it was like having an albino for a brother.

"My mother's name is Victoria Reynosa. Do you know her?"

"Is she related to the woman by the same last name who had an albino for a baby? I remember the story in the newspaper."

Evita curled her legs under her skirt and answered quickly, "No, she's not related."

Isidora walked back slowly with the glass of juice and told Evita to drink it and she'd fix her something to eat.

"You're skinny, Evita. Too skinny! In fact, you're un hueso, a bone that wears clothes." Evita sat up straighter, trying to look more grown-up. Isidora laughed. "Don't worry. I'll make you food, plenty to eat, and you'll put on some weight. Just as long as it's weight from eating and not from getting pregnant. You've never been pregnant, have you?"

The question surprised Evita, and she didn't know what to say. Isidora looked at her closely as if she could tell if she had ever been pregnant.

Even though Evita had never thought about being pregnant, and she had never been with a man, her face turned bright red, and Isidora laughed again, patting Evita's cheek with her heavy hand.

"You look like a fox," she said. "A tiny fox who has lost her way. And some men like foxes, yes they do, but you have to be careful because men who like foxes are sometimes the worst coyotes of all!"

Evita shivered thinking about Isidora's words. Already, she sensed she had made a big mistake following Isidora to her dark house. She wanted to run out, but really there was nowhere to go. She wouldn't go to Lety's because she couldn't stand her husband, Julio, who beat up her sister when he was in a bad mood. She might go to Ofelia's, her madrina. Ofelia was her mother's cousin and became Evita's madrina when she stood with her mother and father at Evita's baptism when she was only a week old.

There was no telling how long her mother would be mad at her. Her mother nursed her grudges, always excusing her own actions with men by saying they were her business partners. Eventually, she'd go to Lety's in search of Evita and demand that she come back home. Evita was glad she wouldn't be there, because that would make her mother worry. She thought of Ricardo and wondered how long he'd stay with her mother. Isidora seemed to read her mind.

"Was this thing over one of your mother's boyfriends?"

"Well, yes. Her boyfriend took me to eat, and a waitress told my mother I was flirting with him, and that maybe we were already sleeping together."

"The nerve of that bitch! It was none of her business, and el mitote drove her crazy. I imagine she ran and told your mother." Then Isidora looked at Evita sideways, one eyebrow arched. "You weren't flirting with him, were you?"

"Of course not!" Evita wasn't sure whether or not wanting to hold Ricardo's hand meant she was flirting with him. She didn't tell Isidora she thought Ricardo was handsome. She was glad Isidora didn't ask her any more questions, as she already felt guilty about staring at him and imagining herself as his business partner.

With a wave of her hand, Isidora dismissed the image of Ricardo, as if she was a queen banishing him from her presence. "Ay, men—I tell you, I'll never know why women fight over them, even though I had a few fights myself when I was young. But you'll be safe here, Evita, as long as you don't run out on the streets alone at night. There are kidnappers loose, murderers who kill girls." Evita looked at Isidora, alarmed.

"I heard they caught them."

"That's only a lie the police tell to make themselves feel better for not doing anything about the murders. Don't worry. You can help me out for now—to get to the doctor and help clean around the house. Would you like that?"

Evita took a drink of her orange juice, sticky sweet on her tongue, and nodded. She had no choice: it was either stay at Isidora's or live on the streets.

"Put your things over there, in that room."

Isidora pointed to one of the four rooms in her house. It was dark like the rest of the house, and Evita looked into it and felt like a real fox crawling into its hole.

The next day, Evita found out there were two other girls living with Isidora. She figured they were girls who had problems with their mothers like she did, and she thought Isidora generous for taking them all in. The girls' names were Anabel and Cristal, and both were older than Evita. Anabel was sixteen, and Cristal was seventeen. Anabel was friendly with Evita, and they shared a room. There were twin beds in the room, set so close to each other they had to go sideways when they walked between them. Anabel told Evita she was from Durango and ran away from home after her mother died and left her with a stepfather and five small children. Anabel was the oldest and was the only one born to her mother from another man. After her mother died, her stepfather got the idea that Anabel could take her mother's place and be a mother to his children and sleep with him at night.

"Every night I slept between the younger children, and ese cabrón would get mad and put his hands all over me and try to make me get up. He breathed on me, and he smelled so bad—tequila, cigarettes. I don't know. One night he spit in my face and said I would regret it. That was the night I ran. All I had was the clothes on my back. I met a man and woman headed for Juárez. I lied to them and told them I had relatives in Juárez and had to get there before school started. I had stolen money from my stepfather, who never gave any of us a nickel. If it hadn't been for that money I would have never been able to get to Juárez. If he ever finds me, he'll kill me—I know he will."

Then she started to cry because she missed her mother. She said her mother made dresses for her and cooked all her favorite meals, and what would she do now that her mother was dead?

Evita thought about her own mother, and remembered her mother singing to her and lying in bed with her, rubbing her back when she didn't feel well. After Fidel's death, Brisa stayed close to Evita, finding comfort in her as she mourned the death of her baby. Then one day her mother found out that her husband, Hermilio, had fallen in love with a woman from Chihuahua City. After that, it was as if Brisa had awoke from the nightmare of her child's death, opened her eyes and noticed, for the first time, her husband's betrayal.

It wasn't very long before Hermilio moved to Chihuahua City to start a new family and forget all the misfortunes he had suffered with Brisa in Ciudad Juárez. Two years passed before Brisa met a young man named Bruno. Evita's mother changed after that, turning into someone Evita didn't recognize anymore. She became a woman who wanted to please Bruno, with money, sex, and gifts. When Bruno moved in, Lety moved out to marry her husband, Julio, even though he had a reputation for beating up on women to get his way. Evita's older brother, Reynaldo, seldom visited them from El Paso, so that left Evita alone to live with Brisa and Bruno.

Evita couldn't help growing up, and the more she matured the more Brisa became impatient with her and on the alert for any attraction between her daughter and her young lover. This made Evita want to disappear as people said she would, but instead of disappearing she became the center of Bruno's attention, because he said she looked like his little sister who was always sick with one thing or another. Evita hated being compared to his sickly sister and didn't want the man's sympathy, but she figured it was better for him to think of her as a sickly sister than someone who was becoming a woman.

Anabel talked to Evita while she put on makeup. She used powder and blue eye shadow, colored her eyebrows with a pencil, and touched her cheeks with pink blush. When she was done, she looked into the mirror and put on lipstick, bright red. Evita thought she looked beautiful. Her eyes were big and dark, her skin smooth and creamy. Her ears stuck out, but she said, oh well, nobody's perfect, and hid them under her long hair.

"I'll teach you how to put on makeup, Evita, when I get the chance. You won't need much. Your skin's light, so you'll look great in bright colors."

Evita asked Anabel where she worked, and she said it was a restaurant not too far from Isidora's house. She worked late, sometimes not returning home until two in the morning or later. Evita wanted to ask Anabel what kind of restaurant was open so late. She didn't want to believe Anabel was a prostitute. She didn't look like prostitutes Evita had seen walking up and down las zonas or sitting patiently on steps or on chairs set up outside cheap hotels, sometimes with an older woman like Isidora sitting close by.

Cristal, the other girl, was much more beautiful than Anabel. Her body was muscular and white and her breasts full. She streaked her long dark hair in lighter shades, auburn and red. Evita wanted to ask her a hundred questions about her work as a dancer, but Isidora told her not to ask Cristal any questions, as she hated to talk about herself.

Cristal wore a cross around her neck, made of shiny red beads. She hummed little tunes and ran around the house in her bare feet and a big man's T-shirt. Evita cooked for her at noon because Isidora told her Cristal danced until dawn and couldn't get up in time for breakfast. Cristal didn't talk much to Evita. She looked like she was angry all the time. She poked at her food—ate this, left that. She was picky but didn't tell Evita what she liked. It made Evita try harder to please her, as she prepared dishes she had learned from her sister, Lety. Evita didn't want Cristal angry with her, so she studied her carefully until she knew the foods she preferred—small dishes of meat, with salads, tortillas, corn, and rice.

Once, Evita saw black and blue marks on Cristal's arms and legs, and without thinking she asked her why she had bruises. Cristal frowned and looked at Evita as if she was an idiot.

"A man," she said. "A man went crazy, and this is the result. Do you think I run around bruising myself?"

"Did he hit you?"

"He liked the way I danced," she said, and refused to eat another bite of the food Evita had made for her. Evita was sorry for what she had said and cleared away the dishes, throwing the leftovers in the garbage.

Cristal gave Evita a little money every week for cooking, washing her clothes, and cleaning her room. Isidora told Evita to keep Cristal's room clean, because Cristal couldn't be bothered with housework. Evita put Cristal's clothes away in her closet, carefully hanging silk pants and blouses of all colors and gowns with plunging necklines, decorated with shiny sequins and rhinestones. In Cristal's chest of drawers, Evita arranged her fancy lace stockings, garters of all colors, see-through panties, G-strings, sexy bras, feathers in the shape of fans, and tiny disks, belts, and bracelets that glowed in the dark. She stacked up Cristal's fancy spiked heels on a shoe rack.

It was as if Evita was looking at Cristal's naked body when she touched her things. Cristal's clothes smelled sweet like gardenias, and Evita held them up to her nose to smell the enticing fragrance. There were spots on her clothes where her sweat stained the material, and the colors ran. Alone in the room, Evita put Cristal's sexiest bra up to her chest and danced in front of the mirror, shaking her shoulders. She wondered if her flat chest would ever grow breasts as big as Cristal's, then worried what she would do if she *did* get breasts as big as Cristal's. Thinking of a man at her breasts made Evita turn pale, and she arranged the sexy bra neatly into Cristal's drawer, relieved that it didn't belong to her.

Sometimes Cristal sat on the couch with Isidora, and Isidora rubbed her back and her legs as they watched telenovelas together and talked about all the stories as if the actors were neighbors they knew by heart. They never invited Evita to sit with them, so she stayed in her room and pretended she was busy listening to the radio.

Isidora didn't say anything to Evita about working at the restaurant, or about dancing. She said she was too little, too skinny. Besides, her mother might send someone out to look for her, and Isidora wanted Evita's mother to think she had rescued her from a life on the streets by giving her a place to stay.

At least twice a week, Isidora took Evita with her to pick up medicine from a doctor's office. She told Evita she was sending the medicine to a clinic in El Paso. "It's stuff they can't get in los Estados Unidos," she said, as she rummaged around in her oversized black purse, which resembled a small tattered suitcase. The purse had bulging flaps, pockets, zippers with missing teeth, and a hazy mirror pasted on the inside. It held all that mattered to Isidora, and she guarded it jealously. It made Evita wonder if Isidora had ever stuffed her clothes into a red vinyl bag like the one

Cristal owned and sighed and danced until dawn for men who bruised her body.

Isidora explained she was doing a favor for someone important by helping los Americanos get the medicine they needed for less money. She had a big heart, she said, and couldn't stand to see people suffering when medicine was available. They put the boxes of medicine in plastic bags that looked like shopping bags, so no one could tell it was medicine. Then they got into a taxi with a chofer who seemed to know when they were coming and going, and he drove them back to Isidora's house in silence. Sitting in the backseat, Isidora positioned her huge purse under the fleshy cushion of her left arm, and with her right arm embraced Evita as if she was really her niece. It made Evita feel that Isidora truly cared for her.

Every day Evita lovingly rubbed Isidora's swollen legs with ointment. She took her time over each leg, wrapping it neatly in white gauze. She cooked meals for Cristal, careful not to ask her any more questions about the bruises on her body, and she waited for Anabel to come home.

3 Reynaldo was in Juárez for only a day, having to return to El Paso where he worked doing landscaping for the Golden Crest Country Club, one of the city's elite clubs catering to famous golf figures from all over the world. When he asked around to find out where Evita was hiding out, someone told him she had been seen in la Zona del Canal. Reynaldo knew the area well and was enraged to think his sister was living on the streets like a prostitute. He was a frequent visitor to la Zona del Canal, often picking up women, and couldn't stand the thought that his sister had joined las mujeres de la calle, common whores who walked the streets at night, luring men to have sex with them.

Reynaldo walked down the streets of la Zona del Canal wearing a pair of dark jeans, a striped shirt, a hat and boots. His face was tanned a deep brown from riding a motorized lawn mower all day, manicuring golf courses for the rich in El Paso. Reynaldo kept his burned arms and chest hidden under the long sleeves of his shirt, and often thought what it would be like to have the freedom to wear short sleeves and collars that unbuttoned midway down his chest. The women he picked up in la Zona del Canal didn't care what kind of scars he had, as long as he paid them for what he got. Reynaldo was good at getting the most he could from them for the least amount of money, and it didn't matter to him if they saw his charred body. He used prostitutes like tools to get a job done, so he could return to his life in the United States. He was angry tonight, because his mother had told him to find Evita and get her back home before she became another statistic in Juárez, the victim of a rape or murder. He would have to wait for another time to pick up a prostitute he had met recently, who for the moment had become his favorite.

It was an early evening in September, and street lights glittered dimly in the darkening sky. Shops were open, selling merchandise, food, and clothing. Loud music floated out into the street as bar owners prepared to entice customers inside. Evita saw her brother from across a busy street, and she knew by his long firm steps and the way he zigzagged through the crowd that he was looking for her. She walked faster, trying not to attract his attention, but Reynaldo had already seen her and rushed across the street. When he caught up with her, he pulled on her arm to stop her.

"You're coming home, right now!" he yelled at her. He looked down at her, scowling, his teeth clenched. His expression made her heart pound away in her chest. She tried to squirm out of his grasp, but he held on tighter.

"You're not going anywhere!"

"I'm not going back home! I don't know what my mother told you, but whatever it is, it's a lie!"

"She told me you were supposed to be staying with Lety, but now I see that you're here, walking around like a common whore!"

Reynaldo's voice filled with rage, and he raised his hand as if to slap her. She ducked to one side, but Reynaldo had already lowered his hand. People on the street were watching them, and one man shouted, "Take her home and beat her; we don't want to see it. We've got our own problems."

Reynaldo pulled Evita away from the street and into a dark alley. He told Evita that their mother was mad at her because she didn't go to Lety's house, and now she was threatening to send the police out to find her.

"And you know what that means. The police can't be trusted—so you had better pay attention, escuincla, before it's too late!"

He let go of her arm, and Evita rubbed the spot where Reynaldo had held her tightly. Evita saw her brother's sun-burned face and his calloused hands. In spite of his anger, she could see that he was weary from working all day in the hot sun, and he still had to deal with immigration officials at the border to get back into El Paso, which might take hours depending on what was going on at the border. She knew her brother would calm down once the yelling was over. He had never been one to be cruel to her and often took Evita's side against their mother. Reynaldo told Evita that Brisa had kicked Ricardo out on the streets after they had gotten into a big fight.

"What else did she tell you?"

"Oh, that you were after him—but I know that's a lie. She's crazy that way."

He told Evita that Lety was pregnant again and was having trouble with her husband, Julio. She had quit her job at la maquiladora, the American factory where she had worked before her marriage, and Julio wasn't working at all, so their problems were many. Then he got serious with Evita, very serious.

"Haven't you heard, Evita? They've found the bodies of two more women, in el Lote Bravo. They were tortured and raped, murdered! You have to go home. Don't believe anybody on the streets who says they can protect you. They can't."

"Everybody's saying the women were prostitutes who walked the streets late at night. I told you, I'm not doing that. I live with a lady and help her clean and cook meals." Evita was ready to tell him that she had heard they had caught the murderers, but Reynaldo didn't give her a chance.

"What lady?" he shouted, with his face pressed into hers. "There aren't any ladies around here! So, you think the murdered girls were prostitutes, do you? They were maquiladoras, girls who worked at one of the American factories. Their uniforms were found next to their bodies. What are you thinking? There are men in this city who kill women. They don't ask questions. They seek out beautiful women, women skinny like you, Evita—women who are easy to kill."

A taxi stopped on the street, close to them, and el chofer waved to Reynaldo and asked him if he wanted a ride. Reynaldo walked to the taxi and talked to the man, pointing toward Evita. He gave el chofer money to take Evita home and then led her to the taxi, opening the back door for her. Evita looked solemnly at Reynaldo, not knowing how to make him understand that she couldn't go back home. Sometimes, if she was patient with Reynaldo, she could make him feel sorry for her and forget what he had been yelling about, but this time was different.

"Don't give me that face! Listen to me—don't you ever come out on these streets again. Do you hear me?"

He didn't wait for Evita's answer. He shut the car's door with a bang and rushed down the street, thinking he might have enough time to meet with one of his favorites, after all.

Evita gave el chofer an address that was two blocks away from Isidora's, but he said that wasn't the address Reynaldo had given him.

"It's my tía's house. I have to pick up my clothes before I go home."

"Your tía's? Reynaldo didn't tell me you were staying with relatives." Then he looked behind his shoulder at Evita in the backseat. "Wait a minute—are you Reynaldo's whore?"

The man asked the question as if it meant nothing to him, something he asked every day of his life.

"No! He's my brother. Didn't he tell you?"

"Well, he did, but I don't believe anything anybody says. And it doesn't look like you're on your way to school."

El chofer turned around to get another look at Evita, who was dressed in a pair of white slacks and a bright red T-shirt with the picture of a woman sitting in a skimpy outfit on a shiny yellow crescent. The T-shirt was one of Anabel's, but Evita didn't bother to explain it to the man. He said she didn't look anything like Reynaldo, then laughed. Evita frowned, angry with him for calling her a whore. Just because she was living in la Zona del Canal didn't mean she was a whore. Suddenly, she felt like kicking the seat in front of her just to make him mad.

"You're too young to be out on the streets like a prostitute. It's girls like you who end up dead in el Lote Bravo. If you were my daughter, I would beat you and make you stay home. That's what women need. They need to be beaten and kept at home for their own safety."

"I'm not a prostitute!"

"That's what they all say."

El chofer stopped at the address Evita gave him.

"Reynaldo won't be happy. He told me to take you home. God knows I don't want to make him mad."

El chofer thought that someday Reynaldo might be his contact for a job on the other side of the border, el otro lado, so he wanted to make a good impression on him. He told Evita he'd wait outside on the corner with the car running.

"And hurry; I run a business. If it weren't for Reynaldo, I wouldn't do this at all."

Evita walked down the street at a normal pace. Then, when she was out of sight of el chofer, she rushed around a corner and crossed one more street to get to Isidora's. There was no one home, and the house was dark and very still. Evita wanted to hide from el chofer and stay with Isidora. There was no use going back home again. She knew her mother would beat her and accuse her of being with Ricardo. Even though he was gone, it would be her fault.

Evita was afraid el chofer would ask someone which house she had run into and start searching for her, so she went out through the back door and into the alley behind Isidora's house, making her way through the dark passage, which was littered with garbage and smelled of sewage and spoiled food. Every movement in the alley terrified her. A drunk rose from a pile of newspapers and yelled at her, then stumbled into garbage cans set up along a wall. In her mind Evita saw the girls who were found in el Lote Bravo, tortured and raped, and she ran out into the street again, her chest aching with each breath, and disappeared into the crowd.

Every day, Evita walked down to el Centro to buy food, tortillas, cosmetics, toothpaste, lotion, hair dye, or whatever else was on the list that day for Isidora, Cristal, and Anabel. She caught men watching her, and she imagined they were thinking she was a prostitute and would approach her, as she had seen men approaching other girls who walked the streets. She had no idea what the men asked the girls, and figured they were setting a price for their services. Evita couldn't get the word "whore" out of her mind, as it reminded her of what her mother had called her when she had kicked her out of the house. Every time she thought of the word, she felt dirty, as if she had gotten mud on her hands. Besides all this, she was worried Reynaldo would come back to Juárez to look for her; so she went out during the day when she knew Reynaldo was working in El Paso.

When she crossed the busy streets, Evita had to jump down at times to reach the street from the steep angles of the sidewalks, being cautious of cars that spun wildly close to pedestrians at crosswalks. The streets were filled with cars, taxis, and ruteras, lined up from one end of Ciudad Juárez to the other. Living in Juárez all her life, Evita was used to the noise of horns blaring incessantly and the rancid smell of exhaust that stuck to her skin, hair, and clothes. She walked past clothing stores, drug-stores, stands set up with carne asada, a bakery, and tables set out on the sidewalks displaying curios: ceramic fish, birds, hand-carved crosses, pictures of la Virgen de Guadalupe. At one corner she saw a man selling *El Diario*. On the cover was the story her brother was talking about. Two more girls' bodies had been found in el Lote Bravo, half-buried in the sand. Evita glanced at one photo: showing the shoe of one of the girls sticking out of the sand. A wave of fear swept over her, and she almost turned and ran back to Isidora's. Ahead of her, two women were talking about the murders.

"Believe me, somebody's being paid to keep silent about who's mur-dering these girls. The first body was found two years ago, and now it's 1995 and still nobody's been charged. Ay, te digo! If people weren't afraid to tell the truth, we'd know who the murderers are."

"It's la mordida," her companion said. "People are being silenced with money, and la policia are the worst. They'd sell out their own mothers for a few pesos. And nobody talks, or it's certain they'll be killed. I'm not letting my daughter go anywhere these days—she's a prisoner in our own house, my poor daughter!" The woman glanced behind her and saw Evita.

"What are you doing on the streets? Don't you know any better? Don't ever walk out alone!" She shook her head as if talking to Evita was useless. "I tell you, these young girls don't know what danger is."

The women turned the street corner, shaking their heads, looping their arms together as if to protect themselves from the murderers, who might be only a few steps ahead of them.

Evita looked up from the sidewalk and noticed a couple walking by. The man had his arm around a girl not much older than Evita. He blew Evita a kiss as they walked by and whistled at her. She looked away from him and acted as if she hadn't heard him.

"Ay, mi chulita! Now there's a vision."

"Her? She's a bone," the girl said. "How dare you even look at her!"

The girl pushed the man away and cursed at Evita. The man only laughed and grabbed the girl in his arms, lifting her up as he hugged her.

"Put me down! If you think you can find something better, then do it!" The girl was struggling but not really trying to get away.

The man only laughed harder and kissed the girl and whispered something in her ear. Then she laughed too. She looked at Evita, pointed at her with one finger, and laughed again.

Evita walked faster, hoping the girl wouldn't recognize her again someday and try to pick a fight with her. Then, before she knew it, el chofer who had given her a ride to Isidora's house came up to her and said, "Hola, how are you this morning, Evita?"

It seemed strange to see him walking leisurely down the street instead of driving his taxi, so Evita didn't answer. She tried to walk faster, but he followed easily beside her. Evita thought maybe Reynaldo was somewhere close by, or that he had sent el chofer out to find her.

"Aren't you talking to me today, Evita? You were smart to fool me once, but you'll get yours today."

And before Evita had a chance to think about what he was saying, she felt someone grab her shoulders from behind. It was a policeman. He pulled Evita's arms behind her back and put a pair of handcuffs on her thin wrists. Then another officer joined him, and between the two of them they picked Evita up as if she weighed less than a feather and dragged her to a police car. Evita was yelling as loudly as she could, and people on the street were standing by, looking at her. Yet no one moved as la policia dragged her away to a police car hidden in an alley.

The police officer who put Evita in handcuffs grabbed her by the throat and told her that this time she was lucky. They were doing her mother a favor, he said, and taking her back home instead of driving her to a place where she would never forget who they were. He pushed Evita into the back of the police car and bent down with his face into hers and yelled at her.

"So, you want to be a whore and run on the streets, do you? Well, see if you like this!"

The policeman unzipped his pants and exposed himself to her. Then he took her face and forced it over his crotch. Evita, struggling and crying, felt sticky wet fluid all over her face. She had never seen a man's private parts before. She only remembered playing naked in the water hose with her cousins, not caring that they were different from her. The officer sitting in the front seat yelled at the other to stop.

"What? Are you crazy? Ya, we have what we want. Let's get this over with."

The man stopped himself with difficulty. He was breathing heavily and now put his head down to catch his breath. His eyes were wild, his face red. His sunglasses had landed on the floor of the car, and his shirt was out of his pants. He unbuckled his belt and tucked his shirt back in, then zipped up his pants, centering the belt buckle tightly over his flabby middle.

"I think she's still a virgin!" he said excitedly. "This bitch is really a virgin!"

The officer in the front seat got out of the car and stood at the back door. At last the other officer got out and moved to the front seat, leaving Evita in the back crying, her face a sticky mess. Evita's arms ached from the handcuffs tight around her wrists, and her mouth went suddenly dry as if every bit of moisture had left her body. She was struggling to sit in an upright position as the police car jerked away. The car traveled at top speed until there was a snarl in the traffic. Then the policeman who was driving turned on his siren to get through.

Evita's only thought was that they were taking her to el Lote Bravo, the empty bloody lot, where they would torture her, rape her, and kill her. She screamed as loudly as she could and kicked the seat in front of her. The policeman who had attacked her said if she didn't stop, he'd tie her up and stuff her in the trunk. Evita calmed down only when she looked out the window and saw they were taking her home. She recognized the streets in her colonia, el Quinto Sol—narrow dirt roads, twisting and turning between houses that looked no better than the ones in la Zona del Canal. When the car stopped in front of her mother's house, the police officer who was driving opened the back door and grabbed her by one arm, pulling her out of the police car. Then he whispered in her ear:

"If you say anything about what happened to you, you'll live only long enough to regret it. What he did to you is nothing compared to what I'll do to you."

He held tightly to Evita's hands, still handcuffed behind her back, and pulled on the handcuffs hard. Then he unlocked them and set her bruised wrists free. Evita's shoulders slumped forward as if sprung from the grasp of an invisible trap. She felt her body trembling and was unable to take even one step.

"You're free—stop making such a big deal about it," he said.

Brisa ran out to the police car with her arms flying in the air, crying and acting like she had been heartbroken over Evita. She held Evita in her arms and cried, telling her what a disobedient daughter she was and how she had been afraid she had been kidnapped or killed. Evita smelled liquor on her mother's breath and felt her breasts against hers when she hugged her. It was obvious her mother wasn't wearing a bra, and she was already half drunk. Evita stood with her hands at her sides, letting her mother hug her, feeling embarrassed and watching how the police officers looked on unconcerned.

"This girl doesn't know how much I love her! Here she is making me go crazy thinking she could turn up like the other girls they're murdering and throwing out like garbage in el Lote Bravo. Y, mirala! Just look at her—not a tear for her mother, not a kind word!"

The two policemen looked at Evita, their faces hard.

The officer who had attacked her said: "She's your responsibility. Keep her off the streets, because next time we can't guarantee what will happen to her."

Then he smiled as if it was all a big joke, and the other officer slapped him on the back as they returned to the police car.

Evita observed the driver of the police car, tall and stiff-kneed, lean on his companion's shoulder. The man who had attacked her was shorter and thicker, with bowed legs. In her mind, Evita relived the pressure of his body over hers and his hand holding her face down, then the feeling of nausea overcoming her as she realized what he was doing. They said something to each other and laughed. She saw the back of their uniforms, their black shoes, their guns, and thought she'd never forget how the officer had exposed himself to her and what his companion said to her when he had whispered in her ear.

The first thing Evita did after she got home was to wash her face, scrubbing every inch with soap. Then she got into the shower and let hot soapy water run all over her hair and body. She said nothing to her mother about the policemen. What good would it do? Everyone knew they had the power to beat people, imprison them, make false charges, even kill them. Evita looked around and felt as if she had come back after being exiled to a faraway country. Her vision and sense of hearing, even her voice, seemed to be drifting in the air. The pattern of who she was had changed after the assault, and she didn't know where the parts of her were hidden. The dark spikes that punctured her skin from within seemed to be gathering strength, reclaiming their power over her.

There was another woman in the house when Evita got home, a neighbor named Cleotilde who drank with her mother. Cleotilde started telling Evita how lucky she was to have a mother who looked for her on the streets, a mother who worried day and night over her. She should be ashamed, she said, to treat her mother so badly. She'd regret it when her mother died, and then it would be too late. Evita hung her head and listened to Cleotilde, pretending she was getting something from her drunken babbling.

Evita found out that her mother knew el chofer and had asked him to help her find her daughter and bring her safely home. She paid him la mordida, and enough for the police officers as well. El chofer lied to her and told her the police officers were friends of his and would do her daughter no harm. He guaranteed Brisa they would find Evita and bring her back home—for a small price, of course. Her daughter's life was certainly worth much more than that.

As night approached, Brisa and Cleotilde got drunker. They started talking about men they had known in their lives and how they had all been machos and never appreciated a good woman. Mendigos! Desgraciados! What does it take for them to appreciate the love of a good woman? They laughed until they were hoarse and played loud music and danced with each other. From her room, Evita heard her mother talking loudly about Ricardo, saying he was a fool to go after children when he had her for a lover. He was a sin vergüenza, shameless, and he deserved to be locked up for preying on young girls. Evita took a deep breath and gathered the bedspread around her, knowing what would happen next. Brisa wasn't so sure it was all Ricardo's fault, so she called Evita into the room and held her tightly by the arm. She slapped her face and demanded to know if she had made love to Ricardo. Evita kept telling her she had never touched

Ricardo, but Brisa wasn't satisfied until she had made Evita cry by calling her names and telling her that Ricardo hated her for going after him and that now he was out on the streets where he belonged. Evita escaped her mother and ran out of the house while Cleotilde sang, "Volver, Volver" at the top of her lungs, and her mother shouted at her: "Don't you dare leave me! After all the money I spent to get you back, you should serve me for the rest of your life!"

Across the dirt road, Evita saw her neighbors, Luis Ledezma and his sister Yvone. They both crossed the road when they saw her in tears. Evita was glad their brother, Chano, wasn't around. Chano was a tecato, always on one drug or another, dirty, shaking, crawling if he had to to get the money he needed for his habit. Evita remembered Chano's fingers trying to pull her underwear down one day as she was coming home from school. He wanted to know if el Albino's sister had the same thing other girls had. He hit Evita and made her nose bleed, then laughed and told her she was lucky she ran so fast or she would be bleeding from somewhere else besides her nose.

Luis and Yvone had seen Evita brought home in a police car like a common criminal, but out of respect for her feelings asked her nothing about it. Evita didn't have the nerve to tell them about the assault by the police officer, as she felt ashamed at what had happened and considered it her fault for having run away in the first place. She was glad for the darkness of the night as the three stood together outside her mother's house. There were no street lights in la colonia Quinto Sol, and only a few stars shone dimly in the northern sky. Evita took comfort from the darkness, knowing that Luis and Yvone couldn't see her face clearly. She felt as if the sour sticky fluid was still stuck to her skin.

"Stay at our house," Luis said to her. "I'll ask your mother's permission." Luis's kind voice reached Evita and soothed her. Still, she shuddered to think of staying at Chano's house, so she told him she'd be all right as soon as her mother stopped drinking.

Lety was the reason Evita ran away again. Her sister came back pregnant from her husband, Julio, limping worse than ever. Her two small children, Joselito and Milito, both under five years old, cried and fussed and wanted Lety to hold them all the time. Evita helped take care of them: playing with them, giving Milito milk in his bottle, changing his diaper.

And she helped her sister wash and iron clothes for people who could afford to pay for such things. Her mother went out to los mercados every day to sell her merchandise. That helped, as Brisa wasn't around to yell at Evita and tell her she was sure she had tried to trap Ricardo, and that was why he had left her.

Julio came to the house regularly to fight with Lety. Evita figured her sister let it happen because her leg was deformed and she couldn't expect anything better from men. One day Julio came by in a nasty mood and beat up Lety, pushing her down on the ground and making her bleed from between her legs. He ran off and left her hurt, screaming for help. There was nothing for Evita to do but bring Lety into the house and put her to bed. Lety wanted Evita to run down to the store where there was a phone and call the police so she could have her husband arrested. The thought of having to talk to la policia sent Evita into a panic.

"No! Lety, don't call the police! They'll do nothing. In fact, they'll defend him and say that he's right to beat you and take you home."

Lety looked closely at Evita and saw her fear. "Why are you so afraid of them?" she asked.

"Haven't you heard? You know how they are. They don't defend women. In fact, they do all they can to abuse us!"

Lety moaned in pain and lay back down on the bed. Joselito and Milito ran in crying and jumping on her, pulling the bedcover over their heads to hide from their father. Evita pretended it was all a game, teasing the children by pulling the covers off while Lety wept into the pillow. It was then, Evita decided, that she couldn't live another day at her mother's house.

4 Evita asked for permission to stay at her godmother's house, su madrina, for a few days. Her mother called Ofelia, and she said yes, she could come stay with her. Brisa said, go, what did she care? Evita had never done anything for her anyway. She told Evita to let her madrina know that she had been sick and to ask if she could come by and help her sell her merchandise. Brisa gave Evita money to get on las ruteras and a little more to give to Ofelia as a gift. She'd have to take two ruteras to get to la colonia San Fernando where Ofelia lived. Evita packed a few pieces of clothing into a schoolbag and hugged her nephews,

Joselito and Milito, kissing their cheeks and tickling them playfully. The two boys loved Evita, and the older of the two, four-year-old Joselito, packed a plastic bag with clothes, wanting to go with her. It took Evita a whole day to convince him that he couldn't come with her. She ended up promising him she would come back and take him to los mercados where he could see the clown who entertained the crowds on Sundays by balancing three children at a time on his shoulders.

Brisa shook her head as she looked at Evita with her schoolbag packed and ready to go. Then she stared at Lety's expanding belly and said that if Evita ever came back pregnant, she'd kill her. She had no patience, she said, for girls who let themselves get pregnant and ended up bringing their babies home as extra mouths to feed. Obviously, Brisa had forgotten that she had delivered Reynaldo in her best friend's bedroom when she had barely turned fifteen, to avoid having to tell her parents until later.

Lety sat with her hands on her stomach, staring out the window at her children in the front yard. Joselito and Milito, naked and burned dark brown from running around in the sun, were playing in a tub of muddy water. There was a large dog splashing in the water with them, and every time the dog shook himself off he sprinkled the boys with more muddy water, and they laughed and held onto the dog's ears and tail.

"Get the boys!" Brisa screamed. "Don't you have any sense? They've been playing in that dirty water all day."

Lety got up slowly and made her way to the door. The weight of the unborn child made her limp so badly she had to put out at least one arm to balance herself. She called the boys, and they came running in, dripping water and mud into the house. Brisa yelled at them, and they started to cry. She slapped Joselito on the head as if she were swatting a fly, and he cried louder and held onto his ear. Then Joselito saw Evita standing by the door and started to wail, hanging onto her and getting muddy water and the smell of wet dog on her white blouse and dark trousers. Lety had to drag Joselito away so Evita could make her escape.

Evita left the house with her schoolbag looped over her shoulder, brushing off her clothes, tears in her eyes over Joselito. She looked back at her mother's house. It was sloping to one side, and the two windows, once glass, were now covered by clear plastic. The blue paint was peeling, and the roof looked like it would be blown away by the next storm. In the backyard, standing next to an outhouse, was a shack Reynaldo used to sleep in before he left for El Paso. The shack was now used to store old tools and two broken-down sewing machines. The outhouse was there for times when the rusty toilet in the house didn't work. The odor from the outhouse reached Evita, forcing her to turn away. Brisa said she'd fix up the shack one day and rent it out. She said there was always some-body sleeping on the dirt, people new to the city, who would consider her shack a palace. Through the haze of one of the plastic windows, Evita saw Joselito's sad face watching her leave. She smiled and blew him a kiss.

Brisa stepped out of the front door and watched her daughter as she walked away. She didn't wave good-bye, only stared at her in silence. Her mother's somber figure was too much for Evita, so she pretended she was busy picking out the coins in her pocket she needed for la rutera. Although her mother had not struck her, Evita felt herself beaten down. She was afraid to wave good-bye. What if she waved and her mother didn't respond? Then she'd have to carry that memory with her as well. Brisa walked back inside, tears in her eyes, and banged the door shut. As she walked away, Evita heard her shout at the children and was surprised to hear Lety's voice shouting back at her.

Evita's madrina lived in a house that her husband, Prospero, had built for her years ago in la colonia San Fernando. Back then, he was working for a trucking company, making deliveries all over Chihuahua and into El Paso. The house was made of concrete blocks, with a small stairway lead-ing up to the roof, where the family would sit and watch the sun set over el Río Bravo, which the Americans called el Rio Grande. Inside, Prospero built Ofelia a kitchen with wooden cabinets and a sink that had running water most of the time. When the river ran dry, water was bought in bottles, and people had to take turns using the water that ran through the faucets. The houses in San Fernando went on forever, with some built into the hills, nestled between rocks and crevices, while others leaned precariously from jagged cliffs that cut into the horizon like sharp-edged blades.

From Ofelia's house Evita could see el Río Bravo in the distance, and across the river she could see, clearly, los Estados Unidos—America, with its fine houses, freeways, and tall buildings. Evita had visited El Paso once, when Reynaldo had gotten his job at the golf course. He had taken them all over in his car to see the Golden Crest Country Club that faced a mountain range known for its golden-colored sunsets. A marker stood on one of the hills, announcing, *Golden Crest, the most beautiful sunsets in the Southwest*, and there were benches set up for tourists to sit and enjoy the late afternoon sky.

Evita knew that the Americans could see Mexico as easily as she could see America. She wondered if she'd ever travel to the other side, like many others had done, and work for a rich family, spying on the poverty of her people from across the river. Someone told Evita that once you crossed the border, you got spoiled and came back with a big head, looking with disgust at what you had seen every day of your life. Then you'd apply for a visa, hoping it would be the beginning of permanent citizenship in the United States.

Ofelia had food waiting for Evita when she arrived: burritos de carnitas, salsa, guacamole, beans—everything simmering and smelling delicious. Ofelia used to be heavy but had lost weight, and now the fat hung from her throat, arms, and hips like a fleshy garment. She was wearing a faded dress, lavender with tiny white flowers, and huaraches with missing straps. She hugged and kissed Evita.

"You're so grown-up now, already a young lady. And so pretty, like a daisy," Ofelia said, holding Evita close. "Soon, you'll bloom and be a beautiful woman."

Evita didn't believe her—beauty was not for her. She thought about Anabel and Cristal and knew she'd never be that beautiful.

Ofelia told Evita she could stay with them for one week, or two, or three. Then she didn't know what would happen. She had relatives coming to live with them from the village of Montenegro, she said. Her cousin Flor's husband was very sick, and she was trying to convince him to come to Juárez to see a doctor.

"You remember your cousin Petra, don't you?" Ofelia said, tasting the rice she was cooking, adding a bit of salt. "The little girl you used to play with when her family would come to visit us."

"Yes, I remember her," Evita said, thinking of how pretty her cousin was in her bright red Christmas dress. They had run in and out of the house together during family celebrations, holding hands, zigzagging past adults who ate tamales and drank copas of tequila, all the while pretending they were twins, even though Evita was three years younger.

"Her father's been very ill. The matter is urgent. But men are so stubborn—Estevan refuses to come to Juárez to see a doctor! He's driving Flor crazy, my poor cousin!"

Ofelia looked around at her small house. "I don't know where they'll all stay. I might ask your mother if she can keep someone at her house."

"Oh, she'll do that," Evita said, "especially if there's money to be made. Lety's there now, but she'll be back with her husband soon."

"Flor says she and Petra have jobs at one of las maquiladoras and should make enough money to get their own place very soon. Petra's never lived in a big city, so you'll need to show her around."

"Maquiladoras? There were girls killed from a maquiladora just the other day. I saw it in *El Diario*." Evita remembered the photograph of the girl's shoe sticking out of the sand. Glancing up at Ofelia, she felt herself flutter inside as if her heart had skipped a beat when she thought of the hot sand covering the dead girl's body.

"Juárez has always been dangerous! I worked in a maquiladora for years and nothing ever happened to me," Ofelia said, setting the dishes on the table for dinner. "It's girls who run on the streets at night who get killed."

"But Reynaldo said—"

"What? When did you see Reynaldo?" Ofelia asked, surprised. "Your mother didn't tell me he had come to Juárez."

Just then, Prospero walked into the kitchen, whistling a happy tune. Evita was glad for the interruption. Prospero was dark and thin, with eyelids that drooped over each eye, and he rushed about as if he had a hundred things to do. He reminded Evita of a ground mole, busily excavating dirt for his next burrow, never finishing one excavation before moving on to the next. He hugged Evita, spinning her around in his arms like she was still five years old. He said Evita weighed as much as she had weighed when she was only five. It was good getting attention from him, and Evita felt like a small child again, ready to play with the dolls made of socks Ofelia used to sew for her. She laughed along with Prospero as he told Ofelia to get him some dinner, because he was so hungry his stomach was playing the Mexican hat dance.

Ofelia said they couldn't climb the wooden stairway to the small deck on the roof anymore to have their dinner, because the beams on the roof were sagging, and they might fall through. She pointed to a patch on the ceiling where, she said, one of her cousins had stepped too hard on the roof, scaring everyone in the kitchen below when his big foot came crashing through. Everyone ran around thinking it was a gun pointed at their heads. Privately, she told Evita that Prospero barely made any money at all now that the trucking company he had worked for had closed down. It was hard for them to live, much less repair the sagging roof.

After dinner, they sat in the backyard under a tree and got dust all over their clothes, face, and hair from cars that passed by on the dirt roads that led through San Fernando. The dust was made of grains of sand, and it settled on everything and looked like a fog all around them. The dusty fog made everything seem unreal to Evita. The children running and playing on the road, teasing one another, looked like silhouettes to her. The fog was like a cocoon and reminded her of the beautiful butterfly she had wanted to become in the second grade. White clouds drifted in the dark sky, and soon a breeze started blowing. Here and there dust devils appeared, and the children laughed as they ran in and out of the swirling dust. Somewhere in the distance a man started strumming his guitar, and people began shouting requests for songs and clapping when he played their favorite. Evita heard the grown-ups talking and joking with each other, and she felt a sense of peace come over her. Unlike the gust of wind she had experienced in her dream, this peace was scattered and incomplete, like confetti sprinkled on her soul.

Neighbors stopped by to say hello to Ofelia and Prospero and to visit with them, while their children took turns racing after a soccer ball in the dark. Evita didn't feel like joining the other children. Since the assault by the policeman, she felt more like a grown-up with adult worries. More like Isidora, with tree stumps for legs and an oversized black purse with hundreds of flaps, pockets, and zippers that weighed her down. Evita wished she had the nerve to tell Ofelia about la policia, but she was afraid she'd say she shouldn't have run away from her mother in the first place and that she was lucky they hadn't done something worse.

Evita stayed with Ofelia for two weeks, happily helping her around the house and enjoying Prospero's attention and compliments, forgetting, for the time being, what she had suffered at the hands of la policia and her life at Isidora's. In the third week, Ofelia told her that Lety had called and said she was back with her husband and that Brisa now had a new man—someone named Alberto. Evita had already sensed a new pattern starting inside her, something gathering and rearranging itself, so she wasn't surprised by what her madrina said.

Ofelia looked sadly at Evita. "Don't worry. Alberto won't be there long."

She had tears in her eyes as she gently stroked her goddaughter's hair. Evita knew it was time for her to go home. Petra's family was coming from Montenegro, and there wouldn't be any room for her. It made her angry that Petra's family was coming now, when she needed her madrina the most.

Ofelia said that if it were up to her, Evita would stay with them forever. She whispered in Evita's ear, pleading with her: "Promise me you'll go back home and not run away again. You know the streets are dangerous! No woman is safe in Juárez! There are murderers, men who—"

"I won't be out on the streets!" Evita said, interrupting her, holding tightly to her madrina's hand. A great longing rose in her to confess the awful secret of her assault by the policeman and her life at Isidora's in la Zona del Canal, but she only sat in silence holding more tightly to Ofelia's hand, her head bowed.

Evita felt her madrina's breath at her ear, her words, sincerely said, the kiss on her cheek, and she promised her she'd go back home, but she was lying. She was going back to Isidora's.

Rabbit on the Face of the Moon

5 Petra de la Rosa knew the story of Montenegro. A volcano had erupted millions of years ago, the people of her village said, destroying everything in its path. Over the years skulls in the form of enormous heads had been uncovered, along with the skeletal remains of small bodies. Maybe the people had been pygmies with bloated heads—no one knew for certain. Here and there a piece of pottery had been unearthed, a scrap of rough material, a primitive shoe, an ancient blanket or headdress. Also dug up were the remains of huge beasts with enough fur and meat to clothe and feed many families. There was evidence that strange creatures had existed with webbed feet, flat bills, fur on their wings, one-eyed, three-eyed, and some with spikes sprouting out of their heads. The animals had lived together with the primitive people and eaten their fill of lush green plants that had grown where a huge river had once flowed. The villagers of Montenegro no longer remembered what the primitive people had called the river, but everyone said the river's rocky banks hid a treasure of silver, making its water run silver gray. Thus it was named el Río Gris. Tall, majestic trees, ahuehuetes, used to grow along the length of the river. They were sacred to the ancients and were offered gifts, food, tobacco, and flowers. The fire from the volcano had destroyed the primitive people, most of the ahuehuete trees, and the strange animals. Hot lava had covered the earth like an enormous fiery canopy, spewing dark ash into the air for fifty-two years.

The primitive people had marked the passing of time by the movements of the sun. There were five suns, each ending in destruction. The first was destroyed by tigers, the second by a hurricane, the third by fire, the fourth by a great flood, and the last, el Quinto Sol, the era of the Fifth Sun, would end by earthquakes.

Petra learned these things from Abuela Teodora Santos de Texcoco, a tiny bony woman who held her granddaughter's heart in the palm of her hand. Abuela Teodora was a descendant of the tribe of people who had come before the Aztecs, possibly the Toltecs. Eventually, one of her great-grandmothers had married a Tarahumara, and her family had migrated to Chihuahua. The old woman could speak Rarámuri, the language of the Tarahumaras, chanting prayers that had lulled the infant Petra to sleep.

Petra had seen a sign, once, now hidden by rocks and rubble, its words all but faded: ZONA ARQUEOLOGICA DEL MUSEO DE ANTIGUE-DAD DE CHIHUAHUA. Many years ago, the government of Chihuahua decided it was too much work and required too much money to uncover the remains of the primitive people with the bloated heads and short bodies and the mysterious creatures, so the work was abandoned. To this day, the mountain peaks of Montenegro rise into the sky in the shape of immense stone figures that crouch together in the dark and whisper prayers and blessings for the civilized people of Montenegro.

Every day there was talk that the wells would run dry and the people of Montenegro would die. Everyone hated the rich Spanish landowner who had built a dam many years ago, so many that no one could remember exactly when. He had forced the water from el Río Gris to flow into his land alone, to his hacienda, to water his crops and fatten his cattle, but the river broke loose and spilled its water wherever it willed, on the land and on the people of Montenegro. There were great floods. Then it dried up as a last act of vengeance, and the people of Montenegro cheered the river's wrath and said they possessed the same power to resist the proud and arrogant.

A deep dry arroyo formed where el Río Gris once ran, and dead trees, hollow with decay, flanked the length of the river's bank, and still the villagers resisted the desert's sentence of death. They dug wells and stored water in huge iron tubs called tinacos and laughed at the rich and powerful who set themselves up as gods when they were only men. Cortés was vanquished, they said, and from his defeat el mestizo had risen, the mixture of Spanish and Indian blood.

The villagers of Montenegro were faithful to their old traditions and taught them to their children. It was a person of courage who didn't complain about every ache and pain suffered and didn't stoop to whine over the hard work of everyday life. You fought for life in Montenegro—that was how it was done. La lucha. You woke up in the morning and looked out to see if the weather was something that would make you happy or sad. If rain was needed for the cornfields, and it was cloudy, already you knew it would be a good day. You could smell the rain in the air, feel it pounding on the cornfields and turning the dry earth into a layer of rich moist soil. If the cornfields were in need of rain, and every husk of green corn was staring up into the sky, and the sun was a shining globe of fire, you knew it would be a bad day and everyone would be miserable, and you prayed harder to the Christian God and secretly to the ancient god of rain, Tlaloc. Days in Montenegro were that simple. Wind, sun, rain, clouds, stars, plants, animals, and, at night, the face of a rabbit glowed on the surface of the moon.

Petra was proud when she lived in Montenegro, and before she left for Ciudad Juárez, which was to become for her the inferno, Abuela Teodora had told her about a dwelling place of the dead from where no news comes, where the doors are left-handed and there are no roads leading out.

6 People described Estevan de la Rosa with one word—caprichoso. He was caprichoso because he wouldn't go to Juárez to see a doctor. He was irrational and hardheaded, and everybody who knew him was angry with him, but nobody could stand up to him. Estevan was a man among men, un macho, who was convinced he had the power to challenge the illness that possessed him and win back his health, like winning at a hand of cards.

Estevan had come from the rich farmlands of Oaxaca to Montenegro to try his hand at mining silver. He was tall, good looking, unbelievably strong, and he feared nothing. He was the kind of man who could create something from the very earth—and that is exactly what he did. With his earnings from the silver mines, he bought land in Montenegro and built a house, brick by brick, until he had a decent place to live in. Then he decided he was ready to get married, and that's when he met Flor, although she had been there all along and he had never noticed her.

Flor was athletic, robust, a woman who wasn't afraid to start from the ground up and wouldn't waste Estevan's money on trips to Chihuahua City or Juárez to buy the latest styles in dresses and shoes, as some of the women from Montenegro were known to do. She had a serene face, dreamy eyes, and Estevan couldn't get her out of his mind no matter how much he tried. He made up his mind to marry her, and once that was done, like everything else in Estevan's life, there was no turning back. It was lucky for him Flor was in love with him; otherwise, he would have had to take her by force, eloping the old fashioned way and winning her heart a step at a time.

Mining silver was one of the hardest things to do, Estevan found out, and a sick, weak body was the price he had paid for his years of refining the precious metal. Now the silver mines produced nothing, nada, ni una moneda de plata, compadre, as the men said—not even a silver coin. Estevan turned to raising cattle and planting patches of corn and fodder for livestock, pigs and horses. He blamed the American government for supporting NAFTA in 1992, which caused thousands of villagers to lose their farmlands and granted big corporations the right to establish themselves in foreign countries, making huge profits on the sweat of the poor. The Mexican government was as greedy as los Estados Unidos in allowing factories to take advantage of Mexico's low wages, paying Mexican employees a fraction of what Americans made for the same work. Both countries were interested in reaping billions by building industrial factories—las maquiladoras—along the border between the United States and Mexico; and thus the rich remained rich, and the poor got poorer. Life for the poor in Mexico took a turn for the worse. Thousands immigrated to the cities to start from the ground up, hoping to get jobs in maquiladoras, or as taxi cab drivers, or cleaning houses, digging ditches, doing anything and everything they could to survive—even joining in the illegal trade of people and drugs across the border.

Tío Alvaro, Estevan's brother-in-law, was one of the men who marched right up to the International Border, Paso del Norte, boldly demanding that the rights of landowners not be ignored. The protestors were pushed back by los federales with loaded guns. Several men were wounded, and two died, leaving Tío Alvaro and the rest to scatter to their villages, or risk being arrested and sent to prison.

With the mines closed and the farms counted as worthless, many villagers became ill and disillusioned. Along with countless others, Estevan suffered a life of uncertainty and despair. Every day there were changes in his body. He lost weight and coughed endlessly into the night. Flor got up and fixed her husband an herbal tea, manzanilla, to soothe him, but it was not enough, and she sighed over him again and again, "ay, Estevan, ay, Estevan," as if he was a baby and she was singing him a lullaby. Petra held her father's hand, as she had when they had gone on walks together, and noticed his fingernails were yellow and brittle and his hand trembled. She smiled at him, but she was afraid of what she saw as her father leaned on her for support.

Flor and Abuela Teodora wove baskets and made pottery, attractive pieces they put in the marketplace at least three times a year to earn extra money. They gathered pitaya, the sahuaro's red fruit, and made jelly and other sugary delicacies to sell to people who lived in the city. Their hands were cracked from handling the clay and sore from tiny stickers that settled into their hands when they harvested la pitaya from the prickly cacti. They soothed their hands with a thick ointment they made out of the aloe vera plant. Other family members made silver jewelry, some of them exquisite pieces they sold in Juárez or sent to El Paso. They talked about Juárez: it was close by, they said, only four hundred miles or so, not so far they couldn't make it there in a day. Flor listened and looked at her husband, worried. She nodded her head.

"See," she said. "See—we can go. You can see a doctor, get the medicines you need. We can stay with my cousin Ofelia and her husband. She's always been good to us." Estevan glared at her. He had no intention of going to Juárez, he said, where the poor lived like rats and the materialistic world of el gringo proved to be a lure, enticing many to run the risk of crossing into el otro lado, never to return.

Petra remembered Juárez as if in a dream. As a child, her family had visited their cousin Ofelia on trips they made to Juárez, and she had played with her little cousin Evita Reynosa, a thin, wiry girl who followed her everywhere she went. There were many people at cousin Ofelia's, more than Petra had ever seen in her life, and she was hugged and hugged again and again by primos, tios, tias, until she thought she couldn't stand another hug. Everyone said Petra was a beautiful child, and they pitied her father, who would have to be trucha, wily and on the alert, for all the men who would pursue his daughter. There was no telling how many men's hearts Petra would break, everyone said, but it was certain there would be many. Petra didn't know what they were talking about, but she knew she was deeply loved. She ate ice cream with her cousins, smooth paletas of different flavors. And that was the best of all. She slept with her lips red or orange, purple or green, depending on the color of la paleta she had eaten.

Flor lit the gas stove, set into a corner of the kitchen, and had coffee brewing in a black kettle. She cooked eggs with bits of bacon, tomato, onion, and chile, then she rolled the eggs into tortillas and made burritos for breakfast. Heat rose from the stove and fogged up the windows, warming up the cold October morning. After a while, the heat became unbearable, and everyone's faces turned red; then Flor opened the kitchen door for relief. Fresh cold air rushed in, filling the kitchen. But then Abuela Teodora scolded Flor and asked her if she was crazy, letting in the cold air. Didn't she know they could all catch el viento, the cold chill that would get stuck in their bones and cause arthritis, or lodge under their skin and make lumps appear? Some of the lumps caused by el viento grew on women's backs, and in time they got hunched over, their backs stiff as boards. Abuela Teodora got up and shut the door, and pretty soon everyone got hot again, and the drama of opening and closing the door would be repeated like a scene on a stage.

Petra and Abuela Teodora sat at the kitchen table with a huge burlap bag of pinto beans between them. They took fistfuls of the beans from the bag and spread them on the table, picking out tiny rocks, small bits of soil, and occasionally the remains of an insect. The task was tedious and boring. Petra wished Nico and Ester, her little brother and sister, would help, but Abuela Teodora said no, Petra was the one who took the job seriously. As they worked, they listened to Flor and Estevan argue, something they had been doing for days. Already the kitchen had heated up with their arguments, and Petra knew her mother would open the door very soon, and Abuela Teodora would sigh and get up and close it. Petra hoped for the fresh air, as her forehead was wet with her sweat, but she didn't want to hurt Abuela Teodora's feelings by siding with her mother.

"I would rather die than go there! Do you hear me? Die than go there!"

"You're stubborn, Estevan! That's your problem. What about your family—can you think of us for once?"

Flor was kneading dough, flour up to her elbows, pounding hard on la masa's soft lumpy surface. When she wasn't talking, her lips formed a hard line on her face that announced to the world how angry she was.

"I *am* thinking about my family. That's why we won't go."

Flor and Abuela Teodora exchanged looks. They were the same face, one young, the other old, mother and daughter who spoke to each other with their eyes. Estevan would die if he stayed in Montenegro.

"I called Ofelia, and she says we can stay with her. She knows a doctor who will see you . . . and—"

Estevan's voice cut in harshly. "Talking about me! Ay, esta mujer! Making it seem as though I'm already dying!"

"Estevan, por favor, try to understand! It's all for your own good. Alvaro told me he met a man from Juárez who says there's money to be made in Juárez, in las maquiladoras. Ofelia worked there for years. I can work there—Petra too; she'll be nineteen soon. We can earn money. You can see a doctor. The best doctors are there. You know there's nothing here. You have to get to a doctor! Don't you understand?"

Flor's voice trembled, and she gasped for air. Strands of hair, wet with sweat, stuck to her face, and she brushed them aside with the end of her apron.

Estevan yelled at her. "Alvaro should know better! He was one of the men who marched to the border. Has he forgotten? Stop, I tell you woman, stop! What do you know about that city? We can't go. It's filled with coyotes who sell out our own people, thieves, murderers of every kind. And do you think that's what I want for my family? Tell your brother to mind his own business!"

Estevan was sitting up in bed, still wrapped in a blanket, drinking a cup of hot tea. He looked like a big bony baby, shriveled and deformed. He got up, slipped his jacket over his clothes, and stumbled off to the outhouse, cursing Juárez and Tío Alvaro.

"How can this man be so stupid!" Flor yelled, pounding hard on la masa's gooey surface with both hands. "So crazy! I tell you, I've married the village idiot."

Abuela Teodora sighed, shook her head, poured water into the pot of good beans, and started washing them out. Estevan came back into the house, banging the door behind him.

"We're leaving for Juárez!" Flor yelled. "You need a doctor!"

"We're going nowhere," he managed to say.

Estevan's weakness had changed his voice. He now spoke as if he was far away from everyone, although he might be only two feet away. Before his illness, his children could sometimes hear him calling them when they had climbed to the top of a mountain peak.

"Die then!" Flor shouted.

In silence, Petra helped Abuela Teodora carry the pot of washed beans outside. On her way out, the old woman left the door open. "It's too hot in here, Flor, ya, get yourself under control. Maybe the cold air will do you some good for once—wake you up!"

Petra turned her face from her mother so she wouldn't see her smiling. Abuela Teodora had a knack for telling the truth. Petra herself was helpless to take sides between her mother and father. She wanted them both to win. She wanted to get to Juárez so her father could get help from a doctor, and she wanted to stay in Montenegro, on the land their father had worked so hard to keep.

It was early October, and the air smelled fresh, new. Petra took a deep breath before she and Abuela Teodora dumped the water out on the ground. They poured more water into the pot of beans and rinsed them one more time. Inside the house there was war. Outside, it was an ordinary day. The sun was shining overhead, warming up the cold morning. Nico and Ester were playing with a long stick, striking a rock between them, chasing it as it disappeared down the dirt road. Nico was twelve, and Ester had just turned seven. The children were playing as they did every day.

The beans were ready for cooking. Abuela Teodora and Petra got the firewood ready for the old wood-burning stove in the backyard. They filled the stove with firewood, ignited the dry brush, and set the pot of beans on top of it. Petra stretched out her back, her hands at her hips, and watched the old goat nudge Abuela Teodora with her head. The goat needed to be milked, as was obvious from her swollen udder. Petra was ready to follow Abuela Teodora to el granero, the old barn constructed of wooden planks and heavy tarp, to be the first to drink of the goat's sweet milk. Then she'd go back inside, pour herself a cup of coffee, and sweeten it with the milk. The day had just begun, and already she was weary. She had no idea how Abuela Teodora could walk so straight and move as quickly as she did from one task to another. Petra heard her mother angrily calling her back inside. Her voice was piercing, the voice of a woman gone mad.

"Petra-aaa!"

She held the last vowel of Petra's name as if she would never let it go. Petra wondered if that was the way she would hold on to her—forever. She stood still, shaking her head, her hands hanging dejectedly at her side. She watched in silence as Abuela Teodora followed the goat into el granero.

"Go," Abuela Teodora said. "Go before your mother comes out to look for you. It will be worse if she does."

Abuela Teodora had consulted with la curandera of Montenegro, Doña Lorena, concerning Estevan's illness. As a partera for the village, Abuela Teodora was famous for bringing children into the world, ministering to women from all walks of life. She had assisted at hundreds of births and had often consulted with Doña Lorena when a child was born with a cleft palate, a clubfoot, a forehead turned upside down, or a malady she couldn't diagnose. Now, she consulted with her about her son-in-law's illness.

Doña Lorena was tiny like Abuela Teodora, but broader and darker in complexion, and smelled of herbs and mesquite wood. Around her waist, she carried two pouches filled with concoctions made from plants, herbs, seeds, oil, and the powdered remains of things she wouldn't mention by name. Villagers said the old woman was over a hundred years old, and consultations with her were a matter of life and death.

All the treatments Doña Lorena had given Estevan had failed, and Abuela Teodora knew that death would soon follow unless her stubborn son-in-law took the old curandera's advice. Doña Lorena said Estevan was suffering from kidney disease and that his skin would turn yellow and he would die unless he got to a doctor to have his blood cleaned out in a process known to modern medicine.

"The matter is urgent," Doña Lorena said. Then she had turned away and refused to say another word.

Tío Alvaro came to the house when Estevan was visiting at his brother's down the road. He was tall, robust, his head almost bald, his manner imposing. He laughed easily and talked loudly. Alvaro was determined to help his sister, Flor, get her husband to Juárez. He walked in with a man from Ciudad Juárez named Gustavo Rios. Gustavo was short compared to Tío Alvaro. He was dressed neatly in a blue shirt and black pants and wore a huge golden medallion of Christ around his neck. His potbelly hung over his belt, and his skinny legs looked like the brittle stems of an ocotillo cactus. His eyes were shifty, taking in everything.

Tío Alvaro introduced him as someone from Ciudad Juárez who was passing through Montenegro. He had met him at a gas station in town. Flor had never had anyone visit them from Juárez except for family. She led Gustavo away from the sagging couch and invited him to sit in the best chair they had. Gustavo sat down casually, his legs extended before him as if he was a rich man waiting for a servant to get him a drink. When Abuela Teodora walked in cleaning off her sweaty forehead with the end of her apron, Flor asked her to bring Gustavo something to drink—water, coffee, una limonada, or even a shot of tequila. Gustavo shook his head—no, he was fine, he said, he had just had a meal. Nico and Ester ran in, excited about having company, and Flor stopped them at the door and told them to stay outside and wait, as the adults had business to discuss.

"Tell them," Alvaro said. "Tell them about the work in Juárez."

"Work? You want work?" Gustavo asked. "Well, what are you waiting for? You'll find it in Juárez. Thousands, yes I repeat, thousands of women work in las maquiladoras and make plenty of money to support their families. The Americans can't get enough of us Mexicans. They bring more and more of their factories to Juárez, and we supply their labor. What do we care as long as we get paid. Women are what they want. They say women make for better employees. They're not out drinking every weekend and demanding higher pay. They work hard, they get paid, they make a living. It's that easy. I work at Western Electronics. You can apply there, and I'll help you get in."

Petra was surprised to hear Gustavo say the name of the American-owned factory in perfect English. She wondered if he had ever lived in los Estados Unidos, or if he had studied English on his own. Gustavo didn't look directly at Petra, although she sensed he was studying her somehow and making it a point not to stare at her.

"What about work for Petra?" Flor asked him. "She'll be nineteen in December."

Gustavo looked at Petra as if he hadn't noticed her until then.

"Oh, is that your daughter?." He stood up, reached into his pocket, and took out his wallet. "Here," he said. "Take it." He handed Petra money, over four hundred pesos.

"No, I can't take this." She tried to give the money back to him. Flor stiffened, bit her lower lip, but said nothing.

"Take it. There's lots more where that came from. Use it for your father. Alvaro tells me he's sick. Is that true?" Gustavo asked the question as if it was a statement. He wanted it to be true, even if it wasn't. He was standing over Petra, looking intently into her eyes as if he was an interrogator forcing a confession from her.

"Yes."

Petra looked at the money in her hand and could do nothing more. She knew he had won, and she had lost. She took the money from him and noticed a look of satisfaction on his face. He grinned matter-of-factly, as if he had made a pact with her.

"So, is it settled? Can I count on you to come to Juárez?" He looked at Flor and smiled.

"Yes," Flor said. "There's nothing more we can do. If we stay here, Estevan will die. At least in Juárez we have a chance. I have a cousin there, Ofelia, and she says we can stay with her."

"Well said. What do you think, Alvaro?"

"I think it's a bad idea. Las maquiladoras have ruined us and have caused more trouble than they're worth. Don't you remember el NAFTA and what we went through? It started the suffering in our villages and all the people starving because they couldn't make any money with the things they grew on their farms. But under the circumstances, I see nothing more that my sister can do." He looked at Flor and said, "I'll drive you there. We can make it in eight hours, maybe less, depending on the roads."

Gustavo turned to look at Petra again. "And, Petra, you'll be meeting lots of other girls there. You'll have fun. You can go to the movies and buy new clothes. Would you like that?"

Petra curled her toes inside her shoes, which were so tight they hurt her feet. Gustavo Rios was bargaining with her, and it made her feel as if she was about to lose again. She thought of her father, fighting for his life, and sensed this stranger was ready to pounce on their misfortune, making it seem as if all that mattered to them was making money.

Shame and anger collided in Petra, and she rose to her feet, surprising herself as she faced Gustavo Rios and said boldly: "I only want my father to get well. I want nothing for myself!"

Flor stared at her daughter in shock. Her look was hard. Then, realizing Gustavo was watching them, she smiled sweetly, trying to reason with her daughter.

"Petra, Señor Rios is only thinking of our needs." Flor's voice became apologetic, and it angered Petra that her mother had to make excuses to this man because they had taken his money.

"Forgive my daughter," Flor said to Gustavo Rios. "She's been under great pressure. She loves her father, and—"

She stopped talking as Estevan walked in, sullenly. He greeted no one. He knew in one glance why Gustavo Rios was there. He pushed aside the curtain that divided the living room from the rest of the house. They heard the bedroom door open, then slam shut.

Petra was ready to run after her father, already feeling as if she had betrayed him by accepting the money from Gustavo Rios. Her mother reached out and put one hand on her daughter's arm.

"No! Petra, wait. There's nothing else we can do," she whispered. "You must understand." Petra saw her mother's eyes pleading with her, her hand on her arm, hard and cold. Petra nodded solemnly, looking down at the floor.

"Alvaro, can you drive us to Juárez?" Flor asked.

"Yes, of course. As soon as you're ready, we'll go." He put one hand on his sister's shoulder, a comforting gesture.

Gustavo Rios walked out without another word.

7 El maize is the gift of the gods and has sustained life since the beginning of time. Petra hoped it would sustain her family now. Padre Valdez, the priest at San Francisco del Desierto, had allowed Petra's mother to sell ears of corn, elotes, at church on Sundays, to help them through Estevan's illness. "How's Estevan?" he asked every Sunday, as Flor simmered los elotes in a huge pot that was set in a pit dug into the ground behind the church.

"Caprichoso as always. He won't go to Juárez where my cousin, Ofelia, says he can find a doctor to treat him."

Padre Valdez shook his head every time he heard Flor's reply and wondered if being that stubborn was a sin. He looked at Petra standing next to her mother and wrinkled his brow.

"Petra, you'll break men's hearts. I tell you, you will. Such beauty will not go unnoticed." Then he looked into her eyes as if he was seeing a ghost. "Stay close to your heart—whatever you do, stay close to your heart." He embraced her gently, and Petra smelled wine on the priest's breath and noticed his eyes, red and tearful.

The steam rose like incense in the cold morning, sending a sweet aroma into the air. It was the last Sunday Flor would sell los elotes at the church before the family left for Juárez. Abuela Teodora arranged salt, fresh slices of lime, chile, and butter for customers to add to the corn. In the summer, the heat in Montenegro was unbearable, and people didn't choose elotes as much. They ran over to the carts where men sold refreshing drinks: tamarindo, limón, mango, horchata, and homemade ice cream served in cups, or frozen in various fruit flavors on a Popsicle stick. The carts had names written in bright colors that were used to attract customers of all ages. Some had animal names like el Osito, the Little Bear, and la Iguana Mágica, the Magic Iguana. Others celebrated love, women, and popular songs: el Mil Amores, the Man of a Thousand Loves, la Princesa, the Princess, and Cielito Lindo, Beautiful Heaven. Every cart offered the same things, but the owners added their own twist to the merchandise and used pictures of cartoon characters to attract the children.

On the church steps, Petra saw Antonio Manriquez waving at her, and she waved back.

"A nice boy," Abuela Teodora said, "even though his grandfather was a drunk. He drank so much pulque that at last he died. They buried him, and I went to his funeral. I can show you the spot where he was buried because an enormous maguey plant now grows there. Everyone said it sprouted from his belly, so now the old man has all the pulque he wants!"

Then Abuela Teodora laughed, and Petra laughed with her, noticing tiny blank spaces in the old woman's mouth where teeth were missing. Petra sensed Antonio staring at her from the church steps, but she didn't turn his way because her mother was now looking at her. Flor said her daughter was in a hurry to become a woman and that she would regret it, just as she had.

Chavela Sabina, a Tarahumara Indian woman, tall, dressed in a long skirt and a blouse with huge red embroidered flowers, stopped to buy elotes for herself and her five children, as she did every Sunday. Flor smiled wearily, and Chavela understood. She held Flor's hand in hers, a gentle touch. Chavela's husband had been murdered in a fight with another man. Since then Chavela claimed no man, but continued bearing children for men who soon disappeared and were never heard from again. Flor charged her only a few centavos for los elotes, smaller ones for her ragged children, who stood staring at the iron pot as if they hadn't had a meal in days. They hardly smiled, or talked. Petra smiled at all of them, and one of the girls shrugged her shoulders and stuck her tongue out at her when Chavela wasn't looking. Her name was Mayela. Petra looked at her closely in surprise, then laughed, and Mayela giggled. The children all giggled and put their hands up to their mouths to hide their smiles.

Petra felt as if Mayela was a member of her own family, as she had been present at her birth when she was only seven years old. It was the first time Petra had ever seen a woman's agony raw and open, as things are in the lives of the poor. Life, death, struggle, blood—always blood. It was Cina, Chavela's sister, who had come looking for Abuela Teodora to help with the difficult birth. She was in a panic, saying that Chavela had been in labor for three days. Abuela Teodora and Flor took Petra with them as they left Montenegro with Cina for a tiny village called Chitlitipin in the mountains close by. When they got there, Chavela was in el granero, an old barn, still in labor. Outside, a terrible storm was about to break. El granero smelled of the excrement of the animals, and the whole place was damp and dark. Chavela lay on a pile of hay, fully dressed. Abuela Teodora, who was never frightened by anything, was alarmed at Chavela's condition. She tore off Chavela's skirt and with Cina's help laid her on a clean blanket she had brought with her. Then Abuela Teodora told Cina that she would have to help her sister bear the child. She told Cina to loop a rope over the wooden beams of el granero's roof, and together they all lifted Chavela to her feet. Abuela Teodora told Chavela to grab hold of the rope and bear down, and each time she asked her to bear down, Cina said the words to Chavela in their own language and bore down with her sister. Before it was all over, they were all bearing down with Chavela, including seven-year-old Petra.

The problem had been that Chavela had twins in her womb. One was born dead—a tiny boy, purple and still. Right after the birth of the boy, the women heard a clap of thunder that seemed to split the heavens in two and rumbled on in the distant sky for several terrifying seconds. It shook el granero and gave Chavela such a scare that she was able to bear down with new strength. Out came the second child, a girl, born purple as well but squirming with life. Chavela named her Mayela. Abuela Teodora cut the cord and saved a piece of it so Chavela could bury it close to their house. In this way, she would be assured that Mayela would follow the old traditions and never venture far from home. The women waited long enough in Chitlitipin to help Cina bury the dead baby under a tree. Abuela Teodora helped her arrange the tiny body in a small wooden box for its burial.

On their way back to Montenegro through the mountains of Chitlitipin, the women picked their way around arroyos swollen with the rain. Petra stared at the highest mountain peak, fearing she'd see el tsahuatsan, a huge serpent with seven heads that villagers said roamed the mountaintops. It was chased everywhere by thunderbolts and made a whistling sound as it was driven through the air by huge storms. Wherever it fell, a lake was formed.

Chavela was grateful to Abuela Teodora and Flor for saving her life and the life of her child, Mayela. She had something for Flor in a cloth bag she carried. Un ojo de Dios. She made them in different colors and sizes to sell, and she gave one to Flor to hang in their house in Juárez, she said, so God would watch over them. The four-pointed star made of colored yarn was red with black in the middle—God's eye, watching.

A dinner celebration was prepared the night before the family left for Juárez. The house was filled with the fragrant smell of fresh tortillas, beans, red chile, and los elotes simmering in a huge iron pot. Flor's sister, Susana, came over with a cake and fruit for the gathering. Susana was short with thin arms and legs, saying her stomach attracted all the fat she ate and there was nothing she could do about it. She laughed loudly, and her laughter annoyed Flor, who was serious and worried over everything.

Susana was full of pranks. She was like an elf, running from one person to another, collecting secrets like charms on a bracelet. She was especially fond of anything to do with love and matching up lovers. Her husband ignored her and let her do as she pleased, brooding silently at times while his wife danced alone at celebrations and acted more like a child than a full-grown woman.

Susana knew about Antonio Manriquez, the young man everyone said was hopelessly in love with Petra, and she also knew that her brother-in-law was very strict and would never allow Antonio to visit Petra. She told Petra that Antonio had been asking about her and was sad that she was leaving for Juárez.

"He'd like to see you before you leave."

"How?" Petra asked her.

They stood in the kitchen, cooking corn tortillas over the stove. Susana looked around the room and checked for intruders, then looped one arm over Petra's shoulder and lowered her voice. "Simple. He'll stop by tonight, and while everyone's busy eating and carrying on, you'll be outside in the dark saying good-bye."

She laughed and held onto her stomach. Then she got serious and asked, "That is, unless you don't want to see him?" She smiled, amused at Petra's solemn face.

Petra grabbed Susana's shoulders with both hands. "Are you joking with me? Of course, I want to see him!"

"Then it's done."

Petra danced side to side, holding hands with Susana, thinking she was lucky Susana acted more like a sister to her than an aunt. Just then, Flor walked into the kitchen, bringing with her a gloom, a dark cloud that made Petra and Susana freeze in their tracks.

"Celebrating already? And I thought you didn't want to go to Juárez, Petra." She looked sternly at her daughter, making her stare at the floor to avoid her eyes.

"I don't. But I'll do whatever it takes for mi papi."

"We're just having a little fun," Susana said. "No crime has been committed." Flor shook her head as if talking to Susana was hopeless.

"Gustavo Rios is going to get us jobs at la maquiladora where he works, didn't Petra tell you?"

"Not a word."

"Why should she? She was rude to him when she met him, and here the man was trying to help us. He said we can make good money working at la maquiladora, and we can save it to get our own house. In the mean-time, Ofelia will let us stay at her place. My poor cousin! She's always been so good to me. When Estevan gets better, we'll come back. I hope it's soon."

"I don't like Gustavo Rios," Petra told Susana. "I don't like the way he looks at me. I think he's one of those dirty old men who chases women."

Flor, who was stirring chile on the stove, looked up at her daughter. "Get used to it. That's the way men are. They'll look at you like they can see right through your clothes. They look that way at all beautiful women. Isn't it true, Susana?"

"Very true," Susana said. "And Petra will be plagued all her life with men looking at her. You can count on that. Just look at her!" She put her hand under Petra's chin and lifted her face. "The face of a queen. Don't you think so, Flor? If I had Petra's eyes and that slender neck—made for wearing pearls. I tell you, I might keep Gilberto's attention for more than five minutes!"

"Don't give her a big head, Susana! You know how her father is. If it were up to him, she wouldn't go out at all until she left the house as a married woman." Then she added: "I've had my share of men looking at me that way. Of course, now it's different. But when I was Petra's age, that's the way it was. Get used to it, Petra. Ignore it."

"Yes, ignore it, Petra," Susana said. "Men can be nasty, and they think nasty thoughts. Thank God, you'll only be working at la maquiladora. You probably won't see much of Gustavo Rios."

Abuela Teodora walked in, having heard the last part of their conversation.

"Men like that should learn to respect. They have no right to treat women like that. We're not prostitutes! If they're so hungry for a woman, they know where to find one."

Abuela Teodora was angry. Petra could hear it in her voice. She sat down at the table still muttering to herself, angrily dicing up onions, jala-peños, and cilantro, ingredients she would add to tomatoes to make the rich spicy salsa she was famous for.

"Don't encourage her, Mamá," Flor said. "I'm trying to prepare her for the way men are." She sighed deeply. "Gustavo probably has his wife and children. It's just that he was here alone, and when they're alone they take advantage of their freedom."

Abuela Teodora wasn't happy with Flor's response, but she said nothing more. Her eyes had tears from the onions she was cutting up, but it seemed to Petra that the old woman had been crying even before that.

"I still don't like him," Petra told her mother, feeling as though Gustavo Rios already had some strange claim over her. "I don't want anything to do with him."

"I don't like him either," Susana said. "And I don't even know him." She winked one eye at Petra, and Flor shook her head in silence, banging the lid over the pot of chile.

That evening, Tío Carlos, Estevan's brother, came by to celebrate the family's farewell with his wife and daughter. Gilberto, Tía Susana's husband, brought their three children. Petra's friends Lizette and Maribel came by with their parents. No one was in a festive mood, but everyone ate and drank anyway. Tío Alvaro walked in with bottles of tequila, and the men all drank, even Estevan who was miserable and ill. As the sun set, the evening turned cold, and the men started a fire with dry wood and brush in a pit dug into the ground. The fire sent warm waves of heat into the cold night, vibrating orange, red, and purple, and spewed tiny sparks that looked like fireflies spinning off into the darkness. Everyone sat outside on old chairs and wooden crates as long as they could stand it without freezing. The men emptied a bottle of tequila and opened another one. Tío Carlos pulled out his guitar and started strumming, playing beautifully, and pretty soon everyone was singing and dancing under the moonlight.

Inside the house, Flor prepared for the trip to Juárez. She packed their clothes and got food ready to eat along the way. Abuela Teodora had made extra tortillas and boiled pumpkin, using it to bake empanadas, Petra's favorite. The dough was fresh and soft, the pumpkin spiced with sugar and cinnamon.

Petra was trying to be casual about meeting Antonio, but she was nervous and kept running up to Susana to ask her if he had arrived.

"Stop worrying; I know how to do these things." She squeezed Petra's hand and smiled.

Lizette and Maribel didn't leave Petra's side the whole time. They looked over pictures they had taken of each other and talked about their school days, holding hands and laughing at their funny hairdos and childish clothes. Time was passing by, and still no Antonio. Susana was making the most of every minute. She was secretive and wouldn't give Petra an answer, playing a cat and mouse game with her. Then, just as Petra began to lose hope, Susana signaled her to a corner of the house and told her Antonio had arrived and was waiting for her behind el granero. Lizette and Maribel said they would take over Petra's tasks and nobody would notice she was gone.

Petra walked quickly, choosing not to run and attract attention as she made her way in the darkness to Antonio. She saw his silhouette, tall and slender, and as she approached, his handsome face overpowered her. People in Montenegro commented on what a fine couple Petra and Antonio made—tall, good looking. They were perfect for each other, the villagers said.

Petra stood with Antonio under a full moon that rose in the sky like a bright silver disk. They had never been alone together, and Petra felt awkward. They looked at each other, neither knowing what to say. Then they moved closer, and Antonio put his hands on Petra's shoulders. She shivered even though his hands felt warm. Wind was blowing in from the mountains, and Petra could smell el granero—hay and animal droppings, mixed in with the smell of gasoline from a small tractor her father owned. They were clumsy together, until the old mare in el granero snorted loudly, and they laughed and then embraced for what seemed like a long time. Petra could feel Antonio's sturdy shoulder against her face, the strength of his arm, the wide expanse of his back.

"It won't be long, Petra. You'll see; you'll be back in Montenegro, or I'll go to Juárez. You know how I feel. I love you so—more than you know—and always will. When your father gets well, things will be different. We'll get married. Promise me?" Although Antonio was whispering, his voice seemed magnified in the dark.

"Yes, I promise. I'll be back as soon as I can. We'll get married just as we planned when we were children."

Then he kissed her, lightly at first. She pressed closer for more, and they kissed again, and the giving was sweet between them. Antonio kissed her hands and put a ring on her finger.

"There, so you won't forget me!" There were tears between them as they held on tightly to each other. Petra heard Susana talking loudly in the distance.

"She's around here somewhere! I think she's out back getting more wood."

Antonio disappeared into the darkness, and Petra stood alone, feeling a bitter cold wind blowing in from the mountains of Montenegro. Suddenly, she felt the cold in her bones and shivered. The crouching figures on the mountains of Montenegro were watching them silently in the dark. In the distance, she saw her brother, Nico, a small lone figure outlined by the moonlight. Nico stopped briefly as he saw Antonio race away, then looked back at Petra. She knew he wouldn't say a thing.

A comet streaked across the sky, one ambitious comet among a million stars. It was a bad omen. In the ancient world, a comet meant disaster would strike. Petra made the sign of the cross over herself as quickly as she could. Villagers said that if you made the sign of the cross over yourself before the comet's tail disappeared, you would cancel any unknown disaster.

Estevan got drunk and made things worse for everyone, saying he wouldn't go to Juárez and would rather die in Montenegro—at least it would be with dignity. The men took him outside to try to reason with him. Petra watched from the window as her uncles, Gilberto and Alvaro, and Lizette's father, Don Eusenio, talked to her father as if he was a child. He was staggering back and forth, trying to get away from them, but the men cornered him, staying close. The moon was a silver globe in the sky, the stars were shining overhead, and her father was drunk and afraid. Petra wanted to go out to him, hold his hand, lead him back inside the house, but she knew it was useless. He'd never listen to her. He was caught up in pain so deep, it had worn him down to a fragment of the man he had been. For Petra this was the worst part of her father's illness.

"I'll shoot myself!" she heard him say. "So help me God! I have nothing to live for."

"So this is the way you'll repay your family for all the love they have for you?" Alvaro asked him.

"Stay out of this; it's none of your business!"

"Hermanito," Carlos said. "Listen to reason. You're ill. You have a fever. I know it. Go inside, rest—sleep. Tomorrow you'll be in Juárez. You'll find a good doctor. Before long you'll be well and able to come back and take over the ranch again. I'll run it while you're gone."

Then Petra saw her father break down, fall into the arms of his brother, and hold onto him as if he was a child. They cried because they had been together since they were born, and now, for the first time in their lives, one of them was leaving.

8   The sun rose over the ridge of the mountains, breaking through thin white clouds, warming up the cold morning. Every morning Abuela Teodora roused her granddaughter by whispering in her ear, *Sing, Petra, sing to the morning,* expecting her to get up silently and follow her outdoors to greet the morning sun. The rest of the family was asleep, breathing deeply under blankets, all except Estevan, who hardly slept at all with all the pain he suffered. The morning was fresh, alive, the air wet with dew.

Abuela Teodora looked first to the east, lifting her elegant face to greet the rising sun. Once it climbed over the mountains, the sun's radiance enveloped her like a mirror reflecting its light on her face. She had taught Petra to sing to the four directions, north, south, east, and west, giving each direction its due. They sang in Rarámuri, mimicking the sounds of the chirping birds, the old woman's voice raspy and trembling and Petra's voice high and full, trilling out the words Abuela Teodora had learned from her Tarahumara grandmother. As they sang, they became the keys spoken about by the ancients, the keys that opened the doors to heaven, which were many. According to legend, each man and woman is a key that fits perfectly into one of heaven's doors. Petra imagined the doors for her and Abuela Teodora would be side by side, and they'd fit their keys perfectly into keyholes and live as neighbors for all eternity. The words of their song sank deeply into mountains and rocks, sky and desert sand. The song was old, primitive.

> Iwéra rega chukú kéti Ono
> Mápu tamí mo nesériga ináro sinibísi rawé
> Ga'lá kaníliga bela ta semáribo
> Si'néame ka o'mána wichimoba eperéame
> Népi iwérali bela ta ásibo
> Kéti ono mápu tamí neséroga ináro ne

Né ga'lá kaníliga bela ta narepabo
Uchécho bilé rawé mápu kéti Onó nijí
Ga'lá semá rega bela ta semáripo
Uchécho bilé rawé najata je'ná wichimobachi
Népi ga'lá iwérali bela ko nijísibo
Si'néame ka mápu ikí ta eperé je'ná kawírali

Uchécho bilé rawé bela ko ju
Mápu rega machiboo uchécho si'nú ra'íchali
Uchécho bilé rawé bela ko ju
Mápu ne chapiméa uchécho si'nú 'nátali
Népi iwéraga bela 'nalína ru
Uchúpa ale tamojé si'néame pagótami

Echiregá bela ne nimí wikaráme ru
Mápu mo tamí nesériga chukú sinibísi rawé
Echiregá bela ne nimí iwérali ásima ru
Mápu ketási mo sewéka inárima siníbisi rawé
Népi iwériga bela mo nesérima ru
Mápu ikí uchúchali a'lí ko mo alewá aale

*   *   *

Be strong father sun,
you who daily care for us.
Those who live on earth are living well.
We continue giving strength to our father,
who fills our days with energy and light.

With great joy we salute our father
with one more day of life.
We are living well following one more day on earth
as you light our way.

One more day to learn new words,
one more day to think new thoughts,

giving you strength you in turn
give energy to your brothers.

Thus I will sing
to you who daily care for me.
Thus will I give you strength
so you will not be discouraged.
With all your strength
care for those you have created
and given the breath of life.

Abuela Teodora blessed Petra with the sign of the cross.

"Father, Creator, for my granddaughter, for Petra, protect her, fill her with wisdom, knowledge, understanding. Above all, love." It was Abuela Teodora's way of saying good-bye. She'd join them in Juárez when they got a place of their own.

Petra was crying for herself, for her family, for Abuela Teodora who sang to the morning. They stood embracing tightly until the sun was well into the sky, white light shimmering. After their prayers, Petra wanted to crawl back into the bed she shared with her little sister Ester, but by then it was too late. Her mother was up, though her father was still in bed, cradling himself into a ball under a blanket, as if that would make his pain go away.

Estevan couldn't get up. The drinking had made him even sicker. His skin had turned yellow, just like Doña Lorena had said it would. Flor made a cup of tea for her husband and was trying to get him to drink it when Alvaro came by to pick them up in his old station wagon. Petra looked out the window at Alvaro's car and wondered if it would make it across the desert, for four hundred miles or more.

"It's morning. I'm ready to go!" Alvaro said loudly.

Hearing his voice, Estevan got up, sick to his stomach. He staggered to the back door and out into the yard. Ester and Nico were up, rubbing their eyes, afraid now that their father was so sick. Ester rushed after her father, her long unbraided hair flying behind her like a cape, but Flor grabbed her daughter in her arms and pulled her back in.

"Get ready! We're leaving. Wash your face, put your shoes on, and get ready to get on the road." Everyone stood still and looked at Flor, wondering what she would do next.

"Are you listening to me? Are you all deaf?" Her face was flushed with anger. She was trembling. Petra knew her mother was afraid. She wanted to see them on the road and in Juárez, at Ofelia's house, with Estevan on his way to the hospital. Petra walked up to her mother and put her arms around her.

"Mamá, we can't go with my father as sick as he is. We have to wait." Her mother was shivering. "Get Mamá her sweater," she told Nico.

He brought it, and Petra helped her mother put it on. They both walked out to the backyard and found Estevan had collapsed on the ground. Flor screamed, and Alvaro rushed out. Between Flor and Alvaro, they lifted Estevan to his feet. He stumbled frantically, trying to balance himself on his own. His ashen face resembled a grotesque mask that made him look as if he was already dead.

"Walk him, Flor, slowly. We'll have him rest for a few hours. I knew it was a mistake, all the drinking he was doing. We can leave by this afternoon. It might be better—the roads will be deserted at night, and I know the way."

Flor and Alvaro walked Estevan back to bed, while he mumbled curses at them and at Juárez. Abuela Teodora was standing by the stove, serving pinole, smooth grainy cereal, in ceramic bowls. There was thick golden honey from their beehives on the table to sweeten it with. The old woman's face was sorrowful as she saw them leading Estevan back to bed.

"Eat, all of you—you must, to keep up your strength," she said.

Sitting at the table, Nico showed them a sketch he had drawn, a picture of their house with the sun shining over it, the ahuehuete tree in the backyard, the henhouse, el granero, and their father's old rusty car discarded behind the house.

Tío Alvaro walked into the kitchen and asked Petra for a cup of coffee. She served it to him, and he sat with them at the table, smiling, trying to soothe the children as they ate.

"Are you ready to make the trip of your lives? It's like going to Disneylandia. One of my cousins who crossed over to El Paso went there. Mickey Mouse and Donald Duck!"

He acted like he was wearing mouse ears, cupping his hands over his ears and saying in a squeaky voice: "You come to Disneylandia, but first to Juárez? No cats, no cats!" Ester and Nico laughed at his antics.

"And you?" he asked Petra. "Petra, the beautiful! I'll have to keep the boys away from you with a big bat."

He got up and acted as if he was swinging a baseball bat. "Stay away from my niece, you bunch of no-good ugly scoundrels! There! There! Take that, and if you don't leave her alone, you'll get more!"

Petra smiled to see her bald-headed uncle swinging a make-believe baseball bat at invisible suitors.

"No, it won't happen. I'm there to work!"

She thought about Antonio and the ring he had given her. She had put the ring away so as not to have to explain it to her parents.

"Look! You're blushing."

Petra sensed her face turning red and thought harder of Antonio. No one would know about him unless they looked into her heart.

"Antonio? Antoooo—nio! Oh, where are you?" Alvaro put his hand up to his heart, calling Antonio's name over and over again, rolling his eyes.

Petra stood up and grabbed the rolling pin, pretending to strike her uncle on the head with it, while Abuela Teodora looked on smiling.

The more Petra told her uncle to stop, the louder he called out Antonio's name, until they all burst into laughter. She wondered if she was that obvious about Antonio and told herself she would have to stop showing her feelings to everyone. Flor walked in and smiled at all of them, even though there were tears in her eyes.

"Alvaro, behave yourself!" she said. Then she looked at Petra. "Your father's feeling better. He's gaining his strength. Pretty soon, we'll be able to leave."

Flor looked at Abuela Teodora's face and knew she had been crying. "It's not like we're going forever, Mamá. As soon as Estevan is better, we'll be back. Ester and Nico will be able to go to school; Petra will work with me in la maquiladora. Alvaro will keep you informed, won't you, Alvaro?"

"Who me? Oh yes, Mamá, you can count on me. I'll keep you informed of everything."

"You can stay here with me," Abuela Teodora said to him. "Stay here, Alvaro." She seemed to be pleading with him.

"Of course, as much as I can. You know the demands of my work. I have to live on the Gonzalez ranch. The whole place would collapse without me. Nobody seems to know what to do next. Besides, Susana and her husband will visit you every day."

By the time they left for Juárez, it was night. Doña Lorena had stopped by and given Estevan a treatment that she said would make him feel better until they got to Juárez. Doña Lorena's dark eyes looked at them compassionately. She said simply: "It is urgent. His blood must be cleaned out—the doctors will know."

As they left for Juárez, Petra looked back at the mountains of Montenegro and at the immense crouching figures that seemed to be dancing in the dark, swaying, as the moon sailed high into the sky. From the road, she made out the rocky arroyo where el Río Gris had once flowed. In the moonlight the rocky crag looked like a silver spoon. The night was dark, and the road was long and lonely. They traveled for hours, until Petra's legs were numb, her hands and nose icy cold. They took with them food that Abuela Teodora and Flor had packed for them in brown bags. There was a weakness in Petra without Abuela Teodora, a sense of things gone wrong. A hole opened inside her, as if a piece of the black sky had forced its way into her heart. She thought of Antonio and knew he was awake and thinking of her, making plans on how he would talk to her father once he got his health back.

Flor and Alvaro whispered to each other about how dark the road was and how isolated.

"Devils and angels everywhere," Alvaro said.

In the dark, Petra saw his head turn this way and that, scanning the landscape. He talked to Flor about how they would deal with Abuela Teodora's worries. They didn't want to add to their mother's troubles and decided they wouldn't tell her about any problems.

"Ya, sabes," Flor said. "You know how my mother is. She'll die just to think we're suffering."

Flor spotted a coyote running across the road and said she saw the color of its eyes—yellow in the car's headlights. It was gone as quickly as it had appeared.

"At least it's not a human coyote," Alvaro said. "I myself prefer the ones with bushy tails, not the ones who carry guns."

In the seat behind Petra, Ester and Nico were sleeping. They were two small bundles covered over by a blanket among suitcases, soda pop, bottled water, bags of tangerines, limes, and pecans for Ofelia. Leaning upright against a back window was a tire and tools for fixing a flat. On top of the station wagon, Alvaro had tied two more suitcases. Abuela Teodora had looked at the packed car and shaken her head, frowning. "Looks like you'll be gone a long time," she had said sadly.

Petra listened to Ester and Nico breathing gently. Once in a while Nico held his breath, then let it out in a short honking snort, as if he was already learning how to snore. She sat next to her father, who was wrapped in a flannel blanket and leaning heavily on a pillow set up against the back window. He said nothing, only sighed, sucked his teeth, groaned, and mumbled things Petra couldn't understand. She put her hand on his forehead. It was hot. Fear seized her.

"My papi's got a fever," she told her mother. Petra leaned over her father. He smelled like stale alcohol and sweat.

"I know, Petra," her mother said, irritated. "There's nothing I can do about it. I've given him aspirin and his antibiotics." She shook her head. "I tell you this girl wants me to perform miracles."

Petra closed her eyes. She was too weary to answer her mother. Her eyes were dry, the lids heavy, and she felt herself drifting off to sleep, sensing Antonio's hand pulling her up out of something she had fallen into—a chasm, a deep dark ditch. Suddenly, the car hit a huge hole in the road.

"Ándale!" Tío Alvaro said out loud. "Somebody's hoping the car will break down so they can climb in with us."

The jolt was enough to rouse Petra. For a second, she had lost her bearings, thinking she really had Antonio's hand in hers. Then she felt cold wind blowing in through the cracks of the car, freezing wind and eerie darkness everywhere, and she remembered: they were on the road to Juárez, and Tío Alvaro had been driving for hours now. She was sure he must be exhausted.

As the car climbed over a rocky hill, the motor pulled hard, making the car shake and rattling the windows. Petra opened her eyes, and there before her, over the crest of a hill, was Juárez. The city's lights sparkled dimly in the night, like a huge canopy of light spread before them, extending as far as the eye could see. She couldn't believe the lights. There were so many! In Montenegro, they slept in darkness, profound darkness, pierced occasionally by an electric lightbulb or a lantern. But this! Was she dreaming?

Then Alvaro said: "There she is, Juárez! But where did she come from? She came up from the dust, formed herself out of the rocks and craters that used to hold dinosaur bones. And now look at her! There's no end to her, or to us. Juárez, how great, how sinful, full of malice—and how we need you!"

Tío Alvaro's voice filled with emotion. In the dark, Petra heard her mother's tired voice: "How many more kilometers? How much longer to get to Ofelia's? She'll be waiting, I'm sure. Poor Ofelia, with a bed ready for Estevan."

Next to Petra her father sighed, shifted his weight, adjusting the pillow under his head and angling his legs in a new position. Petra reached for her father's legs and put them on her lap.

"Papi, rest your legs on my lap. Rest, Papi, rest!"

"Don't worry about me," he said in an irritated voice. "I'm all right." His voice was weak, weaker than Petra had ever heard it before. She put her hand on his shoulder, gently stroking his arm.

"Petra, don't worry about your old father. The doctors will get me well. Juárez has good doctors. If nothing else, they have doctors."

"How many kilometers?" Flor asked again.

"Oh, not long, maybe thirty. Rest, compadre," Alvaro said to Estevan. "Don't get yourself worked up. You've seen Juárez before. Remember when we came here to deliver supplies for the concrete place we worked for. Ah, it was so hard, such a long haul, you remember? How they cheated us! Oh, they made us work nonstop for three days. Then they turned around and told us we had to collect from the American owners. We had to prove we had driven the truck and brought in the concrete all the way ourselves. We had no proof; we had no time cards. We had nothing. We weren't union members. We were poor men, young, working for pennies to support our families. I laugh now because I should have seen through their lies, but then, remember how young we were? Young, stupid, tontos!"

"Don't remind me. If it were up to me, I would turn this car around and go back to Montenegro."

"Stop, Alvaro!" Flor said. "Why bring up the past? It'll be good to get to Juárez. Ofelia says she has a doctor who will see Estevan tomorrow morning. And we can start saving for a place of our own."

"A place of your own? You mean a shack, a cardboard box. I already told you, Flor, you'll find no house you can afford in Juárez."

"You told me, but God will provide."

"Only if he has a powerful political friend. Everything is politics and power. Drugs everywhere. God will have to create a house for you from out of nowhere. That's how you'll get a house."

Estevan mumbled something Petra couldn't understand. He talked like he was crazy when the fever was bad.

"Stop. You're scaring Petra," Flor said. Petra wanted to say, *and my father*, but remained silent.

"Are you afraid, Petra? But no, don't be afraid." Alvaro turned around briefly to look back at her. She saw his silhouette in the dark, his double chin, the nose a straight edge.

"Are you afraid, Petra?" he asked again.

"No!" she said with as much strength as she could. She wanted to sound firm, secure. Why should she be afraid? Her mother and father were with her, Tío Alvaro knew the road, and Ester and Nico were asleep, safe in the backseat. True, it was cold, the road rough and desolate, and they had had no dinner. Besides that, her back and legs were numb, her vision blurred from not sleeping. She felt her father's forehead. It was burning with fever, but there were all the lights, and Juárez was spread before them—doctors for her father, work for her and her mother in las maquiladoras. Gustavo Rios said they would make plenty of money in la maquiladora. Western Electronics. Plenty of work, he said, and they hired women by the hundreds, by the thousands, lots of opportunity. He said they'd make money while her father recuperated from his illness. He needed dialysis, and no one knew how long he would last on the machines. Perhaps one of them would have to give him a kidney—they had not talked about it yet. Maybe it would be her. Yes, she wanted it to be her. Spare everyone else. She'd work at la maquiladora too, learn to speak English, learn the American way of doing things, and how to deal with men like Gustavo Rios. She saw his face in her mind, grinning, self-satisfied, sure that he had made a pact with her. She had given her mother the money he gave her, and she had used it to get them on the road and to buy food and household supplies Abuela Teodora would need.

Petra made up her mind that she would not accept any more money from Gustavo Rios and hoped she wouldn't see much of him in Juárez.

Petra saw her mother shake her head and sigh heavily. Then she leaned her head on the window, while Petra did the same in the backseat. Perhaps they could catch each other in dreams, hold hands, race together over the rough, rocky road, and get to Juárez laughing, free, liberated women, ready to work in la maquiladora and make money—so much they would have to open a bank account.

When Petra woke, dawn was appearing, a thin gray light glowing in the east. In her mind, Petra heard Abuela Teodora's voice, *Sing, Petra, sing to the morning.* She gazed out the window and looked for the sun, singing the ancient song in her head. They were traveling north, the sun at her right shining dimly. She knew Abuela Teodora had already sung her song, greeted the sun, prayed for them.

They entered Juárez, rounding corners of dark streets and driving over holes and rocky ground that made Alvaro's car rattle and sway. It was early, and the city was quiet. City buses, las ruteras, passed them by, headed for las colonias to pick up their customers, spewing trails of black fumes behind them. They were driving along el Río Bravo, and Petra could see los Estados Unidos across the river. Tall buildings and rows of street-lights outlined in the early dawn—that was America. On the Mexican side, there were lotes baldíos, empty lots, old cars discarded here and there, and unpaved streets with dust rising in clouds as las ruteras made their rounds. They drove into la colonia San Fernando where Ofelia lived, and Petra saw dirt roads leading everywhere. There were rows and rows of houses stacked against each other, like a child's lopsided building blocks, and in the distance she saw houses made of cardboard, planks, old tires, and rusty metal pieces from cars and buses. Some houses were built one on top of another, precariously clinging to rocky hillsides. Tiny fires appeared in the distant hills, as people who had no electricity prepared to cook their meals outdoors. Thousands of electrical wires, strung together by the destitute residents of San Fernando, hung between houses and over roadways to secure electricity illegally from Mexico's power lines. It reminded Petra of the people of Montenegro and their will to survive. In spite of el conquistador's greed for the waters of el Río Gris, they had existed in their village for hundreds of years.

A few people walked out on the streets in the early dawn, some of them mothers with their children on their way to nearby stores and tortillerias. Alvaro turned sharply on one of the dirt roads and had to put his car into its lowest gear to get it going up a steep hill. Petra heard a siren sounding far away. She didn't tell anyone, but a sudden, overwhelming fear seized her. It began in the pit of her stomach and spun out of control, making her heart beat wildly. Something was there in the gray dawn with the siren sounding in the distance and the sun rising through a cloud of dust. Something was there—waiting for her.

Love Doesn't Exist, Only Need

9 Evita arrived at Isidora's on her fourteenth birthday, September 25, with her schoolbag looped over her shoulders and Ofelia's words still ringing in her ears. She was on the move again, a tiny gypsy, nameless on the hectic streets, her face a small white blur seen through la rutera's windows. She didn't feel any different now that she was fourteen. In fact, she didn't want to think about it.

Evita walked up to Isidora's door and knocked, but no one answered. So she reached into her pocket for a key Isidora had given her wrapped tightly in a Kleenex. As she walked in, she smelled what must have been breakfast—eggs, potatoes, onions—and from Isidora's room she caught the minty pasty smell of her ointment. Dirty dishes were everywhere, and Evita knew there wasn't anybody doing much to keep the place clean. Anabel was the only one home, and she was lying in bed in the dark. She told Evita to close the door—she was sick. It took a lot of effort for her to talk. Anabel's teeth were chattering as if she was freezing to death, and when she spoke it seemed her tongue was stuck to the top of her mouth. In the dim room, Evita could see Anabel's body curled up into a ball, wearing only underwear. An electric fan was on, blowing around hot air. Evita asked her if she needed help, and she said no, there was nothing she could do except wait for Isidora who had gone out to get her some medicine.

"Close the door," she said wearily. "Close the door."

"Where's Cristal?" Evita asked her.

"I don't know!" she yelled. "And stop asking me questions!"

Anabel had never been hard with Evita, and her words stung. Evita wanted to ask her if she was sick because of something she had eaten at

67

the restaurant where she worked, but she didn't want to make her mad. Anabel moaned and started calling out for her mother. Evita knew her mother was dead, and she was afraid that if Anabel called any louder, her mother might stop by to help her.

Before long, Isidora came in with boxes of medicine stamped with long medical names. Like before, the boxes were inside plastic bags. Evita was in the kitchen washing dishes and fixing a cup of tea for Anabel. Isidora embraced her in her huge lumpy arms.

"Ay, Evita, I've been missing you! There's no one to help me clean this house, run the errands, and pick up the medicine for the clinic in El Paso. No one but you!"

Evita felt good seeing Isidora again. She leaned on Isidora's big body when she hugged her, and something came up in her throat that made her swallow hard to keep herself from crying. She wanted to tell Isidora about her mother's new man, and about her cousin Petra, who would soon come to Juárez and take her place at her madrina's house, but decided it wasn't the right time with Anabel sick in the next room. She told Isidora it was her fourteenth birthday, and Isidora laughed and said "Feliz cumpleaños," and told her that later she'd go down to the bakery and buy her a birthday cake for a celebration.

Isidora opened one of the boxes of medicine and took out various plastic bags of powdered substances, some with labels, others with needles and syringes, and plastic bottles with pills. Evita wondered at all the medicine, thinking there must be more sick people in El Paso than there were in Juárez. She had thought Americans were healthier.

Isidora walked into Anabel's dark room and shut the door. Evita saw a tiny light escape from under the door. Later Isidora came out and said Anabel would feel better soon. She asked Evita to help her stack all the boxes of medicine in her room—someone would come by soon to pick them up. Before she had said the last word someone knocked on the door. Evita opened it and saw a man leaning against the adobe bricks of Isidora's house, acting like it was any other day and whistling a tune. It was Chano, Luis Ledezma's brother. He wasn't wearing all his worn-out wrinkled clothes, but instead had on a white shirt and black pants and looked decent. He wasn't surprised to see Evita and tilted his head to one side to stare at her through dark sunglasses, all the while smiling, showing gray crooked teeth.

"Evita. I had to see it to believe it," he said. "But you're here, it's true. Well, now you're in business just like me!" When he said that, Evita remembered what Ricardo had said to her—that someday she would be in business for herself. She stared at Chano with her mouth open in surprise and remembered how he had tried to pull her underwear down the day he chased her from school, making her run so fast she lost one of Lety's big shoes. Isidora came to the door, opened it wide, and told Chano to come in.

"They're over there," she said, her voice flat, her eyes avoiding his.

Chano walked in, brisk and businesslike, grabbed the plastic bags with all the medicine, and walked out with them. He didn't say anything to Isidora, not even a greeting, and that's when Evita realized that Isidora was helping transport drugs. She wanted to yell at Isidora and tell her she didn't want anything to do with drugs and then walk right out the door before anything else happened. She thought about going home, but Chano lived across the street from her mother's house. All he had to do was cross the dirt road and tell Brisa where she was and what she had been doing at Isidora's. Isidora looked at Evita, seeing the fear and mutiny in her eyes.

"Don't think about leaving, Evita. I'm only doing it as a favor for someone important. It will end soon, and no one will ever know."

She sighed heavily and wobbled away in pain. Evita picked up the ointment she saw on the kitchen table and followed Isidora to her room, knowing no one had rubbed her legs since she had been gone.

By noon, Anabel was feeling better and invited Evita to go shopping. She would buy her some clothes for her birthday, she said. They went out to los mercados and tried on all kinds of clothes, shoes, hats, and underwear. Evita asked Anabel about Isidora and the drugs she saw Chano take out of the house. Anabel told her she must never call it drugs.

"It's medicine for a clinic in El Paso that serves the poor. Los Americanos won't let their people get certain medicines because they have so many rules and laws in los Estados Unidos, so Isidora helps them out. Don't ask questions and don't answer any," Anabel told her firmly. "Always say you don't know anything. Besides, Isidora knows how to take care of herself. She's working for someone important who protects her, and nothing will come of it. No matter what happens, always say you don't know anything. Do you understand?" Anabel looked down at Evita as they crossed the street, and Evita nodded. "You're a child," she said, "and no one will suspect you."

Evita wanted to ask Anabel a hundred questions about the drugs and tell her she was afraid, especially now that she knew Chano was involved, but Anabel didn't let her. She held Evita's hand tightly. "You're like my little sister," she said, tears gathering in her eyes. Evita looked up at her and smiled, pretending she wasn't afraid anymore, but all the while she was looking everywhere for el chofer and any signs of a police car.

Anabel was wearing tight jeans, a small black top, and shoes with big plastic heels. Her face was beautiful, her makeup impeccable, and at times she tossed her head back like a restless colt in a way that made her long shiny hair fall evenly down her back like a silky mane. Men whistled at her and said things when they walked by. She ignored them all and moved on, walking straight and curving her back so her breasts showed round and full. Evita was impressed by all the attention Anabel was getting and walked proudly at her side. They walked into a women's clothing store that specialized in lingerie and sexy gowns.

"Buy yourself some sexy underwear," Anabel said, and she laughed and held up a tiny black lacy bra in her hands. "Yes, do it Evita! You're growing up now."

Evita's face turned red as she looked at the bra and wondered how it would look on her tiny breasts.

"You'll love it!" Anabel said, rummaging around on a display table for matching panties and nylons. Then she turned to a rack of fancy dresses. "Take this dress too," she said, holding up a red silky dress and pressing it up to Evita's body. The dress went down to Evita's knees, but had a big slit on one side that traveled all the way up her thigh.

"I won't look good in it."

"Of course you will. Your skin is light, not dark like mine. You're made to wear red."

"Your skin's not dark!" Evita said, shocked that Anabel would describe herself as anything less than perfect.

"Yours is lighter," Anabel said, smiling.

The woman at the counter knew who Anabel was and gave her a discount when she found out it was Evita's birthday present.

When Evita asked Anabel if she was going to work, she said not today—her boss knew she had been sick. "Don't worry," she said confidently. "It's all been taken care of."

Anabel held Evita's hand everywhere they went, from store to store, just like she was her big sister. It was as if Anabel wanted to make up to Evita for yelling at her when she was sick. A man walking past them with his wife and two children looked at Anabel and lifted an eyebrow at her. Anabel only glanced at him.

She leaned toward Evita and whispered, "He's one of the customers at the restaurant."

Then without warning, she grabbed Evita by one arm and ran into a store with her. "Let's hide!" she said. When Evita asked her why, she said one of her bosses from the restaurant was coming their way, and she didn't want him to see her.

"But I thought you said they knew you were sick?"

"No! Not him, he's one of the sons of the owner. He doesn't believe anyone. In his mind, no one can get sick!"

They walked as fast as they could through one of the stores and out the back door, running into an alley to avoid bumping into the man who didn't like anyone to be sick.

By late afternoon, the girls were back at Isidora's. She had bought a cake for Evita at a nearby bakery and had invited an old man named Don Sancho from la Zona del Canal to stop by and play "Las Mañanitas" on his guitar for her. Don Sancho said he was named Sancho because his mother kept having children by Sanchos all over las zonas and wasn't sure which Sancho was his father. Don Sancho was dressed in tattered clothes and wore a huge sombrero with a frayed silk ribbon and missing sequins that may have belonged to a real mariachi at one time but was now fit for the junk pile. There was a round cake on the table with pink frosting and the sugar face of a girl on it, with the words *Feliz Cumpleaños, Evita*. Isidora told Evita to lean over her lap, and she slapped her playfully on the bottom fourteen times. When it was over, Evita hugged Isidora tenderly, grateful she still had her in her life and already wishing she didn't know about the drugs. They shared a secret now, deep and dark, which joined them together in a pact more powerful than blood. Isidora and Anabel clapped their hands, and Don Sancho poured himself a drink of tequila and one for Isidora. He sang several songs, with Isidora joining him.

Every time Don Sancho sang another song, he had to clear his throat and take another shot of tequila.

Evita cut the cake, licking the frosting off her fingers as she sliced through the pink frosted layers. She served everyone a piece on small white ceramic plates, making sure there was a piece left over for Cristal, although she knew Cristal was picky and probably wouldn't eat it. Isidora said the ceramic plates had been given to her as a wedding gift by a rich uncle in los Estados Unidos who never bothered to even write to her again. The dishes were shiny, and Evita saw her face reflected in them. In her mind, she looked more grown-up, as if her features had rearranged themselves now that she was fourteen and had been given sexy clothes to wear. The cake was sticky and sweet, and Evita's mouth filled with sugary delight. Evita cut another piece for herself while Don Sancho sang more songs, clearing his throat and taking his shots of tequila. They all clapped for him as if he was a famous singer, and Isidora surprised them by strumming the guitar for one of the songs and singing in a sexy, throaty voice.

"Too bad Cristal's not here to dance. I think she'd enjoy the music," Evita said.

"Oh, no! She'd give Don Sancho a heart attack!" Isidora said, and they all laughed as they watched Don Sancho pound his bony chest with his hands to prove his strength.

Hours passed by with everyone singing and enjoying one another's company. By then Isidora was anxious to get Don Sancho out of the house, as he had already demanded another bottle of tequila and started repeating songs he had already sung. Before walking the old man to the door, Isidora helped him tie his guitar around his shoulder with an old leather strap. He weaved unsteadily as he walked by her side, then stopped and whispered something in her ear, at which she roared with laughter, telling him she was too old for that and that he should have been around twenty years ago. Then she pushed him out the door and smoothed down her skirt with her hands as if she was done with him.

"The nerve of that old man. He can barely walk out, much less do anything else." Then, still smiling and shaking her head, she hobbled on her stumpy legs to her bedroom, telling the girls to clear the table—they would wash everything up in the morning.

Later, Evita tried on her new clothes and wondered if she would ever grow any breasts. It would take two of her breasts to make one of Anabel's, and three to make one of Cristal's. She thought she looked like a bone wearing the sexy red dress, but Anabel said, no, she looked just fine, and men liked women who were skinny. Evita asked her why, and she said they didn't like to have to jump on a woman and bounce back like they were on a trampoline. Then she laughed and pulled Evita close, and they lay down on their beds and held hands and talked together until they fell asleep.

That night Evita dreamed of Anabel's long hair. The silky mane that ran down Anabel's back was all over her pillow, and she lay on it and felt a big lump. She got up and put her hand into the pillowcase and found something soft and round. She took it out and shouted with horror. It was a woman's breast. Then she woke up sweating, her body shaking. She looked for Anabel on her bed, but she was gone. In the other room Evita heard a man's voice arguing with Isidora, and she heard Anabel crying. She peeked out through a crack in the door and saw the son of the owner they had run away from. He was angry and drunk, telling Anabel that she was going with him, and there was nothing she could do about it.

"Let her stay!" Isidora said. "Just for tonight. She's had it bad this time."

The man grabbed Anabel by the hair and dragged her out the door. Evita ran out, shouting at him to let her go, but Isidora stood up and blocked her from doing anything else. She held her tightly in her arms, and there was nothing for Evita to do but watch the man drag Anabel away.

"Go back to bed, Evita. Really, there's nothing anyone can do."

As Isidora was talking, Cristal came home, limping and kicking off her spiked heels. She leaned on the door and sighed, then walked unsteadily across the room, stopping to look at Evita. She swayed, as if she would fall to the floor, and forced each word from her mouth.

"What are you doing up? Go to bed. The night's for whores and drunks, thieves and murderers, not for children. Go to bed!"

She stumbled to her room and shut the door with a bang.

The next day, after running errands for Isidora, Evita took time to visit la Catedral to say prayers. She was dressed all in black, feeling as though she was already dead. The streets of Juárez were linked in her mind like a maze of dark alleys, dead ends, twisted streets, and noisy cabarets that wouldn't let her go. Life was dangerous—a cliff she dangled from with one hand waving in the air. She had been helping Isidora transport drugs, and that could get her killed. She thought of the guardian angels assigned to every human being by God, and wondered if they would take care of her now even though she was so sinful.

Evita sat in the last pew, trying to make herself invisible. When it was time for everyone to walk up the narrow center aisle to receive communion, she stayed behind, not considering herself worthy to approach Christ. She shut her eyes tightly, then opened them and pretended she was seeing halos around the statues of the saints. The saints were holy; she wasn't. She hoped God wasn't too mad at her and wouldn't end up leaving her like her father had done when he took off to Chihuahua City. Outside, an old man rang the church bell by pulling on a long rope. Over and over again, the bell clanged, reminding her that she was a sinner, headed for the fires of Hell. The dark spikes inside Evita seemed to glow like embers in la Catedral's dim light. When she looked down at her hands, her palms were bright red, tender to her touch.

She sat in the church a long time. The last mass of the day started, and more people came in to pray and sing and receive communion. She sat in the church after the services, wondering why trouble chased her everywhere, and noticed red blotches appear on her arms. The invisible spikes under her skin were making their way to the surface, piercing her from within. She looked at the big statue of San Francisco, lying in its glass coffin, and saw people put their hands through a round hole in the glass to touch the saint and secure his blessing. Some people lifted his head up with their hands, which meant their prayers would be answered. Evita didn't dare put her hand through the round hole. She thought the saint might frown at her and pull away.

A woman walked up to Evita and asked her if she had a place to go. She told her she couldn't stay there all day, as she was cleaning up the church and had to lock the doors.

"Go home," she said. "Your mother must be waiting for you."

Evita tried to get up but couldn't. Her legs were tired, her bones hurt. She wanted to ask the woman what the symptoms were for polio and already imagined herself in a wheelchair, like one of her cousins who had contracted polio and sat day after day with an old shawl drawn over her shoulders, looking down at her withered legs. The woman said she'd get the priest, Padre Octavio, to talk to her, and they'd arrange for someone to take her home. Or would she like to stay at the orphanage where other children lived?

"I want to go to school," Evita told her. She knew it was a lie, as she hated school, but it sounded like something she should say.

The woman smiled. "Good," she said. "Just two blocks from here is a school. It's a place for children who have nowhere to go. I think you'll be happy there. If you're willing to work and learn, they can help you."

Evita didn't tell the woman that she was the dot at the end of a sentence, little and stupid. She didn't tell her that she wanted to be a beautiful butterfly and only live for a few days. Lately she had been dreaming of joining her brother, Fidel the Albino, in Heaven. In her dream, she saw herself flying freely with Fidel, higher and higher into the clouds, while they fluffed up their white angel's wings and held hands. Evita smiled as she thought of the dream and walked out of la Catedral with the woman. The woman thought Evita was smiling because she was happy about joining the orphanage and starting school, and she pointed two streets down to where the school was located. She said it was called el Instituto de Niños Huerfanos, and she instructed her to ask for Señora Juana del Pilar, the director of the facility. "Tell her Licha sent you." When she asked Evita for her name, Evita said it was Elena. She didn't want to be Evita. She hated Evita. She wanted Evita to die.

10 The next morning, Isidora looked sternly at Evita and told her to stop wearing black clothes and start wearing bright colors—she was taking life too seriously. Evita was young, she said, and if she lived depressed all her life, she would be that much closer to her own grave.

"Take a shower," she said, "and comb your hair. You'll feel better. Life goes on, Evita. You either move with it, like a stone rolling down the road, or you're left behind. Ni modo." Then she sat wearily in a chair and pointed to her swollen legs. "Rub my legs before you do anything else, and wrap them in gauze. They hurt like the devil!"

Isidora cursed her legs and her life in Juárez, mumbling under her breath that she had never wanted to come here in the first place. If her husband had not died and left her with small children, she would have stayed in the country. When she arrived in Juárez, men started whistling at her everywhere she went and wanted to climb into bed with her, and all along she had never appreciated her own beauty. And that's how she supported her children, she whispered, and God knew the rest. Isidora closed her eyes, and Evita thought she had fallen asleep while she rubbed her legs. Then she looked up and saw tears on her face and knew Isidora was still awake.

Before the week was over, Evita had accompanied Isidora twice to get medicine for the clinic in El Paso. They sat in the backseat, Isidora hugging her oversized purse with one arm and Evita with the other. El chofer drove them back and forth in silence and never bothered to even greet them or look them in the face. At night, Chano came by to pick up the boxes, and each time Evita ran into her room until he left. She wondered what would happen if Chano ever told her mother where she was. And what if her mother called the police to report on the activities at Isidora's? And worse still, what if the important person Isidora worked for decided he didn't need her anymore? Would that mean he'd get rid of Isidora and her child accomplice, Evita? It wasn't surprising anymore to hear of a woman's body found half-buried in the desert sand. She was haunted by visions of her own shoe sticking out of the sand in some desolate part of the desert.

One afternoon Isidora sent Evita out on errands to get more ointment for her legs, to pay her layaways at clothing stores, and to do some shopping for food at the supermarket. Evita didn't tell her she was planning to go to el Instituto to talk to Señora Juana del Pilar and finally do what Licha, the cleaning woman at la Catedral, had told her to do. She hated school, but she was determined to end her life on the edge at Isidora's. Evita put on her black clothes again, in spite of Isidora encouraging her to wear bright colors, and went out into the bustling streets, alive with hundreds of people working, shopping, and strolling about—a day like any other. Traffic was at its worst in the afternoons, and today was no different.

Just as Evita headed for la Plaza and el Instituto two blocks away, she heard someone call her name and turned around. It was Ricardo— tall, swarthy, and neatly dressed in dark jeans, a striped shirt, and boots—striding confidently across the busy street toward her. Cars honked at him, and a rutera packed with people nearly hit him, but he laughed it off. He reached Evita and hugged her tightly and held her hands. He looked her over and saw she had been crying.

"Evita, don't cry. Look, I know you've had a hard time. I heard your mother has a new boyfriend. Doesn't waste time, does she? But don't blame yourself."

Ricardo kissed the top of Evita's head and smoothed down her hair. His touch felt good to Evita, but it made her afraid. Her mother wasn't there to see them; no one was there to stop Ricardo from touching her if he wanted to.

"Let's go eat," he said. "You look weak and tired. You can't live like this, Evita."

He took her to a nice restaurant and sat next to her in a booth. He didn't seem to care who saw him sitting right next to her. She leaned her head on his shoulder. He felt so strong, as if he could protect her from everything. The gloomy, disappearing Evita was made stronger by Ricardo's manly vigor.

"Why are you so sad?" he asked her. Evita didn't know what to say. He handed her a napkin from the table, and she wiped her tears away. Then he asked for menus and said they would start with lemonade, tart and icy cold, and then they would eat whatever Evita wanted and she would feel better. While they had their meal, Ricardo was attentive to the tiniest details, arranging Evita's knife, fork, and napkin so they would be at her fingertips, making sure she had the kind of salsa she liked, and that corn tortillas were on the table warm in their plastic insulated container.

After they ate, they walked out into the cool October evening together. Streetlights were on, and the shops were all glittering and blinking with neon signs. Evita took a deep breath, sensing herself coming back to life. Then Ricardo asked her, casually, as if the idea had just entered his mind, if she would go with him to watch telenovelas—he knew a place. He put his arm through Evita's, and they walked to a place at the end of one of las zonas, a hotel with faded letters at the top. El Río de Oro, The Golden River. An old man sat begging at the entrance in soiled clothing, a chipped cup in his hand for donations. Ricardo ignored him.

"We can see telenovelas here, Evita, in one of these rooms, and you can rest." Ricardo looked down at Evita, his eyes taking in her face, her black clothes, and the way her small hand fit into his. She wanted to run away, but Ricardo's dark eyes were looking into hers as if he was pleading. Evita knew he had defended her against her mother and that he had bought her food and stroked her hair. She didn't want him mad at her, but she was afraid of him, of his big hands on her face, and the way he held her hand in his, and how it disappeared into his hot, sweaty palm. She knew if her mother saw them together on the street, she'd beat her up on the spot and report Ricardo to the police. She was ready to tell him that her mother might be sending her brother, Reynaldo, to look for her, but he opened his mouth before she did.

"I can't believe you don't trust me! And here, all this time, I thought we were friends. You know I'd stand up any day for you against your mother. But if that's the way you feel about me, then maybe we should go." He seemed angry and ready to walk away. Evita couldn't bear that he was mad at her and might leave and she'd never see him again. She looked down at her shoes, shrugged her shoulders, and nodded.

The woman at the desk was on the phone and didn't seem to care that they were standing at the hotel door: Evita wearing all her black clothes—black blouse, black levis, black shoes, mourning her own death—and Ricardo next to her in his dark jeans and striped shirt, his black polished boots shiny and new. Already Evita's heart was pounding, and she felt herself to be the tiny fox Isidora told her she was, ready to step into the hunter's trap. She looked up at the woman at the desk, wanting her to help her somehow, but the woman was talking intently to someone on the phone and didn't give Evita a second look. Ricardo told Evita to wait for him at the door while he paid for the room. The woman at the desk got off the phone when she saw Ricardo walking in and looked him over closely, pointing to a list of prices for rooms tacked to the wall behind her. There were prices for an hour, two hours, and for the whole night. "Which do you want?" she asked him, as if she wanted him to hurry up so she could get back on the phone. Ricardo paid for the whole night. "Here's your key," she said. "And be sure you're out before ten in the morning."

Evita's hands were cold and sweaty. Ten in the morning! But they wouldn't be there that long. They'd be out in a couple of hours, after watching a few telenovelas, and talking about the stories like Isidora and Cristal did. As they walked to the room, she told Ricardo she had to get back to Isidora's or she'd send someone out to look for her. She still had errands to run, and Isidora wouldn't like it if she was late. Ricardo ignored her and told her Isidora wouldn't mind if they spent a few hours together. After all, he was her stepfather in a way, since he had lived with her mother.

Before she knew it, they had walked around the building that had plaster and paint peeling off its walls and windows in need of cleaning. They found their room up a dark stairway and through a small door. There was nothing in the room except a bed and a bathroom with two towels hanging on nails. The sink was chipped and broken, with a faded gray mirror dangling on a piece of wire over its basin and a toilet with no top. There was no chest of drawers, no closet, only a small table with a broken leg and an old lopsided lamp on it. One wall was defaced with crude images of women exposing their bare breasts and naked men sexually poised over the women. Evita looked away.

"Diego Rivera style," Ricardo told her. "Remember the great muralist? But never mind all that. Don't look at it if it bothers you."

On a metal folding chair was a tiny television set, secured by a chain to the floor. It was on, blinking bright red, with the sound barely audible.

"What kind of a room is this?" Evita asked. "It has nothing in it. How will we see la tele. It's so small!"

"We'll get close to it," he said, laughing. He took off his shoes and shirt, and there he stood showing the hair on his chest, dark and curly. He took out a knife in a leather sheath from his back pocket and set it on the table with the broken leg and the old lopsided lamp. He said he carried it around with him for protection, and he'd make sure no one would ever hurt her.

Evita froze, her feet refusing to move. The memory of the policeman who had attacked her came to her mind. It was as if the policeman was standing in front of her, and she started to shake. She stared at Ricardo. He looked so old with his shirt off and his stomach showing round over his belt. He lay on the bed, relaxed, his head cradled in his hands.

"We can rest, Evita; it's that easy. See, I can still see la tele. It's not that far away. Ya, Evita, you're nervous because you want to be."

He didn't say anything else and just looked at her. The image of her mother surfaced in Evita's mind, and she looked at the door to see how far it was in case she decided to run. She wondered if Ricardo would chase her down the dark stairway, catch up to her, and force her back into the room. She knew he would be furious if she ran, his money wasted for nothing.

Pretty soon, a look in Ricardo's eyes seemed to change his face, and he got up and reached for Evita. He held her in his arms and told her she was precious to him—like a tiny child that he wanted to cradle. Would she mind if he cradled her in his arms? Evita didn't say a word, only stood there shaking, feeling the room crowd in on her and the naked figures on the wall point their fingers at her. Ricardo sat with her on the bed as if she was a tiny baby and caressed her, rocking her back and forth. He put his face in her hair and kissed her and said he loved her, and would she like to take off her shoes and get comfortable? Ricardo was nothing like the policeman. He was gentle and his voice was soft, soothing, and it made Evita cry. Little by little, Ricardo convinced Evita to take off all her black clothes, until she was lying in his arms—her naked body, a tender white reed he gently embraced. Then Ricardo covered her with a thin sheet and laid her down next to him on the bed. He switched off the lamp, and in the dark he took off his pants and underwear and began to caress her passionately. He said she was the most beautiful girl in the world and he was so lucky to have her close to him.

Evita thought of her mother, and new tears started. She would kill her if she saw her lying naked next to Ricardo. Her mother's image made Evita feel powerful, and something came into her mind, vague at first, then clearer. She wanted to be better than her mother and mean more to Ricardo than her mother ever had. She remembered how Ricardo had defended her the day her mother had thrown her out on the streets, and this made her embrace Ricardo as he gently kissed her lips. Then slowly, very slowly, while the telenovelas were playing in bright red colors, Ricardo calmed Evita down, opened her legs wide, and made her insides burn with pain.

During the night, Evita had to get up and wash herself twice. Her blood was on the sheet. Ricardo put a towel over it and said no one would mind; these things happened between men and women. In the darkness, Evita saw the shadows of the naked figures on the wall, and she thought it was all a nightmare and she'd wake up soon.

Ricardo touched Evita constantly, between her legs, on her tiny breasts, and didn't seem to get his fill. His heart pounded, his breathing was quick. When Evita thought he had fallen asleep, he started touching her all over again, wetting her skin with his lips and tongue. He finally fell asleep, exhausted, and Evita got up, her face cold, hard, feeling the huge black spikes she carried inside her pushing up through her skin. She looked at her arms and could see the red blotches where the spikes were ready to burst through. Sensing the weight of the dreadful spikes inside her, she walked to the table with the broken leg where Ricardo had put his knife. She took the knife out of its leather sheath and felt the blade. It was very sharp. She looked at Ricardo on the bed and thought it was nice of him to keep his knife so sharp. She looked carefully at the knife in her hands. It was just a thing until she made it her own. She plunged the knife into her left arm, deep into her wrist, and blood spurted out onto the floor.

Ricardo jumped up out of bed and grabbed the knife while Evita tried to cut into her right arm. He yelled at her to stop and dragged her back to bed. Terrified at the sight of the blood draining from Evita's arm, he cut up a towel with his knife and bandaged her wound. He pressed on the wound firmly until the blood stopped flowing. Then he ran his fingers nervously through his hair, biting hard on his lips as he saw all the blood Evita had lost. He remembered the woman at the desk had looked him over closely. If Evita died, he knew she would be able to identify him as the man who had been with her.

"Lie still, Evita," he said, trying to soothe her. "Lie still; you'll stop bleeding soon." He put his clothes back on and walked out, telling her he would get her something to drink. He returned with two orange sodas and a bottle of water and told Evita to drink the soda. Then he opened the bottle of water and said drink. That's what he wanted her to do—drink the soda, drink the water, and rest. Evita did what he said, dry-eyed, her face pale, her eyes vacant. Ricardo seemed to be the one who wanted to cry. He talked to her, soothing her, telling her things would be all right. She lay naked on the bed with one wrist bloodied and bandaged. She didn't even have the strength to put her clothes back on and didn't care if Ricardo saw her nude body. She had joined the naked figures on the wall and was surprised that it didn't matter to her anymore. Ricardo sat next to her and watched her closely.

"Your color's coming back, Evita. Pretty soon, you'll be fine." He kissed her cheek gently and said he'd go down to get some cigarettes. He walked out and didn't come back.

Evita left the room at el Río de Oro long before ten in the morning. She washed herself one more time and put her black clothes on, combing her hair through with her fingers and feeling for the deep purple scab on her wrist. The wound was painful and swollen. Evita felt pain in other parts of her body as well. There was pain between her legs that traveled all the way to her breastbone and down her spine. Her tiny breasts were sore, the nipples tender, and there were purple bruises all over her body where Ricardo had kissed her.

Her legs were weak and wobbly as she made her way behind the building and into an alley, avoiding the woman at the desk. A cold wind scattered papers down the street, and Evita shivered. She walked slowly past people already gathering in the plaza, opening up their shops and starting the business of a new day, and realized she still had the money Isidora had given her in her pocket for the errands. She looked at her reflection in store windows—a tiny skinny girl, limping her way down the street. No one seemed to notice her, and she no longer looked around for el chofer or the police car. Evita was glad Ricardo hadn't left her any money. If he had, then she'd be no better than a prostitute. She labored to climb up the steep sidewalks, thinking she was growing stumps for legs like Isidora's.

Isidora let Evita in and seemed unalarmed at her condition. She sat next to Evita on the couch and looked closely at the purple scab on her wrist, then got some of her ointment and rubbed it on the wound.

"What's this about?" she asked.

"Oh, that. Well, I guess I tried to kill myself."

"And why did you try to kill yourself?"

Evita didn't answer, only rested her head on Isidora's shoulder.

"Listen to me, Evita. If this is over a man, don't ever do it again! A man takes and takes and takes from a woman, and when he's done he goes to another woman and starts all over again. Love doesn't exist, only need. Did you hear me, Evita? I learned that a long time ago."

Evita started to cry until her bony shoulders were shaking and her throat felt as if it were on fire. Isidora held Evita in her arms and told her she was safe now, and nothing was worth dying over. Evita told her all about Ricardo and the night they had spent in el Río de Oro, and about his knife and how she had plunged it into her arm.

"Now, I'm his lover—and my mother will kill me when she finds out!"

"And how will your mother find out?" Isidora asked her. "You see, you're crying for nothing. You can stay here, and things will resolve themselves." Then she asked, "Did Ricardo give you any money?"

Evita told her he hadn't given her any money. After all, she wasn't a prostitute, she said.

"So, why did you go to bed with him?" Isidora asked her. "Do you love him."

"No! I don't love him, but he loves me. He says he loves me like a father."

Isidora sighed, shaking her head. "And would a real father make love to his own daughter? You were a virgin until last night, Evita. Ricardo loved you only enough to take your virginity away from you. Evita, listen to me—he used you."

Evita wanted to put her hands up to her ears and stop Isidora's voice.

"I see what he did. He spent all his money on the room at the hotel and didn't have any money left over to give to you. You must never, never give your body to a man without payment. Never. He didn't ask you for special sexual pleasures, but worse, he took your virginity away. That should have cost him plenty! And he may have complained. But look at what a woman has to go through. This is a business, Evita—you must understand. You're a woman now, and a businesswoman at that!" Then she looked at the purple bruises on Evita's neck and said, "If a man wants to bruise you with kisses—that's another charge."

Evita felt nauseated and dizzy, thinking that Ricardo was right when he had told her that someday he would be working for her.

"Go rest, Evita, and when you get up, I'll tell you more about how to deal with men."

Three days later, Ricardo stopped by Isidora's house in the evening with gifts for Evita. He gave her a pink stuffed teddy bear with a red plastic heart and a small bottle of perfume with a fancy flower on the label. Isidora made coffee for Ricardo and sat at the table to talk with him as if he was any other visitor. Ricardo was dressed up and smelled like sweet cologne. He told Isidora he was worried because Evita cut her wrist and tried to kill herself. He didn't mention anything about being with her at el Río de Oro, making it sound like Evita was troubled and he was her father checking up on her. Isidora told him that young girls were sometimes confused about men, and that Evita would soon grow up and see the light. She looked at Ricardo in a way that let him know she knew what he had done to Evita at the hotel. Ricardo changed the subject, looking down at his watch and saying he had time to take Evita out to get something to eat and get her mind off her problems if she was willing to go with him.

Evita dressed up in a pair of shiny black pants Cristal had given her, with a silver belt that gleamed in the light. She wore a blue top with white rhinestones around the collar, one of Anabel's, and black velvet high heels that she bought with money Isidora had given her. She wore makeup on her face for the first time, as Anabel had taught her how to apply it—not too much, but enough to dramatize her light skin and dark eyes. Ricardo looked at her and said he was glad she was wearing other colors besides black, and Isidora agreed. Before they walked out into the night, Isidora pressed Evita's hand as a reminder of all she had talked to her about.

Ricardo took her to a restaurant that was only a small stand facing a busy street with tables set up outside for people to sit and eat their meals. He told her he had to watch his money these days, and he hoped she didn't mind. He asked her if she had been home to see her mother, and Evita shook her head and started talking about something else. There were other couples eating at the place, one of them a man about Ricardo's age with his arm around a girl who looked younger than Evita. The girl was loud, laughing and pulling on the man and kissing him playfully. Evita knew the girl was a prostitute and hoped she didn't look that obvious next to Ricardo.

Evita didn't have much to say, as she stayed home all day at Isidora's. She couldn't tell Ricardo about the medicines she'd seen at Isidora's and couldn't mention Anabel and Cristal without going into detail. After they finished eating, Ricardo put his arm around Evita and told her he'd like to spend some time with her alone. He looked gently at her and said he couldn't forget how they had made love and hadn't stopped thinking about her day and night. He pressed close to Evita, and when she leaned into his chest she could hear his heart beating hard.

This time, Ricardo took Evita to a hotel that had only a few rooms, el Paraiso, and he got a room for them that had no tele at all. The room was smaller than the last one, and he paid for only a few hours, telling her he couldn't afford more. Evita felt shy asking Ricardo for money, as Isidora had told her to do. She couldn't see him as her client, and she imagined that one day he'd tell her mother what she had done and her mother would search for her and kill her. They lay on the bed together, with Ricardo anxious for Evita to take off her clothes. Then Evita started to cry and told him that Isidora would kick her out if she didn't bring home some rent money. It was the first time Evita had used tears to get what she wanted in return for her services. Ricardo was desperate to get to Evita, so he promised that of course he'd pay and pay her well. Then Evita let him take her clothes off. Before he thrust himself into her, she showed him the condom Isidora had given her, but Ricardo only laughed and Evita was helpless to stop him.

Every week after that, at least three times a week, Ricardo met Evita at el Paraiso. He insisted that she see no one else, and he paid her an amount that satisfied Isidora, so Evita saw no one but him. Ricardo stopped taking her out to dinner, saying he had new expenses and couldn't afford it, and he asked her instead to meet him at el Paraiso and he'd have a room ready for them. They spent hours together until Ricardo had exhausted himself inside her and was finally satisfied. He asked her to promise him that he'd be her one and only. Then he told her it wasn't important to wear condoms, as that was for people Evita didn't know. He taught her different positions and how to caress him and kiss him until he lost the sense of who he was.

Then one night, Ricardo told Evita that he'd teach her how to enjoy her own body. He taught her about the places in her body that caused her deep pleasure and how to use them to lose herself in their lovemaking. It was the first time Evita had ever experienced what Ricardo had been experiencing all along, and she clung to him and cried with joy. Then Ricardo told Evita that his wife was having another baby and that he couldn't pay Evita anymore for her services. Evita, still sweating and trembling in Ricardo's arms, was shocked to hear that he had a wife—and a new baby on the way. She had never seen him in her mind as a husband with a wife and children. That night, Ricardo left without paying Evita a thing. It was then that Evita began longing for him and pining over him, wishing he would take her to el Paraiso over and over again.

Isidora found out quickly that Ricardo was no longer paying Evita for her services. She told Evita that either he paid for her services and she ran her business as she should, or she'd have to leave. Evita wasn't to see Ricardo, she said, unless he was going to set up a house for her. Then she told her she was kicking Anabel out because she didn't listen to her. She was hooked on heroin, she said, after she had told her hundreds of times not to start on the drugs.

"Now, she's worth nothing. She'll let a man mount her for two centavos to get her drug." She looked at Evita and told her that drinking was fine, a drink or two to relax with a man, but anything more than that was to step into hell.

Isidora pointed to herself, her face red with anger. "I did that," she said. "The drugs was all I lived for. It's a miracle I'm still alive!"

Evita remembered what Isidora had said to her: *Love doesn't exist, only need.* She knew this to be true, as her need for Ricardo had become so great that she searched for him day and night, hoping to see him on the streets or by el Paraiso. But he never showed up. The spikes that drilled in her from the inside showed up on her body again, huge red blotches of pain, and disappeared only when she thought about hurting herself— running into the street to be hit by a car, or buying a knife to stab herself again. She wasn't afraid of the stories of the girls found dead, their breasts bitten off, their heads, arms, or legs chopped off. Some of the bodies were burned beyond recognition, or left in the desert so long they were only skeletons when they were found. She didn't think she'd be one of them, and if she was, maybe that would end her misery.

Evita walked up and down the busy streets until she couldn't feel her legs under her, until the bright lights of Ciudad Juárez had burned a hole in her heart.

IF I Die in Juárez, Bury Me in Montenegro

11 Ofelia's husband was not home when Petra's family arrived in Juárez on a cold damp Saturday morning. Petra noticed the air was hazy, as if there was a cloud of smoke over the city. Traffic on the busy streets sounded like the rushing of water to her ears, so used to the silence of mountains and deserts. She tried to shake off the fear that had spiraled inside her when Tío Alvaro's car had rounded the corner of the highway into Juárez. Something had happened to her that she couldn't explain to anyone. An unknown *something* was hanging in the air, suspended, threatening, and it made her shiver and rub her arms with her hands for warmth.

Ofelia was standing at the window and pulled aside the curtain, peeking out at them. In the gray morning, she was only a shadow seen for a few seconds before she opened the door. She was wearing a long dress, with socks and huaraches, and her gray windblown hair fell to her shoulders. She had draped a flannel shawl over her shoulders, plaid with bright colors, red, green, purple. Flor opened the car door and ran into Ofelia's arms, and the two women hugged and cried, holding onto each other tightly. Estevan couldn't sit up and had to wait for Tío Alvaro to help him out of the backseat, looping arms with Petra for support.

"We're here, Papi, we're here. Ofelia's house! Everything will be all right."

Her father mumbled something that Petra couldn't understand. Ester and Nico woke up and climbed out of the car, yawning and stretching their legs, staring at everything in amazement. Estevan got out of the car and walked balanced between Flor and Tío Alvaro, with Ofelia rushing ahead, her old huaraches flapping on her feet, leading them up three stone steps and into a small entryway to the front door. Petra looked at the house and wondered how they would all fit inside. Then she looked down the narrow dirt road, crowded with houses and storefronts, and thought of the desolate roads leading to Montenegro, with only a few scattered ranches in sight and with horses and livestock competing at times with cars for use of the road.

Ofelia had a room prepared for Estevan at the back of the house, bare except for a bed, an old wooden dresser, and a kitchen chair. From the kitchen, Petra smelled coffee brewing, fresh tortillas, and chorizo with eggs cooking on the stove, and suddenly she felt as if she was starving and remembered that none of them had eaten since they had left Montenegro.

Flor and Alvaro led Estevan to the bed. Flor asked for a glass of water, giving it to her husband so he could take more aspirin and antibiotics, which he swallowed in one gulp. Petra watched as her father closed his eyes and lay wearily on his side in the fetal position that had become customary. Then he startled everyone by opening his eyes wide and staring at his wife, grabbing her hand, and holding on until his fingers turned white.

"Flor, promise me, if I die in Juárez, you'll bury me in Montenegro."

Flor searched her husband's face, then lowered her head.

"Did you hear me?"

"Stop talking about death! We're in Juárez now. You'll see a doctor, you'll get well."

"I won't let you go until you promise me. Why are you so hardheaded! Caprichosa! Promise me!" The whites of Estevan's eyes had turned yellow, and his face showed the bony ridges of his cheeks. Flor looked at him in fear, knowing this was her husband's death wish. "And you, Petra," he demanded, staring hard at his daughter, "convince your mother—if I die in Juárez . . ."

"Papi, por favor!" Petra said, tears starting, as her father's passionate plea reached them all.

"I promise you," Flor said, lacing her fingers gently through her husband's hand. "Te prometo."

Estevan smiled, something he hadn't done in months. He could already see his grave and himself resting peacefully under the huge cottonwood trees in el camposanto close to their ranch.

He turned his face toward the wall. "I'll feel better once I rest," he said, gasping for breath. The walk into Ofelia's house had wearied him. Flor covered him over with a blanket and patted his shoulder gently. There was a look of relief on her face in spite of Estevan's wish for death. She knew there were doctors in Juárez, hospitals. Tomorrow something would be done for him.

As everyone sat down at the kitchen table to eat and drink coffee, Prospero walked in. He was still boisterous from a night of drinking, his clothes and hair disheveled, his belt hanging loosely at his waist. He reeked of the smell of hard liquor—tequila, cigarettes, and an unwashed body. He pulled off his tattered jacket and walked in confident that Ofelia would not fight with him in front of her family.

"Compadre!" he shouted as he clapped Alvaro on the back. "How long has it been since I've seen you? Too long, too long. But here you are in the flesh. And your hair—what happened to your hair? You're bald!"

"It happens to the best of us," Alvaro said. And both men laughed, clapping one another on the back again in a gesture of affection.

Prospero turned to Flor. "Flor, I swear you get younger by the year!" Flor got up from her chair and Prospero hugged her, though Petra could tell her mother wished he wouldn't. She pulled away politely as Prospero looked around at all of them. Meanwhile, Ofelia ignored him and served everyone more coffee and small glasses of orange juice.

"Somebody needs a bath," she said loudly.

"No!—a kiss!" Prospero said playfully. He tried to kiss Ofelia, but she turned away in disgust.

Prospero looked at Petra. "This can't be Petra!" he said. staring at her in amazement. Petra was standing with Ofelia at the stove, warming tortillas. Prospero rushed toward her and grabbed her in his arms, making the warm tortilla in her hand tumble to the floor. He lifted her up slightly as he hugged her, and Petra felt his arms around her back, bony yet strong. She was conscious of her breasts pressing against his chest and pulled away.

"This can't be the little girl who used to visit us and always wanted a paleta. She could never get enough ice cream!"

Everyone laughed. "You can have all you want here in Juárez," he told her, holding her hands. "What a beauty! I would lock her up for safety and throw away the key!" Everyone laughed, and Petra felt herself blushing.

"Ya, Prospero, you're embarrassing Petra," Ofelia said. "She's a young lady now, not a child."

"Of course, you're right." He released Petra and turned his attention to Ester and Nico. "And these two fine-looking children? Don't tell me they belong to you Flor? No, it can't be!"

He hugged the children and kissed them on the cheek. Petra noticed that Nico smirked slightly but allowed Prospero's kiss. Flor watched Nico sternly for any sign of disrespect.

"You don't know this viejo, because you weren't born when I last saw your mother and father. A beautiful family, don't you think so, Ofelia? We should have had more children, hundreds of children, not just two. And now they're old and married and never visit us." He frowned as he looked at his wife.

"Don't tell me what we should have done," Ofelia said. "You should have been here last night; worry about yourself." Tension rose in the room like an electric current. Tío Alvaro put an end to it as quickly as he could.

"Estevan's also here," he said, "and glad you've opened your door to him, sick as he is. We're all grateful to you and Ofelia."

"Where is he?" Prospero asked, his bloodshot eyes softening. "My heart aches for him, and for any man who is so ill he can't provide for his family. God knows, a man has to provide. I've had my share of illness, and my poor wife has helped me through the bad times."

Ofelia received her husband's compliment in peace.

"We've helped each other," she said. "La lucha, always, the battle to live is before us."

Tío Alvaro walked with Prospero as he moved unsteadily to the back room to greet Estevan. Flor followed. From the kitchen, Petra heard Prospero's shout as he greeted her father and then his loud sobbing as he saw Estevan's condition. Ester and Nico sat quietly at the table, their food untouched.

"Eat," Petra told them. "Drink your juice." She felt tears run down her cheeks.

"He was always so strong, your father, so handsome," Ofelia said.

Petra looked out the small living room window at the street in front of Ofelia's house. The day had begun. There were people and cars passing by. The houses across the street were built one after another, some with iron grills around their windows and doors. It was strange for her not to see the open spaces of Montenegro and the blue sky overhead.

Very quickly, Petra found out that nothing would be as Ofelia had said. Her house was so small, they couldn't all stay with her. Ofelia said the problem had been resolved, as one of their cousins who lived in a colonia nearby had said she would help out. Petra and Nico would stay with Brisa Reynosa, Ofelia's comadre.

Ofelia talked privately to Flor and Petra while the children and the men were helping unload the car.

"I'm madrina to Brisa's daughter. You remember your cousin Evita, don't you, Petra?"

"Yes, of course. We played together when we were children." Petra remembered holding Evita's hand, running in and out of the house, twirling, and playing together. Twins, Evita would say. She wanted them to be twins.

"And her mother, Brisa?" Ofelia asked.

"Brisa?" Flor frowned. "I never got along with Brisa. Wasn't she a drinker? She's from my father's side of the family, and some say she was adopted by one of my aunts and nobody ever knew who her father was. I remember her—a talker, chismosa, and nobody could stand her."

"Well, that's true, but she's changed. Why, just the other day she was here, crying over Evita. Evita's had problems with her mother and has run away from home several times. She's supposed to be at her sister Lety's house, but no one knows if she's really there at all. I tell her not to be out on the streets, but she doesn't listen. It's dangerous for women with all the violence in Juárez."

"This city's always been violent," Flor said. "That's nothing new."

"Yes, and now more than ever. They've uncovered the bodies of women, raped and murdered—young women, left out in the desert to rot. And of course, no one is talking."

Flor put one finger to her lips, looking in the direction of the room where Estevan was resting, and she leaned toward Ofelia.

"Please, I don't want Estevan to know too much about all this. He knows Juárez is violent, but if he knows details of all that's happening, he'll make us leave—and you know we can't go back! He'll die on the way, and I—"

Ofelia interrupted her, putting one hand gently on her arm. "I know. Of course, we'll keep as much as we can from him."

Petra looked at Ofelia, fear in her eyes. "Don't worry," Ofelia whispered, "they say the girls were prostitutes, living a double life, ya sabes, working during the day, then at night running around in bars, I'm sure without their parents' permission. Decent girls are safe."

Then she told them that one of Brisa's children was born an albino but had died when he was only two years old, drowned in a bucket of water. It was truly a tragedy for Brisa.

"I still have the story from *El Diario* about him, if you'd like to see it. She has another son, Reynaldo, but he rarely comes to Juárez. He works in el otro lado, in El Paso, and doesn't stay long when he visits. I've already spoken to Brisa, and she says Petra and Nico can stay in Evita's room."

Ofelia didn't tell them about Brisa's new man, Alberto. She was afraid Flor wouldn't let Petra stay at Brisa's, thinking the man would be a danger to her daughter. Nico could stay with Petra—he was twelve years old, and that would be a protection for her. Ofelia felt bad for her cousin, but there was nothing she could do. She had little money and no room for them.

Flor seemed to be spinning in circles, talking rapidly, moving quickly, clearing the dishes away from the table, washing them, sweeping. She was already nervous about staying with Ofelia, and it was worse now that she knew Prospero was a drunk. She'd be separated from Petra and Nico, even though Ofelia told her Brisa's colonia was only twenty minutes away by car and less than an hour by rutera. As she repacked a suitcase, taking out items that belonged to her, she leaned close to Petra.

"As soon as we start working in la maquiladora, we'll start saving money," she whispered. "You'll see, mija, we'll have plenty, and we'll get us a house. A room for you—all by yourself—and dresses, new shoes." She looked deeply into her daughter's eyes and saw her fear. Petra wanted to grab her mother in her arms and cry, plead for them to go back to Montenegro.

"Watch Nico," her mother said. "Take care of each other at Brisa's. If there are any problems, call me. It's not far from here. I'll be there every day if I can. And I'll find out what school Nico and Ester will go to. I have some money for their uniforms and books. Your abuela gave me some money she had saved up."

When Petra heard Abuela Teodora mentioned, her throat ached and tears surfaced.

"Don't cry, Petra. Gustavo Rios will keep his promise to get us work."

The mention of Gustavo Rios sent a shiver through Petra's body. At any moment she expected him to walk through the door with information on Western Electronics and when to report for work. In the next room, they heard Prospero arguing with Ofelia over his clothes not being ironed. They heard something thump on the floor and found out later that he had thrown the iron at Ofelia because she didn't have his clothes ironed and ready for him. Flor looked up at the ceiling, her eyes closed, and whispered a prayer.

"Tomorrow," she said, "your father will be seen by a doctor at the hospital. Pray that he'll get well."

As Flor embraced her, Petra smelled her mother's hair. It smelled like the shampoo they bought in Montenegro, inexpensive yet perfumed with various fragrances. Her mother's favorite was a sweet lemony smell, and suddenly Petra felt herself a child again, sleeping with her mother in bed, one arm looped over her back, her nose buried in her mother's fragrant hair.

Tío Alvaro drove Petra and Nico in his car to Brisa's house. Once on the street, Petra was conscious of everything. It was as if she was floating everywhere. There was so much to see, people walking, a small band of musicians playing at the corner, food stands with smoke curling up from grills packed with carne asada and vegetables. There were children, some riding on old bikes, two and three to a bike. People called to each other from one side of the street to the other. There was a vendor walking slowly down the street with a cart filled with drinks for sale—soda pop, juice, and paletas—with the name *Mi Amigito* painted boldly in bright blue letters. Men gathered at street corners talking, smoking cigarettes, and staring at them as they drove slowly by looking for Brisa Reynosa's house in la colonia Quinto Sol.

Brisa was as old as Ofelia but dyed her hair black. She pulled it back behind her ears in a short bun held together by a hairpin decorated with rhinestones, and wore slacks, a flowered blouse, and black pointed shoes. She greeted them politely, and Petra picked up the fragrance of the perfume she was wearing—sweet, almost like candy, maybe meringue. She was light-skinned, and in spite of the wrinkles on her face Petra could see that she had once been a very attractive woman. She said she was delighted to have them stay with her, as they were all family and should always help one another.

"Come in, please, make yourselves at home." She helped Tío Alvaro bring in their bags, even though Petra told her Nico could help.

"But you're my guests," she said. "I'm at your service." She smiled sweetly, and Petra noticed her teeth had been worked on by a dentist many times. There were silver fillings in almost every tooth, reminding her of the mines in Montenegro. So, this was one of the things they sold the silver for, to fill holes in teeth like those in Brisa's—her father's life hanging in the balance because of holes in people's teeth.

"Is Evita here?" Petra asked her.

"Oh, that one! She's at her sister's house. You'll stay in her room. It won't be any problem. Evita comes and goes, and most of the time she's gone."

Brisa was especially attentive to Tío Alvaro and offered him coffee and cookies. She served coffee to him at a small round table set in front of a sofa and brought Nico and Petra glasses of lemonade. She arranged small sugar cookies on a glass dish: triangles, squares, rectangles, and circles. The sofa was vinyl and the seats worn, but it was still in good shape. There were fancy pillows set up on the couch, crocheted beautifully in bright colors—blue, yellow, orange, and purple. Glancing underneath the table, Petra noticed a small carpet with designs that looked oriental. She had never seen a rug that looked oriental and studied the designs closely.

"Nice, isn't it?" Brisa said, noticing Petra staring at the carpet. "I got it from a Chinese family I worked for. They owned their own store, and I helped sew for them. They liked me so much they gave me the rug as a gift. Now I run my own business, sewing bedspreads and tablecloths, even those pillows you're leaning on. Some of my things sell for lots of money, but by the time the money gets to me, it's almost gone from the shops taking their cut and everybody wanting something. Rich people can afford the best. There are rich people in Juárez. You know that, don't you, Alvaro?"

"Oh, yes, very rich people. Those who own the poppy fields that produce heroin, for example, that sells around the world for billions of dollars, not to mention la marijuana—that's been around since the world began. A weed, can you imagine—meant by God, I'm sure, to be used for good and not for evil."

Brisa said every word was true. Drugs ruled the world, and those who fell into their power were bound to end in destruction. Of course, drinking was a part of life, she said. A drink here, a drink there, never hurt anybody. She told Petra and Nico to sit on the sofa next to Tío Alvaro and pulled up a kitchen chair across from them, smiling and making jokes, laughing with Petra and Nico and serving Tío Alvaro another cup of coffee. Petra and Nico snacked on the cookies and laughed, trying one of each shape, and all the while Petra was thinking that staying at Brisa's might be good for them after all. She watched Nico enjoying the cookies and Tío Alvaro talking with Brisa about the stupidities of the Mexican government and the hopeless condition of the people in Mexico.

"We need another Benito Juárez," he said. "We need a revolution to rid ourselves of the rich once and for all. The soul, you know, does not feed on money, not at all! It lives on truth and hope, faith and love."

"Beautifully said!" Brisa told him, and she smiled broadly, the silver in her mouth gleaming.

Then, Tío Alvaro got serious, asking Brisa what she knew about all the violence going on in the city.

"Do you mean the murders?"

"Of course, I mean the murders. I saw the story in *El Diario* about the two young girls murdered and found in el Lote Bravo. The man I met in Montenegro, Gustavo Rios, promised my sister and Petra jobs at one of las maquiladoras, but he never mentioned anything about the murders. Now, I'm wondering if this was all a big mistake, and we should all go back to Montenegro. I tell you, if Estevan knew about all this, he'd make us go back tonight, sick as he is and almost dying."

"Oh, no, there's no need for you to go back! I know it's very frightening, and no one is safe. But it's always been that way in Juárez. La policia know more than they tell us. And money silences everyone, las mordidas. But women must also find ways to protect themselves and not put themselves in danger. It's girls who run on the streets that get themselves in trouble."

"I heard the girls who were murdered were maquiladoras—they worked at an American factory."

"It is believed they were—unless they were leading a double life and spending time at night at the cabarets."

Petra looked intently at Tío Alvaro as he discussed the murders with Brisa. When he turned to her, his eyes softened. "Don't be afraid, Petra. If it's all that bad, I'll take you back to Montenegro tonight."

"Don't be afraid for her, Alvaro. Really it's girls who run away from home who fall into the murderers' hands. I tell my daughter, Evita, to stay home, and does she obey me? Absolutely not! I worry day and night that someday they'll find her body—God forbid!" Brisa made the sign of the cross over herself and shuddered. "I tell you, Alvaro, I have no way to control my own daughter."

"Estevan won't rest once he hears this. I'm sure he'll find out what's going on here, very soon," Alvaro said, shaking his head.

"The girl from across the street, Yvone, works in one of las maquiladoras," Brisa explained, trying to lift the sense of doom that had descended on Petra. "Petra can go to work with her. If she always walks with someone else, and tells someone where she's going, she should be perfectly safe. She isn't the type of girl to go off in the middle of the night—are you, Petra?"

"No, of course not. My parents don't allow me any freedom, and besides, I would never go out alone at night."

"And that's so wise! I only wish my daughter was as obedient as you are! And, besides all that, you have your brother here for protection—right, Nico?"

Nico sat up straight in his chair. "You can count on me!" he announced. Petra reached over and put her arm over her brother's shoulder.

"Said like a real man!" Tío Alvaro said. "Nico will keep an eye on Petra, qué no, mijo?" Nico nodded.

Brisa stood up and put her hand on Tío Alvaro's shoulder. "Alvaro, you're welcome to come back at any time."

Petra could tell that Tío Alvaro was suddenly uncomfortable with Brisa's offer and the attention she was giving him. She wondered if her mother was right. Maybe Brisa had been adopted and wasn't their cousin at all.

"Gracias for the invitation, but I have a friend who lives here. He has only a shack, but I can share it when I come to Juárez. I have to go back to Montenegro tomorrow morning. I run the Gonzalez ranch in Montenegro, and it's big, with acres of land, cattle, and crops to harvest."

"But you'll be back, won't you?" Brisa's eyes narrowed, then became huge again. She turned her head to one side, almost as if she was a young girl flirting with Alvaro. He stood up and laughed, which was his way of ending anything uncomfortable.

"Oh, yes! My sister, Susana, has a phone in Montenegro, and Petra here knows the number. If anything goes wrong, any little thing whatsoever, I can be reached through my sister. And of course, I'll be back to check on Estevan's condition. The poor man needs medical attention as quickly as he can get it."

Then he put his hand in his pocket and took out money and handed it to Brisa. She refused it, and he insisted. She refused again, even though it was obvious she wanted the money. When he insisted again, she finally accepted the money, saying it wasn't necessary, not at all. Then she reached over and hugged Alvaro tenderly, as if he was a son she was saying good-bye to.

On his way out of the house, Alvaro wiped his forehead as if to wipe away sweat and whispered to Petra, "I'm glad I'm not staying here! That woman is a flirt!" He held Petra's hand tightly. "You heard, Petra. Absolutely do not ever walk out on the streets alone—and of course, never at night. Take Nico with you every chance you get."

Petra held onto Alvaro's hand as they walked out, feeling his warmth, the calluses on his hands, hard and dry. It seemed to Petra as if she was letting go of Montenegro completely when she let go of Tío Alvaro's hand. She had not known what he meant to her until she had to say good-bye. Then she knew she'd miss his kindness, his funny stories and jokes.

Alvaro sensed Petra's fear, saw her tears, and put his arm around her. "Petra, all will be good. Any problems, call me. Yes?" He lifted her face in his hands and brushed her tears away. She wanted to tell him to greet Antonio for her—tell him she was already dying in Juárez without him. As if reading her mind, Alvaro said, "And don't worry about Antonio. If he really loves you, he'll wait."

Brisa directed Petra and Nico to the room they'd share. It was cold and damp, and Brisa had stripped it of everything except the furniture. She didn't want anything to remind her of Evita, she said. There was a chipped dresser in one corner with a mirror and a closet where Brisa said they could hang their clothes. Nico could sleep on the floor until Flor was able to buy him a cot he could use. She'd give him an extra blanket, she said, but no pillow, because she had no other pillows except the ones on the sofa, and they were decorations, not to be used as real pillows.

"You're from a ranch," she said, "and I know you don't have things like this out there. But you'll get used to it. This is the city, and we try to keep our houses looking nice, even if we are poor."

Petra was surprised to hear an edge in Brisa's voice, as if she was mocking them. She wanted to tell her that Abuela Teodora crocheted beautifully and had made them bedspreads and sweaters and all kinds of doilies for tables and chairs, but decided Brisa didn't want to hear what she had to say.

"Oh, and Nico, you dropped some cookie crumbs on the carpet, so get the broom and sweep them up. I fight cockroaches here every day, and it won't help if you leave crumbs for them to eat." She looked sternly at Nico, and he hesitated, not knowing what to do.

"Did you hear me?"

"Yes," Nico said. "And I'm sorry about the crumbs." Petra could tell Nico was afraid of her.

Brisa ignored his apology. "Well, what are you waiting for? I tell you, children of today need to be told over and over again, when everything's so simple. But then, of course, you are from a ranch. You've never learned how to do things the right way." Petra stood behind Nico and put her hand on his shoulder. She sensed her brother's back stiffen. They both looked at Brisa in silence.

"Now, what's this? The two vagabonds looking at me like they don't have to do what I say." Her face turned into a dark scowl, and she raised her voice and pronounced each word, as if spitting it out of her mouth.

"Get the broom! Are you that ignorant?" She saw Petra's face go red with anger.

"Angry, Petra? Already? And what will you do? Tell your sick father, and your mother—and worry them?" Then she turned her back on them.

"If Evita comes back, tell her you now have her room," she said, and walked out of the house without another word.

Close to midnight, Brisa came home with a man. As they stumbled in, Petra heard his voice, loud and angry. His name was Alberto. She knew this because Brisa called him by his name many times, trying to quiet him, but he wouldn't listen and continued to argue with her.

"No!" he said. "It wasn't that way at all. I should have killed him was what I should have done. I owe him nothing!"

"You owe him nothing, but he'll charge you anyway. You idiot—you know what that means!"

They argued back and forth about someone Alberto was fighting with. After several minutes, their voices turned to mumbling and the sound of muffled laughter. Petra heard Brisa's bedroom door shut with a bang. Then there was silence.

She looked up at the ceiling, watching dark shadows appear. The crouching figures on the mountains of Montenegro had followed her to Juárez. She stared at them, comforted, and drifted off to sleep.

12 Petra woke before the sun rose, feeling as if she hadn't slept at all with all the trouble at Brisa's. Her body had recorded the early morning hours of Montenegro, and she couldn't go back to sleep, even if she had wanted to. Abuela Teodora's voice spoke in her mind, *Sing, Petra, sing to the morning.* She looked out the window and discovered that Evita's bedroom faced west, not east. She couldn't see the rising sun unless she went out the front door and found a place where she could look east. She watched the room's shadows turn from dark to gray in the early dawn and whispered the ancient song to herself.

> Iwéra rega chukú kéti Ono
> Mápu tamí mo nesériga ináro sinibísi rawé
> Ga'lá kaníliga bela ta semáribo
> Si'néame ka o'mána wichimoba eperéame
> Népi iwérali bela ta ásibo
> Kéti ono mápu tamí neséroga ináro ne
>
> Né ga'lá kaníliga bela ta narepabo
> Uchécho bilé rawé mápu kéti Onó nijí
> Ga'lá semá rega bela ta semáripo
> Uchécho bilé rawé najata je'ná wichimobachi
> Népi ga'lá iwérali bela ko nijísibo
> Si'néame ka mápu ikí ta eperé je'ná kawírali

Uchécho bilé rawé bela ko ju
Mápu rega machiboo uchécho si'nú ra'íchali
Uchécho bilé rawé bela ko ju
Mápu ne chapiméa uchécho si'nú 'nátali
Népi iwéraga bela 'nalína ru
Uchúpa ale tamojé si'néame pagótami

Echiregá bela ne nimí wikaráme ru
Mápu mo tamí nesériga chukú sinibísi rawé
Echiregá bela ne nimí iwérali ásima ru
Mápu ketási mo sewéka inárima siníbisi rawé
Népi iwériga bela mo nesérima ru
Mápu ikí uchúchali a'lí ko mo alewá aale

*   *   *

Be strong father sun,
you who daily care for us.
Those who live on earth are living well.
We continue giving strength to our father,
who fills our days with energy and light.

With great joy we salute our father
with one more day of life.
We are living well following one more day on earth
as you light our way.

One more day to learn new words,
one more day to think new thoughts,
giving you strength you in turn
give energy to your brothers.

Thus I will sing
to you who daily care for me.
Thus will I give you strength
so you will not be discouraged.

With all your strength
care for those you have created
and given the breath of life.

Petra thought first of her father, wondering if he had his appointment to see the doctor. Next, she thought of Abuela Teodora, who at this
early hour must be getting the stove ready to make breakfast for Susana
and the children. Antonio should be getting up at this very moment and
getting ready to go to church. She had put the ring he had given her in
the pocket of one of her jeans, still in her suitcase. Someday they'd be
married, and she'd wear it on their wedding day.

Petra's head and stomach ached, nerves she thought, from being
angry with Brisa for talking to her and Nico as if they were idiots. She
walked quietly to the bathroom that smelled of sewage and found out
the toilet wasn't working and the shower was nothing more than a box
constructed of moldy wood and broken tiles. A trickle of water came out
of the faucet at the sink when she tried to wash her face. Seeking another
toilet, she walked out into the backyard, where there was an outhouse
next to a shack. Rushing into the outhouse, she latched the door, all
the while thinking that at any moment Brisa, or her lover, would come
pounding on it.

In the kitchen, Petra couldn't find anything she could cook for breakfast. The cabinets were bare except for cans of food and sacks of beans,
flour, and sugar. She was wondering where Brisa kept everything else
when Alberto walked into the kitchen. He was a fat man with a heavy
dark moustache. He reminded Petra of a homeless person, with his hair
stuck to the side of his head and his legs still unsteady from last night's
drinking.

"I didn't know Brisa had angels living with her," he said. "And to
think, she didn't tell me."

Petra walked past him and back to her room, sensing him staring
after her.

"I'm not good enough for you, am I? I imagine a queen like you would
be used to a king!" Then he laughed and grabbed a bottle of liquor and
poured himself a drink.

Petra heard Brisa yelling for him and telling him to mind his own business and get out of the kitchen. Alberto only laughed louder, taking another drink.

Nico was up, and Petra told him to get dressed so they could go out to buy a cup of coffee and get something to eat. Petra got a jacket for Nico and a sweater for herself, to keep them warm in the cold morning. When they walked out, Petra noticed an old pickup truck parked along the side of the narrow street across from Brisa's house. It was painted bright orange except for its rusty hood, which looked like it had been added to the truck after it was painted. Two men were sitting in the back of the truck and two more were standing outside by the cab door, smoking. The two men outside the truck puffed on cigarettes and laughed. One pounded his thigh in a sudden burst of laughter. Petra was conscious of them as she and Nico got closer, and she held Nico's hand tighter, remembering all the talk about the murders. There were other people on the street, two children and a woman with a child at her hip. All of them were hurrying along, bundled up in coats, sweaters, and shawls. A car turned a corner and sped by, the music from its radio blaring. The driver of the car shouted at the two men standing by the cab of the truck, and one of them, the one who laughed the loudest, chased the car for a short distance and then returned.

"Idiota! Someday he'll run over somebody, and I for one will be there to give him a good beating." The man stood in the middle of the street, then noticed Petra. He whistled through his teeth.

"Finally the neighborhood is looking good! Looks like we have company. My lucky day!"

Petra felt her face turn red and walked faster, but the man hurried to catch up to her and Nico, while the men at the truck commented loudly on her looks.

"I haven't seen anyone that beautiful since Inocenta got married," one of them said. "Now, that was a good-looking woman—but this one is even better looking!" They laughed and passed a cigarette back and forth, cheering their companion on.

"Ándale, Luis, let's see what you can do."

The man quickly caught up to Petra and stood at her side. He was stocky and muscular and wore a blue baseball cap, which he pushed up over his eyes to look at her. She noticed the man's cheeks were red and raw, dry skin showing in places where his skin was peeling.

The man shifted from one leg to another, awkwardly, as if trying to keep his balance. He was polite, apologetic. "Forgive me, señorita, but I believe I'm your neighbor—that is, if it's true that you have arrived in Juárez to live in this God-forsaken colonia. Are you the people from Montenegro?"

Petra nodded and looked into his eyes. She sensed that he wanted to please her. There was a shyness about the man as he stood in front of her as if he was her servant. It soothed her to know he genuinely wanted her approval.

"A sus órdenes," he said. "I'm at your service. My name is Luis Ledezma." He shook first Petra's hand, politely, then Nico's. "It's rare that we have someone who is, how I shall I say, as beautiful to look at as you are señorita, and please forgive me if I'm offending you."

When Nico looked hard at Luis, Luis teased him. "Don't worry, hermanito; I'll mind my manners!"

His courtesy and humbleness moved Petra. "No, of course, you're not offending me," she said. "I'm here, it's true, to stay with la Señora Brisa Reynosa for the time being. I'm here to work in las maquiladoras."

"Ah, sí, you and hundreds of others. Is Montenegro close to Chitlitipin?"

"Very close."

"Ah, well, that's far, over four hundred miles away. So I suppose you won't be going back soon. I'm also from a village, not too far from Montenegro, but I've been here since I was a boy. And your name, señorita, if I may be so bold."

"My name is Petra de la Rosa, and this is my brother, Nico."

Luis put his hand up to his heart, as if he had just heard a poem. "A beautiful name, señorita—yes, music to my ears. A pleasure, señorita, a great pleasure to meet you. And welcome to la colonia Quinto Sol."

Petra smiled when he said the name, remembering Abuela Teodora had told her they were living in the era of el Quinto Sol, which would end in earthquakes. She wondered if Luis knew the story.

"You like the name?" he asked.

"Yes, I do. It's ancient. It belongs to the world of our ancestors."

"Oh that, yes, it goes back to the Aztecs." He smiled broadly, happy to have impressed her with la colonia's name.

"If I can be of service to you, señorita, I know this place. I have sisters, cousins, who can also assist you. There are also friends."

"Gracias, Luis, for your kindness, and certainly we will be calling on you if we need to." Then she asked, "Do you know anything about my cousin, Evita?"

"Evita? Yes, I saw her the other night."

"How is she? I've heard it's dangerous here, and I—"

Luis interrupted her. "You mustn't worry for Evita. She knows how to take of herself. Her mother's always fighting with her over one thing or another. But don't concern yourself with these things," he said, smiling. "I'm here if you need me."

Then Petra asked him to tell her where she and Nico could get something to eat, and he walked with her the distance of the street and pointed to a stand nearby with hot coffee for sale and burritos. She asked him for a church close by, and he pointed to the east, telling her that only three streets away she would encounter la Capilla de la Ascención. They had services there—not big ones, but simple ones, twice on Sundays.

Petra looked at Luis, waiting for what would happen next. She asked him if he would like something to eat, and immediately he realized he was intruding on her breakfast.

"Of course not! Señorita, forgive my bad manners. There's no need to buy me a thing."

Luis's companions at the pickup truck whistled for him noisily and called out to him, telling him to shake himself away from the vision and give them a ride back to town. Luis excused himself, apologizing for taking up her time, telling her his companions had no manners and would she please forgive them for being so crude? She nodded and smiled, feeling lucky she was talking to him and not to the other men. Luis walked back down the street, climbed into the driver's seat, and started the pickup's engine, driving slowly past Petra and Nico. The men sitting in the back of the pickup laughed and waved good-bye as they drove by, and Petra could hear Luis scolding them, telling them they were all uneducated brutes who had no sense of how to treat decent people. Petra and Nico walked up to the food stand, where the man behind the small counter said. "Don't pay the least bit of attention to any of them, señorita.

They're on the streets all the time, making trouble for others." Then he added, "If I may be so bold, may I ask your name?"

Petra told the man her name and asked him for directions to Ofelia's house in la colonia San Fernando. He was more than happy to oblige, describing each step of the way, gesturing with his hands for emphasis. One rutera, he said, then another rutera, and she should be there in less than an hour.

Brisa had coffee brewing on the stove when Petra and Nico returned but didn't bother to tell Petra where she hid the coffee. She was in a better mood, as if she sensed Petra was already making plans to leave as quickly as possible. She invited them to eat breakfast and acted disappointed when Petra told her they had already eaten. Alberto sat at the table drinking coffee, pretending Petra and Nico weren't in the room at all.

Cleotilde, Brisa's neighbor, stopped by to say that Petra's mother had called at her house, wanting to talk to her daughter. Petra's heart raced as she grabbed Nico's hand, and they ran down the street to get to Cleotilde's house, only three houses away. She was thankful the woman had a phone and was worried the call was bad news about her father.

Petra found out from her mother that her father couldn't get into a hospital until Monday morning. She asked Petra how they were doing at Brisa's, and Petra lied to her and said things were going well. Her mother knew the truth—she could hear it in Petra's voice—but she was unable to do anything about it. She only said: "Promise you won't walk out on the streets alone—no matter what—remember there's danger everywhere. We'll be working soon, and we'll go together in las ruteras to la maquiladora. God knows, we both need to work to get us through all this!"

Then she told Petra that Gustavo Rios had stopped by and told her he was almost certain they'd start work at la maquiladora by next week, the same one he had mentioned to them in Montenegro—she couldn't pronounce the name in English. In spite of Petra's distrust of Gustavo Rios, she was relieved that soon they'd be working, and she'd be that much closer to leaving Brisa's house. Flor told Petra that by next week, God willing, Ester and Nico would be attending the school, Primaria Benito Juárez, in San Fernando, Ofelia's colonia. Nico would have to get on las ruteras to go to school every morning, but he was old enough to do it and it shouldn't be a problem.

"And mi papi? How's he feeling?" Petra felt tears surface as she thought of her father curled up in a ball, wrapped in a blanket, suffering intense pain.

"He's noble and brave. He'll be well soon." Flor sighed deeply, and Petra knew the truth—her father would rather die than stay in Juárez. As she walked back to Brisa's with Nico, she sensed herself floating above the dirt road and over la colonia Quinto Sol, which in her mind was a huge puzzle made of tattered, broken pieces, everything confused and sticking out at the wrong ends. Juárez was unreal to her, a chain around her throat, tightening.

Los Tres Magos

13 Mayela arrived in Ciudad Juárez not long after Petra and her family had left Montenegro. Her mother had given her sister, Cina, permission to take Mayela with her to Juárez to help her care for her two small children, Isi and Nabor. Chavela set one condition—that Cina put Mayela in school. Her daughter was bright and talented, but had never had a chance to attend school. Their village was too poor to sustain a school, and walking daily to Montenegro was impossible. She gave Cina money she had saved for months from the sale of los ojos de Dios, the bright-colored yarn woven into intricate designs, for clothes and books for Mayela. She felt good that her brightest, most talented child would have an opportunity to make something of herself.

Cina considered herself Mayela's second mother, having helped Chavela when she was in labor. They had borne down together in el granero, the old barn behind Chavela's house, as instructed by Teodora Santos, Petra's grandmother, and the result had been twins. Of the two infants, only Mayela had survived. Everyone said Mayela was powerful in mind and body because the spirit of her dead brother remained with her. Cina was comforted having Mayela to help her with the children, as she knew Mayela was mature for a child her age, shy but courageous and willing to share the burden of her children with her. She would have been truly frightened to leave Chitlitipin if Mayela had not been with her.

Cina planned to stay with Tía Concha, their only relative in Juárez, until she found a job in one of las maquiladoras or work in the house of a rich family. She hadn't seen Tía Concha since she was a child and couldn't remember what she looked like. She had sent word by way of a distant cousin to the old woman, telling her she was coming.

Cina was desperate to get out of Chitlitipin. Her husband, Zocotl, had already tried to kill her three times, and she bore a scar on her throat from his last attempt. His jealous rages had cost his first wife her life. Cina told Chavela that she either escaped from Chitlitipin or Chavela would be burying her dead body.

Mayela was twelve years old, a girl who liked to laugh, sing, dance, and run free. She was healthy and athletic, a fast runner in the tradition of the great Tarahumara distance runners, who were known to run, without tiring, from sun to moon over rough mountainous terrain. Mayela had two braids that ran down her back and bright black eyes that saw everything. Her skin was dark, and got darker the longer she stayed out in the sun. Around people she was shy and easily frightened, but in the comfort of her own family she was lively, precocious, and always ready to sing a song or dance to the rhythm of drums, rattles, and violins. Leaving the village of Chitlitipin was for Mayela like taking a journey to another planet. She had no idea what she would encounter in Juárez, except that her mother said she would go to school in a bright uniform and learn to read and write. Mayela already imagined herself sitting in a classroom with other children, reciting the alphabet and learning how to write, which was important to her, for she had promised her mother that as soon as she learned how to write, she'd send her a letter from Juárez.

The journey to Ciudad Juárez was a long one—a train ride of over a day from the country, then la rutera into the city. The train made many stops to pick up villagers along steep, mountainous roads. Then the bus broke down as they made their way into the city, and they waited hours until it was fixed. Zocotl had left with a cousin to hunt javelina in the nearby mountains, which meant he would be gone for at least three days. This had given Cina time to pack an old suitcase with her ragged clothes and whatever garments she had for the children and make hurried plans to leave before he got back. Still, at every stop, Cina looked around for any signs of her husband, who was crafty enough to disguise himself and outrun the train to carry out his mission to kill her. Cina's hands trembled every time she thought of Zocotl, and her throat tightened to the point that she gasped for air, turning her bony brown face gray. Chavela said Cina's problems with her husband had made her asthmatic, and she gave her an herbal tea, yerba buena, to drink along the way so she could breath better and calm down.

Cina was relieved when she got to Tía Concha's house in Ciudad Juárez without seeing her husband along the way. The whole distance Mayela had been in charge of Isi, Cina's baby girl, and Cina had taken charge of Nabor, her three-year old son, who was willful and undisciplined compared to his complacent, good-natured sister. Tía Concha lived in la colonia Los Tres Magos, named after the three wise men who had once followed the star of Bethlehem to honor the Christ child with gifts. Los Tres Magos was one of the poorest colonias in all of Ciudad Juárez. The people there lived in tents and in houses made of cardboard, old tires, and pieces of metal and rusty pipes. They were like rats living in hovels, dirt all around, with no running water and no electricity. Long ago the government of Mexico had promised the poor that they would give them land if they voted for its political cause, but the leaders never bothered to tell them that the land they would possess would be worthless.

"Where's the school?" Mayela asked Cina, looking at the dismal surroundings.

"Ay, don't worry about that! It's around here somewhere. Tía Concha will tell us where." Cina grabbed Nabor before he chased a dog heading for a pile of garbage that reeked of decay.

They got to Tía Concha's house by asking people in Los Tres Magos if they knew her. People pointed out trails through the hills, dips, and curves, sharp turns on rocky ground, left, right, and between two hills in the shape of a crescent moon where they said Doña Concha lived. Cina walked in silence with the children, leading them deeper and deeper into Los Tres Magos. Sometimes they walked one behind the other to make way for other families climbing up and down the narrow trails. Chickens were penned in along with people in makeshift dwellings, and families who owned goats tied them to nearby trees or bushes. On ropes dangling between the dwellings, clothes dried in the sun, stiff and colorless.

Tía Concha saw them coming and walked out to meet them as they climbed the last hill to get to her dwelling. The old woman looked like an ant to Mayela, tiny and beady-eyed, covered from head to toe in dirt and grime, and creeping along with a bundle of rags slung over her shoulder. She was happy to see them, putting her bundle down and tenderly embracing them. She held Isi in her arms until the baby started to cry, possibly because Tía Concha's voice sounded like a crow shrieking in midair.

"You're here," she said. "Bienvenidos, welcome to my humble dwelling. Not much, I can assure you, but you'll be safe and have a place to lay your head. It's not much farther," she said, noticing how weary they were. "Just right there, right there . . ." and she motioned with her lips to her dwelling between two hills that formed a crescent moon.

They climbed up, Cina with her tattered suitcase in one hand and Nabor's hand in the other, gasping for air and sweating. The black bag looped over Mayela's shoulder bulged with her clothes, an extra pair of shoes, a blanket, toiletries, and small cooking utensils her mother had packed for them to use along the way to make tea and heat their food. Isi rode on her hip and clung to her neck as they made their way up to the crest of the hill to Tía Concha's dwelling. With the afternoon turning cool, Mayela regretted not wearing her woolen shawl. Isi's small arms and legs were cold. Directly in front of them, the sun was setting—red, orange, with purple fingers spreading like a man's hand into the empty sky.

"How much farther, tía?" Cina asked, laboring for each word. "It can't be far—can it?"

"No! We're here," Tía Concha answered. They dropped to the ground in exhaustion before a structure of old boards covered over with cardboard and tarp that looked more like a chicken coop than a place to live.

Tía Concha apologized humbly for having nothing to offer them but tapetes, crude woolen rugs they could sit on and at night spread on the dirt for use as beds. Visible from the dwelling, on the Texas side of the border, was la chimenea, a tall chimney blackened by years of usage in the smelting of copper. The structure was owned by ASARCO, an American copper company from El Paso, and was built in a manner that allowed the billows of noxious black smoke to drift downhill into la colonia Los Tres Magos. The black smoke, laden with chemicals and toxins, covered everything in Los Tres Magos like a black mesh entrapping the land, the primitive dwellings, and the people. Mayela's amazement came when she looked across el Río Bravo and into los Estados Unidos, where she saw tall buildings outlined on the distant horizon and well-built houses and paved streets that ran everywhere. Mayela had never seen an American up close. Once or twice, she had seen Americans in cars passing through her village with Mexican tour guides. They had stared at her from their cars as they rode away, and one day one of them took her picture.

La colonia Los Tres Magos was close to a huge garbage dump, one of the biggest in Juárez. Tía Concha often spent her entire day there collecting discards she could fix or mend to sell for money and gathering whatever scraps of food there were, competing with goats and dogs who visited the dump site regularly. When Cina saw the huge dump, with its smell of human waste, decayed food, tires burning, chemicals exploding, and muddy pools of water that harbored insects, cockroaches, and rats, she made a promise to herself that she would do all she could to begin work immediately and move to a place that was decent. She planned to take Tía Concha with her, to thank the old woman for letting her stay with her in Juárez rather than die at the hands of her husband, Zocotl.

Desperate to find work and get out of la colonia Los Tres Magos, Cina began to look around and ask questions. She talked to anyone who would listen to her, anyone who might help her make a better life for her children. Late at night, Cina joined others who gathered around fires that burned in the hills and listened to stories, words of wisdom, prayers said to ancient gods and to the modern God, and incantations for using witchcraft to get your way in love, success, and money.

It was during one of these nights around a fire that Cina met Sebastian, who was from the Yucatan Peninsula. He was friendly to her and talked to her in Spanish, although he spoke to his companions in the ancient Aztec language, Nahuatl. Sebastian dressed in white trousers that stopped at his ankles and a serape that covered his body down to his knees. He wore a straw hat and huaraches that were worn to shreds, he said, from walking over the mountains of Mexico to get to Juárez. His face was round and flat, and there was a big space between his two front teeth. Sebastian had nothing, not even a hole to crawl into, but he imagined himself powerful because he carried his machete with him, strung around his waist and encased in a leather sheath. He said he used el machete in Yucatan to cut sugarcane, and once in a while he used it to defend himself, as is the right of any man. Then he laughed and patted el machete at his side and said they would never part.

Sebastian convinced Cina that they should join their fortunes together and told her he'd establish a home for her. Soon he had money saved up from gambling, saying he was lucky in matters of love and money. He told Cina, secretly, that his luck stemmed from the power of el Imán, a magnetic stone he carried with him for protection and counsel. It was a black crystal that came from the same rock used by Christ as His resting place after His death. Sebastian told Cina he had bought it from a powerful curandero in Vera Cruz, and the man was one hundred percent reliable. The stone required service from Sebastian, and often el Imán told Sebastian what to do next and what would happen in the future. He said el Imán had instructed him to take Cina as his woman, and that was exactly what he would do.

One evening, Sebastian came to Tía Concha's dwelling. He looked around humbly, apologizing to Tía Concha for the intrusion and bowing his head in shame. He said that he was in love with Cina and would she beg his forgiveness? He knew Cina was a married woman and that her husband was a treacherous man who no longer merited her as his wife. He wanted to make Cina his woman and someday his wife—that is, if Cina would consider such a thing.

Mayela watched Sebastian closely, noticing how he took off his straw hat and held it up to his chest. He sat cross-legged on the dirt and didn't bother to use one of the tapetes, saying he was not worthy of such comforts. Cina sat on a wooden crate, holding her son, Nabor, and didn't say a thing. She only looked at Sebastian solemnly, observing the huge serape he wore and noting the outline of el machete, which she knew he had hidden at his waist. She wondered about el Imán, which guided Sebastian's life, and was secretly pleased the stone had chosen her as his woman, as she had never considered herself someone who merited attention from a crystal imbued with magical powers. Sebastian explained to Tía Concha that he now had a dwelling he had built himself and needed Cina to complete his life.

"Since you're the only relative she has here, I come to you, Doña Concha, to ask your blessing. Cina's the kind of woman who's strong, fuerte y guerrera. She's not afraid to fight for what she believes in. And I'm willing to make a life with her, Doña Concha, if it pleases you."

Tía Concha scratched her head and ran her hands over her wrinkled skirt, thinking it wouldn't be a bad idea to have a man around who would help her build onto her dwelling and give her some protection from thieves. Still, she felt a dark frightening power emanating from

Sebastian, although Cina had told her nothing yet about el Imán. Pausing briefly, she consented—there was nothing else she could do. She had no right to tell Cina whom to marry, as she was already married in the first place. Besides, she noticed Sebastian had brought a bottle of pulque, and her mouth was already watering for a drink.

"Oh, sí, cómo, no! My blessings are with both of you. Misery unites us all, but love is the key that breaks through and give us hope."

Then Sebastian stood up and smiled, embracing Tía Concha with one arm and Cina with the other. Tía Concha's head barely came up to Sebastian's shoulder, and Mayela could tell by the way her beady black eyes lit up that the old woman was pleased with Sebastian's attention. Cina looked serious next to him, and thin, her hair held back from her gaunt face by a black ribbon. She smiled a crooked smile, while her eyes darted from Sebastian to her children and then to Mayela. Nabor started to cry, and Cina asked Mayela to take the children down the way to play while they celebrated with a toast. Sebastian opened the bottle of pulque with great pomp, as if it was an expensive bottle of champagne, and gave Tía Concha the first drink, then one to Cina, and finally one for himself. Pretty soon, they all took another drink, then another, and started talking and enjoying each other's company. Cina sat next to Sebastian, and he wrapped his arm around her. Mayela watched them while she played with the children and noticed Sebastian held Cina tighter as the evening wore on. Finally, Cina told Tía Concha that she was going with Sebastian to see the house he had built for her. Mayela could tell Cina was excited about what Sebastian had done for her, and so quickly, as it demonstrated how much he loved her. She called Mayela and told her she'd be right back and to get the children to sleep, as it was late.

Mayela watched them as they disappeared into the darkness. The night was cold, the air heavy with smoke from la chiminea and from campfires that flickered among the dwellings. The moon dangled in the sky as if hanging on a string, and Mayela felt a great longing to be back in Chitlitipin with her mother, sitting out in her own backyard, running races with her friends, listening to her mother tell stories to her brothers and sisters. She saw the power Sebastian had over Cina and was afraid Cina was leaving her in charge of the children, and that somehow Sebastian would convince her to run away with him to the Yucatan Peninsula and she would never see her again. Cina had the money Mayela's mother had given her to put her in school, but now that Sebastian was in control of Cina, the money would soon be in his hands.

The children went to sleep, and Tía Concha pulled out a bottle of tesgüino, liquor made from fermented corn. She drank from the bottle and talked to Mayela in the dark.

"Sebastian is a bird of prey. I know. I've seen men like him all my life. Cina's his next victim. But she won't listen to me. She's under Sebastian's power. Her eyes are blinded. Sebastian has put mal ojo on her to make her see only him."

"What can be done?" Mayela's voice was weak, tired from the long day, and afraid now that Cina was under Sebastian's power.

Tia Concha didn't answer. Mayela was about to ask her again when she heard the old woman begin to snore heavily and knew she had passed out from the liquor. Outside, Mayela heard people shouting, men arguing, and a woman screamed. Feet ran past Tía Concha's dwelling. Mayela wrapped herself tightly in a blanket next to Isi and held onto Isi's tiny hand in the dark.

14 Mayela found out the next morning that Cina had spent the entire night with Sebastian. She came back with every inch of her skin, hair, and clothes covered in dirt, sandy and gritty and sticking to her skin, making her scratch herself until her skin was red and raw. Tiny grains of sand were lodged between her teeth, and she rinsed her mouth over and over again and spit. She told Tía Concha that she needed to take a bath. Tía Concha said they had to wait until the water truck came by to fill up two round plastic drums she had found in the dump site, thrown out by the American-owned copper smelter.

The water truck finally showed up at noon, and Mayela helped Cina drag the two plastic drums to the side of Tía Concha's dwelling, where they were connected to a water hose at the back of the truck. Mayela felt pain in her legs as she helped Cina move the plastic drums over the rocky ground, and she started to sweat even though it was the last week in October and the day was cool. Mayela was surprised to feel pain in her legs, having never experienced such pain in her life.

Cina finally bathed herself behind a faded curtain at the back of Tía Concha's dwelling, dipping an aluminum pot into the plastic drum and ladling the water into a round tub where she sat. She washed her hair and body vigorously, scrubbing off the gritty sand with a bar of Palmolive soap. Tía Concha said the nuns from the Catholic church had given her the soap and some towels, shampoo, and even a bottle of perfume that Tía Concha sprayed on herself when she went into town. Cina bathed the two children in the same water she had used, which was now muddy and full of the sandy soil. After their bath, the children began scratching themselves until red blotches appeared on their skin, and still they couldn't stop scratching. Tía Concha said it was because they weren't used to bathing.

"But they bathe in the river in Chitlitipin, and nothing ever happens to them," Mayela said, watching the children scratching themselves while they sat in the dirt waiting for Cina to fix them something to eat.

Tía Concha thought for a second, then looked at Mayela as if a bright idea had just occurred to her. "Bathing in the river doesn't count," she said. "The children aren't used to using soap."

Mayela was about to tell her that her mother bought soap for them in Montenegro, and of course they used it, but she hardly had the strength to say another word. She was dizzy and had to blink rapidly several times to clear her blurred vision.

Cina asked Mayela if she also wanted to bathe, but Mayela told her she'd wait. Secretly, she wanted to fill the tub with fresh water, but didn't want it to look as if the water everyone else had used wasn't good enough for her. Tía Concha bathed next, saying it was hard for her to get water and any water in la colonia Los Tres Magos was a blessing. The old woman enjoyed her bath, laughing like a child and telling Cina that someday she'd own a house with a real bathtub, as soon as her husband came back from el otro lado. Cina was surprised to hear of a husband and asked her when he was expected. Tía Concha said she wasn't sure, as she hadn't seen him in fifteen years. Still, she said she had hope, because no one had reported him dead. He'd come back from America with a sack of money someday, and her troubles would be over.

Cina prepared a meal for everyone, cooking between two rocks that Tía Concha used as a grill. Mayela helped gather dry brush, paper, twigs, and anything else she could find in the dump that would burn. Tía Concha used matches to start the flame going and spread a bit of fuel to make the flames leap and burn hotter over the grill, which was nothing more than a thin slab of iron she cleaned off with a knife, scraping bits of burned food from its surface. She kept guard over the fire until it was hot enough for Cina to cook corn tortillas she had formed from cornmeal Tía Concha had ground on el metate, the stone grinder she had used since she was a girl. Then Cina boiled a piece of meat she had bought from a man who swore it wasn't spoiled, mixing chile into the meat and boiling a pot of beans over a small firebox fueled by gas vapors.

Before long, Sebastian came back to Tía Concha's. This time, he left his straw hat on and didn't offer anyone a drink of pulque, keeping the bottle to himself and saying he had been working all day long and was tired. He was starving, he said, and Cina had to serve him as soon as he sat down on a nearby rock. He ate ravenously and asked for more. No one else ate until Sebastian was finished, and when it was time for every-one else to eat, there was hardly anything left. Sebastian sat back on the rock and sharpened a twig with a hand knife so he could pick his teeth clean. He made his tongue stick out through the wide space between his front teeth and laughed when he saw Mayela looking at him with fear in her eyes. Again and again he pushed his tongue into the empty space between his teeth, as if it was a trick.

"Can you do this, Mayela?" he asked her, laughing and curling his tongue into a point so it could fit into the wide space. Mayela's face turned red with embarrassment. She didn't want to offend him, so she only smiled and looked away.

"Just like my little sister," he said. "Mayela's too serious and doesn't know how to have fun."

Cina smiled and looked at Mayela as if to tell her to be friendly to Sebastian.

"She's not used to having company. We lived on our own in our village—and we didn't get a chance to meet many people."

"Well, she better start changing. This is Juárez, and who knows who we'll meet along the way." Sebastian settled back on the rock and said he felt better now that he had eaten his meal.

Nabor went up to Sebastian, wanting to climb up on his lap to take a look at his tongue close up, but Sebastian pushed him away and told him to stick out his own tongue if he wanted to be a real man.

"That's what happens to boys brought up by a woman. They get soft and don't know how to do their own tricks."

Nabor frowned and stuck out his tongue at Sebastian. "Next time you do that, expect a slap across your face," Sebastian said angrily.

Cina pulled Nabor to her side and laughed as if it was funny. "He wants to be like you!" she said. But Sebastian ignored her.

Cina had to start making food all over again, with Tía Concha lighting more dry brush. She made corn tortillas again, and more chile, and this time she added potatoes because Sebastian had eaten most of the meat. By this time, Mayela was starving, her hands shaking with hunger. Her head ached, something she had never felt before, and every time she took a breath her chest hurt.

After the evening meal, everyone walked with Cina and Sebastian to see the place he had built for her, which was not far off, leaning up against the rocky hillside. The dwelling was constructed of sticks that Sebastian had put together to form a cylinder shape that fit right into the hillside. One of the walls of the dwelling was the hill itself. He had used cardboard to make a roof and walls, securing it with nails he said he had gotten from one of the neighbors. Inside, Sebastian had swept the dirt floor neatly and separated it into a space for himself and Cina to have some privacy by tying two old blankets on poles dug into the ground. He had tapetes rolled up along the sides of the dwelling, to be used at night as beds. He even had crates for chairs and a wooden box he used as a table. He was proud of the dwelling and said that pretty soon, God willing, he'd start hauling adobe bricks a few at a time until he had one wall, then two, then three. Then he'd start on the roof and next add real glass for windows and a bright blue door as a sign of their good fortune.

Mayela woke during the night, her head throbbing, her stomach cramping. When she felt her forehead with her hand, she found it burning with fever. From behind the blankets Sebastian had hung on poles for privacy, she heard terrible sounds, as if an animal was growling and ready to attack. She got up, weak and dizzy, and walked toward the blankets, worried that something was happening to Cina. Suddenly, the blankets collapsed to the ground. Sebastian had kicked them down as he jumped on Cina, up and down, grunting and pressing Cina into the ground with his weight. In the moonlight, Mayela saw Sebastian's brown back and thick arms, and Cina lying under him, naked from the waist down. Cina had her eyes closed, with a look of great anguish. Mayela's first thought was that Sebastian was attacking Cina and was ready to kill her with el machete. She let out a scream. Instantly, Sebastian was on his feet. He grabbed el machete from its leather sheath and brandished it like a madman. Mayela saw the blade shining in the moonlight and was terrified he'd kill her and Cina.

"I'll kill you!" he shouted at her over and over. "You'll pay for this, you little whore. You don't fool me!"

Cursing and screaming, Sebastian stood in front of Mayela naked while she cowered on her knees. She scrambled to her feet, the dark pubic hair showing between her legs. Cina grabbed her skirt and balanced it in front of her naked bottom and yelled at Mayela to get out, while Sebastian cursed louder and swore he'd kill Mayela for spying on them and pulling down the blankets.

Mayela threw up as she ran out, trying to get to the outhouse in time to relieve her loose bowels. She didn't make it and soiled her clothes, crying in despair and all the while looking behind her for any signs of Sebastian chasing her with el machete. She stumbled over rocks and steep ravines to get to Tía Concha's dwelling, waking up the old woman with her cries when she arrived. Mayela was so faint from running away from Sebastian that Tía Concha had to help her wash herself and change her soiled clothing. Then she led her to a small cot she said she had received that day from the Catholic nuns, and had her lie on it while she slept on el tapete, saying she was used to sleeping on the ground and that the mattress was too soft for her. She gave Mayela a cup of medicinal tea to help her with the stomach cramps, then said flatly: "What did I tell you? Sebastian's a bird of prey, and Cina is his next victim."

For days, Mayela stayed with Tía Concha and saw Cina only during the day when Sebastian was out working. Cina asked her why she had pulled down the blankets, and Mayela told her with tears in her eyes that she had never done such a thing.

"I want to go home," she told Cina. "My mother must be worried. Please put me back on the train!"

"You can't go back. I saw someone here who was just in Chitlitipin, and he says your mother's gone to Puebla. Our mother, your abuelita, is very ill, and who knows when Chavela will come back. I myself may be called to take care of my mother, but if I go back, Zocotl will kill me. We have to stay here."

"What about school? My mother wanted me to go to school." Cina looked away from Mayela, not wanting to talk about the money her sister had given her for Mayela's education.

"There's no money for school right now! It's work we need, not school. I need your help with the children. Tomorrow, we'll go with Tía Concha to los mercados, and I'm sure we'll make some money. Later, we can talk about you going to school."

Mayela's neck was swollen and stiff, and she couldn't turn her head. Cina noticed and told her maybe she was sore from lying on the ground and not having anything to support her neck. She'd roll up another tapete for her, she said, that she could use as a pillow. Mayela didn't want to tell Cina she was feeling sick, as this would only put another burden on her and make matters worse with Sebastian. Cina said she'd talk to Sebastian and convince him that Mayela hadn't been spying on them and hadn't pulled down the blankets. In the meantime, she told Mayela to stay away from Sebastian, as she didn't want him to see her and remember all over again what she had done.

All day long Mayela played listlessly with the children, unable to carry Isi in her arms anymore. She fed them pinole mixed with water in rusty tin bowls and dry flour tortillas that broke in her hands. She scattered fragments of the tortillas on the ground for red ants to carry away on their backs, not caring if the ants climbed up her legs. Mayela watched the ants at work and felt as if she was disappearing into the earth along with them.

That evening Sebastian came back happy, saying that someone had hired him to load boxes onto freight trains, and the money they would pay him would be enough to buy food and start stacking up adobe bricks for their dwelling. He was loud and boisterous with such good fortune. He even approached Mayela and patted her on the head.

"You can come back," he said. "I think you've learned your lesson. Never bother adults at night. They need their privacy. Do you understand?" He smiled broadly as if it was all a joke and put one hand under Mayela's chin. "Smile, I'm not a monster!"

Mayela tried to smile but couldn't. She only looked at Sebastian silently, remembering his naked body and el machete waving wildly in front of her face. Sebastian laughed and said Mayela was just like his little sister—too serious and gloomy. Cina was happy with Sebastian's good fortune and smiled at him, grateful that he was no longer angry with Mayela.

Everyone shared a meal, and Sebastian brought out three bottles of pineapple soda he had bought for the children as a surprise. Mayela had no appetite and gave her bottle of soda to Isi and Nabor. One of Tía Concha's neighbors, Don Cipriano, stopped by with two bottles of mescal that he said he had made himself from an old recipe passed on to him by his great-grandfather. Don Cipriano had a violin that was old and battered and held together with pieces of string and glue. He played the violin beautifully and said he had once played for el jefe, his boss, and for all the important occasions in his village. Everyone was in a festive mood, and Sebastian put his arm around Cina and told her that he had found the right woman. Then he pulled out el machete for Don Cipriano to see and said he had used it to chop sugarcane in the Yucatan Peninsula and all along the seacoast. Then he laughed and said he had used it to chop a few other things as well. He pulled out what looked like human hair from the leather sheath, saying that perhaps there was still some hair left over from one of his enemies' heads on el machete. Don Cipriano laughed along with Sebastian, clapping him on the back as if they were two men sharing a humorous adventure story. Tía Concha didn't say a thing and took another long drink of mescal. Mayela looked at the human hair in horror and was now afraid Sebastian would use el machete to cut off one of their heads.

Mayela wanted to run to Cina and tell her what she felt, but Cina was laughing as if it was all a magic trick and not really human hair at all. After Sebastian had put el machete back into its leather sheath, Cina leaned into him and thought that if her husband Zocotl came to Juárez looking for her, Sebastian would use el machete to fight for her. Sebastian looked over at Mayela and said she was welcome to come back to live with them in his dwelling, after which Cina hugged him and kissed his cheek.

Tía Concha made an herbal tea for Mayela to drink and put it into a gourd she had fashioned out of a calabash fruit, instructing her to drink as much of it as she could, as it would make her stomach pains go away. At night, Mayela pulled out the gourd. With her body trembling as she leaned on one elbow, she silently sipped the tea. Her stomach was cramping with pain that traveled into her back and down her legs, and her hair was wet with sweat as her body battled the fever that made her feel as if she was on fire. Her neck and back were so stiff and painful, she could barely move. She lay still on el tapete, again listening to the animal grunts coming from behind the blankets Sebastian had hung on the wooden poles. The sounds went on for a long time, getting louder and more threatening, then stopping altogether. This time, Mayela didn't get up. In the dark, she saw the outline of Sebastian going outdoors to relieve himself. When he walked back past Mayela, he reached into the blanket under her skirt and put his whole hand over her bottom, pressing hard, and whispered that she would like what he would do to her, just as Cina did. Without making a sound that would alarm Cina and make trouble for her with Sebastian, Mayela started to cry.

Early in the morning, Mayela listened to roosters crow and smelled mesquite wood burning, along with the terrible smell of decay and death that blew in from the dump. She labored to stand up and had to walk very slowly so as not to fall to the ground.

In the early dawn she saw Sebastian in the distance performing his services to el Imán. The tiny rock was laid out on a plank Sebastian had set up between two rocks. He stood in front of it as if he was at an altar, repeating his chant.

> Te pongo oro para mi tesoro,
> Plata para mi casa,
> Cobre para el pobre,
> Coral, para que me quite la envidia y el mal,
> Trigo, para que Cina sea mi esposa según lo que desea,
>   se le pide.

> *   *   *

> I give you gold for my treasure,
> Silver for my house,
> Copper for the poor man,
> Coral, so you remove from me envy and evil,
> Wheat so that Cina will be my wife, as fate will have it.

A chill ran through Mayela's body as she saw in secret what Sebastian was doing. Tía Concha was right—he had complete power over Cina. Mayela, too weak and afraid to say or do anything else, lay back on el tapete and held onto Isi's tiny hand for comfort.

Mayela couldn't concentrate on the trip to los mercados. The pain in her head was pressing into her eyes and behind her ears. She carried with her the gourd of herbal tea but didn't have the strength to open the gourd and take a drink. They rode for almost an hour on la rutera, going round and round in circles to pick people up at every stop. The jerking of la rutera and the fumes from its exhaust nauseated Mayela, and she leaned over the side of an open window in case she had to throw up. Tía Concha told her there were yerbistas in los mercados and curanderos who might be able to recommend medicine that would heal her.

Tía Concha and Cina had gotten together a few things they found at the dump that they thought might bring in some money—stockings they had washed and made almost new, children's shoes they had reseamed, and small ceramic animals Tía Concha had made out of clay. They also made burritos and corn tamales to sell, which Tía Concha had cooked in a pit dug into a hole in the ground. Tía Concha said she would ask her cousin, Licha, for help with Mayela if she didn't feel better soon. Licha cleaned for the priests at la Catedral, she said, and knew all there was to know about what was in Juárez and how to get help for Mayela. "Licha attended school and went up to la prepa," Tía Concha said proudly. "She's quite educated."

Mayela had never seen so many people and cars and ruteras flying by, or heard so much noise. They combined into a big ball of color and noise and movement that went round and round inside her head. Isi and Nabor were staring at everything, wide-eyed and solemn, afraid to venture far from Cina. Mayela's weakness made it impossible for her to help Cina with the children. It seemed to her that her life was hopeless and that the purpose for her being in Juárez in the first place had all been forgotten. Along the sidewalk facing one of the busiest streets in el Centro, Tía Concha found a spot for them to display their wares. It was hidden behind other street vendors, but the best places along the sidewalk were already taken, so they had to settle for what they could get. Tía Concha told Mayela to lie on el tapete she spread out for her on the sidewalk—lie very still, she said. Mayela felt so sick, she was thankful that she wouldn't have to do anything but lie down. Tía Concha put her hand on Mayela's back and told everyone who went by in a pleading singsong voice, "Por favor, for my sick child, who's dying, starving. God will repay you!"

There were tourists on the streets, Americans, who walked past them searching for Mexican curios. Tía Concha held out a tin plate, reaching for them as they walked by. Some of them looked sadly at Mayela, then reached into their wallets and put money on the tin plate. Sometimes it was a whole American dollar, or more.

"We're lucky today!" Tía Concha said, looking at a five-dollar bill one of los Americanos had given her. "Mayela, you have brought us good luck!" Mayela didn't respond, as she was so weak she couldn't even open her eyes.

By the afternoon, they had sold a few burritos and tamales but no stockings, children's shoes, or ceramic animals. Tía Concha and Cina were happy with the American money, as it was more than they had expected. When Cina told Mayela that it was time to go home, Mayela didn't respond. That's when Tía Concha feared the worst and hurried to la Catedral to get her cousin Licha.

When Licha arrived, she took one look at Mayela and said she needed to be taken to the doctor immediately. "She's close to death," Licha said, as she put one finger on Mayela's throat to feel for her pulse. "I'm sure the doctor will have her admitted to the hospital as soon as he sees her."

Cina was frightened by what Licha said and by the way the woman looked at Mayela, shaking her head in pity. Now she was worried Chavela would kill her before Zocotl did. Then she thought of Sebastian and knew he'd be angry with her if she wasn't at home with his dinner prepared when he returned from work.

"Would we be able to take her home and bring her back tomorrow morning to see a doctor?" she asked Licha.

"If you do that, I guarantee you she won't live through the night."

Cina wrung her hands in despair at the thought that Mayela could die and she would be to blame. She looked at Tía Concha with tears in her eyes.

"Por favor, yes, tía, take her to the doctor, and I'll forever be in your debt. Tomorrow, early in the morning, I'll go see her at the hospital.

You know how Sebastian is; he'll be angry if I'm not home when he gets there."

"Hmh, sí, ya lo creo. Sebastian should mind his own business—this is family!"

Licha looked at both women. "I can't stand out here all afternoon. I have work to do, and this child must be taken to the doctor." She pointed out to them the way to a clinic, only three blocks away.

"You'll have to carry her," she said. "And hurry." Then she turned away and headed quickly back to la Catedral.

Mayela was too heavy for Tía Concha to carry, and Cina was already walking away with Isi and Nabor. Tía Concha reached into her pocket for one of the three American dollars she had hidden away and ran to the nearest store to change it for Mexican money. Then she called a young man who was standing at the street corner.

"Por favor, here's a bit of money for your services if you will carry a child to the clinic for me."

The young man was courteous and said he would do the job. Tía Concha took him to where Mayela was lying, still and lifeless on el tapete, and the young man bent down and picked her up as if she was a feather. He carried her easily a few streets down to a medical clinic run by la Cruz Roja. At the clinic, the doctor took one look at Mayela and told Tía Concha that he was sure, beyond a doubt, that Mayela was suffering from meningitis and there was nothing else to do but transport her immediately to the hospital.

Mayela stayed in the hospital for two weeks. The doctor told Tía Concha that one more day without medical help and Mayela would have died. She was dehydrated, and the disease had invaded her body to the point that she started having seizures. The doctor instructed the nurses to put Mayela in a room by herself, as he didn't want the disease to spread. The room was more like a closet, with space for only one person to stand at Mayela's bedside. Overhead a tiny window let in gray light.

At night Mayela had nightmares of Sebastian. She saw him naked, waving el machete, and saw his red tongue darting in and out through the wide space between his front teeth, faster and faster, until it became a huge bird that flew out of his mouth and pecked her eyes out. She felt his hand under her skirt, touching her, hurting her, and she screamed.

A nurse walked in and said the fever was giving Mayela nightmares, and she put a cold towel on her forehead and Vaseline on her lips to relieve her of the fever blisters that had erupted. Then she sat on a chair next to Mayela's bed and held onto her hand because Mayela was crying and begging her not to leave.

Cina visited Mayela only once. She told her she was making every attempt to send word to her mother, who was still in Puebla. She said the people who had been forwarding messages to her mother had moved away, and she knew of no one else to call. She combed Mayela's long hair, brushing all the knots out and weaving it into two braids that she tied in bright red ribbon. She arranged the braids on top of Mayela's head to prevent her from sleeping on them. Then she looked sadly at her, holding her close.

"I won't be able to come back to see you. I'm pregnant, and Sebastian's afraid his baby will be contaminated with your disease. In fact, if he knew I was here . . . he, well, he would be angry with me."

Mayela put her arms tightly around Cina, not wanting her to go. "Just last night," she told her, "I dreamed that my mother came here to Juárez to take me home. She is coming, isn't she?"

"Yes, of course she is, as soon as I tell her what's happened to us." Already Cina was wondering how she would explain to her sister that Mayela had never been put in a school and that all the money she had given her had been given to Sebastian. She would have to think up lies and rely on a tragic story to avoid her sister's quick temper.

Mayela didn't tell Cina the rest of the dream. She had dreamed that Sebastian had used el machete to cut off Cina's head. Mayela shivered and cried thinking about it, while Cina soothed her, telling her Tía Concha would stop by as often as she could until Mayela was ready to come home. Then she showed Mayela a beaded purse she had bought for her, with a tiny comb and brush inside. Mayela looked at it and pretended it was something that made her happy.

At the end of two weeks, the doctor said Mayela was strong enough to go home. However, he advised Tía Concha that she not go back to live in la colonia Los Tres Magos. Mayela's condition was delicate, he said, and she needed great care. He explained that Los Tres Magos was the worst place possible for children, and if Mayela went back there, he couldn't guarantee that she would live long. She had never been around the viruses and germs that lived in the water and contaminated ground, and besides that the dump harbored numerous plagues. Tía Concha argued with the doctor and told him that other children lived there and they survived. She wanted Mayela to live with her, to help her with her chores and bring her good luck at los mercados like she had done before. She still had American money left over from the time she had begged on the streets with Mayela, even though Cina had taken most of it to give to Sebastian.

"She's in a weakened condition," the doctor explained impatiently to Tía Concha. He seemed irritated that the old woman had dared to question his advice and looked at her as if she was the most despicable creature he had ever seen. "My advice is for you to take her to el Instituto de Niños Huerfanos, the orphanage run by Señora Juana del Pilar, over by la Catedral."

He told her there was an American doctor working there with the children, doing a study on how poverty affected their health, especially in cases of children with meningitis, polio, and other diseases. He said the American doctor had asked him for any children who lived in la colonia Los Tres Magos, and he had recommended Mayela to her.

"I'm sure there won't be any problem getting Mayela into el Instituto, as Señora Juana del Pilar wants to do all she can to please the American doctor. Ya sabes, I'm sure la Americana's bringing in American money to el Instituto, and considering how many orphans there are in Juárez who need to go there, this is a good thing for Mayela."

Then the doctor walked away, still angry over Tía Concha questioning his advice, and started scolding everyone in sight, telling them that if they had listened to the advice of a doctor they wouldn't be in the sorry condition they were in, suffering like dumb brutes. And now, Americans were in Juárez studying them like they were a swarm of flies, and all because they didn't know how to tend to their health problems until they were nearly half dead. If this was why he had gotten his medical degree, to serve people who didn't take his advice, he might as well go dig ditches.

Tía Concha told Mayela she'd return by the end of the week to take her to a nice place, a clean place where other children lived. She said it would be so much nicer than Los Tres Magos, she might never want to come home. Besides, she would go to school there, and that's really what her mother wanted her to do. Tía Concha didn't mention that the place would be an orphanage and that Mayela would be part of a study carried out by an American doctor.

Babies Who Fly

15 Isidora invited a new girl to live with her. Her name was Josefina, but she preferred to be called Fina. She said she was *fina*, as her name indicated, refined and pleasing. Fina took over Anabel's bed, but she wasn't friendly like Anabel and spent her days talking about how many men she had had and how much they had paid for her and how many times she had gotten to be somebody's favorita. She did her nails, gave herself facials, and dyed her hair at least two different colors in one week. She wasn't much bigger than Evita, but pretended her breasts were so much bigger and her legs longer, more shapely. Besides all that, she said, she had more experience in one of her little fingers than Evita had in her whole body. Evita decided Fina looked like a grasshopper, with her head pointed at the top and her chin dropping into a perfect V. Her eyes were big and round and reflected the world like two tiny mirrors that saw everything at once. All day long, Fina admired herself in the mirror and tried on clothes and did certain dance steps that she said would get men hot and they would pay her more money.

Evita walked around with the hole in her heart that Ricardo had left and imagined that someday he'd return and they'd be together. She was sure he didn't love his wife, and maybe his wife didn't love him either. Ricardo had told her he couldn't live without her, so Evita imagined it was just a matter of time before he returned and they resumed their lovemaking at el Paraiso. She was hoping she would never have to face her mother to defend her love for Ricardo. When she thought about her mother with him, she got crazy inside and couldn't make the thoughts go away until she imagined herself holding Ricardo's knife and cutting into her wrist. Evita still believed she wouldn't have any peace until she killed herself.

Fina laughed at Evita and said she was wasting her time waiting for Ricardo, as he would never return unless it was to meet her at el Paraiso. He had made a fool out of her, she said laughing, and Evita didn't even know it.

Cristal ignored Fina and refused to speak to her at all, saying Fina was una creida, who believed she was better than everyone else. Someday she'd get what she deserved, but in the meantime they'd have to put up with her. Evita still cooked for Cristal and cleaned her room because Cristal said she was no good at anything that had to do with a house.

Now that Evita was one of them, Cristal talked to her and told her about her dealings with men. But she didn't tell Evita the truth about Ricardo. She thought it would hurt Evita too much to know that Ricardo had been one of her customers when she had started in las zonas at thirteen. Men had preferences, and for Ricardo it was little girls. Cristal remembered him as someone who was hungry for her body, like a lion who wanted to eat her up. Then he vanished, and she never saw him again. Now the same thing had happened to Evita.

Cristal didn't mind if Evita saw her naked while they talked together in her room, as wearing clothes or not wearing clothes was all the same to her. Evita unsnapped the clasp on the red beads Cristal wore around her neck so she could take a shower and helped her out of her tight clothes, while Cristal told Evita about Maclovio, an older man she was seeing who was well experienced in trying out women all along las zonas. Maclovio was big and brown, with a short neck and thick chest. He reminded Evita of a big brown dog she had seen once with a thick mane for a neck and dark furry ears. The dog's paws were white, but turned black and muddy after he jumped into a puddle of water, then ran around chasing the children and leaping on them, getting mud all over their clothes. The children shouted and ran away from the dog. Evita wondered if Cristal would someday run away from Maclovio in the same way.

Maclovio had been married at least five times, and his children were scattered all over Chihuahua. He liked Cristal because she kept to herself and didn't bother him with questions he didn't want to answer. He bought her the cross with the red beads that she wore around her neck, and sometimes he came by to pick her up to take her to el Club Exotica, where she danced until dawn. Maclovio sat in the dark, waiting for her, smoking cigarettes and taking his tragos of tequila in shot glasses, one after another, and observing the way other men looked at Cristal, feeling jealous every time a man approached her or tried to touch her. It got bad at times, and Rudy, the owner of the club, had to get his bouncer on him, a man three times bigger than Maclovio who had fought as a guerrilla in the Amazon jungles and was now trapped on the streets of Juárez waiting for the right time to join another revolution. In the meantime, he was staying in practice by beating up unruly customers, shoving elbows into their faces and torsos and putting choke holds on them until they turned limp and pale, and he could throw them out on the streets like so many sacks of flour.

After Cristal's shower, Evita smoothed lotion on her legs, taking her time to massage the muscular, shapely legs until they were glossy and rosy red. She admired the G-string Cristal wore, bright purple, and the stars she had decorated her belly with—shiny plastic tatoos she said would shine when she danced in the dark under the stage lights. Evita noticed a long scar going from Cristal's left underarm down to her ribcage. She asked Cristal about it, and Cristal said never mind, she'd tell her about it someday. Evita thought about her own scar, the pink jagged line made by Ricardo's knife on her left wrist, and said nothing more.

"Maclovio's not hard to deal with. He's easy on me and doesn't demand much. He's at the end of his sexual life and is only trying to prove that he can still get himself going."

Cristal laughed as she talked about Maclovio, and Evita laughed with her. She asked Evita to bring her the bra that matched her G-string, translucent, with purple straps and two lacy dots that clung to her nipples. Cristal lifted her arms, making her breasts go full and round on her chest. They were beautiful, and Evita envied them.

"Help me," she told Evita. "Tie this string around my back." Evita tied the matching purple bra around Cristal's back and smoothed the lacy dots around her brown nipples.

"Don't do that," Cristal said, "you'll make them go hard!" Then they both laughed, and Cristal touched them herself. The nipples stood up under the lacy dots. Then Evita helped her slip on a melon-colored dress, sleek and sophisticated, that showed off her breasts. Cristal tossed her head back impatiently, making her wet hair fall over her shoulders, and asked Evita to get the blow-dryer so she could help her dry and comb out her hair.

"Maclovio owns his own business," Cristal said, raising her voice above the blow-dryer. "He makes plenty to pay me, and I don't have to look elsewhere."

Cristal told Evita that the most demanding customers she would ever encounter were los mejicanos. "They're used to being served by us and know what a woman can give. So they demand and demand, and there's no end to their demands.

"I'm glad when they're too drunk to do much. Then I encourage them, and tell them they're great lovers—their wives should be happy."

Then she told Evita about the American soldiers and schoolboys who travel to Juárez on weekends from los Estados Unidos looking for prostitutes.

"Los Americanos are mostly interested in getting drunk and having a good time. Some of them come in from their military base and are taking time away from their duties. They want to get drunk as quickly as possible, and as they say, *escore*."

Cristal didn't have the courage to tell Evita about the dangerous men, the ones who pulled out a knife and subjected women to all kinds of violence. The ones who refused to wear a condom and ended up telling the woman they were infected with AIDS, when they knew it was too late for her to do anything about it. She didn't tell her the story of a friend who was murdered by a man who turned on her and slit her from her vagina up to her throat.

"It's dangerous—very dangerous, too. Always let someone know where you are, who you're with. That's why I like living with Isidora. She keeps an eye on us, and she pays off the police when she has to, to get us protection."

"I'm afraid of the police," Evita told her. "They threatened me once when my mother sent them out to look for me."

"Oh, they'll do more than threaten you. You must never assume anything from them. They are more dangerous than all the men you will ever meet."

"What about the murders? I'm afraid of all the murders."

"Don't worry about that," Cristal said. "Most of the time they're after las maquiladoras and schoolgirls. They want to inflict the most pain they can, so they choose women who are innocent and certain to have families who will mourn them. And of course, the police accuse the women of being prostitutes and leading a double life—as you know, they always blame the woman. Don't think about it too much, Evita, really—but be as careful as you can, always telling someone where you will be. Maybe someday you'll find a man like Maclovio, and he'll be good to you, and you won't have to look any further."

Evita could hardly believe that she was learning how to be a prostitute from Cristal. She had become a business woman like Ricardo had told her she would. Evita thought about all the curses and names her mother had thrown at her in anger and realized she was now the image of what her mother had accused her of being: a shameless whore. Still, it felt good to sit close to Cristal, smell her sweet body and admire her splendid breasts, sharing secrets with her about men.

Evita was slow about taking up her life in las zonas. She was having trouble getting up in the mornings and didn't feel like going out with Fina to the dance halls to get customers. In fact, she hadn't been with anyone since Ricardo, and made up for it by preparing meals, massaging Isidora's legs with ointment, cleaning up the house, and not complaining when they went to the doctor's office for more medicine. She hadn't seen Chano stop by to pick up the medicine for a while, but other men came in his place. They never talked to Isidora, just walked in brusquely wearing dark sunglasses, picked up the plastic bags, and walked out without a word. Evita was afraid of them and stayed in her room when she knew they were knocking at the door.

Evita started to throw up in the mornings and couldn't eat a thing. Isidora sat next to her, felt her forehead, looked into her eyes, and told her she was pregnant.

"What did I tell you? You always demand that a man wear a condom. Now Ricardo's got you pregnant, and you'll have to get an abortion."

Evita held onto her stomach. "I don't want an abortion! I want to have Ricardo's baby."

"What? Are you crazy? What will you do with the baby? How will you take care of him? Do you think Ricardo will come back to marry you?"

Evita didn't say anything, only curled up into a ball and held onto the tiny baby inside her womb that belonged to Ricardo. She felt her breasts swollen and her body filled with a strange energy. Feeling Ricardo's baby in her body reminded her of all Ricardo had taught her about love, and she began to pine for him again. Maybe if he knew she was pregnant, he'd want to help her and take her to live with him. Then she thought of Ricardo's wife, and of her mother, and knew it would never happen. His baby was all she had left of him, and she was determined to have it, no matter what Isidora said.

When Cristal found out about Evita's pregnancy, she sat with her at her bedside, one hand on Evita's shoulder.

"Evita, you can't have this baby. You're still a child yourself. I know there are girls your age who have babies, some even younger, but look at the trouble they have. And how will you ever go back home with Ricardo's baby?"

"I don't ever want to go back home!"

"But Evita, you will. Someday you'll go back home, and you'll see your mother again. Men come and go in our lives, but our mothers remain forever."

Evita resisted the temptation to cover her ears with her hands, knowing Cristal was telling her the truth. As much as she wanted to keep Ricardo's baby, she'd have to abort it, and Cristal told her it had to be done very soon.

"Will it hurt me?"

"Yes, some. But not more than the birth of a child."

Evita thought of the tiny baby growing inside her, the size of a marble with eyes and ears, fingers and toes, and she held on to Cristal's hand. Cristal smoothed her hair and told her everything would be fine. It was the first time Cristal had been so compassionate with Evita, and it made Evita wonder if Cristal had ever had an abortion. But she didn't ask her, as she knew Cristal didn't like to talk about herself.

"Unborn babies become angels and fly away to Heaven," Cristal said to her "and they don't ever have to suffer on earth."

Evita remembered her baby brother, Fidel, el Albino, making his way into heaven with the red rose she had placed in his hands, and imagined that Ricardo's baby would join him, and they'd fly off together into the clouds and play games all day long.

"Will I go to the hospital for the abortion?"

"No! Of course not. You'll go see Doctor Juárez. He's the one who will do it for you. He has a place that women go to—and he doesn't charge much. No one knows his real name, so they call him Doctor Juárez. He makes a lot of money from desperate women."

Evita's face got pale, thinking of Doctor Juárez and what he would do to her.

"He's harmless," Cristal told her. "He looks like a cockroach, but you won't have to see him for very long—thank God for that! He might even give you pills so you won't get pregnant again." Then she looked closely at Evita's arms. "What are all those red spots on your arms?"

"Allergies," Evita said, and turned her face to the wall.

Isidora gave Evita a tonic to drink that she said Doctor Juárez had given her for girls who found out they were pregnant.

"It may upset your stomach, but it will also start the process of getting rid of the baby."

Evita didn't want to drink the tonic and ended up taking only two spoonfuls, instead of the half glass Isidora told her to drink. The tonic was black and bitter and made Evita throw up. Isidora told her that in two days she would take her to Doctor Juárez, as he performed the procedure only twice a week. The rest of the week he worked at a hospital as a regular doctor.

By the next day, Evita was throwing up and her stomach was cramping. She began to bleed from between her legs. Isidora told her that was a good sign. It meant her body was getting ready to expel the baby on its own. She might not even need to see Doctor Juárez. That night Evita moaned in bed and imagined Doctor Juárez as a big cockroach with the head of a man. He held a knife in his hand and was ready to cut Ricardo's baby out of her body. Alone in her room, Evita screamed in terror as she saw crimson clear fluids on the white sheet and a tiny translucent bag with the microscopic beginnings of a baby in it. Evita saw the baby's head, two pinpoint eyes, and a white body. She screamed, thinking Doctor Juárez had paid her a visit at Isidora's. Isidora rushed in and told her to get into the shower and clean herself up. She'd take care of everything else.

That night, Evita pulled out the pink stuffed bear with the red plastic heart that Ricardo had given her. She had put it away in the closet, not wanting to be reminded of him. She cuddled up to the stuffed bear and pretended she was sleeping with Ricardo and listening to his heartbeat. Evita slept and dreamed she was in a dark room and could hear Ricardo calling her name. Just when she thought she had found him, he stopped calling her. It was as if he was playing a game with her and didn't want her to find him.

In the morning, Evita put the pink stuffed bear back into the dark corner of the closet and noticed her arms and legs were covered with red blotches, as the black spikes inside her pushed up to the surface of her skin. After the loss of Ricardo's baby, she slept for two days in the dark, telling Fina not to turn the lights on, as she couldn't stand to see herself in the light. Fina got mad and complained to Isidora that she'd never be able to put on her makeup in the dark, and how was she going to fix her hair if she couldn't see to comb it? Isidora had to let Fina sleep on her bed and use her room while Evita slept with the door closed. Evita wanted to stay in the dark bedroom, like the room in her dreams, and bump into Ricardo, telling him she didn't want to get rid of his baby but that now his baby was happy, flying around in Heaven with other babies that nobody wanted.

Isidora was kind to Evita and prepared meals for her at great cost—the cost of standing at the stove with her swollen legs. She did all the cleaning and washing of clothes and going to the doctor's office for more medicine. She said she had something for Evita to do, something very special when she was well again. She was asking her only because an important person was making the request.

Evita braced herself, already afraid it had something to do with drugs. She was deathly afraid of drugs and knew what it would mean if a mistake was made or if someone thought a person knew too much. Already, *El Diario* had reported another girl murdered, her body found after months of searching in un lote baldío, an empty lot, right in the center of Juárez, not far from the American-owned maquiladora where the girl worked. The girl was only seventeen and had been working faithfully at la maquiladora for over a year. She had been given a new shift, late at night, in spite of the fact that she had told her supervisor repeatedly that she had no way to get home and could not afford to pay taxi fare. The girl was from Vera Cruz and had been living with her sister in Ciudad Juárez. They had both been assigned the early morning shift until the murdered girl was transferred to an evening shift. At first, a family member was picking her up and taking her home, but one night the family member couldn't pick her up, and that's when the girl took la rutera back home. While walking down a dark street, she was taken by someone, perhaps more than one, and murdered. Her body was found bruised and beaten with one breast missing, lying in a pile of trash in the empty lot. She had been raped numerous times, and investigators said her wrists had been handcuffed. Then later, police said it hadn't been handcuffs at all and claimed the girl's wrists had been bound by shoelaces. A photo appeared of the girl's sister, crying over her body. The girl's colonia came out into the streets to walk in procession to her house on the night of her velorio—men, women, and children, holding candles and crucifixes and singing religious songs as they held up a wooden cross that was painted pink and decorated with a shiny black ribbon. Her remains were placed in a coffin and set up on a kitchen table decorated all in white, with roses and pictures of her alive and smiling—a beautiful girl, slender, warm brown skin, and dark hair that fell below her waist. Her parents demanded justice, and her mother swore she would go right into the Presidential Palace in Mexico City, to el Presidente himself, to show him pictures of her dead child's remains.

16 Evita took up her duties again at Isidora's house—cleaning, running errands, picking up medicine, and massaging Isidora's huge aching legs. In two days, Isidora said, Evita would meet the important person she had been telling her about. She talked to Evita while Evita put her clothes away and wouldn't look at her when she mentioned the important person. She only walked away, laboring with every step, saying she needed to put her legs up on a leg rest she bought at el mercado to stop the blood from forming in her swollen veins. The doctor told her it was dangerous, all the blood pooling in her legs, as the veins could burst and cause hemorrhages. Evita asked her who the important person was that she wanted her to meet, but Isidora only rested her head on the arm chair and pretended to be asleep.

That night, Maclovio stopped by to pick up Cristal. Evita was in Cristal's room, helping her dress, when Maclovio came by. She snapped the hook on the red beads with the crucifix that Cristal wore around her neck and made sure her pink silky blouse was zipped midway up her back. Under the blouse, Cristal wore a pink lacy bra that barely disguised the huge dark circles around her nipples. Her hair was brushed smoothly from her face and gathered into dark curls at the top of her head. She was wearing shiny black pants that shimmered with iridescent colors, pink and blue. Her shoes were tall pink spikes, clasped at her ankles with dainty rhinestone straps. Evita thought she looked like a movie star. She sprayed Cristal with perfume, a tangy gardenia fragrance, her favorite.

As they walked out of the bedroom, they saw Fina sitting on the couch next to Maclovio. It was apparent that she was flirting, smiling and whispering something to him. She stood up quickly as they walked in, and it was then that Cristal unleashed all her fury on Fina. She leapt at Fina and brought her down to the floor, tearing at her face, scratching her, hitting her with her fists while Evita looked on in horror. Fina screamed and tried to push Cristal off her body, her hands flailing like antennae that made Evita think she was a real grasshopper after all. She managed to grab onto Cristal's necklace and pulled it off, sending the red beads all over the floor. Cristal was in such a rage, she didn't feel the necklace breaking and didn't let Fina strike even one blow. Maclovio jumped up and put his big hairy arms over Cristal, holding onto her and getting her to her feet. He yelled at her to calm down, pushing her away from Fina with his big brown body. Evita saw Maclovio as the big brown dog, rescuing the grasshopper from Cristal's frenzy.

"Ya! Cristal, stop, have you gone crazy? Stop, I tell you!"

Evita saw that Maclovio did have feelings for Cristal, as he smoothed back her long hair from her face, holding her shaking body up to his bulky chest, and trying to piece together the silky pink blouse, now ripped to shreds. Cristal's bra had come undone, and she stood naked from the waist up. Evita could see that Maclovio was hypnotized by Cristal's beauty. He looked lovingly at her ample breasts and tried to hold the shreds of the blouse's silky material over them.

The spike on one of Cristal's shoes had broken, and it made her look as if she had one foot on a ladder. She was still cursing at Fina, calling her a common bitch, una perra, who went after any man she could get. Cristal tried to grab Fina as she stood up, crying and spitting blood, and just as Fina was ready to rush Maclovio to get to Cristal, Isidora walked in with more bags of medicine. Her face was long and droopy, her step heavy. She nearly slipped on the red beads of Cristal's necklace, strewn all over the floor.

"Fighting are you! Fighting like bitches who can't do anything right. I should throw both of you out!" she shouted. "Qué cabrones estan pensando! Look at this mess!" She went up to Cristal and was ready to slap her, but Maclovio stopped her hand in midair.

"Don't you dare touch her!"

"Oh, so I see. You like women to fight! Maybe you're the one who set them up to do this!"

Fina ran to Isidora and buried her head on her shoulder. Isidora calmed her down, telling her it was over now and everything would be all right.

"Protecting her, are you!" Cristal shouted. "She goes after my man, and all you can do is protect this puta, who has no respect for another woman! Well, this is the last time you'll ever see me!"

Cristal walked angrily into her room and grabbed plastic bags and a suitcase she had under her bed. She ordered Maclovio to take everything out of her bureau and closet, saying she was leaving. Then she started furiously packing her suitcase, pushing everything down, not caring that it was a scrambled mess.

"I'm taking everything—everything, and I'm never coming back! I don't need an old hag to take care of me." Then she looked at Evita. "Get your things," she yelled at her. "You're coming with me!"

Evita didn't hesitate. She knew that staying at Isidora's would mean fighting every day with Fina, and she wouldn't be able to defend herself without Cristal.

Evita walked into her room and used an old suitcase and her school-bag to pack her things. She didn't have much to take and managed to find a space for the pink stuffed bear Ricardo had given her with the red plastic heart.

"Evita, you're not going anywhere!" Isidora shouted at her. "You're staying here!" Evita ignored her and continued to pack her things. "Evita, did you hear me? You're staying here!" Then Isidora started to cry and began to plead with Evita to stay. "I've treated you like a mother—how can you turn your back on me? Evita, please don't go. Things will be all right; we'll all live in peace."

"I know what you want her for!" Cristal yelled from her room. "She won't do anything you say!" Then she walked out of her room ahead of Maclovio, who held everything she owned in his hands, and waited at the door for Evita. Evita walked out with the old suitcase in one hand and her schoolbag looped over her shoulders, past Fina sitting on the couch crying and Isidora begging her to stay.

Evita missed meeting Isidora's important person by one day.

Western Electronics Inc.

17 Petra received the call she had been waiting for. Her mother telephoned to tell her Gustavo Rios would meet them at la maquiladora Western Electronics, to make sure they were given an interview and were able to fill out their applications all in one day. He told Flor they were to bring their birth certificates and whatever other documents Petra might have on schools she had attended. All Petra could think about was that soon she'd leave Brisa's house and stop worrying about Brisa's sudden bursts of anger and her boyfriend, Alberto, who leered at her and tried to draw her into conversations.

She had made friends with Luis Ledezma's sister, Yvone, Brisa's neighbor from across the street. Yvone worked at Thompson Industries and told Petra that if she worked the same shift, she'd be able to go with her, even if they didn't work at the same maquiladora. Her brother, Luis, drove her there and back, and Yvone said her mother and father wouldn't let her go any other way.

"My parents don't want me to take any chances—you know with all the violence, but we'll be safe with my brother driving us there."

Petra was grateful for her invitation, even though Yvone told her that her brother was hopelessly in love with her.

"I've never seen him act as crazy as he's acting. He seems like a small child who's found the greatest treasure of his life." Then Yvone laughed. Petra smiled and watched Yvone's small round face look up at her. "You're tall," she told Petra, "but that doesn't matter to my brother. He adores you!"

Before they arrived at la maquiladora to meet Gustavo Rios, Prospero drove Petra and her mother to the hospital to see Estevan. As they walked into his room, Estevan was sitting up in bed talking to another patient in a bed close by.

"I'm much better," he told them. "Really, you shouldn't worry."

Estevan told them he had received a series of treatments, and the doctors now thought they could save one of his kidneys. He would lose the bad kidney because of a tumor they had found in it. At least he'd have one kidney, he said, and that would keep him alive. Petra watched her father closely and noticed there were dark circles under his eyes and he had lost more weight.

"What else did the doctor tell you, Papi?"

"Nothing more. What did I tell you? I'm fine. All this trouble, and it wasn't anything more than a little tumor. I'll have surgery next week. They'll remove it, and I should be ready to go back home."

"What kind of a tumor is it," Flor asked him.

"How should I know?" he answered impatiently. "Ask the doctor. Listen to this woman, Prospero. I tell you she should have let me die in Montenegro!"

"No compadre! Don't give up on life. You'd do the same if Flor was sick. I fight with Ofelia all the time, and still I wouldn't want her to die."

"You're right. I'm just not used to this—lying all day long in bed. I want to get back to work."

Estevan saw that he had wounded his wife. There were tears in Flor's eyes. Petra put her arm around her mother, trying to stop her tears while holding back her own.

"Ya, stop, both of you. The doctors will do all they can. And yes, I'll do my best. Stop crying." Then Estevan leaned back on the pillow wearily and closed his eyes. "And Ester and Nico? How are my children doing? God knows, I miss them! I can't stand this place—nobody knows what they're doing. One nurse says something, and the other one says something else. One doctor examines me and says I need surgery before the day is done, and another doctor comes in and says all I need is a few more treatments. I tell you they're all driving me crazy!"

"I'll talk to the doctor," Flor told him. "Let me find out about the surgery. In the meantime, rest, Estevan. Get your strength back so you can come home." Then she told him they'd start working soon in one of las maquiladoras.

"I'd be careful if I were you, señora," the patient in the next bed said. "There are murders going on of women who work in las maquiladoras."

Estevan sat straight up in bed. "What murders? This city's been violent since I've known it."

"And more so now, compadre. Much more," said the man. "They've found more bodies of dead women, and some have been obreras, girls who work in las maquiladoras. A shame, I tell you, when women can't work in peace."

"It's true, Estevan," Prospero told him. "We didn't want to tell you because of your illness. But more bodies have been found, and no one is willing to say who's murdering the women. The police, of course, are all silenced con mordidas. You know how money silences everyone."

Estevan was ready to stand up and demand to know what was happening, but he was too weak to get out of bed. His face turned red with anger.

"What did I tell you, Flor! Why don't you ever listen to me. Now you're in danger, and look at my daughter! She's everything they want. Get your brother back here. You're going back to Montenegro, all of you. I'm staying right here, and if I die here alone, well, at least you'll be safe in Montenegro."

"Estevan, stop! We can't go back."

"Call Alvaro, I tell you, Flor. Get him back here! God, this woman is driving me crazy!"

"There's problems at the Gonzalez Ranch. One of the Gonzalez brothers has come back and is trying to run the whole place, and he's fighting with everyone. If Alvaro leaves now, he'll lose his position. Besides, Gustavo Rios found us jobs in one of las maquiladoras, and why would he lead us wrong? I'm sure he'll guarantee our safety."

"What about you, Prospero? Would you be willing to take this caprichosa back home?"

"I would, but she doesn't want to go. And what should I do—tie her to the seat of the car?" Prospero smiled and told Estevan that if the women were careful about coming and going to work, they should be fine.

Estevan looked at his daughter intently, his sunken cheeks rising like small stones under his skin. "You have to be sure that you are never alone on the streets, do you understand, mija? You must never be alone!" He reached over and held Petra's hand in his own, and she could feel his hand still calloused from years of hard labor, now dry and bony.

"Of course, Papi, I know, and I promise I'll be careful—we'll be safe." Petra tried to make herself sound convincing, cheerfully kissing her father's cheek.

"Ay mija, so beautiful. I remember when you were born, an angel from Heaven. Do you remember, Flor?"

"Of course I remember! We'll work at la maquiladora together, and I'll be able to watch over her as well, so don't worry. And we have Prospero, here, and Ofelia to help us." Flor said nothing to her husband about Brisa, as she knew he didn't like the woman and would get angry thinking that Petra and Nico were staying at her house.

"Ofelia worked for years at a maquiladora, compadre," Prospero said, "and nothing ever happened to her. Of course that was before they brought so many of them to Juárez. Now, there are women from all over Mexico working here, and with them come more men. Some of the men are worthless, to tell you the truth, and more than this, they're mad at their wives for making money. You know, el machismo rules their lives. They feel worthless because their wives support the family, and so they take it out on them, beating them up and making their lives miserable. Then there's women who get big heads and think they can wear the pants in the family. Pretty soon, the couple fights, and the man takes off to el otro lado, to make his fortune in los Estados Unidos. That leaves more children on the streets for gang members to recruit, and so it goes on and on."

Estevan nodded his head. He said Prospero was absolutely right. Then he angrily cursed Gustavo Rios and told his wife that if he ever caught Gustavo out on the streets he'd fight him man to man. As soon as he was strong enough, he'd get even with Gustavo Rios for all the damage he had done his family.

The man in the next bed spoke up: "Well said, compadre. I'd do the same thing if I were you."

Western Electronics Inc. was an enormous building, tan with white trim, that seemed to extend for acres. A chain-link fence ran around the entire property, and there was a security checkpoint at the gate. There was a Mexican flag next to an American flag waving outside the steps of the front entrance. Prospero had to park outside on the street, as the security guard said he couldn't come in because he wasn't applying for a job. Petra gave the guard Gustavo Rios's name, and he looked up quickly and stared at her with curiosity. She read his name, Barriga, printed on the plastic ID clipped to his shirt pocket.

"Oh, sí, of course, el Señor Rios—no problem. I already have your IDs ready."

He handed them each a clip-on plastic card that said *Aplicante* and motioned them through the gate. Flor looped her arm through Petra's, already feeling intimidated by the immense building and the fact that she was wearing an ID that said she was coming in to apply.

"What if he's not here? What if it's all a lie and they send us away?"

"No," Petra told her. "It won't happen, Mamá. Didn't you see how the guard responded when we told him Gustavo Rios had sent us?"

"He must be powerful, then. But what if all the positions are filled and we have to wait longer. We have to start working!"

Petra felt her mother's arm tighten around her own and sensed her fear as they climbed the stone steps up the entrance of la maquiladora. Then she regretted she had been rude to Gustavo when he had visited them in Montenegro and had offered her money. Now she was at his mercy, and her family was dependent on the money la maquiladora would provide. She made up her mind to treat Gustavo with respect no matter what he said or did, and patted her mother's arm, trying to comfort her as they went up the stone steps.

They walked into the front office and up to the receptionist, who was wearing a small black earphone plugged to a phone on her desk that had several buttons blinking. Another woman was just walking through a door that led into la maquiladora as they walked in. The receptionist, plump, courteous, and neatly dressed, looked at their IDs with the word *Aplicante* and told them they were to follow the woman who had just walked through the door. Then she paused between phone calls and looked Petra up and down, noticing her trim figure in a lavender skirt and blouse, black patent leather pumps, and dark hair flowing in glossy waves down the middle of her back. The girl remembered Gustavo had told her to call him when she saw a girl and her mother come in to apply. He had met them in their village, he said, and made up a story that he had known the mother's brother in Juárez years ago. The girl noticed Petra was tall, stately, and walked gracefully beside her mother, as if she was gliding over the floor rather than putting one foot in front of the other like everyone else.

"Wait, just a minute, por favor." She looked down at notes written on a pad of paper on her desk. "Are you Petra de la Rosa?"

"Yes—and this is my mother."

"Señor Rios asked me to tell him when you came in. So if you don't mind, please sit down and I'll call him."

They sat together at a small couch facing the windows and glass door of the entrance and watched a woman and man walking in wearing the same IDs. The receptionist motioned them through the door as she called Gustavo Rios on the phone. Flor smiled nervously, whispering to Petra that they were lucky Gustavo Rios was speaking up for them and for sure they would be hired. Petra thought about the others who were applying and wondered why Gustavo Rios had singled them out for special treatment. She remembered his eyes looking at her even when he wasn't staring her way and shifted uneasily at her mother's side.

Within minutes Gustavo walked in, brisk and businesslike, wearing black slacks and a white shirt and tie. Petra and her mother stood up to shake his hand. Petra sensed an energy around him that repulsed and frightened her, making her feel as if his power would somehow swallow her up. He held onto her hand and looked into her eyes, lingering for several seconds on her face. Finally, Petra broke his gaze by looking down at his hand still clasping hers. Gustavo let her hand go, turning his attention to Flor. He explained to both of them that he was one of the supervisors for la maquiladora and wouldn't be able to spend much time with them, as he had a meeting to attend that day in El Paso. The receptionist tapped her pen at her desk and told them, laughing, that Gustavo ran la maquiladora.

"But he won't tell you that. He's not presumptuous, are you, Señor Rios?"

She smiled at him as if she knew that was exactly what he was. Gustavo laughed and told her to mind her own business and answer the phones—couldn't she see the lines were all lit up? He talked briefly to Petra and her mother, then told the receptionist to be sure they got in on the next orientation. "I've already talked to the training personnel about them," he told her. Then he looked at Petra and smiled broadly. "What did I tell you, Petra? Nice place—right? You'll like the work here, much better than out in the country. Just think, you won't have to work out in the heat or cold." He rubbed his hands together. "Very nice!" he said.

Petra wondered if he meant very nice because they would have a job there, or very nice because she would be working there. But she nodded and smiled back. She didn't want to worry her mother over how she felt about Gustavo.

"I'm looking forward to it," she said, "and really, my mother and I are very grateful for your help."

"Sí, Señor Rios, we very much appreciate your telling us about la maquiladora," Flor said.

"Good," he said. "I think you'll like it here—hard work but steady, and you won't get laid off."

While answering calls, the receptionist looked Petra over, balancing her head this way and that, arching her eyebrows as if to study the situation.

"Oh, and Vina," Gustavo said to her. "Since you're so interested in them—be sure you get them into the next orientation. Bueno—I have to leave."

More applicants arrived for the orientation, all looking as nervous as Petra and her mother. They gathered as a group and were led to an upstairs training room. Petra looked at the name of la maquiladora written on a chalkboard in the room, Western Electronics Inc., noticing papers with advertising on the company stacked neatly at a nearby table. The words in English looked strange to her, and she knew why her mother couldn't pronounce the name—she couldn't either. Petra's hands were cold as she sat stiffly in a chair along with the other applicants. She was worried about working for Americans, having heard that they had rules for everything and that their one goal was to make money—millions, maybe billions, who would ever know for sure? All she knew about Americans was that they were rich and hard to please and lived in a country that thousands of Mexicans risked their lives to get to every year. She expected to see Americans talking to them during the orientation with translators, but there were Mexican employees instead, personnel trainers, a man and a woman who explained what kind of work was done at la maquiladora. They made electronic parts for cars and appliances and some electrical parts for computers, the man explained. Then he showed them a chart listing, in Spanish, all the products they produced. The woman took down their names and any other information they could offer, in some cases writing down information for people with limited reading and writing skills. She told them that they'd take short tests to see how fast they were with their hands and how well they could concentrate. Each one would be placed in the spot where she or he would do the best job according to their skills, their age, and their physical condition. The man told them that the rules of la maquiladora were very strict, and the work demanded that they be present every day, on time and ready to work.

"If you can't be here daily, on time, and ready to work, you can leave right now and save us the trouble of firing you. Los Americanos demand that we run this maquiladora to its greatest efficiency. Excuses won't help you here," he said in a loud voice. "Those who do well on their tests and have their papers in order will be considered for employment."

He told them to come back in the morning, 8:00 a.m. sharp, to do the tests, then asked if there were any questions. Petra wanted to ask about the murders of girls who worked in las maquiladoras—had anyone from Western Electronics been murdered? But she knew just by looking at the man that he wouldn't put up with anything that made la maquiladora look bad and would most likely find the question offensive. She couldn't risk anything that might make it hard for her and her mother to get hired; so she said nothing.

On their way out, Petra saw the inside of the massive building and people working at stations, each busy at a task as they stood or sat on stools at long counters and worked on one part of a moving display. Some were doing their jobs like puppets on a string; others were talking, some joking and laughing. The aisles were numbered, and there were colors to identify different stations. The place was spacious, clean, and busy, with men carting away boxes of finished products in forklifts. Petra had never seen a place so big and with so many people working together. As the small group of new applicants was taken back to the front office, the other workers watched them. Men looked closely at Petra and whispered to each other about her, hoping she would be assigned a job at their workstations.

Prospero was waiting for them outside in his pickup truck. The security guard, Barriga, was ushering more applicants in for another orientation.

"Look," Flor said, "more people for another orientation. We have to do well on our tests or we might not get a job!"

"Gustavo Rios will get us in," Petra told her mother. "No matter what else happens, he'll get us in." She looked back at la maquiladora and wondered if Gustavo Rios was staring at her through one of the windows.

On the way back home, Prospero showed Petra and Flor other industrial parks with maquiladoras just as big as Western Electronics and told them that las maquiladoras were making a fortune in Juárez.

"Too bad it's all for the American foreigners and others who own las maquiladoras. The money paid out for wages to our people is nothing compared to what the companies make. In fact, it's crumbs. Just like always, nothing for Mexico unless it's all going to the government, which doesn't care if the poor live or die. Some people say our problems will end when las maquiladoras leave Juárez, but then what will the people do? They've come to depend on wages from las maquilas—and if there's no work, the people will starve and more disaster will fall upon us. I tell you, there are no answers for the poor, only more problems."

As they made their way through el Centro, Prospero honked his horn at two girls who were crossing the street.

"Look, there's Evita!" he said, sticking his head out the window and calling her name.

Evita was wearing a pair of black jeans, high-heeled boots, and a translucent sleeveless blouse that outlined her tiny breasts. The girl next to her was attracting attention from several men, who were staring at her, whistling, and pointing her way. She was tall, graceful, her hair flowing down to the middle of her back. As they walked up to Prospero's pickup, Petra noticed the girl had on a purple blouse that plunged between her ample breasts, a miniskirt riding high on her thighs, and spiked heels that showed off her shapely legs.

Prospero frowned when he saw the girl next to Evita. "Look at that! Everything we tell Evita not to do, and here—" He didn't finish his sentence before Evita walked up to his window. She had on makeup, bright red lipstick and mascara that Petra thought made her look like a doll with a painted face.

"Does your mother know you're out here?" Prospero asked her angrily.

"We're just shopping, don't worry. I'll be at Lety's before dark." The girl next to Evita stared at them, her dark eyes sweeping over them with one glance. "My friend, Cristal," Evita said, and the girl nodded in greeting and walked away, joining a man who was standing at the corner of the sidewalk. The man put his arms around her and kissed her cheek.

"Flor and Petra are here. Aren't you going to greet your cousins?" Prospero asked.

Evita looked in surprise at Petra, who was sitting next to Prospero. She reached into the pickup and took Petra's hand in her own. "I didn't even recognize you!" Then she rushed to the other side of the truck and greeted Flor, kissing her cheek, reaching again for Petra's hand. "Twins!" she said. "Remember how I always wanted to be your twin?"

They both laughed, and Petra said, "How could I forget?" Then she noticed tears gathering in Evita's eyes and was grateful she didn't have to explain that she now slept in her room.

"Call your mother!" Prospero said, raising his voice. "God knows she worries about you. And stay off the streets!"

Evita ignored his words, saying she had to go. Petra watched as Cristal motioned impatiently for Evita to hurry. Then, leaning on the man's arm, Cristal walked down the street, her miniskirt gliding up and down her hips with each step. Evita followed after her, clumsily walking on her high-heeled boots, and turned around once to wave good-bye before they disappeared down the street.

"You stay away from her!" Flor said to Petra. "Imagine, that little girl on these streets!"

18 Petra and Flor started working the late afternoon shift, which ended at midnight. They got into a routine of riding la rutera together to Western Electronics, then waiting for Luis Ledezma to pick them up after he dropped off his sister, Yvone, at Thompson Industries. Flor said they were lucky that Luis picked them up after work, so they didn't have to walk down dark streets after getting off la rutera at one in the morning. Still, she was worried because Luis was in love with Petra, and she knew that would go nowhere and what would happen when he lost her to someone else? Flor didn't bring up Antonio's name, but Petra knew whom she meant. What man would pick them up at midnight and take them home without asking something for himself? They couldn't afford to give Luis much, maybe a little money for gas. He didn't ask them for anything, which worried Flor even more. She said

the money they'd make at la maquiladora would barely be enough to get them started saving a few pesos for a place of their own.

"Luis doesn't want anything, really," Petra told her mother. "He thinks he's in love with me, and there's nothing I can do to change his mind."

"Pretty soon, mija, we'll have our own place, maybe even buy a car, and Luis won't have to pick us up anymore," Flor said, looking into the distance as if she could already see the future. "Then your father will come home, and we'll all be together."

"What about mi abuela?"

"We'll send for her, and she'll come stay with us until your father gets better."

In her mind, Petra saw Abuela Teodora walking straight and bold as ever, navigating the busy streets of Juárez in her long skirt and black lace-up shoes.

Humberto Ornelas showed up at lunch at least twice a week to sit with Petra in the cafeteria. He was a tall man with thinning hair and a gray moustache. He was one of the engineers and had been working at Western Electronics for over ten years. As an engineer, he got to go to El Paso and attend meetings and talk to the American bosses who owned la maquiladora. He said it was routine to sit with new employees, as he wanted to know how they were doing.

Lola Sesma, one of the girls Petra met on her shift, told her Humberto was lying. Engineers didn't sit with new employees; they kept to themselves and only spoke to supervisors about the work they needed done. They checked and rechecked the women's work, and if they found too many mistakes or the quality was poor, they reported it to the supervisors. Lola said Humberto was attracted to Petra, and that's why he was taking time to visit her at lunch.

Lola was a gentle girl, soft-spoken and shy, and she quickly became Petra's friend. Petra knew she could trust her, as they shared the same loyalty to their families and wouldn't think of going out with some of the other girls after work to dance and visit the clubs in el Centro. Lola wore her hair in a long ponytail held together by a colorful bow, which made her look as young as Petra although in reality she was older. She had two children, ages six and three, that she left alone for hours until one of her neighbors came home from her work to take care of them.

She worried for her children, even though a teenage girl from across the street said she'd help keep an eye on them until the neighbor came home. Lola was from Hermosillo, and had plans to return there as soon as she saved enough money for the trip back. There she would start a new life for herself and her children. Living in Juárez for Lola was like being stuck in a deep hole from which she could find no way out. It got worse for her when her husband moved to Obregon after the birth of their last baby, saying he would return as soon as he settled some business for his father. That was the last she had seen of him. She figured he had found another woman and would never come back.

"I can't tell my parents all my troubles," she told Petra one day during their afternoon break. "They have no money to come to Juárez, and besides that, they never liked my husband in the first place." She sighed heavily and looked down at her hands. "Every day, I have to wear a mask and plastic gloves to protect myself from the chemicals I handle—and look, I still have a rash on my arms no matter what I do."

"Tell your supervisor," Petra said. "She'll have to do something."

"I did, and she tells me to quit complaining—it could be worse. As soon as there's an opening on another line, she says she'll get me there. But this has gone on for the last two years. She'll never do it. But I'd rather have this rash than have someone like Humberto Ornelas chasing after me!"

"I don't want anything to do with him!"

"That doesn't matter, Petra. Men like him don't take no for an answer."

Lola told Petra there was no question that Humberto Ornelas was falling hard for her. Everybody at la maquiladora was talking about it and wondering what his third wife would say when she found out. Humberto's marriages had been the subject of many conversations at la maquiladora. His first wife had given up on him years ago and only demanded that he support his two children through high school in El Paso and visit with them on weekends. Some of the women knew his second wife, who was a mouse compared to the first. They said Humberto married her so he could treat her like a dog, como una perra, and the only good thing for her was that she had borne no children for Humberto. He finally left her for the most colorful of all his wives, Bridget, a woman who prided herself in training at the gym and looking picture perfect. The women at la maquiladora had seen her pick up Humberto for lunch, wearing expensive clothes, shoes, and purses, everything perfectly matched down to the color of her lipstick and nails. Bridget looked disdainfully at the women who worked at la maquiladora and haughtily passed by everyone, leaving a fragrance of expensive perfume for the men who worked at la maquiladora to sniff and pretend they were getting dizzy and lovesick over her. The women said Bridget had held Humberto on a leash until Petra came along. Now, no one knew what would happen.

Petra wanted to tell Humberto to leave her alone, but Lola advised her not to do it.

"If you insult him that way, he'll hold a grudge against you, and maybe you'll be fired or given a job that nobody likes. I've seen girls stand up to supervisors before. They always end up losing."

Petra was already working at a job she didn't like, putting together electrical circuits, matching wires and looping them into plugs that would make electrical circuits work. She didn't think her task could be worse than what it already was. She repeated the same movement over and over until her mind seemed to go blank and her arms and shoulders shook with fatigue. By the end of the day, she wanted to drop down on the floor to spare her aching legs. The girls told her she'd get used to it—maybe another two weeks or so, and she'd be fine. Petra was glad her mother had been put in a workstation where she could sit all day, examining tiny lightbulbs to be sure they blinked on and off as they should. Her mother's back ached from sitting all day, and her shoulders and neck were sore, but at least her legs were spared and she didn't have to work with chemicals and wear gloves and a mask over her face as others did.

Every day Petra watched the men and women working around her, all wearing blue rayon coats over their clothes with *Western Electronics Inc.* embroidered on the pocket and a name tag. She noticed they didn't pay much attention to their work. They did it as if in a trance while they talked to each other or looked away or dreamed about some place else they'd like to be. Some women, like her friend Lola, had small children at home and couldn't call them to find out how they were doing, as they were unable to afford a telephone. One of the women told Petra she locked her three children at home alone, as she had no one to watch them and no money to pay for their care. The oldest was five and the baby was only four months old. The woman was already wondering what she'd do when her five-year-old son turned six and had to go to school. She prayed for her children before she left and told them they were to stay in the apartment until she returned. She left food for them, burritos, fruit, juice, anything they could eat without turning on the stove. At lunchtime, when the woman sighed and looked out the window, Petra imagined she was thinking about her three children locked up in the apartment.

Lola told Petra not to pay attention to the gossips, las chismosas, at la maquiladora, especially Amapola Nieto and those who followed her. Amapola Nieto was a dark heavy woman who had worked for years at la maquiladora and thought she owned the place. She led a group of women who sneered and scoffed at everyone else. They started rumors and got the greatest pleasure when someone suffered from what they had started. Lola said they whispered about others all day long and made up stories about what might be going on in their lives. They said Petra was headed for trouble with Humberto. He was an older man, experienced in life, and she was una escuincla who didn't know the first thing about men. Besides that, she was a peasant compared to Humberto, and he wouldn't ever be seen publicly with her. So, what do you think he wanted? What every man wants. And when he got it, he'd throw Petra to the side, como una perra, just as he had thrown out his second wife. And that's what Petra deserved for being una facilota and sleeping with a married man. In their minds, it was only a matter of time before Petra gave in to Humberto, if she hadn't already, and broke up his marriage to the flamboyant Bridget. They'd be happy, they said, when Bridget found out and stopped by to settle the score with Petra. They were hoping they would be at work on the day Bridget arrived, so they could see her go wild, pulling Petra's hair and scratching her face with her long manicured nails. Some of the men wanted to start taking bets on who would win, saying that Petra was younger and would fight back like a young lioness. Besides that, Petra was from a ranch and was used to hard labor, and that made her stronger than Bridget, who had never seen a day of hard labor in her life. It was certain Bridget would have her hands full fighting Petra, no matter what the outcome.

Lola told Petra that it wasn't just the women who gossiped; the men were just as bad. They'd look a woman over to see if she was someone they could take advantage of or someone who would resist their advances and be hard to conquer. Then they'd lie in wait to see who would be the one to conquer her, even if it was only that the woman would talk to him during breaks or sit with him at lunch. If the woman went out with a man after work, well, that was a different matter. Pretty soon everyone would be saying they were sleeping together.

"The girls are envious of you," Lola told Petra, sipping the last of her Coca-Cola. "La envidia's driving them crazy, and now that Humberto's after you, they figure no one can touch you because he'll find out and can make big trouble for them. Maybe he'll say they're not making their quota, or bring up some false evidence about the quality of their work. In some ways Humberto is your protection, although by no means can you get involved with him. It will mean your job, and his third wife will come looking for you."

Petra looked at Lola in shock. "I would never want to get involved with Humberto! I have someone in Montenegro, my boyfriend, Antonio. We're in love with each other; we're planning to get married as soon as my father gets better. Why would I be interested in anyone here?"

"The men here don't care that you have a boyfriend in Montenegro. He's over there, they're over here. That's just the way they think. Don't you understand? You're someone a man would want to conquer to prove his machismo. Women are prey to men. Haven't you read about all the murders?"

Lola was ready to say more when Petra saw Gustavo Rios in the distance waving at her. She waved back, and Lola said, "Ay, Dios mio! He's the worst of all! Don't even look at him."

"What are you talking about?" Petra asked her. "He's the one who got me this job!"

Lola put her hand gently on Petra's shoulder and looked at her with pity. Just then, the buzzer sounded in their department, signaling the end of their afternoon break. Petra jumped as if a gun had gone off. Lola reached for her hand and steadied her as they stood up together.

At Brisa's house, Petra dreamed about the moon shining over Montenegro. The face of the rabbit appeared on the moon's surface and took on a life of its own. Its eyes opened, its ears twitched, then a body formed. She watched as the rabbit hopped along on the surface of the moon and was happy for the rabbit's freedom. Suddenly, the rabbit jumped from the moon all the way to earth. Petra watched helplessly as it landed on her body. She felt the rabbit's body crushing her and woke up in the darkness, sweating and frightened, her heart beating hard. She could still feel the fur and paws of the gigantic rabbit on her body.

The next morning, Nico told Petra he wasn't getting on la rutera to attend school. He said he'd wait until they got back to Montenegro to start school again.

"Nico, you can't wait! You have to go to school. Besides, Mamá will never let you stay here all day long and not go to school."

"I'm not going. And there's nothing you or anyone else can do about it."

Nico sat with his hands folded over his chest, saying he would look for a job instead, so they could move out of Brisa's and find a place of their own.

Petra was ready to go to Cleotilde's house to make a phone call to her mother at Ofelia's and tell her what was happening with Nico. But just then Cleotilde knocked on the door and told her that her mother needed to talk to her on the phone. Cleotilde looked at Nico and asked him, "And what about you? Did Los Rebeldes scare you into staying home?"

"Not at all," Nico said bravely, puffing up his chest. "Esos chavos don't mean anything to me. I don't like the school here. I'll wait until we get back to Montenegro."

"That may not be until you're grown up. Then you'll be too old to go to school!"

Petra didn't have a chance to question Nico about Los Rebeldes before she left for Cleotilde's house to answer her mother's phone call. It was early in the morning as she stepped onto the street, in time to see Luis Ledezma yelling at a man who was kneeling in the back of his pickup truck among tools, old tires, and two big plastic containers marked with black numbers. He put his hands on the man's shoulders and forced him to sit on the bed of the truck. Then he looked up and saw Petra and straightened the cap on his head. He waved to her as his sister, Yvone, walked out of their house wearing her uniform from Thompson Industries.

"Where are you going?" Yvone called out.

"To answer a phone call from my mother at Cleotilde's." As she said the words, the man in the back of the truck stood up and stumbled forward as if drunk. He had on a ragged jacket over faded Levis and wore a pair of dark sunglasses. He was scrawny and shaking violently, as if he was freezing to death.

"Sit down!" Luis yelled at him. "You're not staying here!" He pushed him roughly back into the bed of the truck, and the man fell over the tires, shouting at Luis that someday he would get even with him.

"You'll pay for this!" he shouted at the top of his lungs, but Luis ignored him and got into the cab of the pickup next to Yvone. Black smoke blasted from the muffler as he started the engine, and the man's body jerked forward and back as if he was attached to a slingshot. Then Petra remembered that Yvone had told her she had another brother— Chano, a drug addict—and that she should stay away from him. She was sure the man in the back of the pickup was Chano.

Over the phone, Petra's mother told her she had good and bad news from the hospital. The tumor in her father's kidney was cancerous and the whole kidney would have to be removed. That was the bad news. The good news was that he had one kidney left, and it was healthy and free of cancer. She'd have to miss work on Friday, she said, to stay at the hospital with her father for his surgery. She'd talk to Gustavo Rios about it, so there wouldn't be any problems for her at la maquiladora.

Petra offered Cleotilde money for the use of her phone, which Cleotilde gladly accepted, telling Petra that Los Rebeldes were one of the worst gangs in Juárez and that Nico had better watch every step he took now that they were after him.

When Petra questioned Nico about Los Rebeldes, he told her there was nothing he could do about them. There were too many of them, and they hated him.

"Why do they hate you?"

"Because I won't join their gang, because I won't steal and fight for them, even kill for them. They do drugs and work for mafiosos."

Nico's eyes filled with fear as he described who the gang members were. He told Petra not to tell their mother. She had enough worries, he said. Petra looked closely at her brother and saw in his eyes the same fear she herself felt.

"I'll talk to Luis about this. He must know a way to help us," she said.

The next day Petra stood outside Brisa's house having a conversation with Luis Ledezma about Los Rebeldes. He told her Los Rebeldes was one of the worst gangs in Juárez. In fact, he said, every member was expected to murder someone to stay in the gang. He said that when he was Nico's age, he feared them and even got involved with them for a while. He had no choice. They threatened to rape his sister Yvone, and she was only six years old. He joined and got beaten up by them, which is their way of testing a member's loyalty. The only thing that saved him was that he played pranks and acted the fool. He dressed in a clown's outfit and set out to entertain the gang and raise money for them by doing magic tricks on the street corners. Little by little they looked at him as a fool and not as someone they wanted in Los Rebeldes.

"They beat me up so bad, my poor parents thought I would die," Luis told her. "To this day, my hips are bad and I'm missing feeling in my left leg. As for my skin, well, they didn't do anything to that. I've worked for years hauling chemicals for American companies in El Paso. We bury the chemicals in remote parts of the desert and hope no one will ever find them. They are poisonous and tear up a man's skin."

"Why don't you quit and find another job?" Petra asked him.

"Oh no! They pay me well, and I can afford to give money to my parents. Soon I'll get a new pickup truck, and I'll be able to take them to visit our relatives in Mexico City. The only problem I have is with my brother, Chano. I must apologize to you for the trouble you saw us having the other day. Once in a while he tries to come home, when he's sick with la malilla and doesn't have any money for his drugs. You should never speak to him. He's a tecato and will steal, beg, or borrow money for his drugs from anyone. He steals from my parents, and now they have to keep their money at my tío's house."

"I'm sorry to hear that."

"Really, there's nothing anyone can do. We've lost hope for him, but never mind about that. I'd like to hear more about Nico."

"He won't go to school! Los Rebeldes are threatening him. Is there anything we can do about them?"

"No! Nothing can be done about them. You have to move, Petra. Los Rebeldes won't leave Nico alone until they hurt him, or worse still, kill him. They have a new leader now, a boy named el Cucuy. And he lives up to his name! He's frightening, a real monster. I'm even afraid of him. He's only fourteen years old, but he operates as cold-heartedly as a veterano mafioso. He has no conscience and will do anything for a price. It's rumored that he killed his own father at twelve years old. His mother's so afraid of him she won't dare cross him. She even uses her own money to buy him drugs if that's what he tells her to do. It's very sad."

Petra sighed wearily, glad for Luis's company, his easy way of talking to her. He was telling her what she needed to hear. She wanted to tell him all about her troubles with the women at la maquiladora, but stopped herself. It would lead to him getting closer to her, and her mother told her that there would be trouble when he realized she'd never belong to him. She looked past his skin, red and peeling on his face and hands, and saw that Luis truly had love for her. She decided to tell him about Antonio.

"I'm going to wear my boyfriend's ring," she told him. "It's the only way to stop a man who's after me at la maquiladora."

Luis looked steadily into her eyes to let her know that he understood her dilemma and that she didn't have to hide anything from him.

"Your boyfriend's a very lucky man! As I've said, I know that I'll only be your friend. A woman like you, so beautiful—" And he stopped himself, looking down at his hands.

Petra wanted to tell Luis that he had no idea how grateful she was for his friendship. Instead, she put her hand in his and pressed tightly, feeling his skin dry and hard in her hand. He looked at her gently, then lifted her hand to his lips. Tears came to her eyes as she saw how tenderly he kissed her hand.

Luis offered Petra money to help her and her family get a place of their own. He said it was the only way to save Nico. They had to move as quickly as they could to another colonia, as this would keep Los Rebeldes off Nico's track for the time being. Luis said Nico's life was in great danger. He was sure the young ruthless leader of Los Rebeldes, el Cucuy, would stop at nothing to force Nico to join the gang or suffer the deadly consequences.

Petra and her mother sat close together in a patio area of la maquiladora, trying to keep warm during their evening break. The light from inside la maquiladora shone into the outdoor patio and made the night around them seem darker. Petra knew she had to make her mother understand how urgent it was for them to find a place of their own. When she tried to give her mother the money Luis had given her, her mother refused to take it.

"What did I tell you! Now he'll think he owns you. Now he'll think he can take advantage of you. And what will Antonio say?"

It was the first time Flor had ever mentioned Antonio to Petra. Petra held out her hand and showed her mother the ring Antonio had given her.

"I'm wearing the ring he gave me, to show everyone here that I have a boyfriend and that we're planning to get married."

Flor was surprised to see the ring. "And when did he give you this?"

"Before we left."

Flor closed her eyes, shaking her head. "Things are happening too fast, Petra. And to make matters worse, there are women here saying that Humberto Ornelas is interested in you and that you—"

Petra cut in angrily. "Another reason for me to wear this ring! It's all lies!"

Flor sighed. "Men are easy to charm, Petra, and often think they mean something to a woman when they mean nothing at all."

"There's only one man who means anything to me—and that's Antonio. There's nothing wrong with us wanting to get married. Luis understands that. He's offered us money because Nico won't go to school. Los Rebeldes are after him, horrible gang members who can hurt him or kill him. We have to move to a place of our own!"

"Gang members after my son! Ay, Dios mio, what else can happen to us? Why is God sending us all this suffering?" Flor buried her face in her hands. "This is a nightmare—a terrible nightmare."

Petra noticed Amapola Nieto walking slowly by, staring at them.

"There's Amapola. Mamá, don't act as if there's anything wrong. She'll start another rumor."

"I don't care what esa desgraciada does! I tell you, I'm tired of these people. All of them! They're not civilized. They're savages. Worse than that, some are demons. If it weren't for your father needing to be here, I would leave tonight! We'll have to find a place of our own, for Nico's sake. I'll get Prospero to help us."

Flor took Luis's money from Petra without another word.

Before the night was over, Amapola Nieto spread the word that she had seen Flor crying outside on the patio with Petra, and she knew why. Petra was showing off a ring she said her boyfriend in Montenegro had given her. Amapola knew that was a big lie because her boyfriend hadn't even been in Juárez, and if he had given her the ring, why hadn't she worn it before? No! The truth was that Humberto Ornelas had given her the ring. He was pledging his love to her, and Petra was playing hard to get. But everything would catch up with her once Bridget found out about the ring.

The next day, Lola told Petra that everyone was saying Humberto had given her the ring and that even Humberto himself didn't dare show his face with the scandal he had created.

"He didn't give me this ring, Lola! Don't you believe me?"

"Yes, of course, I believe you. But I'm the only one who does."

On the day of Estevan's surgery, Gustavo Rios called Petra into his office for a talk. He was cordial and asked about her father's health, expressing his concern. Then he told Petra he was happy with the quality of her work and had gone over her application again, including her school records, and was impressed with her grades and her fine reputation in school.

Petra held her hands on her lap, looking solemnly at Gustavo Rios. It always seemed to her as if he was an interrogator who was about to force information from her.

"You graduated with honors from school. Is that correct?"

"Yes."

"But you didn't pursue any more education?"

"Only one year in la prepa. With my father's illness, there wasn't any money."

"Too bad. An intelligent girl like you could be so successful." He looked intently at Petra, his look boring holes through her clothing.

"I'm going to put your intelligence to good use. From now on, you'll be working here in this office: filing, keeping records and accounts. I'll have someone train you, and you'll be making three times as much money. Would you like that?"

Petra looked up at Gustavo and again felt his strange engulfing energy that seemed to reach for her, trapping her somehow. She smiled at him and he smiled back, genuinely pleased with his decision. She thought of her father ill, and of Nico hunted by Los Rebeldes, and of the move they had to make, and she knew that now they'd have the money they needed, more money than she had ever expected to earn at la maquiladora.

Gustavo Rios stood up and seemed about to put his arms around her, then stopped himself.

"You'll start on Monday. Oh, and Petra, buy yourself another ring. In fact, buy two or three. It's always good to keep people guessing."

When Petra walked out of Gustavo Rios's office, no one said a word to her. But behind her back the vicious rumors started. She had sold out, una vendida. She'd give it to anyone. That's how she had gained a promotion in only two months.

La Niñita Frida

19 Tía Concha came to the hospital on the day Mayela was released, smelling of stale pulque. The old woman could hardly stand it, she said, the terrible headache she had. She told Mayela that Sebastian had conferred with el Imán, and the stone had related to him that Mayela was not to come back to Los Tres Magos, as she would contaminate his unborn child, which el Imán said would be a son.

Tía Concha told Mayela not to worry. She had talked to her cousin Licha, who worked at la Catedral, and to the doctor at the hospital, and they had both said that el Instituto de Niños Huerfanos would be the ideal place for her. Licha had spoken to Señora Juana del Pilar, the director of el Instituto and she had said Mayela was welcome as long as she was free from meningitis.

"And my mother? When will she come to take me home?"

"Soon," Tía Concha told her, blowing her nose on a ragged handkerchief. "In the meantime, you'll be safe at el Instituto, and we'll stop by to see you every chance we get." Then the old woman rubbed the back of her neck with her hands. "Ay, this headache! I tell you, if I live until tomorrow, I'll never take another drink of pulque in my life!"

Tía Concha had a few coins she had gotten from la Cruz Roja to take Mayela by taxi to the orphanage, as Mayela's legs were so weak she had no strength to walk the distance. Mayela had lost weight and now looked like a shadow of the bright-eyed girl she used to be. One of the nurses had combed her hair into two long braids and pinned the braids to the top of her head like Cina had done. She had used the red ribbon Cina had left to tie the braids together and make them look festive.

"Doesn't Mayela look like the famous artist Frida Kahlo?" the nurse asked Tía Concha.

"Yes, I suppose she does, with her braids up like that," said Tía Concha wearily.

Mayela remembered seeing a picture of Frida Kahlo once, and thought she didn't resemble the artist at all. Compared with Frida's thick, bushy eyebrows, hers were stray dark hairs. She glimpsed herself in a small mirror as the nurse combed her hair and saw her own small brown face looking back at her with sunken eyes.

"There! Now you look glamorous!" the nurse said cheerfully.

On the way to el Instituto, Tía Concha told Mayela that she was not to tell anyone that Cina was still in Juárez, as that would only make trouble for them.

"If they know that you have a relative from your village here, they'll ask us why she hasn't taken you home."

Mayela turned to Tía Concha in fear. "Is Cina still here?"

"Oh, yes, she's here, but Sebastian forbids her from coming to see you. He's afraid for his own child." Pressing her fingers to her temples to keep her head from throbbing, she told Mayela that Cina would end up destroying herself by listening to Sebastian.

Mayela shivered in her thin sweater as they rode in the taxi to el Instituto. Her lips trembled with emotion as she asked Tía Concha: "When is my mother coming for me?"

"We can't find her. She's with your abuela, and it should be only a matter of time before she comes to Juárez to take you home." Mayela was glad to hear this and leaned her head on Tía Concha's arm.

"You're bringing me luck again, Mayela. My headache is going away." The old woman put her arm around Mayela and kissed her forehead.

"They'll treat you well at el Instituto. My cousin Licha knows the place and tells me they're sincere and good people." She didn't tell Mayela about the American doctor who was working with the children at el Instituto, as she thought this would frighten her.

Señora Juana del Pilar, friendly and courteous, met them at el Instituto. She was a middle-aged woman, energetic, with a quick step and a manner that made you feel as though she was looking at you and thinking about something else. She led them through a room with a couch, chairs, and tables for visitors. There were parakeets in a cage in one corner of the room that chirped endlessly and two potted trees by the window. Framed pictures of landscapes and cities in Mexico hung on the faded walls, and there was a sign over a crucifix with Christ's words: *Les aseguro que todo lo que hicieron por uno de mis hermanos, aun por el más pequeño, lo hicieron por mí.* I assure you, whatsoever you do for the least of my brethren, you do for me.

Señora Juana del Pilar took down information about Mayela in her office as Tía Concha related it to her, sometimes making up information she wasn't sure about. It didn't matter to Tía Concha if something was true or not, as long as Mayela got into el Instituto and she could go back home to lie down for the rest of the day.

"Mayela came with an aunt from Chitlitipin, and her aunt has returned to their village to tend to her aging mother and has abandoned Mayela in Juárez."

"What kind of a relative would do that?" asked Señora Juana del Pilar. "Doesn't she care about her niece?"

"Well, she does, but she's under the control of a man—who, well, how can I say this, in my mind is crazy and will kill her if she doesn't do what he wants her to do. So, they're gone."

Mayela's heart raced, thinking she was alone in Juárez and that Cina was really gone, but Tía Concha touched her leg with her foot when Señora Juana del Pilar wasn't watching to remind her it was a lie.

Tía Concha told her she wasn't able to take Mayela back to Los Tres Magos because Mayela had been in the hospital with meningitis. The doctor had advised her not to take her back to la colonia, as her body was too weak to sustain another illness, which he was sure she would contract there.

Tía Concha scratched her head. "Other children live there, and they survive. The doctor's rich and doesn't know how the poor have to live! And that's the way it is with the rich: they don't know that the poor do the best they can and are forced to live like animals."

Señora Juana del Pilar tapped her pen impatiently on her desk. "I'm not here to argue with you, señora! Now—is there anyone else here who might know the girl?"

It was then that Mayela remembered that Petra de la Rosa and her family had come to Juárez to seek a doctor for her father, Estevan.

She tugged at Tía Concha's ragged sleeve. "I know someone else in Juárez, friends of my mother from Montenegro. Petra de la Rosa and her family are here. They came to—"

Tía Concha didn't let her finish. "They're not family!" she said, raising her voice, and under the table she pinched Mayela's leg.

The phone rang, but before Señora Juana del Pilar picked it up, she asked Mayela if she would like to live at el Instituto.

Mayela didn't answer and only buried her face in Tía Concha's arm. Señora Juana del Pilar spoke on the phone briskly to someone and answered questions, yes and no, then hung up.

"You'll live here for a while," she said to Mayela. "Then your mother will come by and take you home." She looked at Tía Concha as if she believed Mayela's mother would never come back. "I like your hair that way," she said to her. "It makes you look like Frida Kahlo." Then she smiled and stood up, telling Tía Concha to take Mayela out into the courtyard so she could meet some of the children.

Mayela hung on to Tía Concha's hand and wanted to run away, but she knew she had nowhere to go except back to Los Tres Magos with Cina and Sebastian, who flicked his tongue at her through his teeth and reached under her skirt to hurt her. She thought of Sebastian's naked body and of el machete waving wildly in front of her face, and she followed Tía Concha into the courtyard without another word.

The American doctor was intrigued by Mayela, as she was exactly what she was looking for—a child who had lived in one of the worst colonias in all of Juárez and who was also from an indigenous community in the farmlands of Chihuahua. As a pediatrician, the American doctor specialized in the welfare of children who lived in third world conditions. Her name was Doctor Sylvia Huddleston, but the children called her Doctora Silvia because they couldn't pronounce her last name in English.

The doctor told Mayela she was from New York City, and she worked for Columbia University, a big school she said Mayela would like to visit if she ever got to New York. Mayela had no idea what New York City was and thought Columbia meant the country in South America.

Doctora Silvia showed Mayela postcards and photographs of New York City and of Columbia University and explained that she was not from the country of Colombia but from los Estados Unidos. She spoke

Spanish with Mayela, and when she couldn't think of the right word, she asked her, "y cómo se dice?" Mayela smiled and whispered the answer in her ear, as if she was telling her a secret. La doctora listened intently, then tried to pronounce the words slowly, until Mayela nodded her head and told her she had pronounced it right.

Mayela was afraid of the American doctor, who was so different from anyone else she had ever seen. She was tall and her skin ghostly white. Mayela wondered if la doctora had ever seen the light of day. Her brown hair hung in thin strands down her shoulders, and she wore matching brown glasses and a big white coat that made Mayela think she was hiding something under it.

Mayela didn't want to talk to la doctora, but little by little Doctora Silvia won her trust. She showed her more photos and postcards of New York City and Columbia University, describing everything to her. Mayela had never seen such buildings, tall with spires and cylinders at the top. They seemed to be built right into the sky. This frightened Mayela, as she had never been in a building with stairs, nor taken a ride on an elevator. She couldn't imagine what she'd do in the buildings except look down, and that would make her dizzy to see everyone on the street looking like ants.

Doctora Silvia told Mayela she could have the postcards and maybe she could draw a picture of the one she liked best. She gave her a pad of paper and colored pencils. Mayela hesitated, having used a pencil only a few times in her life. Once, in her village, she had found one in the dirt that had been dropped by a schoolchild, and she had used it for a while until the lead was gone. Mayela was used to drawing in the dirt with a stick or painting on clay or wood to decorate vases and cups, plates and water jugs with brushes made of animal's hair by people in her village. Doctora Silvia showed Mayela how to hold the pencil and how to write with it. She told her that when the point got dull, she was to use a small pencil sharpener she gave her for the purpose of making a new point appear. Mayela smiled as she saw the beautiful colors the pencils made on the paper, and she felt happy for the first time in months. She chose the postcard with the Empire State Building because she liked the building's long sleek look and the way the top pointed up into the sky like a mountain peak. As la doctora stood up to leave, she told Mayela that el Instituto had a school and that very soon she'd be attending it with the other children to learn how to read and write. This brought tears to Mayela's eyes, as she knew that was why her mother had let her come to Juárez in the first place.

For hours, Mayela worked on her sketch of the Empire State Building, meticulously drawing every detail as she saw it on the postcard. By the end of the day, she had completed her sketch, and the next morning she showed it to Doctora Silvia. La doctora looked at the sketch in astonishment, then turned to Mayela, her brow wrinkling in surprise. "You did this?"

Mayela was afraid to say yes, thinking maybe she had done something wrong. Perhaps she hadn't used the colored pencils as the doctor had intended. She hung her head sadly, saying nothing.

"Mayela, you don't have to be afraid!" La doctora put her arm around her. "I just want to know if you did this all by yourself."

Mayela nodded, feeling guilty. Maybe she had used too many colors, or made a big mistake and insulted la doctora's city in America. Then la doctora held her close and told her that her drawing was beautiful and that she was an amazing artist. She told her she had never seen the Empire State Building drawn as elaborately and with such an eye for detail. She patted Mayela's braids on the top of her head and said maybe she really was a relative of Frida Kahlo. She called in Señora Juana del Pilar to take a look, and she expressed the same amazement. The women looked at each other and said they had a true Frida Kahlo living among them.

Mayela remembered her eyebrows weren't thick and bushy like Frida Kahlo's, and now she was afraid everyone had made a big mistake and maybe she should wear her braids down like she used to. She had never considered herself an artist, as everyone in Chitlitipin drew on clay and wood and sometimes on leather. They admired one another's work and learned to perfect their craft by looking carefully at designs, colors, and images for new ideas. When someone created a new design, another person would come along and add on to it until the design became so intricate it was hard to follow. Then someone else would start on a new design and the process would begin all over again.

La doctora told Señora Juana del Pilar that Mayela was to be given a space at el Instituto where she could draw and paint. This suited Mayela, as she liked to be alone and didn't make friends with the other children. There was no room anywhere in the overcrowded orphanage, so they had to set up a space for Mayela in the front room with the parakeets chirping in their cage, the potted plants by the window, the framed paintings of Mexican landscapes, and Christ's words hanging over the crucifix.

La doctora had Narciso Odin, who worked for el Instituto, construct a studio for Mayela like real artists had out of wooden planks. La doctora brought in an easel, paints, brushes, pencils, and pads of paper for Mayela and told her to draw anything that came to her mind.

Pretty soon, the room was filled with Mayela's paintings, and la doctora told Señora Juana del Pilar to take down the framed pictures of Mexican landscapes that were there to impress guests and to put up Mayela's paintings, which she said had no equal.

20 Narciso Odin had been employed at el Instituto for over six years. He made friends with Mayela, telling her she was lucky to be at el Instituto, as she had won la doctora's favor. Narciso was dark and slender, with thick black hair and graying eyebrows. On his left hand he had a tattoo of a ladder, which he said he would someday use to climb to Heaven. He told Mayela he was a Huichol from the village of Nayarit. His tribe was a neighbor of the Tarahumaras, and both tribes had been around since the beginning of time.

"Who knows who came on the earth first," he said. "No one kept any records, except in song and dance." Then he chanted a song in his language, and Mayela listened to it, enjoying Narciso's voice but not understanding his words.

Narciso brought Mayela a small table for her paints and a stool she could sit on while she painted. He told her that if she painted with all her heart, people would remember her like they remembered Frida Kahlo.

Mayela didn't see Tía Concha for weeks and worried the old woman wouldn't ever come back to see her. She knew Cina wouldn't come, as Sebastian controlled her with the messages he received from el Imán. In desperation, she wondered how she could find Petra de la Rosa's family in Juárez, knowing they would help her get to her village.

At night Mayela had nightmares, dreaming over and over again of Sebastian, naked and waving el machete in front of her face. She saw him pushing his tongue through the wide space between his teeth. Again and again, the tongue darted in and out, until it became the huge bird she had seen before in her dreams that pecked her eyes out. Each time, she woke from the dream sweating and shaking with fear.

Doctora Silvia wrote in her notes that Mayela was suffering a great trauma and asked her if anything had happened to cause her pain. Mayela couldn't tell la doctora about Cina or Sebastian, and said only that she couldn't remember.

Then one day she painted the image of her nightmares, using bold colors—black, white, blue, red, and yellow. Sebastian was a black silhouette, and the blade of el machete bright yellow. It shone in the dark, making it seem as if el machete would rise out of the painting to strike anyone unfortunate enough to be in its way. Sebastian's teeth were white, and his tongue red and pointed. The bird was blue and its beak red, with blood that dripped from two eyes Mayela had drawn. She painted Sebastian's hand, huge and heavy over her own head, and an ugly spider at her feet.

When Doctora Silvia asked Mayela about the painting, Mayela responded only that she was afraid of machetes and of wild birds that pecked people's eyes out.

"Have you ever seen birds like this?" la doctora asked her.

"Well, yes and no."

"And el machete? And this tongue? Can you tell me anything about why this big hand is over you—or is that you?" La doctora pointed out each part of the painting calmly, as if she was in no hurry to hear Mayela's answer.

Mayela looked away, not saying anything, and la doctora wrote in her notes that something had happened to Mayela that had frightened her so much that she was unable to talk about it.

Narciso's wife, Nubia, came to el Instituto to help clean the place for Señora Juana del Pilar, as some of la doctora's friends were expected to arrive soon from los Estados Unidos. When Americans came to visit, every effort was made to impress them with cleanliness and order in the hope of getting contributions and of having some of the children adopted by Americans who worked with Christian churches along the border.

Narciso's wife looked many years older than he did, and at first Mayela thought it was his mother. He explained that Huichols sometimes took two wives or more, depending on how rich they were. He had another wife, he said, much younger than Nubia, so he didn't care.

Señora Juana del Pilar told Nubia to help her husband hang all of Mayela's paintings on the walls and to arrange them in an attractive manner for los Americanos to admire. Narciso crafted frames for all the paintings, and soon el Instituto looked more like an art gallery than an orphanage. There were sketches of the Empire State Building and the Brooklyn Bridge and a sketch of la Catedral in el Centro. There was a painting of a gigantic butterfly with emerald wings that shimmered with iridescent paint that glowed in the dark. Mayela's bold and beautiful paintings lifted people's spirits, but Señora Juana del Pilar was hoping they'd do even more—that they'd sell for good amounts of money so more rooms could be constructed for the children and a playground finally built. Doctora Silvia told her that she was sure Mayela was a child prodigy and that she had been born to paint.

At the end of November, Tía Concha visited Mayela and told her that Cina and the children had fled to Montenegro. She said el Imán had been telling Sebastian all kinds of crazy things, and Cina thought the next thing it would tell him to do was to kill her or one of the children. El Imán had told Sebastian that Cina was out with another man and she was not to be trusted, as she wanted to run away from him and get rid of his baby. The stone had instructed Sebastian to take Cina's shoes away from her and make her walk barefooted. This would keep her close to his dwelling. Walking barefooted, Cina had developed huge welts from stepping on shards of glass and contaminated water and garbage. One day she told Tía Concha she was going to Montenegro, as it was better to let her husband, Zocotl, kill her, because then he'd have to take care of his children.

Tía Concha told Mayela that Cina had resigned herself to death and no longer cared what happened to her. When Zocotl saw her pregnant from another man, he'd do all he had promised. Cina hoped Chavela would be back in Montenegro so she could bury her body. She'd join hundreds of other women, Tía Concha said, who had been slain by their husbands and thrown out into the desert to rot. Cina expected her fate to be no better than theirs. Mayela thought about Cina and of Sebastian's machete and how Cina had leaned on his body when he had shown them human hair on the blade that he said came from the head of one of his enemies. She was worried she'd never see Cina again and wondered if Sebastian would catch up to her and her children Nabor and Isi. She cringed to think of Cina's hair on Sebastian's machete.

Mayela looked anxiously into Tía Concha's face. "And what have you heard about my mother? When is she coming to take me home?"

"Oh, that. Well, as soon as Cina gets to Montenegro, she'll send word to Puebla and tell your mother where you are. You're not to worry. I'm sure that as soon as your mother knows, she'll get on the train and come to Juárez. Then your problems will be over."

Tía Concha was impressed with Mayela's paintings and asked her what they planned to do with them.

"As you know, I am a relative of your mother's, and they should put them in my care. In fact, they should have told me you were an artist. I never knew!"

Tía Concha told Señora Juana del Pilar the same thing, but la directora reminded her that she had signed papers when Mayela entered el Instituto, stating that she could not care for Mayela and relinquishing her rights as her guardian. Tía Concha walked away angry, as she was hoping to sell some of the paintings at los mercados and make much needed money. Cina's disappearance had also hurt her, as she was counting on Cina to help her sort through garbage to find items they could mend to sell at los mercados and to help her make ceramic animals and tamales. She also had plans to use Isi and Nabor to make herself seem more pathetic when they went out on the streets to beg. Tía Concha left with vague promises to Mayela that she would return. On her way to la rutera, Tía Concha stopped in a bar located in one of las zonas and used the money she had saved to buy herself drinks and sit for hours relating all the injustices done to her by everyone around her. No one paid her any attention, as they had seen her before and knew she would drink until she ran out of money, then stagger away. She ended up sleeping in a dark alley all night long, listening to men violating a young woman who was too drugged up to know the difference.

All the attention Mayela was getting at el Instituto was more than she could bear. In spite of her success as an artist, she would have been happy to go home to Chitlitipin and never see el Instituto again. Other children were quick to make fun of Mayela and told her she wasn't anything like Frida Kahlo. She was a crazy girl, una loquita, who painted stupid pictures. The children taunted her. One of them pulled her braids off the top of her head, telling her she had a hole there and used her braids to hide it. Mayela couldn't tell la doctora or Señora Juana del Pilar about her problems, as the children said they'd beat her up and destroy her paintings when nobody was looking.

Narciso Odin found out what the other children were doing to Mayela and took action to protect her. He told those who were leading the others to taunt her and make her life miserable that if they didn't stop they'd end up doing the worst jobs at el Instituto, and he'd make sure they never got gifts, clothes, and other things that were donated to el Instituto for their use. Mayela came to depend on Narciso's protection and to see him as the father she had never known in Chitlitipin. She began to trust Narciso and often talked to him about her paintings and about her desire to go home. La Navidad, she said, was always celebrated in her village with song and dance and going to church to honor the birth of el Niño Cristo, and now she would have to pass the Christmas season at el Instituto away from her family for the first time in her life. She showed Narciso a scene she had painted from Chitlitipin, showing the villagers dancing before a huge fire, dressed in elaborate costumes with a leader, el monarca, directing them with his wand.

"We have many things in common," Narciso said, looking gently at Mayela. Then he invited her to visit with his family at his home on Christmas Eve, la Noche Buena. La doctora wouldn't mind, since she'd be in los Estados Unidos until late in January. Mayela was happy to think she'd spend some time with Narciso and Nubia, and asked Señora Juana del Pilar for permission to go with Narciso to his home in la colonia Primer Lucero.

Narciso's colonia reminded Mayela of Los Tres Magos. It spread for miles along dusty roads and followed haphazard paths into the hills. It was crowded with dwellings made of cardboard, newspapers, sticks, and tarp. Some of the houses along the main road were constructed of adobe bricks and had wooden doors and small glass windows.

Narciso's house was adobe, with sheets of metal for a roof. Narciso had added three rooms to his house, each with a small glass window, making his house the most prosperous looking one in la colonia. There was a front door, painted blue, and a narrow hallway leading through the house to a door that opened into the backyard where there was an assortment of chickens and goats. The family had their own outhouse in the backyard, with a canvas covering over it that looked like a tiny circus tent.

There were many children, of all ages, living in Narciso's house. They slept on small cots or on tapetes. The adults slept on beds that looked like the ones at el Instituto. There were chairs as well and a kitchen table that resembled furniture Mayela had seen at el Instituto. In the kitchen, the dishes and eating utensils were identical to the ones at the orphanage. She wondered if Señora Juana del Pilar knew that Narciso had furnished his house with what he took from el Instituto.

Outdoors, there was a pit dug into the ground with mesquite wood burning and a goat roasting over the flames that the men had slaughtered for the family's celebration. The women made tortillas like the women of Chitlitipin, kneeling on the ground to grind the corn on el metate, then cooking the tortillas over el comal set on top of a grill that was also used to cook vegetables and meat.

On a small patio, Narciso had fashioned a wooden altar for the Christ Child and for their gods. It was beautifully decorated with candles and small wooden ladders made of sandstone that signified the steps of life Huichols had to take before death. The tiny ladders reminded Mayela of the ladder Narciso had tattooed on his left hand. There were also disks of different sizes, nealikas, set at the altar, elaborately painted with faces of the gods of the sun and fire and the goddess of corn, as well as images of cornfields, plants, snakes, and winged serpents. Narciso told everyone that someday Mayela would paint nealikas for their altar, as she was a true artist.

There was a young woman helping Nubia with the cooking. Narciso said she was his second wife. She was skinny and dark, and one of her eyes was shut tight, as if she had suffered a blow to her face.

"These women are lucky," Narciso told Mayela. "They have a man who takes care of them!" He laughed and both women ignored him.

Neighbors and relatives arrived all day long dressed in their best clothes. Nubia gave Mayela a white dress with blue embroidery and earrings and necklaces that matched. There were flowers for the girls' hair, and some of the men wore flowers around their necks like wreaths. Mayela had never seen such finery and was inspired to join in their dances by the fire to the sound of drums, guitars, and violins. The dancing made her feel free and alive for the first time since she had left her village.

Then the feasting began. Bottles of liquor were opened, and everyone drank, including some of the children. The men sat on the ground to smoke el peyote, and soon everyone was drunk or drugged up. As the night wore on, the dancers got wild, and some of the men started kissing and touching the women. Girlfriends and boyfriends ran off in the dark together. By this time Mayela had stopped dancing and was frightened to see that no one seemed to care what anybody was doing. Narciso told her to sit by him and not to be afraid. When he offered her a drink of tesgüino, she told him she had never had liquor before and refused to take it. Then she saw Nubia and Narciso's second wife, both drunk, eyeing her and pointing their fingers at her. The women whispered together and laughed, and Mayela felt as if she was back at el Instituto with the children laughing at her.

"I'd like to go back to el Instituto," she told Narciso, raising her voice above the music and laughter of the dancers.

"What? On la Noche Buena? There's no way for you to get there. There's nothing running tonight, no ruteras, nada. Everyone's at home, celebrating. Calm yourself, Mayela." He offered her another drink, and when she refused everyone laughed at her.

Mayela walked away from the celebration, but Narciso followed her. He grabbed Mayela in the dark and lifted her up in his arms.

"You're beautiful, Mayela, more than my two other wives, more than any other woman I've ever seen. And your paintings are magic. You're a goddess, for sure!"

Then he kissed Mayela on the mouth. She struggled to escape his arms, her mind racing with images of Cina, Sebastian, and el machete. She was screaming at the top of her lungs, but no one heard her cries. Narciso, drunk and unsteady on his feet, swayed back and forth and finally fell to the ground holding her. She got up and ran in the dark over ground that was rough and full of holes and stones and began to climb a nearby hill, scratching at the ground, her fingernails and knees bleeding from grabbing onto jagged rocks and rubble. Narciso caught up with her, but she kicked him hard with her foot. In the darkness, she heard him cursing and scrambling to keep his balance on the hillside. She saw the light of a fire somewhere ahead of her, and thought there must be people nearby that could hear her, yet no one answered her cries for help. She got to a small clearing on the hillside, where a trail led around the circumference of the hill, and ran down the strip of sandy soil visible by the moonlight. She ran until she no longer heard Narciso behind her and hid in a small crevice she found, a space between two rocks that held her like an icy cradle.

In the morning, Nubia found Mayela still hiding on the hillside between the two rocks, nearly frozen to death, and brought her back to Narciso's house. Crying, and with every bone in her body aching, Mayela looked wildly around for Narciso.

"He's gone!" Nubia yelled. "Did you think he would make you his wife?"

Then she told Mayela to get into a tub of water she had ready for her, and she had her wash off all the dirt and the blood that had crusted under her fingernails and on her legs and arms from climbing over the rocky ground.

Then she looked at Mayela, her eyes blazing with anger. "If you dare to tell anyone at el Instituto, there will not be a place where you can hide. We will find you." She threw Mayela's clothes at her and said, "Get dressed; I'm taking you back to el Instituto."

From the other room, Mayela heard the voice of Narciso's second wife: "Get out and don't ever come back!"

Mayela started sleeping for long hours during the day. Her body felt heavy, like it did when she had meningitis. Her head ached, and her chest felt as if someone had sat on it and crushed it. She wasn't strong enough to curl her fingers around a paintbrush and lift it to the canvas, so she quit painting. She was pale, her eyes vacant. Nubia told Señora Juana del Pilar that Mayela had fallen from one of the hills and been injured. She showed her the scratches and bruises on Mayela's face, arms, and legs. La directora looked at Mayela's pale face and asked her if it was true. Mayela nodded and lay back down again.

La directora decided to take Mayela to the clinic anyway, to have her checked for meningitis, since she was losing weight and didn't look well. The doctor told her Mayela didn't have meningitis and was probably suffering from the fall she had suffered on la Noche Buena. On her return to el Instituto, fluid began to flow from between Mayela's legs, pink, then red. One of the older girls reported to Señora Juana del Pilar that Mayela had started her menses. La directora sat at Mayela's bedside and explained to her that what was happening to her was a natural thing, something God planned since the beginning of time so women could bear children. Mayela looked right through Señora Juana del Pilar as if she was seeing a ghost.

"Is it that you miss Doctora Silvia? Is that why you're so sad? She'll be here soon. In the meantime, rest. Get your strength back."

She called Narciso Odin in and told him to have the cook bring Mayela a bowl of hot soup. Mayela saw Narciso and started to throw up, jumping off the bed and running to the bathroom. She didn't reach it in time and threw up all over the floor and over Narciso's shoes. Señora Juana del Pilar instructed him to clean up everything and make sure Mayela got her bowl of soup.

At the end of January, Doctora Silvia returned to el Instituto and was shocked to see Mayela's condition. She said Mayela was suffering from a virus and something more—a trauma. Señora Juana del Pilar told her the Christmas season had brought it on, and her fall down the hill in Narciso's colonia. Besides that, she told her Mayela had started la regla and was now officially una señorita.

At night, Mayela's twin brother, dead at birth, came to her in her dreams. He was a beautiful baby, always smiling with her. He sat on her shoulder, or rode around in her pocket, a tiny baby with paper-thin wings like an angel's and microscopic feet with toenails that glowed like neon lights. Her twin brother told her she was not to be afraid of anything, as he would protect her now that she knew he was near. He began by putting thoughts in Mayela's head—thoughts that told her she was stronger than Narciso. Over and over, her twin brother told Mayela she was stronger than Narciso. He flew close to her face, and even when she was awake Mayela could feel his paper-thin wings flutter over her cheeks, eyes, nose, and lips.

One morning, she drew her twin brother and painted an orange glow surrounding him, a warm heavenly glow that took over the entire paper.

Her twin was a tiny blue baby flying in the orange glow with pink wings and bright yellow toenails. Doctora Silvia saw it and told Mayela that it was the most beautiful of all her paintings. She told Señora Juana del Pilar that the painting was in the style of the greatest Mexican artists of magical realism, but Mayela didn't know what she was talking about. She named her twin brother Popo, like the famous lover of Ixtla, in the ancient story of the young couple whose love was so great it became two fiery volcanos that can be seen to this day in the Valley of Mexico. Soon, Mayela was painting her twin brother Popo and adding him to paintings she had already completed. Over and over again, she painted Popo, a blue baby flying, with pink wings and shiny yellow toenails.

Villa de las Rosas

21 Evita and Cristal moved to a zona not far from Isidora's house. It was hemmed in on one side by an industrial park and on the other side by a railroad station and busy streets that curved into a maze of old storefronts, bars, dance halls, and crumbling apartments. The apartments were one block away from an elementary school, and Cristal told Evita that prostitutes, hooked on drugs, lived in the apartments and had sex with schoolboys who wanted their first experience at little cost. No protection, she said, for the kids. What if they got HIV or a venereal disease? The girls didn't care, as long as they got their fix. Evita shook her head sadly, knowing Anabel was probably one of the girls who lived there.

Maclovio stopped by almost every day to see Cristal, spending his time sleeping in her bed and waiting for her to join him when she finished her work at el Club Exotica. Evita fixed food for them, cleaned, dusted, and made sure Cristal's bills were paid. Cristal trusted Evita with everything she owned and relied more and more on her each day to run her life. Evita didn't feel like the dot at the end of a sentence anymore, as she was too busy making sure Cristal's money got to the bank on time to make payments on furniture, jewelry, clothes, rent, and utilities.

Evita took care of Cristal as she had at Isidora's. When she folded her fancy sexy underwear, she inhaled, deeply, the fragrance of Cristal's sweet perfume. Evita stacked the lacy see-through underwear neatly in Cristal's chest of drawers and worried that her body would never be as desirable to men as Cristal's. Maybe Ricardo made love to her out of pity for her bony body, and now he was laughing at her for believing he would return. The thought of Ricardo always brought to mind her mother and made Evita feel ashamed of getting involved with Ricardo in the first place. Yet, her next thought would be of being with him at el Paraiso. Then the longing for him would start all over again, like an ember fanning itself into a flame, until the spikes inside her would show up under her skin, making huge blotches on her arms that she tried to hide under long-sleeved blouses.

Evita liked it when Cristal hugged her, even though the hugs were only casual expressions of affection. She looked forward to helping Cristal dress and was mesmerized by her perfect body and the confident way she showed it off. Cristal didn't seem to notice her effect on Evita, and lay on her bed naked for Evita to massage her from head to toe. Years of dancing had left Cristal with no shame about being seen naked. Evita massaged Cristal's body tenderly, lovingly, with a fragrant lotion that smelled of gardenias. Again she noticed the scar on the left side of Cristal's rib cage, a pink line that ended above her hip, and took a chance in asking her about it.

"What is this from?"

Cristal sighed impatiently. "Men, Evita, what else. My own brother tried to assault me—have sex with me when he was drunk. And now he's in prison—but not for attacking me, no; he's in prison for killing another man."

Cristal turned her face away from Evita, and thought of Ricardo and of Evita's brother, Reynaldo, both of them her lovers when she was younger. She'd never tell Evita, having learned how to keep secrets, how to welcome men into her bed and how to let them go without shedding a single tear or ever talking about them again.

Evita massaged the circumference of Cristal's full, round breasts, admiring their perfect contours and smooth brown nipples. Under her fingertips, Cristal's breasts were supple yet firm to her touch. They made Evita feel as if life was big, bigger than she knew, and that it was good and full of things yet to come.

Rudy, Cristal's boss at el Club Exotica, decided to rent Cristal out to some of his friends for private parties in their homes. He told her she'd be paid well, as long as she pleased the men, and there wouldn't be any danger to her, as there was a signed contract. She was a commodity, a product men bought to spice up their celebrations. The men who rented Cristal were very happy with her services, and she quickly became a favorite in their circles. Maclovio fought with Cristal over the private parties. He told her that all the men wanted was to see if they could get their hands on her and take her to bed before she left. Cristal told him she had a job to do, and she did it well. She danced and led the men on to where they were crazy with lust; then el Club Exotica provided the women and men they needed to satisfy their needs. Maclovio shook his head, not believing Cristal and frustrated by her stubbornness.

Evita had her own room in Cristal's house and, using money Cristal had given her, decorated it with new sheets, pillows, a bedspread, and a small carpet. She also bought an armchair for her pink stuffed bear with the red plastic heart. The bear sat stoically on the chair's cushion. She got a radio with a tape player for listening to her favorite music and a small TV set. Through the thin walls of her room, Evita could hear Cristal and Maclovio making love. She listened to Maclovio's low voice, saying words of love like a chant to Cristal, and her answering sighs and gasps. Then there was silence, and Evita imagined them asleep in each other's arms. Sometimes she was tempted to open the door to see them and lie next to Cristal, to share in the warmth of her body, but she knew she'd never do it. She missed Isidora's huge body, and the way Isidora hugged and cradled her in her arms like a mother hiding its baby under her wing. She remembered Isidora asking her if she was one of the children who needed a mother. She had never answered her question. There were tears in Evita's eyes as she thought of Isidora's embrace, a motherly touch she had to learn to forget. Evita was restless sleeping alone, remembering her body over Ricardo's and how he told her he loved her and rocked her back and forth like a newborn baby.

Evita walked from Cristal's apartment to la Catedral, not talking to anyone except Licha, the cleaning woman, who thought her name was Elena. She was Elena when Ricardo took her to el Río de Oro, dressed in black, and she wanted to forget that day and how she had stuck his knife deep into her arm.

"You're looking better, Elena," Licha said to her, pausing to look at her with a dust rag in her hand. Evita glanced quickly at the image of la Virgen de Guadalupe hanging over an altar with candles blazing. The beautiful face was silent, the eyes cast downward, and Evita imagined she had disappointed la Virgen by lying to Licha.

"You seem like you've put on some weight. That's good—I thought you might fly away with the next gust of wind." Then she smiled and patted Evita's head tenderly, and Evita sensed that Licha suspected the truth about her life.

"Are you back with your mother?"

"Yes, of course."

"So you didn't have to go to el Instituto after all. Well, that's for the best when you have family. Not too long ago, my cousin took a girl there who was sick with meningitis. Poor girl. My cousin called me to take a look at her, and she was all but dead when I reached her. She's completely recovered and is now painting pictures at el Instituto that are making her famous. She's an Indian girl, a Tarahumara, who's a gifted artist. When you step outside on la Plaza, you'll see some of her paintings on display. El Instituto's selling her work to raise money to expand their facility. There are orphans in Juárez who live on the streets, as you know, and they are prey for thieves, rapists, and murderers. But you're not one of them—are you, Elena?"

"No, of course not. I have my family."

"And why doesn't your family ever come with you to mass?"

"They work. My mother sells her embroidery in los mercados—and really, she's gone all day long."

Licha told Evita she was glad things were going well for her, as God was watching over her, and la Virgen of course was blessing her. Evita walked out onto la Plaza, past the old man pulling on the cord to ring the church bell, and saw what Licha had referred to. In the midst of people walking and talking, of families buying food at the stands that circled the plaza, of children scampering everywhere, and of cars whizzing by on the busy streets, sat a small girl with her braids tied up in colorful bows piled high on her head. She was sitting at a canvas, painting—very serious at her task. A group of people stood watching her. There was a sign posted on a table nearby: *La Niñita Frida*.

Paintings leaning on wooden stands portrayed huge trees decorated with ribbons dangling from their branches and gifts set up on altars at the base of their trunks. In another painting, smoke curled from fiery pits and people danced in brilliant costumes. There were paintings of an American city with tall buildings, growing into the sky like an orchard of trees. She saw angry paintings, in black, red, and blue paint, frightening pictures showing a huge red tongue exploding through the front teeth of an enormous mouth and a machete spinning wildly in the air.

Then, Evita saw in the distance a painting of an immense butterfly with bright emerald wings that seemed to flutter magically on the paper. It was the kind of butterfly Evita had always wanted to be—beautiful and free of life's disappointments, sailing high into the clouds, finally at peace. She walked up to the painting, her heart pounding, and saw a tiny blue angel sitting on the emerald butterfly, with pink transparent wings and bright yellow toenails. She held her breath and imagined it was Ricardo's baby flying toward Heaven on the wings of the emerald butterfly. The painting was lit up by an orange glow that suspended the emerald butterfly and the tiny angel in the air as if rocking them in a heavenly cradle. If only she had kept Ricardo's marble-sized baby in her womb! This very moment she'd be pregnant, filled with a power she had never known before, brimming, like Cristal's breasts, with life. Hidden in one of the corners of the painting, Evita saw a name, tiny, barely visible—*Mayela*.

Evita walked up to the girl at the easel and watched her, fascinated by the girl's work.

"Your paintings are beautiful, truly beautiful," she said. "I love butterflies, like the one you've painted over there—and the little angel." Evita pointed to the painting of the emerald butterfly.

Mayela only smiled.

"My name's Evita Reynosa. Are you Mayela?"

Evita could barely hear the girl's answer. "Sí."

Suddenly, Evita wanted to throw her arms around Mayela and beg her for the painting of the emerald butterfly and the tiny blue angel. She had no money and couldn't imagine what it would cost.

"The butterfly—Mayela, will you save it for me, sí? Save it for me—you have no idea what it means to me! I'll get the money to buy it, I promise."

Mayela looked at Evita and smiled again.

Standing nearby was an American woman talking to a Mexican

woman in perfect Spanish. Evita overheard her telling the woman that Mayela was from Chitlitipin, a place close to the village of Montenegro.

"You know Montenegro?" Evita asked Mayela.

Mayela stopped painting and looked intently at Evita. "Why do you ask?"

"I know someone from Montenegro. She's my cousin, Petra de la Rosa. She's staying at my mother's house, unless her family's found a place of their own by now."

To Evita's surprise, Mayela stood up and rushed over to la Americana, speaking excitedly to her, her hands gesturing toward Evita. Mayela had been so still and serious, her behavior made everyone think something was wrong. La Americana called Evita over.

"I'm Doctora Silvia," she said, smiling at Evita. "Do you know someone from Montenegro?"

Evita was afraid she had said something wrong and didn't know what to do.

"Don't worry, you can tell me. Mayela's been waiting for her mother to come to Juárez to take her home. She lives in a village close to Montenegro."

"My cousin Petra de la Rosa is from Montenegro, and she's come to Juárez recently to work in las maquiladoras."

"I know Petra!" Mayela said, her eyes brightening. "She knows my family. She was there when I was born—my mother gave her gifts. Her grandmother is Doña Teodora Santos, and her mother's name is Flor. They left because her father was sick—very sick."

"Yes, that's it. That's their last name, and that's why they came to Juárez. Petra's mother is staying at my madrina's house, and Petra was staying at my house with her brother, but I'm not sure if she's still there. I've been living with my sister . . ." Evita stammered, hoping Doctora Silvia wouldn't see she was lying.

Mayela stepped up to Evita and put her arms around her as if she was a long-lost friend.

"I'll save the emerald butterfly for you, but you must find Petra for me. Tell her I'm at el Instituto, not far from la Catedral, and that I have to talk to her about my mother. And if she's going back to Montenegro, tell her I want to go with her!"

Evita walked away with the promise of the painting—the emerald butterfly and the blue angel flying to Heaven, hers for the price of finding Petra de la Rosa.

Evita told Cristal all about Mayela and the beautiful painting she had asked her to save for her. A Tarahumara Indian girl, she told her, the sweetest little girl—and her paintings were beautiful. Now she had to find her cousin Petra, which shouldn't be hard to do, as her madrina was sure to know where she was.

Sitting at the kitchen table, Cristal ignored what Evita had to say and told her to polish her nails in a hurry, as she had a special party to dance at that night in the house of un rico, a man both wealthy and dangerous. The combination wouldn't surprise anybody, she said. He lived in el distrito Villa de las Rosas. Cristal told Evita you couldn't get much wealthier than that. She told Evita she could come with her. Who knows, maybe she'd find someone and forget Ricardo once and for all. Cristal shook her hands in the air, drying off her nails as Evita applied the polish, impatient for her to finish.

"Stop moving; I can't do this right!" Evita had to stop and dab polish remover on Cristal's fingers in tiny places where she had gotten polish on her skin. She was angry at Cristal because she never listened to a word she had to say. She tried again.

"Really, you should go with me to el Instituto, over by la Catedral. You'd—" Cristal didn't let her finish.

"I've got problems right now, Evita! Big ones! What do I care about some Tarahumara girl who can paint? I had another fight with Maclovio today, and I told him to get out. I'm tired of ese viejo. I've been too patient with him, given him too much. So now his money's gone."

Evita was worried now that Maclovio was gone, afraid of what Cristal might do—maybe bring in another man she'd have to put up with, cook meals for, and listen as he argued with Cristal, then made love with her in the next bedroom. Maybe he wouldn't be old like Maclovio, but more like Ricardo. Then what would she do? Living with Cristal was starting to feel like being back at her mother's house.

"You have to go with me tonight, Evita. You haven't worked for months, and it's time you forgot about ese pinche, what's his name? Ricardo—forget him! We need money!"

The thought of another man touching her body made Evita feel weak and dizzy. "What about the murders? Only two weeks ago they found another girl my age in las Lomas de Poleo, dead. Didn't you hear about it? Her head was wrapped in a black plastic bag, and she had been tortured and raped like the others. They said her tongue was bitten off—and her left breast was cut off!" Evita shivered thinking about the murder and the girl's mutilated body.

"We're protected. I told you: my boss, Rudy, has a contract with these people. They sign business contracts with him. What's he there for except to protect us? Of course we'll be careful. We won't walk out alone at night. And when the party's over, Rudy will send a chofer to pick us up. Stop being scared about everything, Evita. You just can't live that way."

Before they left for the private party, Evita called her madrina to see what she knew about Petra, but Ofelia's phone number had been disconnected. Evita knew the only way for her to find Petra was to go to Ofelia's house, or try to find Luis Ledezma and his sister, Yvone. They would know if Petra was still at her mother's or if her family had found a place of their own. With the memory of Ricardo still haunting her, she couldn't think of going to her mother's house to look for Petra.

Cristal was at her best, wearing an outfit under her sleek white coat that was hardly there at all. It was a black veil that twisted around her white skin, with purple loops that looked like tapestry with fringe dangling at the ends, which she'd untie one at a time to expose herself. She was wearing a matching G-string with only a few strands of fringe and matching purple tassels on her nipples for effect as she danced. Her plastic spiked heels had rhinestone straps that laced over her ankles, and her skin shimmered with a lotion she had bought that had specks of glitter in it. Her hair was loose, thick and glossy, and it covered her shoulders like a mantle. She told Evita that men preferred long hair, but she had to be careful that it didn't fall over her breasts, as she was famous for her huge breasts. Men wanted to see them over and over again. Cristal's face was covered in layers of makeup, and her dark eyes were outlined in heavy black mascara and purple eye shadow.

"You'll see, Evita. The men get wild, but don't be afraid—it's all a show. Don't drink anything unless you see others doing the same. You don't want somebody to put something in your drink that will make you pass out. And if somebody wants to take you to bed, be sure he shows you the money first. The men who will be there have plenty—so don't settle for just anything. You're not part of the show, so they have to pay for you separately. You can give Rudy his portion tomorrow. That's the way it works. Our money isn't our own—we have to share it. Isidora made enough off me, vieja pinche, that's why she didn't want me to go—and you, she was saving for big money because you're still so young."

"What if I don't want to?"

Cristal frowned and looked at her. "Want to what?"

"Want to have sex."

"Well, then what *do* you want? Do you want to live off me? I told you, I don't have any money now that Maclovio's gone!" Cristal turned away. Evita hadn't seen her angry since they had lived at Isidora's.

"I'll try," she said weakly.

Evita wore the sexy red dress and black lacy underwear Anabel had bought her for her fourteenth birthday. The dress fit Evita perfectly except for the shiny sleek straps that fell down her shoulders, exposing the curves of her tiny breasts. She wore a black velvet jacket for warmth that hid her shoulders and breasts and fit perfectly over her waist. She had highlighted her hair in copper shades, and it hung smooth and shiny over her shoulders. Cristal had helped her with her makeup. Evita thought she had on too much, but Cristal said it was perfect for a party in the evening.

"You have to put on more makeup when you go out at night," she told her. "It's hard to see in the dark, and men enjoy a beautiful face. Remember, we have to give them what they want."

Cristal's own face was a mask of colors blended on her skin, with eyes painted boldly in purple and black. Evita thought perhaps it was Cristal's way of hiding from what she had to do.

Rudy sent a car from el Club Exotica to pick up Cristal and Evita. Cristal knew the man who was driving, a man named Ponce. He told them to sit in the backseat and he'd drive them around like they were movie stars. He picked up one more girl, who got into the front seat, her cheap perfume instantly filling the car with a fragrance that made Evita want to sneeze. The girl's skirt was so short, it looked like she was wearing her underwear, but it didn't seem to bother her that when she sat down she exposed her slim thighs and showed off her black garters.

"So, how are you putas doing tonight? Ready to do it with the rich and nasty? Oooh, just think, Villa de las Rosas. Now that's a place my mother visited—to do laundry, that is! Give me a poor man any day, right, Ponce?"

Ponce laughed out loud and leaned over and kissed the girl on the mouth. The girl turned up the car radio and started singing along with the song. Evita looked at the girl closely and recognized her as the one she had seen weeks ago on the street, the girl who had fought with her boyfriend when he had whistled at her.

Cristal whispered to Evita: "She's a disgusting tramp. She'll do it with a monkey for the price of a banana."

The girl turned around and stared at Evita. "I know you! You're that bitch who was after my boyfriend!"

"I wasn't after him—he's the one who whistled at me!"

Cristal looked at Evita with surprise, and Evita shook her head. "I don't even know her boyfriend."

"She doesn't know what you're talking about, puta, and if you want to do more about it—we'll settle it before we get to the party!"

Cristal's voice was loud, and she leaned toward the girl and put her hand on the seat, close to the girl's shoulder.

Ponce laughed out loud. "Ya, all of you—you should know better! Men aren't worth fighting for. Haven't you learned that?" He hit a huge hole in the street, and everyone bounced up together. "There, maybe that'll make you come to your senses! Fighting over men! If anybody should know better, it's you."

The girl in the front seat laughed along with Ponce. "He wasn't worth it anyway. He was one of my customers—and I can barely keep count of them." She opened her purse and took out a marijuana cigarette, creasing it over with her fingers and lighting it up. Cristal angrily opened the back window to let in some air.

"Beto's got some good stuff," the girl told Ponce. "Here, try it." She handed him the cigarette, and he took a drag and said he knew where she could get stuff that was better and maybe he'd tell her later. He put his hand on her thigh and reached under her short skirt. The girl only laughed and told him to get in line.

The house was one Evita had never seen before, in the very center of Juárez. Though not far from las zonas, it was separated from them as if it was in another country. Evita had seen the houses of the rich from las ruteras on her way through the city. They looked like palaces to her, immense and ornate, some with elegant marble pillars on the front steps. The homes had cameras at every entrance and security people who watched from cars on the street.

Cristal's name was known to some of the men. They had requested her for this special party in honor of a man who was celebrating the birth of his first son in a few months. Evita thought it was a strange way to celebrate a new baby coming into the world. But then again, the rich did as they pleased and didn't have to explain anything to anyone.

Ponce drove to the rear of the house and waited for the ornate wrought-iron gates to open wide. The house looked like an immense dark castle, with a silver twisted cord of barbed wire strung along the length of a high block wall that surrounded the estate. Motion lights went on as Ponce drove in, and there were two men standing at the back door watching them as they approached.

Even though it was early December and the night was cold, Evita's palms were sweating. Her heart was pounding, and her senses were alert to every movement, every sound.

She whispered in Cristal's ear. "This looks like a prison!"

"Don't exaggerate. They have to protect themselves from kidnappers," Cristal whispered back.

"What if they *are* the kidnappers?"

"Why would they want us? They have plenty. Stop being so scared. We won't get murdered."

"Who lives here?"

"They call him el Junior. All the rich men's sons are called los Juniors—and he's one of them. Nobody calls anyone by their real names."

"What about our names? Should we change our names?" Evita asked.

"No, silly, nobody cares what our names are." Cristal shook her head at Evita's naïve question. "They say el Junior's got red hair, like the feathers on a rooster. He's a pervert, like the rest of them. He's got a wife, too. She probably closes her eyes and pretends she doesn't know what he does. What women won't do for money! She's gone to visit her mother, in France of all places, so el Junior's throwing a party for her—to honor their first baby. Except she won't be here! Just like a man, to plan everything behind his wife's back."

There were cars parked under the trees and between bushes in the backyard that could not be seen from the street. Mercedes, Porches, and BMWs looked eerie in the darkness. Evita picked up the smell of gardenias, Cristal's favorite fragrance, as they approached the house.

"It's beautiful—the smell. There's gardenias growing here."

"Probably in the patio somewhere," Cristal said. She grabbed Evita's hand as Ponce stopped near the back door, lacing her long fingers through Evita's small bony ones. Her hand was icy cold. Evita had never known Cristal to be afraid of anything, and it made her want to jump out of the car and run out the back gate, before the wrought-iron doors banged shut.

Ponce stopped near the backdoor entrance that was overhung with ivy. The vines covered the outside walls of the house, climbing up to the rooftop and down over the entrance. One of the men at the door grabbed part of the vine dangling close to his head and snapped it off, throwing it on the ground and kicking it away. Evita watched the vicious, abrupt movement and was ready to tell Cristal that she was leaving the first chance she got, but Cristal had the car door open and was pulling on Evita's hand to get her out. Evita heard music coming from inside. The girl who had been sitting in the front seat led the way, her black garters showing under her skimpy skirt. Evita and Cristal, still holding hands, followed.

22 The huge room Evita and Cristal walked into was dimly lit by Tiffany lamps burning with red lightbulbs. The room had an aura of heat and passion, sex and rage. The music was loud, a hard steady beat set into a confusion of drums and electric guitars that sounded more like a heavy metal band than traditional Mexican music. The ceiling formed a huge curving dome, elaborately decorated with a mural that showed scenes from the Mexican Revolution. On either side of the ceiling hung chandeliers dimly lit by hundreds of tiny glass globes. There was a stage at one end and a wooden floor extending a few feet

around it where couples could dance. Evita's high-heel shoes sank into the carpet as she walked past gleaming mahogany tables set with hors d'oeuvres, bottles of liquor, marijuana ready to roll into cigarettes, and cocaine in long thin white lines. She watched men and women sharing marijuana cigarettes, and no one seemed concerned when someone stopped by to snort a line of cocaine.

"I'm getting out of here!" she shouted in Cristal's ear, but Cristal was already talking to a man who was telling her what time she should dance.

"This is Rudy. And Rudy, this is Evita."

The man was fat and not much taller than Evita. He had two red spots, one on each cheek, and eyebrows that connected on his forehead. He looked Evita over and said to Cristal, "You didn't tell me about her."

"Yes, I did. I told you we moved in together—don't you remember?"

Rudy looked at Evita again. "If you play it smart and don't act like a stupid escuincla, you'll make a lot of money tonight. I'm fair, and I'll give you what you deserve, but you have to work for it. Do you understand—entiendes?"

Evita nodded.

"She's terrified," Rudy told Cristal. "Why did you bring her?"

"We work together now. We have to—Maclovio's gone."

"Maclovio comes and goes. I don't want any trouble, no cabronas who are gonna get nervous and say too much. We're private here. We leave, and nobody says anything to anybody and nobody knows anybody's name—entiendes, Evita?"

Evita nodded again, a queasy sensation rising in her throat. Rudy put his arm around Cristal and they walked away.

"Wait for me, Evita!" Cristal called out to her over her shoulder.

Evita noticed the girl who had been in the front seat sitting casually on a bar stool. She realized she didn't even know the girl's name, but even if she had, she wouldn't want to talk to her. The girl might get mad at her all over again and pick a fight over her boyfriend that Evita didn't even know. She was sitting with an older man. Her legs were open and the short skirt she was wearing hugged her hips tightly. Evita could see the man had his hand between her legs, and the girl was laughing and leading him on.

Evita sat alone at one of the tables in a dark corner, trying to make herself invisible. The room was filled with men of different ages, mostly middle-aged and well-dressed, and women, obviously prostitutes, wearing heavy makeup like Cristal and skimpy clothes, skirts slit up to their thighs, necklines cut to their navels, and perfume that mixed in with the pungent smell of marijuana. The men and women were drinking, talking, laughing, and getting high, as couples kissed and fondled one another.

The lights flashed on and off in the room, and one of the men laughed loudly and said, "There's el Junior, playing with electricity again!" Everyone laughed, and Evita heard people making comments about el Junior's fascination with electricity.

Then, as Evita was about to get up and find a way to get back to Cristal, a man walked in through the French doors on the wall opposite the door they had come in. His hair gleamed bright red in the haze of the red lightbulbs. He was impeccably dressed in a black tuxedo. Men were reaching over to shake his hand as he walked in, and women gave him admiring sensual looks. There was power emanating from him, authority, a sense that at any moment he could do whatever he wanted to and no one would say a thing. He was handsome, unbelievably so. His red hair reflected back a golden light, and his dark moustache against his light skin made for a striking contrast. At his side was a girl who looked no older than Evita, slender, dressed in an exquisite white gown that shimmered with pearls and tiny rhinestones. The neckline and bodice of the dress was made of fine lace and curved over the girl's breasts sensually. The dress dipped down the girl's smooth brown back, exposing the perfect curve of her spine. Embroidered white lilies with long golden stems on the hem of the dress caught Evita's attention, reminding her of her mother's embroidery. The pattern was intricate, delicate, and Evita knew it had been made by hand at a huge price. She was awed by the pattern, able to see the whole thing in her mind just as she had seen her mother's patterns, knowing every stitch had been meticulously arranged to create an illusion of perfect balance, although the material must have been cut at an angle. The gown looked like a wedding dress, and for a moment Evita thought it was el Junior's wife. Then she remembered his wife was pregnant, and this girl's body was far from pregnant. Her figure was trim and sleek, her breasts silky bulges under the material that seemed to be painted on her body. She was wearing jewels, a glittering necklace and earrings. Evita was stunned by the girl's beauty, her poise and grace.

The girl turned her head and looked straight into the dark corner where Evita was sitting, as if she had caught her looking at her. Her dark eyes showed a helplessness Evita had never seen before. It was as if the girl was standing there but not there at all, her eyes distant and vacant. Then she looked away from Evita, and el Junior kissed her on the mouth and walked ahead of her to talk to another man. She followed looking down, and he grabbed her hand as if she was a little girl and he was teaching her how to stand up straight.

After seeing the girl held captive by el Junior, Evita became desperate for a way out of the room and decided to try one of the French doors to see where it led. The door opened to an immense hallway, set with an exquisite pattern of polished red tile, shimmering with light from chandeliers hanging overhead. A man walked up to her, stiff-kneed, blocking her way. He clenched his teeth.

"What do you think you're doing?"

"Nothing." Evita looked closely at him and saw he was the same policeman who had been driving the car when she was picked up off the city's streets. She stopped abruptly, unable to take another step.

"Oyes, I remember you. You're la mocosita we picked up to take home to her mother. I see you haven't learned your lesson yet! Maybe I should teach you what happens to las mujeres de la mala vida. So, you really are a prostitute!"

The policeman took her by the arm and pushed her roughly back into the room.

"Don't open this door again, if you value your life!"

Evita turned pale to think that the policeman she still saw in her nightmares was guarding the door, threatening her life.

She walked back in and looked for a way to get behind the stage, to tell Cristal that they were in danger. Just then a man approached her.

"May I accompany you?"

The man was elegantly dressed in a three-piece suit. His black hair was slicked back from his face, and his eyes were slanted, as if he was Mexican mixed with Chinese or Filipino. He seemed kind, and she looked up in relief.

"Come with me," he told her. "We'll watch the show together."

He looped his arm through hers and led her to a table secluded in a dark corner. Twice, Evita saw one of the two French doors open and couples slip out into the hallway, where there must have been private rooms for their use.

The man brought Evita a drink in a tall spiral-shaped glass, pink liquid with foam at the top.

"Drink it. It will relax you." Evita wanted to say, *you drink it first*, but she only nodded and thanked him. After she had taken a drink, he told her to take another. The drink tasted good, a rich strawberry flavor. He told her it was a beginner's drink, fruit flavored, and she wouldn't get drunk. He lifted up a shot glass and drank along with her.

"Let me take off your coat. It's too hot in here for that." He reached over to help Evita, standing behind her, his hands on her shoulders. Evita was trembling as he took her velvet wrap off and ran his hands over her shoulders and down to her hips. He kissed her neck gently, pressing himself up against Evita until she could feel him hard against her back. Evita stumbled forward trying to sit down again, and he caught her and turned her around, kissing her hard on the mouth and holding her close. Evita's mouth filled with the bitter taste from the man's mouth, and she gasped for air.

The music in the room changed, suddenly, to an erotic sexual beat made for stripteasers. Colored lights flashed on, whirling wildly on stage. The man sat down next to Evita to watch the show, putting one hand on her thigh and pressing firmly down until it turned moist and hot on her leg.

Evita looked up at the stage and saw Cristal dancing to the sexy music—swaying, gyrating, moving to the beat, her hair whipping around her face in a black maze. She untied the purple tassels one by one to the rhythm of the music, unwinding the thin layers of black veil to the whoops, whistles, and shouts of the men until she was standing on stage wearing only her G-string. Her perfect body glowed white under the colored lights, then changed to pink, violet, red, and blue as the lights switched colors. She removed her G-string and strutted around the stage, finally spreading her legs on a rug set up on the floor and allowing one man to have sex with her. Evita was in shock, as she hadn't realized Cristal's act involved a man.

The man with the slanted eyes motioned for Evita to sit on his lap.

"No—let's watch the show—later." Evita's head felt as light as a balloon, and she struggled to speak to the man.

His dark eyebrows came together and his eyes narrowed to slits.
"Now!"

He sat Evita on his lap and began clutching at her, pulling her dress up to thrust himself inside her. Evita screamed and pulled away, but he held her down hard.

All night, in the red haze of the room, Evita saw faces over her that blurred and changed into monsters, appearing and reappearing: el Junior, Chano, the policeman, the man with the slanted eyes—and Rudy, saying take her out, she's too drugged up to walk. And finally Cristal's hands on her body, Cristal's voice, telling her something that Evita couldn't make out, an echo in her head like the voice of her mother calling her home.

Neruda and Nightmares

23 Prospero was not very convincing when he told Petra and her mother that Ofelia had to go tend to their daughter in Chihuahua City and would be leaving Juárez before the week was over.

"Our daughter just had a baby and needs her mother," he said. "She's very persistent and won't stop asking for Ofelia."

Ofelia seemed weary of her husband and prepared dinner in silence. She had bruises on her arms and face that Flor thought had been caused by Prospero, but Ofelia didn't explain how she got the marks. Flor thanked them for all they had done to help them in Juárez. A great debt was owed them for their hospitality, she said, and now they were ready to move to a house of their own. It had become a matter of life or death, for Nico was in danger with Los Rebeldes. God had blessed them with Petra's promotion. She'd be making three times more than she had before and traveling with people from la maquiladora Western Electronics into El Paso to meet with supervisors and executives of the company in los Estados Unidos. She would have to buy new clothes and shoes to look every bit the professional.

"My daughter, la muy profesional!" Flor said to Ofelia. "Gustavo Rios wasn't lying when he told us he would get us jobs. Now, Petra will get a chance to work in the office, learn English, and make good money. Who knows, maybe someday she'll get permission to live in los Estados Unidos, and we'll all make a new life there."

"I'm happy for you," Ofelia said, setting the plates on the table. "America is a place where fortunes are made. I don't know anyone in el otro lado, but I imagine that Petra will meet los Americanos and maybe get us all visas to travel there."

Flor was happy with their good fortune and expected to get Estevan out of the hospital soon. Things were looking good for them, but still, her heart was not at peace. She didn't tell Ofelia and Prospero that women at la maquiladora hated her daughter for her beauty and now for the promotion Gustavo Rios had given her. She didn't tell them about the man who had fallen in love with Petra at la maquiladora, Humberto Ornelas. It would only be a matter of time, some of the women said, before Humberto's wife, Bridget, would get even with Petra for trying to break up her marriage. Then Petra would be sorry for sleeping with a married man. In the minds of women like Amapola Nieto, Petra had slept with Humberto, and nothing could convince them that she hadn't.

And to add to her problems, Flor's younger daughter, Ester, was having nightmares of men chasing them in the streets and of Petra missing. In one dream she saw her sister's picture in the newspaper, just like the girls being murdered in the city. Tears flowing, her dark curls a wavy frame around her face, Ester told her mother that a huge question mark came up in her mind, black and shouting, when she had the dream—and no answer came. Ofelia said Ester was suffering susto, terrible trauma, from hearing about the murders, and was creating dreams to go along with the reality. Flor had to turn her attention to Ester and comfort her, while feeling little comfort herself. Secretly, she cursed her husband. He had resisted going to Juárez so long that now his recovery would be a miracle.

Prospero located a house for rent in la colonia Nuevo Leon, not far from Western Electronics. It was not an old house, like many in Juárez that are over a hundred years old. It was newer and built for women who worked at las maquiladoras. The house was block in construction, with a roof that didn't leak and glass windows. There was a small kitchen with a gas stove, a refrigerator, and shelves for storing food and dishes, pots and pans. There were two bedrooms and a large room that served as a living and dining room. The bathroom was set in a small hallway between the bedrooms, and the toilet was connected to a septic tank set up in an alley outside the property. It was the first time the family would have a bathroom that wasn't an outhouse, and a shower that worked once Prospero repaired the water pipe and bought a showerhead that made the water spray out like a real shower of rain. Flor said the house would do just fine, especially as it was close to la maquiladora and they might be able to take la rutera for the short ride rather than depend on Luis Ledezma to drive them to and from work.

"It doesn't matter what it looks like," she told Prospero. "All these houses look the same to me. These people have forgotten the beauty of the country, the peace of the fields, the animals waking you up, and the sun rising every morning. They work every day to get to the end of the week, as if the weekend will give them some refreshment! Then they start all over again. I don't know how long Estevan will be able to take this."

The first thing Flor did after they moved into their house in Nuevo Leon was to hang el ojo de Dios that Chavela Sabina had given her in Montenegro. She still remembered Chavela's gentle touch, her hand reaching for hers on the last Sunday they had sold elotes at church. To Petra it seemed like such a long time ago, almost as if she had dreamed her life in Montenegro. She remembered Chavela's children, and most of all her daughter Mayela, who had stuck her tongue out at her and then laughed, covering her mouth with her hand. She wondered if she would ever see her again, the girl whose birth she had witnessed.

Flor gave el ojo de Dios a special place in their living room, hanging it on the wall over the couch. El ojo's red and blue yarn, tightly looped over sticks, formed a diamond shape that added color to their house. In the center of the diamond, the yarn was black—God's eye watching.

Petra now worked the day shift, while her mother was still on the evening shift. She took la rutera to Western Electronics alone, and just as she returned home in the afternoon, her mother left on the same rutera. Her mother said this was perfect, as the children were never alone.

"Your father will be home soon," she told Petra, "and he can help care for the children and the house, as much as he can while he gets better."

Petra had forgotten what it was like having her father around, and she couldn't imagine what he'd say about the gangs that threatened Nico, Ester's nightmares, and her problems at la maquiladora. She'd also have to prepare him for Antonio's visit at Christmas. She hoped he'd accept Antonio as his future son-in-law.

Luis Ledezma said he'd pick up Petra and her mother whenever they needed him to, but Flor thought he had done enough and felt uncomfortable asking him to drive out of his way now that they lived in another colonia. Petra didn't tell her mother, but she missed talking to Luis and telling him her problems. He listened and gave his opinions carefully, making her see the truth in situations where she might not have seen it at all. He told Petra that Nico's days of trouble with gangs were far from over. The notorious leader of Los Rebeldes, el Cucuy, might be out of sight, he said, but there were other gangs just as powerful, and Nico would have to be sure he stayed only in Nuevo Leon and didn't walk into the territory of an opposing gang. This went for all members of the family as well. When Petra tried to tell Nico this, he said not to bother, he already knew—his steps were being watched.

"I'll have to fight them or join them," he said flatly. "There's no other way."

Petra shared an office with Vina Salcido, the girl who had been the receptionist when Petra had come in with her mother to apply for the job. Vina had been employed at la maquiladora for over two years and had recently been promoted to assistant to Gustavo Rios. Now, Gustavo was asking her to train Petra on her new job of invoicing accounts and mailing out correspondence to companies that did business with Western Electronics.

Vina's father had known Gustavo Rios in the days before Gustavo had taken over as one of the supervisors of la maquiladora. He was retired but still held stock in the company and dealt directly with the American board of directors in El Paso. He had used his influence to make sure his daughter had a job in the office rather than on the assembly line and that she had the chance to be promoted to higher positions. Vina was a plump lively girl, who was married and had two boys, both under the age of five. She had her boys' photos displayed on her desk and constantly talked about their latest adventures: the teeth they had lost, their haircuts, the peewee soccer team they belonged to, and the pet fish they cried over when they found its lifeless body floating in the fishbowl. Lola Sesma warned Petra about Vina, telling her she was ambitions and would stop at nothing to get a top position at la maquiladora. Gustavo Rios didn't trust her either and told Petra not to say too much to her, as she'd go directly to her father and tell him everything.

"I hate Gustavo. He's a pervert," Vina told Petra one day at lunch. "Don't let him talk you into anything."

"Like what? What would he talk me into?"

"Do I have to write it out for you? He wants to take you to bed. Can't you see all the attention he gives you? Between him and Humberto Ornelas, they don't know what to do about you!" Vina laughed, telling Petra she couldn't win for losing.

Petra's face reddened with anger just thinking of Humberto and all the trouble he had caused her.

"Humberto's a liar! The worst possible liar. There's never been anything between us! And Señor Rios—he knows I have a boyfriend in Montenegro. Besides, what do I want with him? I can barely stand to talk to him! Antonio will be here at Christmas. We're going to make plans to get married, and all of this will end."

"Your engagement doesn't matter to any of these perverts," said Vina. "They'll go on trying just the same."

Before the day was over, Vina had spread the word that Antonio was coming for Christmas and that he'd probably marry Petra by next year. She told everyone that Petra was already making plans for a big wedding and an elaborate celebration. The news angered Amapola Nieto and the women who had banded together to hate Petra. During their breaks and in the cafeteria at lunch, they laughed about Petra and Antonio. He's un idiota, an ugly, stupid, country idiot—and that's what Petra deserves, they said, for acting la creida and making herself out to be better than everyone else. An expensive wedding was nothing more than her own pride talking, and they were ready to stop its progress at all costs.

24 Gustavo Rios gave Petra English-language tapes and signed her up for English classes provided free to a group of Western Electronics employees by the sister company in El Paso. Every Wednesday evening after work, an American woman came to la maquiladora to spend two hours teaching them conversational English. The woman spoke perfect English and Spanish and was able to teach with greater efficiency. She clasped and unclasped her hands absentmindedly during the class as she explained to them that the company had plans to

expand into South America. Those who learned English would be worth twice as much, as they could better understand the workings of the company that was based in El Paso, Texas.

Petra learned English quickly, and soon she was able to converse with the teacher exclusively in English. She challenged herself and learned to read first the newspaper in English, then books on history, her favorite, then poetry and novels. Petra's world in English became a joy to her as she discovered the words of Pablo Neruda translated in English.

Petra repeated Neruda's words in English, slowly, methodically: *And it was at that age, poetry arrived / in search of me . . . / . . . from a street I was summoned, / from the branches of night.* The words reached her heart, and for the first time in her life the English language touched her soul.

Petra also felt as though she had been summoned, like Pablo Neruda, to do something she had never thought possible. In her mind, she saw the crouching figures on the mountains of Montenegro and remembered that on the night she and her family had left the village the crouching figures had been dancing in the moonlight.

Antonio phoned on a Sunday morning, a few days before November 1, All Saints' Day, and el Día de Los Muertos on November 2. He asked Petra how they were going to celebrate the Day of the Dead when they were so far away from San Francisco del Desierto and el camposanto where their relatives were buried. Petra didn't answer, as she didn't even know where the nearest church was in Nuevo Leon and didn't know anyone in the neighborhood she could ask for directions. He was coming to visit at Christmas with Tío Alvaro and Abuela Teodora, he said. Petra talked to him from a phone they had connected in their house, grateful that she had been able to provide her family with this convenience. When Antonio asked her about her job, she told him nothing about Gustavo Rios and her promotion, nor about Luis Ledezma giving her money to help them move. If she opened her mouth about what was really happening to her, she knew it would come out all wrong and Antonio would worry.

"Yes, I'm coming . . . I'll be there, and who knows if I'll ever come back to Montenegro again," Antonio said. "I'll talk to your father and tell him how much I love you. I can't take this anymore; it's killing me not to be able to see you."

His voice was serious, strained. Petra could see him in her mind, holding onto the phone, his knuckles white over the receiver—hanging on, not caring anymore about what her father might say. She wanted to cry and tell him all they had been suffering since they came to Juárez, but didn't know where to begin. She only told him she was learning English and would be going to meetings in El Paso with employees from la maquiladora Western Electronics.

"I'll teach it to you. It's not that hard, once you practice it."

"I don't think I want to learn English," he told her flatly. "Be careful with los Americanos. I don't trust them. Look what they've created in Juárez—factories that are making them rich, and the poor remain as poor as ever."

Estevan left the hospital with strict orders to remain in bed and take his medications. He was not to do anything strenuous, and of course he was to follow a healthy diet to help the one kidney left function normally. Estevan was tired of doctors and of his medical treatments, and said if it were up to him, he would have left the hospital in the first week to avoid the expenses that had accumulated for his family. Now that Flor and Petra both worked, the hospital was insisting that they pay a percentage of the costs, which was well over 100,000 pesos. Estevan said it would take a century to come up with the money, and now wished he had never allowed his family to put him in the hospital in the first place. He said Juárez was una cosa ajena, a foreign thing that he didn't recognize anymore. He stared at the houses in Nuevo Leon and scoffed as he saw the outside walls of houses and small markets covered with graffiti: LA TRECE, LOS GALANTES, and many other gang names that were crossed off by warring gang members then repainted in bold letters once again. He gazed at everything as if seeing things from behind a glass, his eyes looking but not comprehending. He didn't want to be a part of it, didn't want to think he'd be doomed to walk the rough streets that twisted and turned between houses set so close together that there was barely any space between one front door and the next. Estevan felt as if he had landed on another planet and would never find his way back home.

Tío Alvaro surprised everyone by showing up a week before Christmas with Abuela Teodora and Antonio. He was supposed to arrive two days before Christmas, but said he needed the extra time to take care of some business for his boss.

Estevan pretended he was feeling fine and greeted Alvaro with smiles and an affectionate clap on the back. Abuela Teodora got out of Tío Alvaro's car wrapped in a woolen shawl, her white hair caught at the nape of her neck with an ivory hairpin. She had on her gold cameo earrings, ovals that dangled from each ear. She smoothed out her blue dress with both hands and shook out each leg, her black stockings loose around her thin calves. She was as healthy as ever, her brisk step intact as she walked into the house. Estevan hugged the old woman gently, glad to see her, as he knew she'd manage the household while he recuperated. Flor hugged her mother joyfully, crying and pressing her close. Already she felt lighter, as if a huge burden had been lifted and her power as a woman had returned now that her mother was close by. Abuela Teodora hadn't forgotten Petra, and had brought soft doughy empanadas filled with spicy pumpkin, Petra's favorite, wrapped carefully in a linen cloth.

Estevan greeted Antonio Manriquez formally, as if he hardly knew him at all. He didn't want to show Antonio just how weak he was. He knew Antonio had come to Juárez to ask permission to marry Petra, and this angered him. He felt as though Antonio was taking advantage of his weakened condition to rush into a marriage with his daughter. Secretly, he respected Antonio for his serious hardworking ways and for the way he took care of his parents. He was sure Antonio would make a good husband for Petra, but still he was afraid to consent to their marriage and lose his favorite daughter.

Antonio wanted to surprise Petra at la maquiladora after her shift. He asked Tío Alvaro for his car so he could drive Flor to Western Electronics and bring Petra home. Flor was more than glad that Antonio was taking her, as she wanted Amapola Nieto and her crowd of followers to see how handsome Antonio was. She knew they had been mocking Petra, saying there was no Antonio, and if there was he must look like un idiota de los ranchos, with nothing to distinguish him from those who lived their lives in ignorance and poverty.

Flor herself had forgotten how handsome Antonio was. She now studied his clear light skin, the square jaw, his neatly cut moustache, and high forehead. He was tall and muscular, his hands calloused from doing hard labor on the farms. He wore dark jeans, a pale blue shirt, a belt with a silver buckle etched with his initials, and polished leather boots. His dark brown eyes, intelligent and compassionate, glanced over at Flor as he drove her to la maquiladora. Happily, Flor told him all about Petra working in the office and learning English. She told him that pretty soon her daughter would be attending meetings with company employees in El Paso, and she'd get the chance to travel to other maquiladoras in South America. Antonio listened courteously, telling her he was happy for Petra's good fortune. Then Flor's voice became serious, as she told him Petra had enemies at la maquiladora, women who envied her.

"That's the way it is, señora. Women envy other women who are beautiful and intelligent like Petra."

"That's why I'm glad you're here. Now, they'll see that Petra does have someone who cares deeply about her, and—" Flor stopped herself before she said anything about Petra marrying him.

Antonio looked carefully at Flor's weary face, noticing she had lost weight and her hair was turning gray. She bit her lower lip nervously, and her hands trembled as she spoke.

"What about the men at la maquiladora? They're not blind; I'm sure they've noticed Petra. Has there been any trouble?"

Flor sat up in the seat, holding her hands tightly on her lap. "There have been some problems—lies someone said about her. She'll tell you herself. I'm sure that now that you're here, all this will be over."

"And the murders? I've read about the murders, women from las maquiladoras hunted down by men. Discarded in trash piles like so much garbage. Feminicidios, that's what they're calling the murders. But how can men have this much hatred for women? And I say this as a man—I don't understand it. Life is too dangerous here, señora. It's time Petra and I made a serious commitment to start our lives together. Don't you think so?"

"Of course, por su puesto. I'm sure this is what Petra wants too. The murders frighten us all. As you know, if it were up to Estevan, we'd leave this very moment!"

They arrived at Western Electronics during the shift change. A few cars were lined up on the street, waiting for workers, and two ruteras stopped in front of la maquiladora as women made their way to the street. Antonio was quickly out of the car, looking intently for Petra. Women passed by him, whispering, giggling, and trying to attract his attention.

Antonio searched every face for Petra's. He didn't have long to wait. At the end of the file of women he saw Petra walking out with her friend, Lola Sesma. Petra met her mother at the gate and walked up to her, and Antonio watched as her mother told her, smiling, that there was someone she would recognize standing across the street. Petra looked up and saw Antonio. Instantly she shouted his name, her voice making everyone turn to look. She raced across the street, zigzagging between cars and ruteras, her high-heel shoes pounding the rough asphalt, her dark hair flying. And in front of both shifts of employees coming and going, she rushed into his arms and didn't let him go until he had wiped away her tears. Holding her securely in one arm, Antonio led her to Tío Alvaro's car.

Now that Antonio had arrived, Juárez took on a new color for Petra, a new sense of excitement and beauty. She wanted to show him everything in the city—the parks, el Centro with all its stores, la Catedral, and the historical buildings and amazing architecture of a city that was almost four hundred years old. Tío Alvaro and Antonio rented rooms in a hotel for their stay in Juárez, as Alvaro didn't want to overcrowd his sister's house. Besides all that, it was cheap, he said, Christmas rates.

One afternoon, Antonio borrowed Alvaro's car and took Petra to el Sanborn, a big modern coffee shop that sold food, candy, books, birthday cakes, gifts, everything beautiful and arranged in attractive displays. Petra loved the smell of the coffee and the aroma of pastries baking. They sat together holding hands, eating club sandwiches, and drinking rich coffee sweetened with thick condensed milk. Juárez wasn't like Montenegro. They didn't have to worry that everyone would know them and report on their activities. For the first time, Petra was allowed to go out with Antonio alone, even though her father had said she could only go out during the day, to do shopping and walk around where there were crowds of people. Her newfound freedom made her giddy, and she wanted to hold onto Antonio and tell him over and over again how much she had missed him. She was conscious of Antonio's need for her. His desire to make love to her was like a vibration around him, a magnet that drew her closer.

Antonio lifted one of Petra's hands to his lips. "The sooner we get married, the better. If it were up to me, I'd marry you tonight, and we'd leave for Montenegro in the morning. Yes . . . tonight!"

Petra laughed to think how simply Antonio put things. She thought of returning to Montenegro with its lonely country roads and hard life, and wondered if she wasn't better off now that she worked in an office and made more money than she had ever imagined. She might even be able to save some of the money to pay her way to the university and get her degree.

She smiled at him, stroked his cheek, told him she loved him and that things would work out for them. His hands over hers were hot and sensual.

After their meal at el Sanborn, they walked together through the bustling streets of Juárez, which were decorated with strings of Christmas lights, every store warm and open. They walked arm in arm, laughing, making plans to buy everyone a gift. Antonio didn't mention to Petra that he had already bought her an engagement ring, with the wedding ring to match, for Christmas. He was planning a special night for them, when he'd take off the ring he had given her in Montenegro and place on her finger the ring he had a jeweler make especially for her—gold, with a fine silver design and a small solitary diamond.

Antonio felt as if he was floating on air as he walked next to Petra in her professional-looking clothes, sleek and sophisticated. He saw the way other men looked at him, envious that he had such a beautiful woman at his side. She made him feel proud, but nervous as well. What if he wasn't good enough for her now that she was a professional businesswoman? And worse, now that she was learning English. She seemed to have a strange power over him when she spoke English. It was as if he was uncouth and primitive next to her because he knew only Spanish. He was unsure how to deal with Petra as a woman who was now working and making a life in Juárez for herself apart from him, a woman feeling for the first time her own independence. Antonio had never worked in an office or attended staff meetings, and no one had ever told him he'd travel to other countries to do business for a big company. While the world held new promise for Petra, Antonio wasn't sure what it held for him.

As they walked around a street corner, they saw a man selling *El Diario*. On the cover was the story of two young women, murdered, their bodies discarded in las Lomas de Poleo. The girls had been buried for weeks in shallow graves dug into the sand. Their bodies had disintegrated, leaving mostly bones stripped of clothing, but still wearing shoes.

Petra turned away, feeling what she had felt when Tío Alvaro's car had entered Juárez—fear starting in the pit of her stomach, gripping at her, making her feel she would lose control. Antonio stopped in front of the man and took out money to buy the newspaper. All the while the man shook his head, saying over and over again that it was a shame women were being murdered in Juárez. He had lived in the city all his life and had never seen such violence.

"Don't buy it," Petra said helplessly. "There's nothing anyone can do about it."

Antonio looked at her in disbelief. "I want to know what's going on-this is serious!"

"Very serious, señor," said the man to Antonio. Then he looked over at Petra and, thinking she was Antonio's wife, said solemnly, "My advice to you is to take good care of your beautiful wife." A car horn honked, and the man rushed away to sell a newspaper to a passing motorist.

Antonio grabbed Petra's arm. "I'm having a long talk with your father," he said. "He must already know what's going on, and I for one will tell him that I'm ready to take you back to Montenegro as my wife. You're in danger here, and—"

Her heart racing, Petra interrupted him. Already she was anticipating her mother's weary face, looking up at her helplessly because there was nothing they could do but stay in Juárez.

"Antonio, please don't do that! My father's too ill; he's just had surgery. Try to understand—we have to stay here. He needs to continue his treatments, and it's my wages from la maquiladora my family's depending on. I can't go back! Later, yes, when my father's better."

Antonio looked at her sternly. "What are you telling me, Petra? You can't go back, or you *won't* go back? Which is it?"

"I can't go back right now," Petra said. But in her heart she knew that even if she could, she wouldn't go back, and that thought brought tears to her eyes.

That afternoon they shopped halfheartedly, with *El Diario* stuck into one of the plastic bags along with presents they had bought for Ester and Nico. Petra heard the bell toll at la Catedral and suggested they visit there and say a prayer. As they approached, they saw an old man pulling a long rope, ringing the bell over and over again. La Catedral was beautiful in the afternoon sun, its white walls reflecting back the last rays. There was a sign out on la Plaza stating that la Catedral had been founded in 1659 by Fray Garcia de San Francisco. Mass had just ended, and the candles at the altar had been extinguished, sending small swirls of smoky wax into the air. Antonio and Petra knelt down and held hands. It was all Petra could do not to cry as she asked La Virgen for her help with all her problems, and now with her engagement to Antonio, as he seemed to be angry with her for delaying their marriage.

When they walked out of la Catedral, Petra felt at peace holding Antonio's hand, grateful they had taken the time to pray together.

As they crossed the busy street, Petra saw Cristal in the distance, walking through the crowd wearing tight sleek pants and red spiked shoes. Petra looked around for Evita and didn't see her.

"Look at that!" Antonio said, pointing toward Cristal. "No wonder there are murders in Juárez! Look at the way these women dress. I hope I never catch you dressing like that," he said sternly.

Petra didn't have the nerve to tell him she knew who the woman was, and she was glad when Cristal disappeared into a crowd gathered outside a noisy cabaret.

25 In spite of their happiness as a couple, Antonio got moody and demanded Petra's attention. He was petulant if she said she had to stay a little late at work, or when he saw her busy doing her English homework. Petra wanted to shower him with attention, but found it difficult with her job and the English classes she took at la maquiladora.

As Christmas day approached, Gustavo Rios told Petra that she had been invited to a special Christmas party in El Paso for employees who were learning English and would be traveling to other maquiladoras in the future.

"What about Antonio? Can he come too?"

Gustavo hesitated before answering. "Well, yes, I suppose it will be all right. Others will be there—Humberto Ornelas and his wife—" Petra didn't let him finish.

"Humberto should tell his wife the truth! There's never been anything between us."

"We know that. He knows that. But his wife doesn't. And that's the source of the problem."

"Then I won't go to the party! I have nothing to say to either one of them."

Gustavo looked intently at Petra, and again she felt as if he was ready to interrogate her.

"Petra, I would like you to go—very much. There are people there that I think you should meet, people who can help you in your career. In fact, I've told them you will be there." Petra knew Gustavo was telling her in no uncertain terms that she must go. He had gotten her promoted to a position that other women envied. If it weren't for him, she'd still be on the assembly line working for next to nothing. Petra felt an impulse to tell Gustavo what she really thought of him—he had made her dependent on him, and she hated him for it.

"I'll see you there, right?" he said, leaning over her desk. "Vina Salcido and her husband are going—you can go with them. Not many office personnel are invited, but I made special arrangements for you."

Gustavo got so close to Petra she could smell his cologne and see the gold chain with the cross tucked under the collar of his shirt.

When Antonio drove to la maquiladora to pick up Petra after work, she told him she had to attend a Christmas party in El Paso. It would be a time for her to meet the owners of Western Electronics and others, people who might help her in the future. When she asked him if he would like to come, he told her he wasn't used to those kinds of parties, and what would he do while she celebrated with strangers? He imagined himself standing at her side like an idiot, watching her talk casually to people he didn't know. Maybe she'd even speak to American men in English, and he'd feel embarrassed when she had to explain that he didn't understand a word of English.

"I'm not from here. I don't know anyone who's going to that party. And what will I do while you're meeting all these people from la maquiladora? And what about *el* Humberto who was after you? I'm sure he'll be there too."

Antonio's voice was harsh when he mentioned Humberto's name, making "el" sound like the man was beneath him, undeserving of any respect. Petra regretted telling Antonio Humberto's name, after he had questioned her for hours, asking her to at least let him know the name of the man who was bothering her at la maquiladora in case he ever met him on the streets.

Petra felt her face flush with anger. "He means nothing to me! I already told you—"

Antonio cut her off, his voice rising. "I have plans to return with you to Montenegro so we can start our life there. Don't you remember, Petra, what we talked about? What do I care about these people. They mean nothing to me!"

"I can't go back, Antonio. You know that. My father's health isn't good, and what should I do? Abandon him now that I'm the one making the most money? As soon as he recovers, we'll go back."

Antonio took a sharp turn and picked up speed down a boulevard on their way to Nuevo Leon. Petra saw the city as a blur through the windows. Her heart pounded as she realized how angry she was with Antonio. He was hardheaded like her father, caprichoso, stuck in traditional ways.

"I don't want you to go to that party!"

Petra said nothing, only looked ahead at children riding on bicycles and others walking on the sidewalks or crossing the street. As the car rounded the corner into Nuevo Leon, Petra saw several boys, some Nico's age, standing out on a street corner. They were members of Los Trinquetes, a notorious gang from Nuevo Leon that got its name from the gold jewelry its members wore, trinkets—gold earrings, necklaces, and bracelets. The leaders had gold watches dangling at their waists.

"Look at that! What a mess. I tell you, if those pandilleros were in Montenegro, their fathers would come out on the street and beat them up publicly and take them home. But here, they stand where they want, do what they want, and get away with it. And how do you think they get all the money for the gold they're wearing? Drugs—they sell drugs for a living! Nico's still in danger—we're all in danger from these sin vergüenzas, who have no consciences or morals."

Antonio pounded the steering wheel angrily with one hand as he talked about Los Trinquetes. When they arrived at the house, Petra got out and slammed the car door behind her. She noticed her mother had put up a holiday wreath with a small electric candle glowing bright red at the window. She walked quickly up to the door, while Antonio got out of the car and called to her.

"I'm going back to the hotel! Alvaro needs his car back. I'll try to get back tonight."

Petra wanted to tell him not to bother coming back but didn't say a thing. She walked into the house alone, slamming the door and kicking off her shoes in anger.

Her mother was in the kitchen preparing dinner with Abuela Teodora. Her father was reading the newspaper in the living room and, noticing her abrupt action, looked up at her, Nico was watching a baseball game, while Ester did her homework at the kitchen table.

"Where's Antonio?" Flor asked.

"Gone."

"Gone? Where? I've made dinner for all of us."

"Ungrateful, is what he is," Estevan said angrily. "He should have at least walked in to greet us. Bad manners. Doesn't he know any better?"

"Tío Alvaro needs his car. He had to go return it."

"He should still have come in to greet us. What are you—a piece of baggage he can dump at the door? He lacks manners and common sense. I'm sure that's not what he learned from his parents."

Abuela Teodora looked at Petra closely. Petra sensed she knew everything.

"He'll be back," she said. "He's madly in love with you, poor man." She sighed and poured water into the coffeepot.

Petra felt Abuela Teodora's hand on her shoulder. Dawn was breaking over the horizon. A thin strip of white light appeared, making the sky turn gray. *Sing, Petra, sing to the morning*, Abuela Teodora whispered in her ear. Petra felt the warmth of the bed, sensing Ester's small body next to hers, and couldn't make herself get up. She hadn't slept well, thinking about Antonio and his anger over the Christmas party. Antonio had not returned to Petra's house and hadn't even called her on the phone to explain what had happened. Petra was worried he was doing what thousands of men did in Juárez—looking for a prostitute. There were plenty of zonas spread throughout Juárez, hundreds of prostitutes, and Tío Alvaro surely knew where they were. Abuela Teodora whispered again, hesitating, realizing Petra wouldn't get up.

"Sing for both of us," Petra said to her. "I'm too tired." She sensed

Abuela Teodora's sadness, but only pulled the blanket up to her chin, feeling her body a heavy stone.

Petra had been worrying all day. The Christmas party was on Saturday, and it was already Thursday. She was nineteen today and felt no different. Her problems had multiplied rather than lessened. She was afraid of facing Antonio, as he seemed to get gloomier by the day. To make matters worse, her father had joined with Antonio in telling her not to go to the party in El Paso. He had never trusted Gustavo Rios, he said, and he was rarely wrong about a person's character.

Petra's head throbbed with pain as she walked out of the office she shared with Vina Salcido and toward the front entrance. Across the street, she saw a man in a suit, tall and handsome, and she stared at him along with all the other women walking in and out of la maquiladora.

"It's Antonio!" Lola said, walking up to her. "He looks like a movie star, all dressed up. Are you going somewhere?"

"He's dressed up for my birthday," Petra said, as she hurried across the street to meet him. She hugged Antonio tenderly, kissing his cheek, holding onto his hand. She told him he looked like a real movie star, and they both laughed as they turned to wave good-bye to Lola standing across the street.

Amapola Nieto walked out in time to see Petra kissing Antonio and shook her head in dismay, telling another woman that Petra had no shame, making out with a man in front of everybody. She probably felt guilty, she said, after trying to break up Humberto's marriage, and was now trying to play the role of la inocente. Both women laughed out loud, and as they passed Lola, they rearranged their purses so she would have to step back to avoid bumping into them.

As they drove away, Antonio told Petra he had a surprise for her, and she guessed he'd give her an engagement ring. She knew her mother was up to something as well, because she had seen her buying extra food and noticed Abuela Teodora up early boiling meat and chopping up chilies and onions for salsa while she whispered prayers under her breath.

All at once Petra felt happy about her marriage and confused at the same time. In the back of her mind a thought appeared like a dark shadow forming, casting doubt on her happiness. Within seconds the thought had disappeared. She reached anxiously for Antonio's hand to steady herself, and he smiled, pleased with what he thought was a sign of affection.

Petra at his side, Antonio sat with Estevan and Flor, Tío Alvaro and Abuela Teodora, to ask Estevan for his daughter's hand in marriage. The traditional ways of Montenegro required this, and he knew that Estevan would expect nothing less. Estevan was sitting uncomfortably on a kitchen chair, smoking a cigarette and staring intently at Antonio. He had positioned himself sideways on the chair, protecting the side of his body with the missing kidney. It was as if he was still not used to something in his body not being there. Estevan scarcely had the strength to draw on his cigarette, yet he pretended he was perfectly well and looked at Antonio with all the manly strength he could gather. He finished the cigarette and put it out in the ashtray, then leaned unsteadily on the table. He already had the same symptoms as when his other kidney had given out on him, so he knew he could play no games with this man who loved his daughter.

"Señor de la Rosa," Antonio started slowly. "I am here tonight to ask for your daughter's hand in marriage. As you know, I'm deeply in love with her and would like to make her my wife."

The words were simply said but also formal and required a response. Estevan said nothing for a few seconds, staring blankly at Antonio as if seeing him from a long way off. Petra saw her father's lips quiver under his tattered gray moustache as if he would cry. He looked away from Antonio and cleared his throat.

"Yes, I think you will make a suitable husband for my daughter," he said. "I know you love her, as I love her mother. I want you to be happy. I want you to take care of my daughter, as I've taken care of her mother—as long as you can," he added, sighing heavily. He looked at his wife's weary face, saw her tears, and reached for her hand.

Antonio put his hand in his pocket, searching for the engagement ring he had hidden there.

"Close your eyes," he said to Petra, smiling.

Instinctively, Petra put her hand in his and closed her eyes. Antonio took off the ring he had given her in Montenegro and placed the new ring on her finger. Petra opened her eyes and looked at the new ring, gold, inlaid with silver and a small diamond shining brightly.

"Will you marry me, Petra. Te amo, deveras, I love you."

"Yes! I'll marry you."

Petra looked over at her family. Their cheeks were red from the warmth of the pot simmering on the stove, filling the house with the delicious smell of chile con carne, savory and spiced to perfection by Abuela Teodora. There were no boundaries between them; they were one family, and now Antonio had joined them.

Petra was crying for herself, for Antonio, for her parents, and for the things she couldn't control that seemed to weigh her down. In spite of her happiness, she felt herself buried under heavy burdens, as if the rabbit in her nightmare was ready to leap from the moon once again, crushing her under its weight.

Lola stopped by at Petra's birthday party for only a few minutes. Her children were over at her neighbor's, and she had to hurry to pick them up. She congratulated Petra on her engagement to Antonio and told her the ring was truly beautiful. The neighbors from next door, Cruz and her husband, came over with their little girl, Denise, who played with Ester. They were humble people who had made their way to Juárez from a small village in Sinaloa. They were glad to be invited to the celebration, as they had no family in Juárez.

Petra cut the cake for her nineteenth birthday, and everyone sang for her. The cake was thick with creamy frosting and rich layers drenched in sweet milk, tres leches, with fresh strawberries, Petra's favorite fruit, piled generously on top. Everyone clapped. Petra stood next to Antonio, their fingers intertwined, her engagement ring pressing against his flesh and hers. Already, she felt as if she was Antonio's wife.

That night Estevan toasted too many copas of tequila with Tío Alvaro. He got sick and wept until dawn over losing his daughter to Antonio.

Petra drove with Vina Salcido and her husband, Cayetano, to the Christmas party at a private home in El Paso. Vina and her husband picked her up at her house in a late-model gray Toyota with a hubcap missing. Vina had a special visitor's pass, signed by Gustavo Rios, that would let them through the border. Vina said she had been invited because her father knew the board members of la maquiladora, and he wouldn't be happy if he found out she hadn't been invited.

"And you, Petra? I guess you're being set up to do something important for la compania—who knows?" Then she laughed and elbowed her husband as if the thing Petra would be doing was something forbidden.

"I'm learning English—that's why I'm going. Señor Rios wants us to get to know the maquiladora in El Paso and meet the American bosses."

"Really? Then where are the other students from your class?"

Petra hadn't thought about the other students. "I hope they'll be there," she said.

"I doubt it. This pass was the only one Gustavo gave me, and they can't get in without it."

"Too bad your boyfriend didn't come," Cayetano said. "Now I'm alone with two women. But I'll get my consolation. There's wonderful food at these parties. Remember last year, Vina?"

"Oh yes, anything you can imagine. And people all over the place. You're about to meet the rich, those who don't know a day without some kind of luxury. I can't imagine such a life! Antonio should have come to keep an eye on you, Petra." She smiled and looked at her husband. "Right, Cayo?"

"True, so true—even though I'm only there for the food."

Petra thought of Antonio and the way he had looked at her when he saw her dressed up in a black gown, simple yet elegant. The dress was borrowed from Lola's sister, who told her to return it after the party because she had to wear it for a Christmas celebration the next day. Antonio was relieved to see that the dress completely covered Petra's full round breasts. The dress was sleeveless, exposing her arms, so Antonio told her to keep her shawl on. She wore a necklace of fake pearls at her throat and her hair swept up. Beautiful, he thought, and became angry with her all over again for going to the party without him.

"Come with me," she had pleaded with him, but he had ignored her and walked away.

Vina read Gustavo Rios's directions carefully to Cayetano. Cayetano was acquainted with El Paso from having worked at a resort in the downtown area when he was a teenager. But the house they were going to was not in the downtown area, but in the mountains somewhere, where the rich lived. As they got closer, Petra noticed the houses had become more like mansions, some as big as the houses of the richest families in

Juárez. Finally they climbed a hill, and Petra saw two rows of small lights, luminarios, leading around a circular driveway and up to the steps of a stately house with marble pillars and high glass windows. An immense Christmas tree glowed in the window. Suddenly she had a feeling in the pit of her stomach as if something inside her was out of control. She remembered she had had the same sensation when her family had first made their way into Juárez in Tío Alvaro's car—the feeling of something lurking, waiting for her. She was ready to ask Cayetano to please let her go back home, or wait for them in the car. Vina turned around and stared at her.

"You're pale, Petra! Stop being so nervous. I'll be with you the whole time. If there's any trouble, Cayo will fight for you—right, Cayo?"

"Oh yes, perfectly true. I didn't get trained as a boxer for nothing!"

"And to think, we brought this old car to a place like this," Vina said. "I'm glad it's dark. No one will notice it if we don't park it too close to the entrance."

The house was owned by Arnold Laverne and his wife, Fatima, who had been born in Juárez and now had American citizenship through her marriage. Inside the house were polished wood floors and oversized Mexican furniture, plush chairs, and fine woodwork. The Christmas tree was the biggest Petra had ever seen, and there were hundreds of presents set under it. Vina told her they'd be allowed to pick one of the presents from under the tree before they left. The instant they walked in, Petra commanded admiring looks from several men. When one of the waiters came up to her to take her shawl, Petra hesitated, remembering that Antonio had told her to leave it on. But Vina took off the wrap she was wearing and gave it to the waiter, so Petra did the same. "They're watching you," Vina whispered in her ear. "Some of these men are wolves in disguise!"

Petra was amazed by the tables piled high with hors d'oeuvres set on silver trays and decorated with Christmas garlands and tiny white lights. Bottles of fine liquor, beer, and tequila were set up next to crystal glasses, and waiters poured out whatever you asked for. Petra noticed that no other clerical staff and no students from her English class were present. She followed inches behind Vina and her husband Cayetano, afraid of losing them among the other guests.

The Lavernes were an elegant-looking couple, both in formal dress.

Arnold Laverne was tall and imposing, boisterous in nature compared to his slender dark wife, who stood stoically at his side.

"Welcome," Arnold said to Petra, lifting one of her hands to his lips. He caught his wife watching him and patted her arm affectionately, signaling her to converse with other guests standing nearby. Petra smiled at his wife, but the woman ignored her, her eyes suddenly mournful.

"Gustavo tells me you're learning English."

"I try," Petra said in English. "I have much to learn."

"Good," he said, nodding his head in approval before walking away to greet other guests.

Gustavo Rios arrived late, saying there had been an incident with someone ahead of him at the border. Everything had stopped until the border patrol sorted out the problem. Gustavo had brought his wife with him and a daughter about Petra's age, dressed in a gaudy purple dress. Petra had never heard Gustavo talk about his wife, and now she knew why. His wife looked older than he, a heavyset woman with frizzy black hair. But she was friendly enough and talked and laughed with everyone.

Humberto Ornelas was there with Bridget. She was everything everyone said she was—slender, haughty, and immaculately dressed. Petra instantly turned her back on Humberto when she saw him. His wife was hanging onto his arm and talking loudly as they moved around the room balancing their wine glasses in their hands.

Petra moved to a table with Vina and Cayetano, who had already started eating everything he could pile onto a small china plate. Petra was deciding what to take when a man walked in. Gustavo Rios rushed over to greet him along with Humberto Ornelas and many others. The man brought a presence into the room like a change in the weather. Petra could feel it from where she stood. The Lavernes were at his side, walking him in. The man was wearing a three-piece white suit with a red rose on his lapel. He was light complexioned, with light eyes and a muscular body that stopped short of being heavy. Petra noticed his hair, golden red under the lights. There was power emanating from the man that seemed to envelop everyone around him. She heard Vina whisper, "Madre mia! That's the new owner of la maquiladora. And he's alone! I tell you, if I wasn't married, I would go right up to him and introduce myself! He looks like a superstar, don't you think so, Petra?"

Petra only stared at the man, her arms prickling with goosebumps. She was surprised at her reaction and wanted to stop looking at him, but couldn't. Finally, she shook herself as if from a trance and picked up a plate to serve herself something to eat. Her hands were trembling as she put crackers on her plate, cheese, and a creamy dressing. After choosing a chocolate-covered strawberry, she dropped it on the floor. Her face turned red as she bent down to pick it up. with a napkin.

She noticed Gustavo Rios walking toward her with the man at his side.

"Here she is—the one I've told you about! My star pupil in English."

Petra looked up at the man and held her plate tightly so her fingers wouldn't tremble.

"This is Señorita Petra de la Rosa," Gustavo said to the man. "And this," he said to her, "is Agustín Miramontes Guzmán." The man looked deeply into Petra's eyes.

"Good choice," he said in perfect English as he looked at her plate. "I like chocolate-covered strawberries—even ones that have landed on the floor!" Then he laughed, and everyone laughed with him. Petra blushed and smiled awkwardly, feeling like a little girl stripped of a childish secret.

French Lace

26 Mayela couldn't stop thinking about Evita Reynosa and her promise to find Petra in exchange for the painting of the emerald butterfly. Already she saw herself traveling with Petra's family back to Montenegro and walking the short distance through the mountains to Chitlitipin. Even if her mother wasn't back from Puebla, she would find someone close by to stay with until her mother's return. Tía Concha hadn't stopped by to visit at Christmas, and Mayela had no idea if she would ever see the old woman again, or Cina and her children. She found it difficult to rid herself of the nightmares about Sebastian, his machete, and el Imán. And now new nightmares haunted her about the old Huichol, Narciso Odin, who was determined to find a way to make her his child-wife.

Narciso Odin wanted to possess Mayela more than he had wanted any other woman or child in his life. His lust for young women had gone unopposed for years in his colonia, Primer Lucero, and he was known to have fathered several children from young girls no older than Mayela. Mayela's paintings spoke to the old man secretly of things that people carried deep in their hearts: longings, fears, and rays of light that broke through the mind like waves of electricity. Her work made him feel powerful, as if he could fly into the sky like an eagle, while his lust, dark and evil, sank deep into his heart and gnawed at him like a disease. Night after night Narciso imagined himself a young man sitting under a sheet with Mayela, naked, in the old tradition of los Huichols who allow a young couple to explore their bodies while the wedding feast is still going on.

Narciso didn't come into Mayela's presence directly, but he found ways to give her small gifts—fruit, flowers, a book, her paints neatly arranged at her easel. He protected her from children who called her names, threatening to punish them in one way or another. Once, he left her a pair of earrings and a necklace and pretended someone else had sent them to her. Mayela refused his gifts and gave them away, or threw them in the garbage.

One of the children told Mayela that Narciso was a medicine man and could put a spell on her if she accepted anything from him. Mayela was afraid of magic and curanderos, remembering Sebastian's terrible worship of el Imán, and was now afraid Narciso had put an evil spell on her like Sebastian had put on Cina.

In her dreams, Mayela's twin brother, Popo, appeared over and over again, a tiny blue baby with pink wings and shiny yellow toenails. He smiled and told her she was stronger than Narciso and that Narciso's magic wouldn't work on her because he was there to protect her. He showed her a castle where he lived and a small golden key that fit into a lock. When he fit the key into the lock and turned the knob to open the door, Mayela saw a beautiful place filled with light and beauty such as she had never seen on earth. The dreams made Mayela strong. Before long she drew the castle and the golden key, and outside the door a snarling black wolf that chased her as she eluded its clutches.

Señora Juana del Pilar got a call from an employee of Gabriela LaFarge, who said she had been instructed to invite the young artist Mayela, also known as la Niñita Frida, to visit at her home in el distrito Villa de las Rosas. She said Gabriela LaFarge had heard of Mayela through a priest who was acquainted with the American doctor working with the children of el Instituto. Señora LaFarge was an aficionada of the arts and took pride in finding authentic native work and being the first to discover some unknown artist who would be a curiosity she could discuss in artistic circles. She found the child artist Mayela intriguing and invited her, as well as Señora Juana del Pilar and the American doctor, to visit at her estate.

After the call, Señora Juana del Pilar rushed into Doctora Silvia's office. "I've just received a call from one of the richest women in Juárez! She's interested in meeting Mayela!"

La doctora had her notebook out on a wooden table and was writing detailed accounts of the children she had treated at el Instituto, with the names of drugs she had used and how well the children had responded to the different medical treatments. It was a long list, as most of the children who came to el Instituto had serious health problems: cancer, polio, malnutrition, meningitis, heart conditions, dysentery, and a variety of problems with their skin, blood, lungs, and bones.

La doctora put her pen down and smiled. "So, our little Mayela's reputation as la Niñita Frida is spreading."

"It seems that Gabriela LaFarge found out about Mayela from one of the priests in the diocese, someone who knows Padre Octavio from la Catedral. So now our Mayela will get attention from the very rich. Can you imagine where this might lead her?"

"Yes, I'm acquainted with Padre Octavio. As a matter of fact, it was he who gave us permission to display Mayela's paintings in la Plaza." Doctora Silvia looked closely at Señora Juana del Pilar and knew she was already calculating how much money Gabriela LaFarge would bring into el Instituto.

"She lives in el distrito Villa de la Rosas—the most exclusive in all of Juárez. You and I are invited too!"

"Señora Juana del Pilar's face was bright, her voice childish, as she related that they'd be able to walk right into a house that she was sure looked like a palace. "I've never been in one of the houses of the rich! And now, for the first time, we'll have that opportunity. And for my orphans, this means so much."

"What about Mayela? Have you told her yet? She's been suffering, as you know. Something's disturbing her, and now she's waiting for someone she met in la Plaza, a young girl named Evita Reynosa, to get her in touch with her friend from Montenegro. Her wish, of course, is that her mother come to Juárez and take her home."

"Yes, every child wants to go home, and Mayela's no different," Señora Juana del Pilar said casually. She stood up to leave, determined not to let anything get in the way of her meeting with Gabriela LaFarge. "I'll go tell Mayela the good news and see what she says. It was my lucky day when she came to el Instituto!"

She disappeared down the hall to find Mayela, leaving Doctora Silvia shaking her head, wondering if all the attention Mayela was getting was good for her, considering all she really wanted was to go home.

27

The house looked like a palace in a fairy tale book. It was hidden from the street by a high block wall that circled the property, with coils of barbed wire slung over the top of the wall behind the house. A wrought-iron gate with a security man posted at a small guard station marked the back entrance to the house. The grounds were lush green with plants, trees, hedges, and flowers. El distrito Villa de las Rosas took its name from hundreds of flowers that grew there—exotic roses, some as high as ten feet, in all shades, bred and crossbred to perfection. As they approached the house in a taxi, Señora Juana del Pilar put down the car window so she could smell the rich fragrance of the flowers. As they turned into the driveway, the smell of gardenias reached them, an intoxicating smell that made Mayela feel dizzy. She was sitting in the backseat with Doctora Silvia, wearing a new dress, white lace with blue trim, that Señora Juana del Pilar had bought her for the occasion. Her braids were piled on top of her head, plaited with colorful ribbons.

Mayela was nervous about meeting Gabriela LaFarge, and she held tightly to la doctora's hand in the backseat, intertwining her fingers through la doctora's. Señora Juana del Pilar sat in the front seat talking excitedly to el chofer, telling him what a lucky day it was for all of them and what a splendid artist Mayela was. La doctora had taken photos of Mayela's paintings and had put them behind plastic covers in a photo album. In this way, she had made a portfolio of Mayela's work to show to Gabriela LaFarge.

As el chofer rounded the circular drive up to the marble steps, he was met by a security man with a gun visible at his hip.

"Are you bringing in the young artist, Mayela?"

"Yes."

"And these ladies?"

"They've been invited as well."

The man made a call from a walkie-talkie. The person who answered said, yes, they had all been invited and bring them in through the side door. El chofer asked the man if he should wait for them until the visit was completed or come back to pick them up. The security man called again, and the person inside said el chofer should go home—the women would be driven back in one of the family's cars.

Listening to the conversation from the man with the gun at his hip made Mayela start to sweat. Her hands felt numb and her legs as loose as rubber bands.

La doctora looked at her kindly. "Mayela, it's okay." She stroked her hand and smiled. "We'll be together—don't worry."

A woman wearing a gray dress with a lacy collar and a crisp white apron opened a side door and motioned them to come in. They walked into a hallway lit by chandeliers, white tiles gleaming brightly. To the right was an enormous sitting room with rich carpeting and tapestries. An elaborate fireplace with an ornate brass mantelpiece was at one wall. Hanging over the brass mantelpiece was a coat of arms in the shape of a sculpted plaque in silver and gold that looked like it belonged to the king of Spain. There was a name on it written in script, unreadable from a distance. The design on the plaque was a gold cross held together by two silver swords.

The woman showed them into a smaller room whose walls were lined with ornate bookshelves. The room's French doors opened to a pleasant patio, where Mayela stared in wonder at a gurgling fountain, with water flowing gracefully from a three-tiered spout. She found a seat next to la doctora on a silk-covered loveseat embroidered with tiny white blossoms. Señora Juana del Pilar sat opposite them in an overstuffed wing chair, close to a polished grandfather clock that chimed on the hour. Besides the birds chirping and the grandfather clock ticking away, the room was very still. On the walls were portraits of family members, ancient ancestors, unsmiling and pompous, all resembling faces of Europeans Mayela had seen in magazines.

The woman who had led them in arranged coffee for them on a shiny round table and juice for Mayela. There were fancy cookies and small powdered cakes arranged on colorful glass plates. Chocolate mints were piled high on a silver tray shaped like a pedestal.

"Estan en su casa," the woman said courteously. "Help yourselves. La señora is still getting ready and should be down any moment."

After the woman left the room, la doctora got up and walked over to the bookshelves, reading off titles and remarking on the family's excellent taste in books. Mayela listened to the titles, proud of her newfound ability to read. La doctora moved away from the books to study an image of Saint Francis of Assisi, a huge figure sculpted to the size of a real man, with birds on his shoulders and a wolf at his feet.

"Marvelous," she said. "Simply marvelous. I wonder where she got this?"

"The statue is from Oaxaca," a woman's voice answered from the doorway, speaking Spanish with a French accent. "It's made of a very light wood, like birch or something similar. It's carved in such a way that it can be carried on men's shoulders in procession. Mexicans are fond of processions—don't you agree?"

"Yes. I've seen processions in my travels all over Mexico."

"Mucho gusto." La doctora walked up to Gabriela LaFarge and shook her hand, while Mayela and Señora Juana del Pilar stood in silence.

Gabriela LaFarge was a tall slender woman, her skin pale, translucent. Her dark auburn hair fell smooth and glossy down to her shoulders, and her eyes flashed a turquoise green. She was wearing a simple white dress, soft and flowing to her ankles, and on her feet sandals with golden straps. Her slim body showed a protruding belly under her dress.

As the woman walked in, Mayela picked up the fragrance of a wonderful perfume, fresh, aromatic. She stood up as Señora Juana del Pilar had told her to, and Gabriela LaFarge walked up to her and embraced her tenderly in greeting.

"And this, oh yes, this is la Niñita Frida! Are you the famous artist, Mayela?"

Mayela was speechless for a few seconds, then responded. "Sí, yo soy Mayela—at your service."

"And you are so welcome in my home! Bienvenida!" The woman smiled broadly. "You're everything I thought you would be! We must take a picture together to prove to my family that I do have friends among the native people. They would be so surprised!"

Then she turned to Señora Juana del Pilar and walked toward her with her hand extended in greeting. "And you must be Señora Juana del Pilar. Yes, it's a pleasure. I've heard of your work with the orphans of Juárez. Please, all of you, make yourselves comfortable." Gabriela sat with Mayela on the flowered couch.

"Take all you want of these desserts," she said, gesturing toward the cakes and chocolate mints. "They're for you, Mayela. In fact, take them all if you'd like to share them with your friends at el Instituto. My husband loves desserts, so the more you take with you, the less he'll have to eat. He can do with less sugar." She joined Mayela as she shyly reached for a chocolate mint. The mint was rich chocolate with a soft creamy center. When Mayela put one in her mouth, it melted on her tongue, filling her mouth with flavor so rich, she smiled broadly at all of them.

"Gracias, señora, these are very good!" Gabriela smiled, amused at Mayela's first taste of French chocolate.

Doctora Silvia sat down and reached into her satchel, bringing out the photos of Mayela's work for Gabriela LaFarge. She explained that Mayela's talent had taken them all by surprise.

Gabriela leafed through the album slowly, saying that everything she saw was marvelous, esplendido, intenso. She shook her head and said she couldn't believe they had been painted by Mayela at such a young age.

"And which one is your favorite, Mayela?"

"The emerald butterfly."

Gabriela turned to the photo of the painting, and said she agreed—yes, it was perfect. "It would look beautiful in this house," she said. "We have other houses, but I think this painting would be perfect for this house—don't you agree?'

"I am sorry, señora," said Mayela. "It's already sold." Gabriela LaFarge looked up at Señora Juana del Pilar.

"Sold—to whom?"

"I don't know," Señora Juana del Pilar stuttered, unable to understand why Mayela had made such a claim.

La doctora spoke up. "Mayela is saving it for a young girl she saw in la Plaza. The girl knows a friend of Mayela's from her village, and she wants to give it to her. She's anxious, you know, to find her mother, and this girl says she's acquainted with people from Montenegro who know her mother."

Gabriela smiled reassuringly. "Yes, that's fine—a good idea to want to go home. You see, I'm far from my home. I was born in Paris. That's where I met my husband, Agustín Miramontes Guzmán. He'll be a father soon, as you can see."

"When is your baby due?" la doctora asked her.

"Oh, I still have a ways to go—I'm five months along, but already I feel as if I've been pregnant half my life. Agustín is so excited about the baby. Of course he wants him born here in Mexico—and won't allow me to go to Paris except to visit. So I come back as quickly as I can, because he's afraid I might get it into my head to stay and have the baby born a French citizen. Oh, he wouldn't like that!"

Gabriela stared at the photo of the painting of the castle and the tiny golden key, the blue angel and the snarling wolf outside the door.

"This one looks like a nightmare. Is it a nightmare?"

Mayela didn't answer. She couldn't explain the painting to this woman, who would never understand her fear of Narciso and Sebastian.

"Mayela paints from her imagination," la doctora told her. "Sometimes she can't explain things, but can only feel them."

"There's danger in some of her paintings, and then there's this little angel. Very strange."

Mayela said nothing.

"Artists, I guess, don't have to explain their work. They have the right to remain mysterious. I was thinking maybe the murders in Juárez had made Mayela afraid and were inspiring her to paint this way." She looked closely at Mayela. "Are you afraid of the murders? Many women are, and it wouldn't be abnormal. Wouldn't you agree?" she asked la doctora.

"Yes. Women of all ages are beginning to feel the danger in this city. They've uncovered more bodies of women, and still no one has been charged with the murders."

"Is this about the murders?" Gabriela asked Mayela, pointing to the painting of the wolf.

"I don't know—no, I guess not."

"But you're safe at el Instituto, and you mustn't worry about a thing."

"Yes, she's safe with us," Señora Juana del Pilar said, trying to sound confident, erasing from her mind doubts about Mayela's strange behavior around Narciso Odin. He was a bothersome old man, and maybe Mayela had had enough of his snooping around at her paintings and giving her special attention. She made a mental note to give Narciso more work outdoors to get him out of Mayela's way, or get rid of him entirely. She wanted nothing to stand in the way of Mayela's paintings and the money she might be able to make selling them in Mexico and abroad.

Before ending the visit, Gabriela picked up a framed photo from a nearby table. It showed her posing in an elaborate room, wearing a white gown with fine French lace at the neckline, outlining her full breasts. The dress was trimmed with pearls and rhinestones, and on the hem was a row of embroidered white lilies with long golden stems.

"This dress was my husband's grandmother's, then his mother's, and now mine. I wore it for my engagement party in Paris. It was made by a famous French designer. Maybe someday you can paint it—a portrait of me in this dress. Would you do that for me, Mayela?"

"It would be an honor, señora."

"Here, take it. I have many photos of me wearing this dress, but no paintings."

Mayela was enchanted with Gabriela LaFarge. She stood next to her, nodding at everything she said, and already saw in her mind the beautiful painting she could make of the photo.

As they walked out, Doctora Silvia asked Gabriela about the name inscribed on the coat of arms hanging over the fireplace.

"The name is that of my husband's family—Cortés Miramontes Guzmán—but they haven't used the name Cortés for hundreds of years. A tragedy, all the loss of lives and the slavery of the Indians by the Spaniards for centuries—don't you agree?"

The three women agreed with Gabriela LaFarge that the story of the Indians was indeed a tragic one. Mayela shivered and reached for la doctora's hand as she walked by the coat of arms bearing Cortés's name.

The Emerald Butterfly

28 Evita was convinced she had been assaulted at the private party, not only by the man with the slanted eyes but by others as well. There were purple bruises all over her body and teeth marks on her breasts, neck, and thighs. In the morning, she had found herself sleeping in a long T-shirt, her red dress and shoes lying in a heap on the floor. Her lips were bloody, and one side of her face ached, as if someone had punched her hard. Images flashed into her mind: the elaborate room, dark red lights, the older man with the slanted eyes forcing himself on her, the drink he offered with pink foam in a spiral glass, Cristal dancing on stage and opening her legs for a man who had sex with her, and the policeman telling her to get back in the room. She remembered the beautiful girl wearing the exquisite gown looking at her helplessly and el Junior next to the girl, his hair a red haze in the dim room. A shudder ran through her as she thought el Junior, or someone like him, might have been the important person Isidora had wanted her to meet. Finally, she remembered hearing Rudy, Cristal's boss at el Club Exotica, telling someone to pick her up and take her outside.

Evita dragged herself to the bathroom to throw up and relieve herself of the nausea that had come over her. She looked at her arms and noticed the pattern of red blotches appear, as the invisible spikes surfaced like sharp daggers and made her skin burn with pain. She was aware of drifting in and out of a dark tunnel, and she wondered if the whirlwind she was sensing would suck her in so far she'd never crawl out alive. There was a part of Evita that wanted to sink deep into the tunnel and rest, tucked away, have peace, care about nothing. And there was another part of her that was alive, legs twitching and hands shaking, that made her think about living.

Evita was drawn out of the dark tunnel by a loud knock. Someone was pounding on the door and wouldn't stop. She heard a man's voice demanding that she open the door. She tried to ignore him, thinking it was Maclovio returning to fight with Cristal. Now she knew Maclovio's suspicions about the private parties were correct. She looked at Cristal's bedroom door and saw it was shut. She didn't know if Cristal was still sleeping or if she had spent the night somewhere else. Evita got up slowly, struggling to walk, as her head spun in circles and her vision blurred.

"Who is it? I won't open the door if you don't tell me who you are," she mumbled. Dark shadows formed in front of her eyes, black clouds that made her blink hard and hold onto the wall for balance.

"Open the door!" someone was shouting at her, and finally she did.

It was Reynaldo standing there, ready to break the door down. Evita looked at her brother, transfigured by the bright sunshine around him, and collapsed to the floor.

Later, Evita claimed it was Reynaldo who had saved her from dying that day. The level of drugs in her body had been dangerously high, and he had taken her to a nearby clinic where she was treated for an overdose.

Reynaldo knew his sister was in trouble when he found out she was living with Cristal. Cristal's reputation on the streets and her friendship with violent men were something he understood only too well. El chofer who helped Reynaldo before had alerted him in El Paso, telling him Evita had gone with Cristal to a private party. El chofer was still hoping that his service to Reynaldo would result in a job in los Estados Unidos.

Reynaldo had asked permission to leave his job at the golf course in El Paso. It was Sunday, and a busy day at the golf course, as there was a tournament going on. His boss was angry with Reynaldo and let him go only reluctantly, telling him this was the only "emergency leave" he would ever get.

"Now, you see, my job may be at stake," he told Evita as they left the clinic together. "Los gabachos don't care. They want their tournaments to be perfect. And all because you did what I told you not to do! I told you to go to Lety's house, and you deliberately disobeyed me. And where would you be if I hadn't found you?"

"Dead." Evita's voice sounded to her like an echo—a thing carried by the wind briefly, then it faded away. She still thought it might have been better for everyone if she had just died.

Reynaldo helped Evita gather her things into plastic bags and an empty box he found in the apartment. Cristal was gone. Reynaldo walked by her bedroom, opened her door, peered in, and saw her clothes scattered on the floor. The room smelled like the Cristal he remembered, sweet gardenias. She drove him crazy when she was Evita's age, and he spent many nights with her, amazed by her beautiful body and repulsed by knowing that what she was giving to him she was giving to others.

It's a wonder she hasn't been killed, he thought, and counted himself lucky to have been one of the first men who had ever slept with her. He said nothing to Evita, only closed Cristal's bedroom door and tried to forget the memory of her childish tender embraces and her warm body over his.

By the middle of January 1996, Evita was living at Lety's house. Reynaldo had given Lety money for Evita to live at her house, and that's what finally convinced Lety's husband, Julio, to let her stay. Julio worked for a concrete company and came home so tired he could barely put one foot in front of the other. He worked from dawn to dusk to make enough money to pay the rent on the tiny house they lived in, which had only four rooms. Evita stayed away from Julio, but still he tried to talk to her through Lety.

"I can only imagine what Evita went through in la Zona del Canal," he said to Lety, who was sitting on the couch with her big belly protruding under her clothes. "With all the murders of women going on—she's lucky she's still alive! And look at her . . . she's a mess. I tell you, Lety, you're lucky to be married and not living a life like your sister lived on those streets." Then he whispered, with Evita only a few feet away watching TV with Joselito and Milito. "Your brother is too kind; he should have beaten her until she couldn't get up. That's the way to stop a woman who wants to run around like a whore."

Evita let Joselito and Milito play with the pink stuffed bear Ricardo had given her. It didn't matter to her anymore that they got the bear dirty and tore off its red plastic heart. She hadn't seen Ricardo for months, and his memory was fading like the purple bruises on her body.

Lety's neighbor, a woman named Rosario, told Lety she had been ill and unable to work at her job in a small flower shop. She had cancer, she said, and now doubted she'd ever return to the flower shop. She told Lety the job might be something Evita could do, if she was a good worker and could learn to create floral arrangements for funerals, weddings, and other special occasions.

"Evita's perfect for the job," Lety said confidently to Rosario. Then she began to worry. Evita had never accomplished anything in school, and what would happen if she couldn't follow simple instructions? Then Rosario would look bad for recommending a girl who was so stupid she couldn't do a thing right. But Lety knew that the money Evita would make at the flower shop would help support her family, and Julio wouldn't be so mad at her for taking her in if he knew she was bringing in some money. She told Rosario she'd tell Evita about the job, and she was sure there would be no problem.

Rosario stopped by the next day and explained to Evita how to get to the flower shop, which was located in el Centro. She told her to talk to the owner, Jazmin, and explain that she had recommended her for the job. Evita rode on la rutera for over twenty minutes until she got closer to the center of Ciudad Juárez, close to los mercados and Cuauhtémoc Square. She saw la Plaza and la Catedral, and instinctively she looked around for Ricardo and for her mother perhaps walking to one of the stores with her merchandise. Every police car signaled danger for her. She knew that handcuffs could be put on her, and she could be taken away in broad daylight, assaulted by the police, maybe even raped before it was all over. By the time anyone found her, it would be too late. El Instituto de Niños Huerfanos was close to la Catedral, and that reminded her of Mayela. She resolved to call Yvone, Luis Ledezma's sister, to find out if they knew where to find her cousin, Petra. Yvone had told her that her brother was in love with Petra, and Evita was sure he would know where to find her.

After getting off la rutera, Evita quickly spotted the small flower shop with its pink doors open to the street, Flores de Jazmin. She walked inside and found Jazmin at the back of the shop working on a flower arrangement. The woman's long droopy face looked sad, like a flower that had wilted in the sun. She looked Evita over, and told her she was terribly skinny and small. How old was she anyway? Evita lied and said she was fifteen, almost sixteen, but looked younger because of her size.

"You're the smallest fifteen-year-old I've ever seen in my life! Did you have a quinceañera for your fifteenth birthday?"

"Oh, yes! A big one. My mother gave me a celebration—it lasted all night."

Jazmin didn't say anything, only turned away and walked out to the patio to fill a vase with water at a nearby sink.

Evita looked around the shop, noticing flowers of all colors stuck into buckets of water with long leafy stems supporting delicate blooms. She inhaled the fragrant scent of flowers, moist earth in potted plants, and a vanilla fragrance that filled the air. On shelves against a wall, she saw ribbons, bows, ceramic decorations, ornaments, photos, and cards. Evita wanted to work there more than she had ever wanted anything in her life, but she was afraid Jazmin would not hire her because of her age. She had managed Cristal's accounts and knew she could help Jazmin with that too, but she didn't want to tell her she had lived with prostitutes in la Zona del Canal and been responsible for their care. Jazmin was scrubbing a stained enamel sink with a brush, ignoring Evita.

"You might have known my mother, Brisa Reynosa?"

Jazmin looked up at Evita. "Was that the same woman who had a child who was an albino?"

"The very same one."

Jazmin stared at Evita with curiosity. "So, you're her daughter . . . It was sad, the death of your little brother. And how's your mother now?"

"Very well, and still working at her needlepoint. I used to help her with it—I mean I helped her create all her patterns. It was easy for me. I'm good at art. If you hire me—"

Jazmin interrupted her. "Come back tomorrow by eight in the morning, and don't even think of being late!"

She had decided to hire Evita, but not because Evita had designed patterns for her mother. Jazmin had suffered just as Brisa Reynosa had, when one of her own children had drowned in a canal.

29 Every day, Jorge visited Evita at Jazmin's flower shop. He was tall, ruddy, and athletic. He played soccer at la prepa, where he took classes that would prepare him for the university. He told Evita she should go back to school, make something of herself, prove herself to the world. He worked part-time for one of the restaurants close by and saw Evita one day on his way to work. He was

intrigued by Evita, because she was quiet and delicate looking, like one of the flowers she shaped into wreaths and arranged in vases and bouquets. Sometimes Jorge was tempted to put a rose in Evita's hair, just to see how she'd look. He wanted to put his arms around her, lift her up, kiss her, and never let her go. The more he thought about her, the more he wanted her, and his nights were spent dreaming about her, imagining himself making love to her. Evita ignored him, but the more she ignored him the more Jorge sought to attract her attention. It was as if her rejection was food for his soul.

Evita was uncomfortable with Jorge, as he reminded her of Ricardo somehow. His mannerisms, the affectionate way he had with her, and his constantly wanting to be with her began to drain Evita of her energy. She was on edge when he was in the flower shop, and kept her eyes on him, afraid he would sneak up on her and kiss her, maybe even caress her breasts like Ricardo had done.

One day Jorge convinced Evita to walk with him down to the restaurant where he worked and get something to eat. He promised her he'd cook something special for her, and the treat would be on him. She walked with him out into the street, conscious of his tall confident stride and the way he leaned toward her every time he said something to her. Just before they reached the restaurant, she saw a familiar figure in the distance. She looked again to make sure it wasn't a nightmare she was having in the middle of the day, then felt an urge to run for her life. Ricardo was walking toward them, and next to him was a woman with long straight hair caught up in two blue barrettes, like something a child would wear, pinned on each side of her head. The woman was pushing a stroller with a baby in it, and beside her walked a little girl with her hand on the woman's arm. The woman was not much taller than Evita, yet round and plumb, her shoulders square, her breasts blending into the bulge of her belly. When the little girl saw Jorge, she ran ahead toward him. Evita then realized this was Jorge's family. Ricardo, dressed in work clothes and boots, looked haggard, as if he had been working all day long in the sun and hadn't even had time to go home and change his clothes. When she saw him up close, a jolt of electricity ran through her body. Instantly, she remembered their lovemaking and the times she had lain naked in his arms, the sweet smell of his body next to hers, his kisses, sometimes salty, over her lips.

"There's my family," Jorge said. Evita stopped walking, her feet frozen, her skinny legs suddenly stiff. It was too late for her to turn and run; Ricardo and his wife and children had already reached them.

"Don't be nervous, Evita. They're good people. Papá y Mamá, I would like to present to you Evita Reynosa."

Ricardo's wife greeted Evita with a smile, her broad hand extended, while Ricardo stood next to her in silence staring at Evita.

"Mucho gusto," she said. "Do you work at the restaurant?"

"No—I don't work there."

"She works at the flower shop," Jorge said. "She makes beautiful designs—you should see her work!"

Ricardo didn't take Evita's hand, only mumbled that he was glad to meet her. Then he told his son that his soccer coach had called to say he must get to practice, as there was a big game tomorrow.

"You need to get home so you can change and get out on the soccer field," he told his son. "Now!" he said impatiently, motioning for Jorge to start walking with them.

Evita pretended to pay attention to the baby in the stroller and asked Ricardo's wife how old he was.

"He's seven months old, but looks bigger because he eats day and night!"

Evita looked at him and remembered the marble-sized baby that had lived in her womb—Ricardo's baby. In her mind, she could see her baby's white microscopic body and its black pinpoint eyes. He was flying now in heaven, like the blue angel she had seen in Mayela's paintings—happy and free. Evita knew she'd never tell Ricardo about the baby she had lost—she would never give him the pleasure of knowing how much he had hurt her. She hugged Ricardo's baby and kissed his cheek, and the baby smiled at Evita. He was friendly and tried to get out of his stroller and into her arms.

"No, Tomás, she belongs to me!" Jorge said to the baby. Evita looked up at Jorge, wondering why he had said that. She noticed Ricardo glaring at her, and it made her angry. She should be glaring at him for all the lies he had told her, how he loved her and they would never be apart. And what if he knew he had gotten her pregnant—now, that would be something to tell his wife! Evita didn't feel like she had before, when she had walked the streets of Juárez looking for him, her legs aching, her heart broken.

"You have to go to practice," Evita told Jorge, "and I have to get back to the flower shop."

"No! I want you to go with me to the practice. You can wait for me—it won't take long. Please, Evita!"

Jorge's little sister held onto his hand. "She's pretty," she said, and Jorge smiled.

"If you'd like, you can come to the house to have dinner after the practice," Ricardo's wife said. "We're humble, but the food is good."

Ricardo looked hard at his son. "She just told you she can't go to your practice. She needs to get back to her job. Let's go!" And he ushered his son away, his hand pressed tightly into Jorge's arm.

Early the next morning Ricardo stopped by the flower shop. When Evita saw him through the window she wanted to run out the back door. She knew he was angry at her, and she didn't want any trouble at the shop. Jazmin had gone to los mercado to do her morning shopping and would be back soon.

Ricardo walked in boldly. Evita noticed he looked older, as if he had aged and gotten fat and sloppy since the last time she had seen him. His hair had grayed, and his moustache was overgrown, drooping raggedly over his lower lip. He held no attraction for her anymore. In fact, she wondered what she had ever seen in him and felt her face burn with shame.

Ricardo leaned menacingly across the counter where Evita was working on a flower arrangement. Her hands started shaking as she felt his hot breath on her face. She continued to work without looking up at him, meticulously trimming stray leaves off long-stemmed roses to show off the bright red blooms.

"I don't want you to see my son—ever again!" Ricardo's words were harsh, sounding like he was hissing at her, ready to strike.

His voice ignited anger in her. She put the scissors down on the counter, aware that they were pointed toward him.

"Tell him to stay away from me! I don't want anything to do with him!"

"I don't believe you! You're a liar, una puta—that's what you've turned into. Remember me, Evita? Do you remember? Where did I pick you up—where? At Isidora's, another puta who runs a business for whores like you."

Then he bent down and whispered close to her ear, and Evita smelled cigarettes on his breath, stale and bitter.

"You went to bed with me, and YOU—WILL—NOT—TOUCH—MY—SON!" He said the last words with force, as if he was slamming his fist into each word.

Evita stepped away from him, the scissors back in her hand. "I don't want your son! He's the one who can't stay away from me. Like his father—do you remember?"

"Why don't you use those scissors to cut yourself again, Evita?" Ricardo said. "You were right the first time. You deserve to die!"

Evita gripped the scissors tightly and thrust them toward Ricardo. He flinched and was reaching across the table to wrestle the scissors from her hand when Jazmin walked in, her hands filled with packages. Evita was trembling, her skin turning into the red blotches that betrayed her pain. She let the scissors drop on the counter and shook her hand out, as if the scissors were a stick of dynamite that had burned her fingers. Ricardo walked out past Jazmin and into the street without another word.

"Is something wrong?" Jazmin asked. "That man looked like he was upset."

"No—nothing wrong. He's upset because his wife died. He wanted to buy her something special and couldn't make up his mind. He'll be back."

Jazmin looked around at all the arrangements Evita had created and clapped her hands in approval.

"Fiestas are forever in Mexico," she said, smiling, "and someone is always in need of flowers."

She walked happily to the back room with her shopping bags and didn't notice Evita's face wet with tears.

Lety went into labor late one Sunday night, and Julio called in la partera for the delivery. The woman said she'd come by in a few hours, as she was busy delivering another baby. Julio told the woman he couldn't miss work on Monday; his company had a job to do on a stretch of highway outside of Ciudad Juárez, and the job had to be completed in less than a month. He was hoping the baby would be born before he had to leave for work at 4:30 Monday morning. He told Lety he'd have to live at the work site in tents that the company would set up for them until the job was done. Evita was glad when she heard Julio had to leave. She told Lety she'd handle everything. Julio would not be back until the baby was over a month old, and that would help because the baby wouldn't cry so much and Lety would be feeling much better. Before he left, Julio spoke to Evita for the first time since she had come to live at his house. His voice was formal, cautious.

"Here's some money for Lety and the children. Use it to buy food and the things they need. If there are any problems, I'll leave the phone number of the company with you. And, of course, call when the baby's born." He handed her a wrinkled envelope. "Don't lose it," he said, looking firmly into her eyes. "Or you'll have to replace it with your own money."

The baby didn't come before 4:30 in the morning. Julio left feeling the cool breeze of morning on his face. He breathed deeply of the moist air and smiled as he looked up at the stars shining overhead. He felt like a free man, ridding himself of all the burdens of his family—his wife's moans and complaints, the boys crying, and Evita in the house sitting around like an angel, tempting him with her skinny white body. He had never dared to talk to Evita or approach her in any way, as he knew the next step would be to take her to bed to find out what she had learned on the streets. Sometimes when he made love to Lety, Julio imagined it was Evita. He held her tightly, feeling his blood rushing through his body, sensing himself a teenager again, until Lety told him he was crushing the baby inside her and if he didn't stop she would scream.

All night long Julio had smelled the fluids from Lety's body mixed with the blood she was expelling, a heavy, pungent odor, and now he was glad his child's birth would take place without him. He hoped Evita would learn a lesson when she saw Lety delivering the baby and stop running around like a whore on the streets of Juárez.

Evita called Cleotilde, her mother's neighbor, to tell her to give her mother a message that Lety was in labor, but having problems. La partera showed up and was confused about what to do next. It was a difficult birth, she said, and Lety didn't have the strength to deliver the baby. There was nothing left to do but take Lety to the hospital to get help from a doctor. When Evita called the flower shop to explain to Jazmin what was happening, Jazmin told her to take care of her sister, as she understood what it meant to bear children. God knows, she had delivered two by cesarean.

Evita was standing at Lety's side when she finally delivered her baby after seven grueling hours of hard labor. The doctor had to come in and cut into Lety to allow the baby's head to emerge. After that, Lety was able to deliver a baby girl, beautiful, with dark curly hair, pink skin, her black eyes open wide and her lips a tiny dot on her face. Lety named her Evelina.

Brisa arrived at the hospital right after Evelina's birth. Her first granddaughter was wrapped in a pink blanket and resting peacefully in Evita's arms.

"She's so beautiful! I can hardly believe it," she said to Evita. There were tears in Brisa's eyes as she remembered the births of her girls. "Your father was standing by my side when you were born, so proud of you, and now look—I haven't seen him in years, and he doesn't even know he has a beautiful granddaughter!"

Brisa took the baby in her arms, holding her tenderly, amazed at the baby's beauty. She didn't scold Evita for living on the streets, as she assumed she had been staying with Lety the whole time. In fact, she was grateful to Evita for the care she had given her sister and for having a job at the flower shop. In her mind, Evita was finally growing up, and maybe she'd get married someday and have children of her own.

As Evita watched her mother with the baby, she saw that she truly loved her newborn granddaughter. She sat down on a nearby chair and closed her eyes briefly, weary from staying up all night with Lety and now feeling a terrible dark sensation rise in her body with her mother sitting close by—the memory of sleeping with Ricardo. It was a secret Evita was prepared to carry to her grave, and she counted it a blessing that she had not borne his baby.

"She looks so much like you did, Evita, when you were born! Oh, she's so beautiful. I can hardly wait to start making her dresses like I used to make for you—do you remember?"

"Yes, I remember." In the back of Evita's mind was the memory of her mother standing her up on a chair to measure her for a dress and trying pieces of material on Evita's light skin to see which one would look the prettiest.

Brisa gave the baby back to Lety and handed Evita a package.

"Open it. I think you'll like it. I thought of you when I bought it, and

I—" Brisa was ready to tell her daughter she was sorry for kicking her out of the house, but she couldn't say the words. She wasn't accustomed to apologizing to anyone for the things she did wrong. She only brushed away her tears.

Evita opened the package and found a brown leather purse inside, shiny and beautiful, with a strap for her shoulder and a golden clasp in the shape of a butterfly that seemed to spread its wings each time the purse was opened and shut.

"I remembered the big butterfly you drew when you were in school. It was so beautiful, and you colored it so brightly. I hung it on the wall—do you remember?"

Evita started to cry as she looked at the gift, remembering what Cristal had said to her. Men would come and go in her life, but her mother would remain forever.

The next day, Jorge came to see Evita at the flower shop as soon as he got out of school. He said Jazmin had told him about Lety having a baby and that he was happy about it. He gave Evita a package, wrapped beautifully in pink foil with a big pink bow to match.

"Pink is for girls, blue is for boys," he said, smiling. "Here, take it."

Evita was cutting pieces of ribbon with scissors and pretending to be very busy. She barely looked at Jorge when he talked to her. After seeing her mother and making peace with her, Evita was more determined than ever to close the door on Ricardo's son.

"Evita, are you listening? Look at me. Don't you care? It's for the baby."

Evita paused in her work and looked at the pink package. She knew that whatever it was, it would help Lety and Evelina. Yet, there was a part of her that wanted to yell at Jorge, scream at the top of her lungs, that he was to leave her alone.

"Take it, Evita; it's for the baby," he said. He put the present in her hands. "Please, Evita."

Evita looked closely at his face and saw the pain she was causing in his eyes. She was attracted to him and wanted nothing more than to treat him like her boyfriend, but the truth about his father would be too much for him to bear.

"Evita, what have I done to you? Why do you treat me this way, when all I want is to be near you. I don't want to hurt you . . . I—"

Panic gripped Evita's mind. Jorge sounded just like his father. She put down the scissors she had threatened his father with and looked up at him angrily.

"I don't want any trouble with anybody! My parents are very strict with me. I can't have any boyfriends. You're making things very hard for me, and if you keep coming here, I may lose my job."

"I don't want you to lose your job, and I don't want your parents to be angry. I don't know how to leave you alone. You mean so much to me, more than anyone else I've ever known."

Evita heard Jazmin in the back room calling for her, and she told Jorge that she had work to do—maybe they'd talk after she got off work. She noticed a look of joy come over Jorge's face, and in that moment she saw Ricardo's face when he had looked at her from the bed in the hotel el Río de Oro.

Jorge didn't come by for Evita after work. Instead, Ricardo met her as she walked out onto the sidewalk on her way to the bus stop. He said he had picked up his son and had taken him home after they had argued about her. He wanted his son in school and strictly forbade him to see her again.

Evita hurriedly walked past him. On one arm she carried the present Jorge had given her for Evelina in a plastic bag, on the other the leather purse her mother had bought her, the golden butterfly clasp shining in the sun. Ricardo caught up to her easily, staring hard at her tight-fitting black pants, bright red blouse, and black shoes with tall wedged heels. Men looked at Evita as she walked next to him, and Ricardo felt jealous, knowing he had been the first man Evita had ever known. She was a child still, and he had made her a woman. Now he couldn't sleep at night, imagining his own son making love to her.

Evita walked as fast as she could over the uneven sidewalk, almost jumping at times to get down from a curb.

"Are you listening to me, Evita?" Ricardo's voice was harsh. He was talking to her between clenched teeth, trying not to attract attention from people they passed on the street.

"I told you, I'm not interested in your son!"

"He told me you asked him to meet you after work."

"Because he was begging me! Don't you understand? He finds me attractive; there's nothing I can do about it."

"There *is* something you can do about it. You can leave from here. Go back to your mother, to Brisa. In fact, send her my greetings."

Ricardo mentioned Evita's mother with disdain, almost as if he had spit her name out on the sidewalk. This enraged Evita, as she now felt Ricardo had also preyed on her mother, and that maybe it wasn't all her mother's fault as she had once believed.

"Leave my mother out of this!"

"Oh, so you've made up with her! Well, isn't that nice. I had both of you in bed! Don't you remember, Evita? You, and your mother! Did I rape you, Evita? No! You came to me all by yourself. You listen to me, hija de la chingada, porque con migo no juegas. You won't play with me, Evita, like you're playing with my son. There are women's bodies being found in Juárez, thrown out like so much trash—what's one more body? Who will believe that you didn't return to the streets and were killed by some narcotraficante, or a crazed maniac? You will do what I say, or you'll live to regret it!"

Evita felt a knot in her stomach. Her face flushed with anger and fear. He was threatening her life, and there was little she could do about it. She couldn't tell her brother, Reynaldo, as this might put him in danger of being murdered as well. She couldn't tell her mother or Lety. Cristal would understand, and Anabel, even Fina and Isidora because they dealt with men who made threats all the time, and somehow they bore it all and survived.

Evita turned away from him and rushed to board la rutera, leaving Ricardo behind glaring at her.

Lety was happy for the gift Jorge had given Evita for Evelina. It was baby clothes and a soft pink blanket. Lety told Evita that Jorge must be a very nice boy to be so considerate. Why didn't she invite him to the house for dinner? That's the type of boy she should consider as a boyfriend, she said, someone hardworking and caring. Evita didn't say anything, only held Evelina close and walked outside with her to see the sunset.

With Julio gone, Lety was at peace, taking care of Evelina and collecting part of her husband's check every Friday at the company office in town. Without their father yelling at them and pushing them around, Joselito and Milito fought less with each other, often playing in peace. Evelina proved to be a perfect baby, sleeping through the night and enjoying her mother's breasts every chance she got. Her dark eyes lit up every time she saw her mother, Evita, or her brothers. She lifted one tiny eyebrow, as if she was observing everything they did. It made them all laugh and wonder what she was thinking as she watched them so closely. Evita whispered in the baby's ear.

"Don't grow up, Evelina. There's too much pain in the world."

30 Harry Hughes was far from St. Louis, Missouri, where he had been born. He was a young soldier, only eighteen years old, stationed at Fort Bliss in El Paso, Texas. Little by little he had learned to appreciate the deserts, mountains, sunsets, and the Mexican culture of the area. Mexico was only a short ride from Fort Bliss, across one of the bridges that connected El Paso to Ciudad Juárez, but for Harry Hughes, Mexico was like another world. He couldn't get over the beautiful architecture of the buildings in the center of Juárez, elegant churches, marketplaces, and hundreds of shops filled with colorful curios and souvenirs. He loved the gaiety of the Mexican people, their humility, warmth, and their music.

However, Harry also saw the poverty of Juárez, spread out as far as the eye could see into the hills where the people lived in cardboard houses, and it struck at his heart. He told his buddies it wasn't right for so many people to live in that kind of poverty—like animals. Something had to be done. Harry observed toothless beggars on the streets of Juárez in rags, sticking out a hand or an aluminum can for money, their eyes dark empty circles.

"Don't give them any money," one of his buddies said. "They're running a scam for their next bottle of booze."

Women sat patiently with their children on sidewalks, their wares spread out on tattered rugs, and Harry gave them dollar bills whenever he could, though his buddies told him to save his money for the booze and the whores—that's what they were there for anyway.

Harry's uncle Al lived in El Paso with his wife, a Mexican woman he had met in Tijuana when he was stationed at the military base in San Diego. She had lived in poverty on the streets of Tijuana, a child nobody wanted, and now she was a good wife to his uncle. Their children attended school in El Paso, and they had friends on both sides of the border. Harry saw the Mexican people in a different way through his aunt Dominica, who was a gentle woman, always ready to serve him when he visited his uncle's house. Dominica had gone out of her way to teach Harry some Spanish and had enrolled him in Spanish classes when he was on leave from the base. Harry practiced his Spanish with her and could understand more than he could speak. He wondered what Dominica's life had been like—maybe like the lives of the women he saw in Juárez selling their wares on the street and others trying to get his attention so he would take them to bed. As an American soldier, he was just the customer they were looking for.

On leave for three days from Fort Bliss, Harry decided to get his aunt Dominica a gift. When he walked into the flower shop where Evita worked, his head was still pounding from a hangover. He wasn't dressed in his military uniform, but Evita knew he was a soldier who had had too much to drink and too much fun the night before. He started looking at floral arrangements made with silk flowers, beautifully arranged in colorful vases. He thought one of the arrangements would be perfect for his aunt.

"Cuanto?" he asked Evita in Spanish. How much? Evita looked up at his dark hair, clipped short, military style. He had a stubble of beard and a broad tired smile. He towered over her, and his hazy blue eyes stared down into hers.

Evita was nervous around him because he was an American. Jazmin had told her to treat Americans extra nice because she could always sell things to them for more money. Evita surprised herself by telling him an amount that she knew Jazmin would say was too low. She was glad Jazmin had gone home to tend to one of her grandchildren who was sick with the flu and wasn't there to correct her.

"Es todo?" Harry asked, a bit surprised.

He looked closely at Evita, who was dressed in a simple bright blue dress, caught at her slim waist with a belt that had a white rosebud for a buckle. When she walked around the counter, she looked so tiny, her skin light, almost translucent, her hair falling to her shoulders in smooth dark waves. She looked up at him and smiled, and to Harry she looked like a fairy princess in a King Arthur story. He fumbled for his money, his head pounding harder as he looked down at the wallet in his hand. He gave her twice the price of the vase of flowers. Evita told him no, please, take back some of the money.

"Take it," he told her in Spanish, trying to impress her. Evita put the vase in a box and wrapped it in gold foil because Harry told her it was a gift.

"For your mother?" Evita asked him.

"No—my aunt—mi tía."

Harry didn't speak enough Spanish to be able to tell her that his mother lived in St. Louis, Missouri, and wouldn't like it that he was talking to a Mexican girl on the streets of Juárez and giving her twice what she had asked for just because he liked her so much.

He asked Evita for her name and told her there was a famous Evita in Argentina. He told her his last name, Hughes, was that of a famous millionaire in America—too bad he wasn't related to him. Harry left with the gift for his aunt Dominica under his arm and with promises to Evita that he'd return next weekend, no matter what he had to do to get off the base. Before he left, she called him back to ask his first name.

"Harry," he said, looking embarrassed, and laughed when she pronounced it "Har-ee."

"That's good," he said, "or you can call me el Cadet, like my aunt Dominica does." Evita liked that better, as she could say el Cadet in Spanish, and it sounded perfectly correct.

Harry kept his word to Evita, and the next weekend he walked into the flower shop ready to purchase whatever he could to impress her. Evita didn't know Harry had bribed his buddy, Tim, an Italian from Minnesota, for his weekend pass, with the promise of taking him to his uncle's house in El Paso for a home-cooked meal that would rival any spaghetti dinner his mom had ever made. He also told his buddy that if he was nice, his uncle would take him under his wing, and he'd be able to stop by any time for another meal. It took Tim only five seconds to hand his weekend pass over to Harry and immediately start making plans for his first home-cooked meal at Uncle Al's.

Harry bought corsages at the flower shop for four of the secretaries at the base and an arrangement for the mess hall that he was sure would wind up in the trash. His buddies told him to snap out of it—she was just another Mexican girl, and they were there for the taking.

"That little ol' Mexican gal's done a job on you. She must be good," one of Harry's buddies said. "She's young, too—looks like a kid. Maybe she's got a papacito who'll blow the hell out of you. In the States, she's jailbait. I can't believe you let this happen!"

To everyone's surprise, Harry stepped up to the guy and yelled at the top of his lungs. "I've never touched the girl—and if I ever did, it's none of your damn business!"

"Take it easy, pal, don't get hyper over this. I'm only kidding—whatever you do, hey, go for it. It's Mexico, who cares?"

The guys walked away shaking their heads, laughing at Harry because he was really serious about a Mexican girl.

Jazmin told Evita it was her lucky day now that an American soldier was interested in her. She already imagined Evita living in los Estados Unidos as an American citizen. It would go good for her as well, she thought. She could go visit in El Paso, maybe even start a flower shop with Evita managing it.

After work, Evita walked out with Harry into the streets of Juárez. He helped her over the rough parts of the sidewalk, putting his arm out for Evita to hang onto. When people looked at them, Evita knew they were thinking she was a prostitute sleeping with an American soldier. Harry pointed out shops to her and asked Evita if she wanted anything— clothes, shoes, hats, blankets, anything, and she said, no, no—please don't do this. She wasn't used to anyone treating her with such generosity. Evita saw Jorge standing outside the restaurant where he worked, his arms crossed over his chest, and she asked Harry to cross the street with her. With Evita holding onto Harry's arm, they made a mad dash through a rush of cars. She felt bad for Jorge and could sense him staring after her for a long time after they crossed the street. Harry left his uncle's phone number with Evita and told her to call if she had to, as his aunt Dominica could speak to her in Spanish and pass on the message to him at Fort Bliss. Evita pronounced "Fort Bliss" as "Four Blees," and Harry said it sounded real cute. When she tried to pronounce his last name, it came out as "Hooguez," but Harry said it sounded better to him in Spanish. He was worried for her, as he had heard of the murders of women in Juárez. He told her that very soon he would take her to visit his aunt and uncle in El Paso. Evita felt safe for the first time in her life, as she realized that el Cadet would be a protection for her from other men. She asked him if he would take her to talk to a friend of hers, Yvone Ledezma, next time he was in Juárez. And he smiled and told Evita he'd take her to la luna, the moon, if that was what she wanted. Then he leaned toward her and gently kissed her cheek.

Jorge told his father he had seen Evita walking down the street arm in arm with an American soldier. Ricardo said yes, of course, that's exactly what he'd been saying all along. She was a little prostitute, it was obvious, and it was a good thing he was rid of her. He was glad that his son had his eye on a bright young girl from la prepa. He had plans for Jorge and didn't want him to fall into the trap of having to provide for a woman at a young age, as he himself had.

Thinking of Evita in bed with his son had been eating Ricardo alive, like a huge ulcer growing bigger each day. He had made up his mind that he would rather die than see this happen. Ricardo found out that el Cucuy, the notorious leader of Los Rebeldes, had a way of teaching women a lesson they would never forget. It was rumored that el Cucuy had recently killed his own sister, and no one in his family had the guts to stand up and accuse him of the crime. El Cucuy was always ready to teach a woman a lesson, for the right price—and Ricardo was ready to pay the price. But now, with the American soldier at Evita's side, the price would be too great. If anything happened to Evita, the American would be the first to know, and there was no telling what would happen after that. Even el Cucuy, as deadly as he was, wouldn't want to get involved with the American military. This made Ricardo even angrier with Evita. She was dangerous for him now, untouchable. However, Ricardo comforted himself with the thought that the American soldier was getting the leftovers. Then, in the next moment, Ricardo remembered Evita in his arms, and if he hadn't been a grown man, bred to be a macho, he would have wept out loud.

31 Harry returned in three weeks, eager to see Evita and take her out on their first date. She asked him if he'd pick her up after work so they could drive to Yvone's house. She didn't tell him Yvone lived across the street from her mother's house, or that she was really looking for Luis Ledezma so he could help her find her cousin, Petra. The emerald butterfly would be her prize. She'd explain later.

Harry arrived at the flower shop on a cool evening in early February.

He was dressed in dark pants, neatly ironed and creased, and a green knit pullover. He smelled like he had just showered and sprayed cologne on himself. He had to wait for Evita to finish cleaning up at the flower shop and ended up buying a few things for people he said he knew in El Paso. Jazmin met him and said he was good-looking for an American. His skin was too pale, and she wasn't used to his blue eyes, but she said he seemed very nice and courteous, and most important he spent a lot of money every time he came to the shop.

Evita wore a long black skirt and a light blue ruffled blouse for her first date with Harry. She wore a black sweater to match and high spiked heels, as el Americano was very tall, and she didn't want him to have to keep bending down so low to speak with her.

Harry was trying hard to speak Spanish to Evita and had brought his Spanish dictionary with him, a pocket-sized edition. "Cómo se dice," he asked her over and over again—how do you say this? how do you say that?—as they drove in Harry's car, a Chevrolet sedan, to Yvone's house. Then Harry asked Evita how old she was. He was thinking maybe his buddies were right, and he'd end up making big trouble for himself on both sides of the border. Evita lied to Harry and told him she was sixteen, but was small for her age and looked younger. Harry was relieved to hear that at least she was sixteen, although he didn't really believe her. His aunt Dominica was only fifteen when she had married his Uncle Al, and they had been together ever since. Harry caught himself off guard thinking about marriage, and shook his head, wondering why he had even thought of such a thing. He still had three more years in the service, and there was no telling where he'd be stationed next year.

Evita was relieved that her mother was out selling her merchandise and wouldn't return until late. She wasn't ready to let her mother see Harry, and told him that he'd meet her mother someday soon. He was hoping Alberto wasn't around either, as she'd have to tell Harry that he wasn't her father, only one of her mother's boyfriends.

Yvone had just gotten home from her shift at Thompson's Electronics when Evita and Harry drove up to her house. Evita knocked on the door, afraid at any moment to see Chano close by. But he wasn't there, and only Yvone answered, telling Evita that her mother and father were visiting at one of her sister's houses. Yvone was sleepy after her shift at la maquiladora but woke up when she saw Evita with el Americano. Evita introduced Harry to her and told her she could call him el Cadet, because it was so much easier to say and he didn't mind.

Yvone invited them in, rushing to move clothes off the couch and clear dishes from the kitchen table. She whispered in Evita's ear: "You should have told me you were bringing him!"

Evita smiled and told her she didn't think el Cadet was the type to judge anybody. They sat at the kitchen table, even though Yvone had encouraged them to make themselves comfortable in the living room. Standing at the sink, Yvone nervously rinsed out dishes and set up the coffeepot. The stove was on for warmth, and the coffee started to brew on one of the burners, filling the kitchen with a rich aroma.

Yvone served coffee and put out a plate of cream-filled crescent rolls. Harry had learned to appreciate the taste of the rich dark Mexican coffee and the sweet bread that was baked daily all over Juárez. He sweetened his coffee with thick brown sugar and sat back enjoying the taste of the sweet rolls.

"Can you tell me where I can find my cousin, Petra?" Evita asked Yvone. "I've tried calling my madrina's house, but her phone's been disconnected, and I remember you said Luis had fallen madly in love with her. I imagine he would know where she is."

Yvone smiled. "My poor brother! He's such a romantic. I'm sure he knows where she is. In fact, he talks to her on the phone once in a while. He'll be here any minute, if you want to wait."

"Your brother's a good man, someone a woman could trust. I'm sure Petra can see that. Good men are hard to find," Evita said, looking over at Harry. "And your other brother? Where's Chano?"

"We haven't seen Chano in weeks. And to tell you the truth, we don't want to see him at all!"

Evita relaxed at hearing that Chano wouldn't be around while she was there with el Cadet. Yvone asked if Harry was her boyfriend, and Evita saw Harry smile, as he understood the word *novio*.

"Novio? Amigo, yo!" he said, pointing to himself. And they all laughed.

Yvone was sure Evita was sleeping with Harry for money. Her brother Chano had told her he had seen Evita on the streets, living with prostitutes, and there was no telling what she was up to.

"Maybe it's a coincidence, but Petra called here this morning looking for Luis," Yvone said. "Something about trying to buy a car. She asks my brother for advice sometimes."

Before long, Luis showed up in his old pickup truck. He was surprised to see Evita at his house with el Americano, yet extended his hand in greeting to him and hugged Evita warmly. Luis pulled his cap up to get a good look at him, and when Harry told him his name, Luis repeated it in perfect English. Evita was amazed at Luis's ability to speak English, but then realized he had probably learned it from dealing with his American bosses.

"I'm here to find out where my cousin Petra lives," she explained to Luis. "I met someone from a village close to Montenegro, a little girl, an artist—very talented. And she wants me to tell Petra she's in Juárez. Do you know where I can find her?"

"Petra? But of course I know. She's moved to la colonia Nuevo Leon."

"Oh, and she called for you this morning," Yvone said to him.

Luis's eyes lit up. "She called for me? Why didn't you tell me?"

"Because you just got home!"

"Is there an emergency? What is it?" Luis was already rushing to the phone to call her. He dialed Petra's number and found out from her brother Nico that she was at the hospital visiting her father.

"Tell Nico we'll be over later to visit," Evita said. "I have a message for Petra from someone she knows."

After Luis hung up, Evita told him about meeting Mayela in la Plaza and about the painting she had bargained for—the emerald butterfly.

"Mayela knows Petra, and she's desperate to get in touch with her. She's been abandoned in Juárez by her aunt and wants to go home. I told her I'd find Petra for her."

Evita invited Luis to go with her and el Cadet to Petra's house, to show them the way, as she had never been to Nuevo Leon. The truth was, she was afraid to be alone with el Cadet. She had heard the girls in la Zona del Canal talk about American soldiers—they spent money on Mexican women, but expected them to sleep with them. Evita's memory of the private party made her feel as if she wouldn't ever be able to let any man touch her again.

Luis climbed into the backseat of Harry's car and directed him through a series of twists and turns and down a busy boulevard to Nuevo Leon.

As they turned the corner into Nuevo Leon, Luis told Harry it was the territory of Los Trinquetes.

"Look there—on the wall." He pointed to the scribbled name of the gang, with a heavy black line drawn through the letters.

"Looks like they have some problems. Another gang is challenging them. If you hear gunshots, get down!" Then both men laughed, and Evita forced a smile. They arrived at Petra's just as she and her mother were walking into the house after returning from the hospital.

Evita stared at Petra's tall perfect figure. She wore a plaid skirt, orange, reds, with a matching jacket, shoes, and purse. She reminded Evita of the beautiful girl she had seen next to el Junior wearing the exquisite gown. The girl had looked right into Evita's eyes, helplessly, as if she was a trapped animal asking for help. Evita had never forgotten the look.

Luis rushed out of the car to Petra's side. He hugged her briefly. It was obvious she was crying. Petra's mother was in tears as well.

"Es mi papa!" Petra told Luis. "He's sick from his other kidney now—the cancer's back."

"Was that why you called me?"

"Yes, of course, and also to ask for your help in buying a car. We need it now that my father's so sick. We have to be prepared to get to the hospital at any moment."

Evita walked up to Petra and her mother, embracing them. Petra was surprised to see el Americano at her side. She remembered seeing Evita walking next to Cristal in el Centro and her mother warning her that she should stay away from her. It was obvious she was up to no good, her mother had said. Cristal was one of the prostitutes who walked up and down las zonas. Now here was Evita with an American soldier. Petra hoped he wasn't one of her clients.

Luis introduced Harry to Petra, and she shook his hand, pronouncing his name in near perfect English.

"I didn't know you spoke English," Evita said, surprised.

"A little. I've been taking classes."

They walked into Petra's house, where Abuela Teodora welcomed them with embraces and had everything clean and dinner prepared. Ester was sitting with her friend Denise, playing with dolls in the living room. Flor told her to put her things away and make room for Petra's guests. When Nico walked into the room, Evita noticed he was wearing jewelry—gold necklaces, a ring, and a small earring looped through one ear. She knew it was a sign that he belonged to Los Trinquetes and looked over at Luis, locking eyes with him. Luis nodded, showing her he understood, then reached over and put one hand affectionately on Nico's shoulder.

"How are you, hermanito?" he asked.

Nico looked at him and shrugged his shoulders.

"Nico—say hello to our guests," Petra said to him.

"Hola," he said, then turned his back on them and walked into the kitchen.

Flor sighed, shaking her head. "Young men of today—I tell you, they lack respect."

Evita sat on the couch next to Harry, conscious that everyone was looking at them. The family was uncomfortable with el Americano, and Flor asked Luis to tell him they didn't know any English and that he was welcome, with everyone else, to stay for dinner. Harry smiled, understanding what Flor had said, and explained in a few Spanish words, "La comida, buena!" Everyone smiled in relief, telling him that was good Spanish, and yes, the food was good.

Petra thought Evita looked very pretty and petite next to el Americano, and she could see that he truly had love for her.

"Do you know a girl named Mayela from a village close to Montenegro?" Evita asked her.

"Mayela, from Chitlitipin?"

"Yes, I think that's her village."

Petra turned to her mother and Abuela Teodora. "Chavela Sabina's girl—remember?"

"How can we forget? They bought elotes from us every Sunday, whether they had money or not!" The women laughed, remembering the faces of Chavela's children all in a row.

"There, on the wall," Flor pointed to el ojo de Dios. "That's a gift that her mother, Chavela, gave us to hang in our house here in Juárez. We most definitely know her!"

"Is she here in Juárez?" Petra asked Evita.

"Yes, I saw her in la Plaza. She's living at el Instituto de Niños Huerfanos, over by la Catedral. She's been under the care of el Instituto and an American doctor, a woman, who has helped her with her artwork. She paints beautifully! They call her la Niñita Frida."

"Mayela? An artist?" Petra smiled at Luis in wonder. "She was the little girl who stuck out her tongue at me before we left Montenegro!" Everyone laughed except Nico, who sat sullenly in a kitchen chair ignoring their conversation.

Evita told Petra about her bargain with Mayela for the emerald butterfly, and Petra told her she'd like to go visit Mayela at el Instituto, and of course she could go back with them to Montenegro.

After dinner, Harry drove Evita, Luis, and Petra to el Instituto, to see if they could visit with Mayela. Luis was in heaven sitting next to Petra in the backseat, talking together as if they had known each other since they were children. Luis told her he'd ask around and find a car for her and would make the deal himself, as women were cheated when buying cars and he knew what to look for.

They arrived at el Instituto and were shown in by Narciso Odin. Yes, he said, he knew the child, Mayela Sabina, and what business did they have with her? He was defensive with them, abrupt.

"What business?" Petra said firmly, surprised at the old man's rudeness. "We'd like to see her. Please tell la directora."

Narciso hesitated, then asked them to sit down. He said he'd tell la directora, but who knew if she'd even allow the visit.

"A miserable old man," Luis said, watching Narciso walk away.

"Look at all her paintings!" said Evita, walking around the room with Harry and admiring Mayela's work on the walls of el Instituto. She looked for the painting of the emerald butterfly, and was glad to see it wasn't displayed, as that perhaps meant Mayela had saved it for her. Evita peered around a small wall made of wooden planks and saw Mayela's easel and her paints, everything neatly arranged. On the easel was the beginning of another painting, of a woman posing in a long elegant gown. Evita moved closer and noticed next to the easel a photo of a beautiful young woman in a gown, identical to one she had seen the girl wearing at the private party as she had stood next to el Junior, her eyes distant and vacant. There were the rhinestones, pearls, the French lace neckline, the lilies with the golden stems worked into the material on the hem. She stood with her mouth open because the woman in the dress was not the same one she had seen at the private party.

"What's wrong?" Harry asked her. "Qué paso?"

"Nothing, no es nada." Evita was stuttering, not knowing what to say. "It's . . . ah, . . . her paintings are beautiful, don't you think?"

"Yes, very professional for a child her age."

Evita sat down, suddenly dizzy. When Narciso Odin walked back in, he noticed she was pale and frightened.

"Don't worry," he said in an irritated voice, "Señora Juana del Pilar will permit the visit."

"The photo . . ." Evita said to him.

"What photo?"

"Is there something wrong?" Petra asked with concern.

"No, nothing . . . I thought I recognized someone . . . but I guess I was mistaken."

Before Petra could say another word, Señora Juana del Pilar walked into the room, warmly inviting them to el Instituto, noticing quickly that there was an American with them who might prove a good benefactor for el Instituto if she could convince him of their cause.

"Mayela will be here momentarily," she said. "I understand you'd like to visit with her. Perhaps you're interested in her work?"

"I'm from Montenegro," Petra said. "We've known Mayela's family for years, and my cousin here, Evita, met Mayela in la Plaza not too long ago. Mayela promised her the painting of an emerald butterfly if she would relate the message to me that she was here in Juárez."

Señora Juana del Pilar's eyes narrowed as she realized she had made a mistake in letting them see Mayela. She had thought they were interested in buying one of her paintings, when in fact they might be the ones to take her away from el Instituto. "Wait a minute!" she said, hoping to stop them from seeing Mayela. "I don't think she's awake."

"But you just told us we could see her," Petra said.

Señora Juana del Pilar stood up and was about to ask them to leave when Mayela walked into the room. She was wearing a bright blue dress that went down to her ankles. Her long dark hair was piled up on her head in braids, tied up in ribbon. Seeing Petra, she ran across the room and into her arms, holding onto her and crying as if her heart would break.

Evita was moved by the love she saw between Petra and Mayela. It was the same feeling she had felt for Cristal before she had led her into danger. Evita wept in joy because the emerald butterfly was hers, and in fear because the woman in the photo Mayela was painting was not the same one she had seen with el Junior.

In a month's time, Mayela finished the painting of Gabriela LaFarge in the beautiful French gown. Señora Juana del Pilar called the Miramontes home to let Gabriela's secretary know that the painting was done. The secretary told her la Señora LaFarge had gone to Paris to visit her mother and would be gone for several weeks. When she returned, she'd give her the message.

Sing to the Morning

32 Agustín Miramontes Guzmán made everything else in Petra's life appear meaningless. It was all she could do to say good-bye to Antonio as he left for Montenegro without betraying what had happened to her at the Christmas party in El Paso. Agustín's presence had been like a magnet for Petra; she was startled by his power to reduce her to helplessness. Shame and guilt had descended upon her, making her treat Antonio especially kind even though he had insulted her about going to the party. She hid her feelings from Vina Salcido, knowing that if she found out, she would tell Amapola Nieto and her followers, and things would be ten times worse than the lies said about her and Humberto Ornelas. She was later to find out that no one could stand up to Agustín Miramontes Guzmán, and whatever the women said, for the time being, would be said in secret.

On the day Antonio and Tío Alvaro left for Montenegro, another story came out in *El Diario* about the murders of yet more young women. Three girls had been found in las Lomas de Poleo, side by side, stripped of their maquiladora uniforms, their arms cut off, and their stomachs ripped out. Las Lomas de Poleo, a huge area of sandy desolate desert, was becoming famous as a burial place for the victims of the brutal murders that everyone now called feminicidios—hate crimes against women. The girls had been tortured, raped, and murdered. Everyone was talking about the murders, and about the two choferes who drove ruteras and were now in custody, accused of the crimes. The men maintained their innocence, saying they had been tortured by the police into confessing. Each day more and more people spoke out against the police, saying their silence had been bought with las mordidas. The police defended themselves by saying that the murdered girls had led a double life and were known to frequent bars and dance halls, acting more like prostitutes than honest hardworking girls. Their parents appeared on television and spoke up on radio programs, saying their daughters had never been known to go out at night and that one of them had been attending school part-time, studying to be a nurse.

Ester's nightmares started all over again with news of the murdered girls. Estevan vowed they would leave Juárez in a month, even if he had to be carried out in a coffin. As if his desire for death had been answered, his one good kidney became cancerous and had to be removed. There was nothing left for him, the doctors said, but to be put on a dialysis machine that would function in place of his kidneys. When he heard this, Estevan started making plans for his burial, saying he couldn't stand machines and wouldn't be on dialysis for very long. He refused a kidney from anyone in the family, even though his brother Carlos and Petra proved, through blood exams, to be perfect matches as donors. Three times a week, Estevan lay in a hospital bed for hours, staring at the ceiling, his blood flowing round and round through plastic tubes.

At home, he would lie around all day feeling sorry for himself, blaming himself for the difficulties his family was in. He was miserable in Nuevo Leon, la cosa ajena, as he called it, and was worried that Ester had too much freedom for a child her age. He said there was no way of knowing whom she'd encounter when she went to visit her friend Denise or walked to the market to buy candy and gum. No one was safe from the violence on the streets, most of all women. He read story after story of women who had been found murdered, their bodies destroyed beyond recognition. So many women had disappeared, that when a body was found, many families went to view it thinking it might be their daughter, their sister, who had never come home. "Las desaparecidas" is what they were calling the girls—those who had disappeared.

"One more month," Estevan said to Petra. "If the doctors can't find me a kidney by then, we'll leave."

"Be patient, Papi," she said, trying to soothe him, but he only shook his head and told her that she was to trust no one, absolutely no one, and especially not Gustavo Rios. She wondered what her father would say about Agustín Miramontes Guzmán. Would he consider him the most dangerous of all? She shuddered to think of Agustín as dangerous. His image haunted her: his face, the smooth square chin, his eyes, faded blue, his hair, golden red—everything about him was stunning. Power pulsed around him magically, and it reached for her. She had never experienced anyone like him.

"I should be the one working—not you and your mother!" her father said, interrupting her thoughts. His voice broke with emotion. Then he sighed and said, "You can marry Antonio in one year, mija—one year. He has to prove his love for you."

Estevan thought of the pistol he had bought from a gang member, telling his wife it was for protection when in reality it was for himself. One day, when he couldn't take it one more minute, Estevan was planning to use the gun on himself to spare his family. He remembered the promise Flor had made, to bury him in their village if he died in Juárez, and he felt comforted.

To make matters worse, Nico wouldn't go to school and came home late most every night. Estevan waited up for his son until the early hours of the morning and cursed him, hitting him with his fists in anger. Flor would wake up and make him stop, shouting at Nico that he had to obey his father. Nico took it all, until the night he came home angry about something that had happened on the streets and smelling of marijuana and liquor. Estevan grabbed him by the throat and accused him of being a member of Los Trinquetes. He threatened to send him back to Montenegro to live with Tío Alvaro before he got himself killed, or got the whole family in trouble with the gang he was running around with.

Nico shouted at his father: "You'll do nothing to me! You're lucky nothing's happened to this family. You know nothing about these streets! You lie around all day long and let everybody support you . . . at least I bring home some money."

"What money? From the gangs? From drugs? Get out of my sight with your filthy money!"

Nico was ready to attack his father, when Flor ran in and stopped him. Petra rushed up to Nico and put her arms around him as in the old days.

"Talk to me, Nico! What's wrong? Why are you acting like this?"

"Don't treat me like a child!" he shouted. "I'm a man now. There are no children on these streets!"

"No! You're still my little brother," Petra pleaded.

"Tell that to Los Trinquetes," Nico said as he pushed her away, cursing as he walked out into the dark street.

One morning, Petra mentioned to Vina at work that Luis Ledezma was helping her locate a car she could use to drive her father to the hospital for his treatments.

"Gustavo Rios can help you find a car," Vina said.

"Don't mention it to him," Petra said in alarm. "Amapola and her crowd already hate me. There's no telling what they'd do if they found out Gustavo was helping me get a car."

"Don't worry about ese veijerio. Those old ladies will talk no matter what happens. But what about Agustín Miramontes Guzmán? I certainly didn't see you try to get away from him!"

"I'm engaged!" Petra said firmly, sensing herself blushing.

"Your face is turning red! But, ya sabes, men talk, and my father said el Señor Miramontes was very impressed with you at the party, and soon you'll get invitations to attend corporate meetings—maybe even travel to South America to la maquiladora they have there, which is what they told me I would do."

Petra looked at Vina over a stack of papers she was mailing out, surprised at the tone of anger in her voice. "I can't go to South America. My father's ill . . . and—"

Vina broke in: "If I wasn't married with two kids, I'd be at Agustín's side in no time! You have to stop being such a baby, Petra." Then she got up and walked out of the office without another word.

Petra leaned on her desk, her hand on her forehead, and closed her eyes, wearily thinking about her father, his illness, her marriage to Antonio, the problems with Nico, and her mother crying every day as she saw her husband's body wasting away. The image of Agustín Miramontes Guzmán surfaced again and again in Petra's mind. Vina had seen right through her. She remembered the way he had looked walking into the house of Arnold Laverne at Christmas, so self-assured, causing a stir as people ran to his side. When he had looked at her, Petra had frozen and could barely answer his question about the chocolate-covered strawberries. She wanted to forget Agustín, and at the same time she wanted to see him again.

The car was a Honda Accord, white with matching white bucket seats. It was brand new, a '96, and it had been sent over to Western Electronics on the last day in February, a Thursday. Vina ran into the office and grabbed Petra, who was on the phone with a customer. Petra wasn't even able to finish her conversation.

"What, are you crazy? What's happened?" Petra was always expecting bad news about her father. She searched Vina's face for signs of sadness and saw only smiles.

"Is he here? Is Agustín here?"

"He's not here, but he sent something for you!"

As she was talking, Gustavo Rios walked in, also smiling.

"There's good news for you today, Petra. Agustín Miramontes found out that you needed a car and has sent one of his own for you. He says you can keep the car and use it—take it back to Montenegro if you want to. You don't have to worry about paying for it—it's a gift."

Petra stood with her mouth open, unable to believe what Gustavo was telling her. She stammered for words.

"But . . . but . . . he shouldn't have done this! Someone is already helping me get a car. I don't want him going to this expense for me."

"Expense? You're talking about one of the wealthiest men in Juárez . . . watch what you say. This is nothing to him. He knows your father's been ill. He's only trying to help you."

Vina grabbed Petra's hand and took her out to the parking lot where the car was parked close to the entrance of la maquiladora.

"One of his security guards brought it over," she told her.

"Guards?"

"Of course, guards! He's from a rich family—they all have people to guard them. Come on . . . get in! The car's yours. The payment comes later!" She laughed out loud as she saw fear come into Petra's eyes.

Petra wondered how she would drive the car, as she had practiced only once or twice in Tío Alvaro's old car with Antonio sitting close by.

Gustavo Rios was like a child with a new toy. He opened the door on the driver's side and admired the interior. "I can't believe this! This is beautiful."

He motioned for Petra to get in on the passenger side, so he could test-drive it. Vina climbed into the backseat. Workers from la maquiladora were watching them from the entrance, and others were coming out to the patio on their lunch break. As they drove away, Petra saw Amapola Nieto and two of her friends at the back entrance, standing with their hands on their hips. Humberto Ornelas ran out to the parking lot, past the women at the entrance, as if he wanted to catch up to the car as they pulled away. Petra watched as Amapola and her friends burst into laughter at the sight of Humberto chasing after the car.

His voice was low, cheerful, as if he was talking to her about the weather and there was nothing to be concerned about. His voice in her ear was rich, intoxicating, and she wanted to hang onto it forever.

"Petra? This is Agustín. How are things going?" She could hear him chuckle.

"You sent me a car! I don't know what to say. I really can't accept it. It's too much! I never—"

Agustín's voice broke in casually, almost as if he was sitting back in a chair. "Oh, the car? Yes, I'm glad you like it. Use it for your family, for your father. I lost my father a few years ago, and I know what it means when your father's sick."

"Gracias. I don't know what else to say to you." Petra felt her throat tighten as she held back tears.

"Petra . . . I'd like you to come to one of our meetings, to introduce you to the corporate side of our business. Gustavo Rios can bring you . . . and if you have any time to spare, I'd like to see you someday soon . . . maybe for coffee. If you're uncomfortable about it, don't worry. There's no pressure."

Petra wanted to shout with joy. She stood up and walked back and forth in front of her desk, nervously knotting and unknotting the phone cord. She wanted to crawl through the phone line and reach for him, but she only said, as casually as she could: "Yes. That would be fine. Gustavo told me something about the meetings. And whenever *you* have time, please call, and we'll plan a time to go out for coffee."

When she hung up, she laughed out loud to think Agustín was asking her if she had time to spare—so humble, she thought. He reminded her of a young boy, trying to please her—so different from Antonio constantly demanding her attention. Her face flushed and her hands trembled with an energy she had never experienced as she thought of Agustín's handsome face, his muscular body, his hair golden red, and the way he had looked at her at the Christmas party.

Vina walked in. "You talked to him! I can tell by the way you look!"

Petra nodded and could say no more.

The day after Agustín's gift to Petra, Luis Ledezma called her after work, excited to tell her he had found the right car for her. Petra was in the kitchen, waiting for her mother to finish getting dressed so they could pick up her father at the hospital. He had been hooked up for hours to a dialysis machine and was now anxious to get home. Petra knew her father would lecture her again about the new car when she picked him up. He had told her it was another plot by Gustavo Rios to soften her up, so he could control her life. When Petra told him it wasn't Gustavo who had given her the car, her father said that was worse, as that meant he had been talking to other men about her, and who could tell what they would do. He shook his head worriedly over his daughter and her position at la maquiladora. As for Flor, any other time she would not have allowed Petra to accept the car, but Estevan's illness had made her desperate and she remained quiet about things she would have never allowed in the past.

As Petra picked up the phone, she looked out the window at the Honda parked in front of the house. It hadn't taken her long to learn how to drive it—the car almost ran by itself. Taking care of the car was another thing. Everyone in the family, and close neighbors as well, were already weary from having to protect the car from thieves day and night.

Luis told Petra over the phone that he had found a Chevrolet Caprice, an older model but in excellent condition. He had made a down payment on it, and it wouldn't take long to pay. He told her he had checked it over carefully, and he was sure the car would run for years to come.

"I think you'll like it, Petra. It has air-conditioning, and everything's in order. It's your favorite color—blue."

Petra was silent as she listened to him, knowing that what she had to say would hurt his feelings.

"Gracias for finding it for me, Luis, but I've got good news to share with you. Someone from la maquiladora gave me a car—a new car! I'm looking at it this very moment through the window. I think you'll like it when you see it. I'm very grateful for your help, but I think you'll understand that I couldn't turn it down."

Luis didn't say anything for a few seconds; then his voice came over the line, soft as if he was whispering, forcing himself to share in her good news.

"I'm happy for you, Petra, deveras. I know you can use the car for your father, and for trips back to Montenegro. And . . . I'm thinking that whoever gave it to you must think you're very special."

"Don't you want to know who gave it to me?"

"Only if you want to tell me."

"He's a man who owns interests in Western Electronics and in other maquiladoras as well. He's very wealthy and has other cars. It didn't hurt him, I guess, to give me the car, although I certainly didn't expect it or ask for it."

Petra felt as though she was apologizing to Luis for accepting the car. Luis was silent on the other end.

"Gustavo Rios knows him. I met him at a Christmas party. You might have heard of him, Agustín Miramontes Guzmán."

"Miramontes Guzmán? Is that what you said?" Petra heard Luis's voice rise in pitch, tense and brittle.

"Yes, is there something wrong?"

"Wrong? Petra, listen to me very carefully. This man is dangerous, extremely so, if the rumors about him are true. It's said that he holds interests in businesses because he's part of a cartel, a group of powerful mafiosos, who make their living through drugs, prostitution, corruption, and every kind of criminal act they can commit. Petra, please . . . "

Petra didn't let him finish. First, she was struck by fear. Then anger.

"That's what everybody says when people are rich. I've heard it all my life. It could be nothing more than envy! He's trying to help me. He's offered me a position in his corporate office. What should I do? Return the car? I can't do that! It would be an insult."

"Yes, an insult, and he deserves it for thinking he can get involved with someone like you! He has a wife, a French woman he married a few years ago."

Petra was silent when she heard of Agustín's wife. It was something not even Vina Salcido had told her about. She ended her conversation with Luis feeling betrayed. First, Humberto had gotten her in trouble by chasing after her and making it seem as if she had been after him, and now this man—the most handsome and powerful man she had ever met—was offering her so much and had never bothered to tell her he was married.

Every morning, lying in her bed in their house in Nuevo Leon, Petra fought with herself, hoping not to have to get up to face a new day. She heard Abuela Teodora get up at dawn singing to the morning sun. Her voice sounded like the sweet chirping of birds.

> Iwéra rega chukú kéti Ono
> Mápu tamí mo nesériga ináro sinibísi rawé
> Ga'lá kaníliga bela ta semáribo
> Si'néame ka o'mána wichimoba eperéame
> Népi iwérali bela ta ásibo
> Kéti ono mápu tamí neséroga ináro ne
>
> Né ga'lá kaníliga bela ta narepabo
> Uchécho bilé rawé mápu kéti Onó nijí
> Ga'lá semá rega bela ta semáripo
> Uchécho bilé rawé najata je'ná wichimobachi
> Népi ga'lá iwérali bela ko nijísibo
> Si'néame ka mápu ikí ta eperé je'ná kawírali
>
> Uchécho bilé rawé bela ko ju
> Mápu rega machiboo uchécho si'nú ra'íchali
> Uchécho bilé rawé bela ko ju
> Mápu ne chapiméa uchécho si'nú 'nátali
> Népi iwéraga bela 'nalína ru
> Uchúpa ale tamojé si'néame pagótami
>
> Echiregá bela ne nimí wikaráme ru
> Mápu mo tamí nesériga chukú sinibísi rawé
> Echiregá bela ne nimí iwérali ásima ru

Mápu ketási mo sewéka inárima siníbisi rawé
Népi iwériga bela mo nesérima ru
Mápu ikí uchúchali a'lí ko mo alewá aale

*   *   *

Be strong father sun,
you who daily care for us.
Those who live on earth are living well.
We continue giving strength to our father,
who fills our days with energy and light.

With great joy we salute our father
with one more day of life.
We are living well following one more day on earth
as you light our way.

One more day to learn new words,
one more day to think new thoughts,
giving you strength you in turn
give energy to your brothers.

Thus I will sing
to you who daily care for me.
Thus will I give you strength
so you will not be discouraged.
With all your strength
care for those you have created
and given the breath of life.

Instinctively, Petra put her arm around Ester's warm little body, inching closer to her sister lying peacefully next to her, and wished the day away. Abuela Teodora walked into her room and gently touched one of Petra's shoulders. Her light warm touch was healing.

"Get up, Petra. You'll be late for work," she whispered. She didn't invite her granddaughter to sing to the morning with her any longer, as she knew that in Juárez the ancient traditions of Montenegro didn't exist.

Somehow, the magic of all that had belonged to them in Montenegro had been left behind.

As Petra made her way to the kitchen, she thought she heard Nico's voice whispering to Abuela Teodora. When she opened the kitchen door, she caught a glimpse of her brother as he disappeared down a dark alley. Abuela Teodora looked up at her, an empty plate of food in her hands.

33 By the middle of March, Petra hadn't heard a thing from Agustín. Now she was worried she had done something wrong. Maybe she hadn't been thankful enough for the car. Or perhaps it was because he was married and no doubt in love with his wife, and she was an intruder, a misfit who was picked on by married men.

At work, Vina told Petra she had heard Agustín was separated from his wife, a French woman whom people said had a mind of her own. Someone told her they had had a big fight over the baby she was expecting, and she had left to stay with her mother in Paris. Now he was alone, and no one knew if his wife would ever come back. She came from a wealthy family in France and didn't need him.

"Don't worry. He'll call and explain everything to you," she said, eyeing Petra with envy. She finished filing a stack of records and sullenly banged the cabinet shut, wishing she had Petra's problems. She wondered what else Agustín would give Petra—maybe the promotion to Buenos Aires that was rightfully hers. If that happened, then she'd have to get her father's help in changing Agustín's mind. He was still a prominent member of the board of trustees and had a vote in the company's future. She figured she had done her time in a clerical position at la maquiladora for two years—something had to pay off.

Antonio sent Petra a letter telling her how much he loved her. It was filled with descriptions of Montenegro—the sun rising, the mountains he climbed, thinking of her. He told her of the hard work it took to keep the ranch going and that he wasn't afraid of working from sunup to sundown to make a future for them. One of his horses was sick, he said, with a fever. It was a stud they thought they would mate with a prize mare. Now it looked as if they wouldn't be able to mate the stud at all, and they'd have to borrow a horse from a nearby farm.

He told her they had a feast before Ash Wednesday, the last day they'd be able to eat meat on Fridays. He missed her, desperately, and would come to Juárez for Easter. He asked her if she was wearing her engagement ring every day and staying away from danger. By *danger*, Petra knew he was talking about other men. Petra looked at the ring on her finger, the small diamond Antonio had given her, and didn't know how she'd tell him about the new car Agustín had given her. She decided she'd tell him it was given to her family by Western Electronics to help them during the time of her father's illness. It was a lie, but she couldn't face Antonio with the truth—her own attraction to Agustín Miramontes Guzmán.

Petra could sense the energy of Antonio's love for her in his letter. The way he signed his name, the letters drawn boldly but scrawled, as if he could barely write fast enough to keep up with his thoughts. And the kisses he said he put all over the letter. She touched the letter over and over again with her fingers, embracing him, crying because what Antonio was telling her sounded like it was coming from someone who lived on another planet.

Antonio had mentioned Ash Wednesday. Petra had forgotten it was Cuaresma—Lent, a time of penance, of cleansing and sacrifice. Abuela Teodora would make capirotada, the sweet bread pudding prepared during Lent with piloncillo—brown sugar—nuts, raisins, bananas, and a huge tortilla for a delicious crust. She resolved to hear mass at la Catedral as soon as she could. Maybe God would hear her prayers, see that she was not to blame for Agustín's attention and for the coldness she felt for Antonio.

On Tuesday, while Petra was eating a sandwich at her desk, Vina answered the phone. Petra heard her voice rise in excitement as she turned to face her, pointing to the receiver and mouthing Agustín's name.

"No, not a problem. She's right here—no, not busy at all!" She put the phone on hold and whispered, "It's Agustín. He wants to talk to you."

"Why are you whispering?" Petra asked, but didn't wait for an answer before picking up the phone, her heart racing.

"Petra, this is Agustín. How's everything going?"

It was the same cheerful relaxed voice she had heard before. Instantly, her hands turned cold as she remembered all Luis had said about him.

"Is something wrong?" he asked.

"No, nothing. I was just eating a little lunch."

"Vina told me you weren't busy. I won't bother you if you're eating lunch. I'll call back later."

"No. Please, I'm finished eating! It was a small lunch."

Petra couldn't bear to have him hang up. Who could tell when he'd call back? She wanted to ask him about his wife, the French woman. Were they really separated? Then she looked down at her engagement ring, with its small diamond sparkling, and wondered why it should matter to her at all.

"We're having a luncheon meeting tomorrow at one of the restaurants—Gustavo knows where. I'd like you to join us. Will you be able to come?"

Petra looked up to see Vina staring at her, then stand up abruptly and walk out of the office without waiting to hear what Agustín had to say to her.

"Tomorrow? Yes, I'll be there."

"By the way, how's the car running?"

"Like a dream—gracias."

Gustavo Rios said they'd leave by eleven o'clock for the restaurant, as he wanted to make sure everything was in place for the meeting at twelve. Reservations had been made, he said, but there were always details that had to be worked out. Petra asked him if Vina was coming along, and he said no, she had to stay behind and take care of the office.

Gustavo was dressed up in a suit, the gold chain he wore around his neck hidden under the shirt's collar and tie. Petra had learned to tolerate the way Gustavo walked next to her, brushing up against her whenever he could, and the way he put his hand on her arm or shoulder when no one was around. Sometimes he'd come up silently behind her when she was filing papers or doing accounts and put his hands on her shoulders.

"Would you like a massage," he'd say softly. "You're tense and need to relax." He'd start massaging her shoulders and Petra would stand up.

"I'm fine, really. I don't need a massage." She wanted to tell him to save his massages for his wife, but didn't. Without his help, she would still be on the assembly line with el viejerio glaring at her.

Gustavo drove Petra to the meeting in his car and told her she looked perfect in the suit she was wearing, a soft shiny material, black with a fancy white blouse showing under the jacket. She had her hair up, brushed smoothly back into a bun at her neck, and wore fake pearl earrings that matched her suit perfectly and shiny black pumps with stockings that had a single black seam running up each of her legs.

When they arrived at the restaurant, Petra looked nervously around for Agustín.

"He's not here yet," Gustavo said. "I don't see his black Jaguar. It's hard not to see a car like that."

The restaurant was built in elaborate Spanish architecture, with huge pillars at the entrance and an immense courtyard with a fountain in the front patio. It was set among an exclusive strip of shops filled with fine clothes and expensive jewelry. "We've rented the back room," Gustavo said.

"How many people are expected?" she asked, suddenly feeling like a misfit in such surroundings.

"Don't be nervous. It's just a few people this time—maybe fifteen. They won't bite!" He walked next to her, looping one arm over her shoulder. Petra felt herself tense up, then relax as he drew his arm away.

In the back room everything was ready for the meeting. The table was set with fancy dishes, colorful floral arrangements, napkins, and fine silverware.

"This is beautiful!" Petra said.

Gustavo ignored her, having seen this setting many times. People started coming in. Some Petra had seen at la maquiladora; others were from other maquiladoras in other parts of Mexico and in El Paso. When Humberto Ornelas walked in, she instantly turned away.

Gustavo introduced Petra to everyone, telling them she was in training, and was learning English as well, to assist with business in El Paso. He told them she would soon travel to one of las maquiladoras in South America. He was proud to introduce Petra to everyone, feeling as though he owned her, since he was the one who had found her in Montenegro. It looked good for him that she was so beautiful, and intelligent besides. Other men congratulated him on finding such a treasure, joking privately with him about finding a diamond among the rocks and filth of Montenegro.

Petra knew when Agustín walked in without turning to look. Conversation stopped for a few seconds around the room, and in its place rose the sound of waiters clattering serving trays and ice clinking in glasses. When she did turn to look, he was at the entrance talking to two men, dressed impeccably in a dark suit and tie. Petra was distracted as she talked to a woman who was telling her where she was from and how long she had been with la maquiladora in Juárez and in El Paso. As the woman rambled on, Petra noticed Agustín walking toward her. She took a deep breath, hoping the woman wouldn't notice the effect he had on her.

He walked briskly toward her, smiling broadly. "Petra, mucho gusto! I'm so glad you could come." He took her hand in his—it was warm and moist—and held onto her, pulling her gently to his side.

"And Imelda," he said, looking at the woman talking to Petra, "how are things over in El Paso? I haven't had a chance to visit the corporate office lately."

"Todo bien, except they just hired another manager from San Antonio, and he's already made so many mistakes they're ready to throw him out. But he's still there . . . you know how that goes."

As they were talking, Petra looked around at everyone dressed in their best business attire. As her gaze took in the elaborate room and its plush furnishings, she couldn't believe she was really there, attending the meeting, and next to Agustín, who casually talked to her as if she had been a part of the business for years.

As everyone walked to the table to take their seats, he whispered in Petra's ear: "Sit next to me. These meetings bore me. We'll eat our dessert first and play with our food. Would you like that?"

Petra nodded, feeling an energy surge through her body. She let him guide her gently to the chair next to his.

The following Wednesday afternoon, Gustavo Rios gave Petra a ride to a business meeting in El Paso, but couldn't stay long, so Agustín told him he'd take Petra back to Juárez. It had been a long day for Agustín, as he had just returned from Buenos Aires after a series of business meetings related to the expansion of the company. At the meeting, Petra noticed the way he tapped his pen impatiently on the conference table and prompted anyone who took too long to speak. Agustín discussed his meetings in Buenos Aires and plans the company had to send a team from Western Electronics to train new employees. He looked at Petra when he mentioned the team, as if to tell her she would be one of the ones who would travel to Buenos Aires.

After the meeting, Petra sat next to Agustín in his black Jaguar, admiring the way he looked in his sunglasses, Ray-Bans he told her he had bought in Spain, and a casual maroon knit shirt, tucked into black pants. Petra was conscious of everything: the beauty and speed of the car, the smell of the leather seats, the power she felt as she looked at the car's shiny black hood, and all around them, the darkening sky of early April, with the hint of a purple sunset.

Agustín gunned the motor, driving at top speed to get back to el Puente Santa Fe. Petra watched other motorists' faces for seconds at a time, curious, apprehensive, their features blurred from the windows of the Jaguar. Unconsciously, she pressed her foot down on the floorboard as if she was pressing down on a brake pedal.

"You look beautiful, as usual," he said, "but I like your hair down. Wear your hair down; it makes you look like an angel. And bright colors, good choice. You look good in bright colors."

Petra thanked him, thinking of the woman who had sold her the pink skirt and jacket she was wearing. The woman had told Petra that her daughter had run away with her boyfriend and hadn't even stopped by to pick up her clothes. And who knows if she really had run away? The woman had no proof. She wanted to believe her daughter was with her boyfriend, because she didn't want to think she was one of las desaparecidas, lost forever, or worse than that, murdered. The woman shuddered when she said the word "murdered," then shook her head, trying to convince herself that her daughter was still alive.

Petra had hesitated and was ready to refuse the outfit, but the woman had urged her on, telling her she needed the money desperately to pay her utility bills.

"She'll be back," the woman assured her. "I'm sure she's not one of the murdered women. May God hear my prayers!" She made the sign of the cross over herself and handed Petra the pink outfit.

Focusing her attention on Agustín, Petra noticed he had lost weight and wondered if it had anything to do with the separation from his wife. She wanted to ask him but couldn't get her courage up. He seemed distracted and anxious.

"So, Petra, when do you plan to get married?"

"Well, it won't be for a while. My father, as you know, is very ill, and he's getting treatments at the hospital. We have to stay in Juárez. He's stubborn—my father—and won't accept a kidney from any of us. That would be the only way he'd ever get better."

"You mean, you offered him one of your own kidneys?"

"Yes. And so did his brother, my Tío Carlos."

"That's very self-sacrificing of you. You must love your father very much. I like that—your loyalty to a man. That's the kind of loyalty I would want from a woman."

"I'm surprised. I thought you might already have that kind of loyalty."

"I did, once. But that's gone. The woman who pledged her love to me is gone, just like all her promises. She went back to France."

Petra's body jerked backward as Agustín stepped down on the gas pedal and cut off the car ahead of them, making it veer to the right. The motorist honked at him, but Agustín only laughed while Petra clutched the armrest for balance.

"I'm sure she'll be back. Why would she leave someone like you?" she said nervously.

"French women are hard to please. The French have always been arrogant—don't you agree?" Petra was ready to say she didn't know anything about the French, when Agustín banged his hand down on the steering wheel, exasperated with the traffic ahead.

"No! I'm not getting caught up in this mess!" he said as he looked at cars lined up for what seemed like miles to get over the bridge. "Hand me the phone that's under the seat, will you, Petra, por favor? Amor? Querida? In English, it's 'Pretty, please.'"

Petra found the mobile phone and handed it to him, and he took her hand in his and kissed it, staring at the engagement ring on her left hand.

"Is that the ring he gave you?"

"Yes—at Christmas. He's from Montenegro." Petra was conscious that she didn't give him Antonio's name.

"Nice ring. Cute. I gave one like that to a girl once when I was only twelve years old. But she lost it. I'm glad I didn't give her a big diamond—then I would have had to get my security people on it."

"Your security people?"

"Just kidding."

He held the phone in his hand and asked Petra to guide the steering wheel while he dialed the number. With the speed of the car and the congested freeway, she struggled to navigate, the lightest touch on the steering wheel making the car sway dangerously. He kissed her cheek and whispered.

"Hmm, tastes good. Can I have some more? I won't tell your fiancé. It will be our little secret—just kidding!" He smiled, and instinctively Petra backed away. Then she heard him on the phone telling someone to inform Mexican officials that he was headed for the border. "Tell them to speed it up—get everybody through. I don't want to waste time. Besides, I've got a beautiful woman with me, so they better move fast."

Petra was glad when he hung up and took over the steering wheel again. He stared at her as if he would reach over and kiss her again, but by then they had reached the border and the long line of cars snaked before them, reflecting the colors of the dimming sunset from windows and chrome fenders. She watched him maneuver the car in and out of tight spaces on either side of the long line of cars. Motorists honked at him, some shook their fists, and others let him go through as he waved at them, opening his window and yelling, "Emergencia!"

Petra wondered if they really believed there was an emergency or were making way to save themselves from a madman.

"This is fun!" he said, and laughed as if he was playing a game of chess and he was the only piece moving. "I should have used our helicopter. We do have one for this type of problem, but someone else is using it."

They made it to the front of the line, whizzing past people selling curios, *El Diario*, burritos, tortillas, candy. He rolled down the window as they approached the border patrol.

A Mexican official saw his black Jaguar and quickly waved him through.

"See, Petra, that's the way to do it. I hate delays. Life is too short for all that. Would you like to get something to eat? Chocolate-covered strawberries?" He laughed.

"I'll take you to a restaurant that I think you'll like. But I don't know if they have any chocolate-covered strawberries. Will that be a problem?" He smiled at her. "I'm teasing you—don't be so serious."

"Really, it doesn't matter to me," Petra said, sensing herself blushing as she had at the party in El Paso.

They drove up to a fancy restaurant in white-washed adobe, La Posada, built in the manner of an old hacienda. They were early for dinner, so it wasn't busy. An attendant opened the ornate oak door for them, and a waiter appeared in a white suit to welcome them in. The hostess, an elegantly dressed young woman, led them to their table. Petra was impressed with the way everyone gave way to Agustín and to her. It was obvious they knew who he was. The waiter pulled out her chair as if she was royalty and waited for her to sit down, then made sure she was comfortable. Petra had never been treated with so much respect, and all because she was at Agustín's side.

Agustín spent several minutes off to the side arguing with someone on his mobile phone. Petra watched him at a distance as he gestured with his hands, turning his back to her as he became more intent on his conversation. Finally he appeared to calm down and came back to the table and sat down beside her. He sighed and rolled his head from side to side, saying he was trying to relax the muscles in his neck and back.

"I've got tension, Petra," he sighed. "Too much stress. Why don't you give me a massage? With your tender hands, I should feel good in minutes." He was like a little boy, his light eyes staring into hers, his eyebrows lifted, his mouth pouting.

"You're a beauty, Petra, did you know that?" He moved closer to her, smiling. "Just a little massage? Pretty, please?" he asked in English.

Petra looked around, already embarrassed, thinking of the spectacle she was about to make of herself rubbing Agustín's neck in a public place. Then she looked at him and was helpless to say no.

"Well, yes, I guess, if you're that tired."

She stood behind him and he put her hands on his neck, pressing with his own hands the areas he wanted her to massage. "Here, here— and here. Ah, I'm feeling better already." He moved his head slowly from side to side and sighed in relief.

Petra looked around and saw a couple at another table staring at them. Agustín ignored them, and Petra continued rubbing his neck slowly, feeling the nerves in his neck and shoulders, taut under her fingertips. She sensed Agustín's power as she touched him, and her hands got hot. She was afraid she was rubbing too hard, as the friction her hands produced was like a fire between them.

"Yes, that feels good . . . that's the way to do it. Oh, I could take you with me everywhere, pull you out of my pocket like a genie out of a bottle, and say—look what I brought with me. Everybody would be so jealous!"

Petra wanted to hide from the other people in the restaurant. What she was doing seemed intimate to her, yet it didn't bother Agustín. He moved his chair close to hers after the massage and rested his head on her shoulder, saying he could stay there and sleep all night long, like a baby. The waiter stopped by, and with his eyes still closed, Agustín ordered champagne for them and chocolate-covered strawberries. He told the waiter to bring the strawberries before the meal, as he ate his dessert first.

"Señor Miramontes, lo siento, but we don't have the strawberries."

Agustín opened his eyes and frowned. "Get some!" he said in a loud voice. "Put them on my bill."

The waiter stared at Agustín, then at Petra.

"Si señor. I will do all I can to get them."

"Just get them," Agustín said. "Don't I spend enough money here? And now, all I'm asking for is a small favor."

He stared hard at the waiter, who was already filled with fear. The man walked briskly to the kitchen as Agustín reluctantly had Petra sit across from him at the small table, telling her he wanted to enjoy her beauty as they ate their meal.

In a few minutes, the waiter brought them chocolate-covered strawberries in a silver bowl. Agustín complained that they were too small— what did he do, pick them off a dead plant? The waiter apologized, and Petra wanted to tell him they were fine. But she couldn't go against Agustín, who had already pushed the dish away, saying never mind, pour us some champagne. The waiter popped the cork on the champagne bottle and poured two glasses, and Agustín offered Petra a toast.

"To your beauty," he said. "And your innocence, and your charm, and your—and everything else." He looked into her eyes, and Petra felt as if he was holding onto her from deep inside. She drank the champagne, rich and sweet, and the drink made her feel lightheaded. She wasn't used to drinking and refused a second glass, even though Agustín said it was bad manners not to drink at least half a bottle. Agustín ordered beef steaks for them with a rich sauce, rice, and a tangy salad. He seemed distracted as he ate, often looking at the door and at his watch.

"I'm running late for an appointment. In fact, I should already be there," he said. Then he looked at her, intently. "I know you're nervous about being out with me, Petra, but this isn't really a date. We're all about business—you know, the American way of life in Mexico. Capitalism has to win out." He winked one eye at her playfully.

As they left the restaurant, Petra noticed a man dressed in a suit watching them from the entrance. He motioned with one hand to Agustín, who responded with a nod of his head. As they drove away, the man followed behind the Jaguar in his car, a dark brown sedan with a black top.

"Who's that man?" Petra asked.

"Oh, that? One of our security people." Seeing her apprehension, he was quick to add, "Don't get nervous. He works for my family. It's only a little security. You know how people like to take down others, especially if they think they have a little money." He reached for her hand and kissed it tenderly. "The curse of having money!" he said, laughing out loud.

Luis Ledezma's words went through Petra's mind. *One of the most powerful cartels in Juárez. Those are the rumors.*

Petra told Agustín she had to go home, as her mother would get out of work later, and she had to pick her up. He told her he'd drop her off at her car at Western Electronics, as he had some things to pick up at la maquiladora before his appointment, but he said he'd take her there only if she promised to spend some time with him on Saturday.

"Otherwise, we'll drive around until midnight, and by then you'll say yes," he said, sighing wearily. "You won't make me drive around all night, will you? You know how tired I am."

"No, of course not. But I have a few things I have to take care of on Saturday, and—"

Agustín ignored her. "So, it's settled? Saturday, we'll see each other again." He yawned and shook his head as if to wake himself up. "Don't you want to see me again?"

"Yes, I do," Petra whispered.

"But you don't sound very convincing. I guess I'll have to prove myself to you. Is that right, Petra? I'm ready to do it, if that's what will please you."

She said nothing, only clenched her hands tightly in her lap, nervously staring at the road ahead. They drove up to the guard station at la maquiladora, and Petra saw the security guard she had seen when she was hired.

Agustín rolled his window down. "Cómo estás, Barriga?" he asked. The man peered into the car for only a few seconds. Petra was sure he had seen her, yet he said nothing to her.

"Bien, I've never been better. My wife just had another baby—a boy!"

"Congratulations. There's nothing like having a son to make your life worth living." Then he mumbled something about his wife, and Barriga laughed.

"What did you say?" Petra asked as they drove away, remembering that Luis had told her Agustín was expecting a baby from the French woman.

"Nothing—just that you have a nice car." He looked at the Honda Accord in the parking lot and let the Jaguar's motor idle next to it.

"You've got good taste."

Petra smiled. "Gracias. It's meant a lot to me—and to my family, especially now that my father's been so ill." She put her hand on his arm shyly, thinking she should do more.

"Saturday. Are you going to let me prove myself to you? I'll pick you up."

Petra thought of the black Jaguar driving the streets of Nuevo Leon, her family in shock, and Los Trinquetes watching from every corner and making plans on how to take him down. She wanted to explain to him that she had several things to do on Saturday. She remembered Mayela was coming by to visit with Evita and her American boyfriend, and there were things her mother needed her to do—shopping, washing clothes, and getting her father to one of his treatments. Besides, she was engaged, and how would she explain all this to Antonio? But she said nothing.

Impatiently, Agustín reached for her, putting one hand on her shoulder.

"Saturday? We'll call it a business meeting. Deveras, it won't take long. It will be a short boring business meeting."

"I'll meet you here, in the parking lot," she told him, quickly making up a lie. "My mother works on Saturday, and I have to drop her off anyway."

Petra was trembling as she got out of the car. Agustín waved goodbye to her as he sped away. At the gate, she noticed the man who had met them at the restaurant waiting in his car. Petra watched the dark brown sedan trail steadily after the black Jaguar until both cars disappeared down the road.

When she drove past the guard station on her way out of the parking lot, Barriga was talking on the phone. She waved to the man, but he turned his back on her, pretending he hadn't seen her at all.

34

Petra met Lola on the patio during their afternoon break. She sat uncomfortably at one of the picnic tables. Lola sat next to her, serious, staring at Petra intently.

"What business meeting? On a Saturday? Will there be other people there?"

"I don't know. He told me to meet him in the parking lot, and we would go from there. It will be a short meeting, he said, and boring."

"Where? Did he say where the meeting would be?"

"No. Only that it wouldn't take long, and he has some things he would like to discuss with me. He said he wants to prove himself to me."

"Prove himself to you? What does that mean?"

"I guess he wants me to trust him. Don't you see, he's concerned about my feelings."

Lola smiled nervously, shaking her head, making her ponytail swish from side to side. "Why doesn't he wait for another meeting at la maquiladora? They have meetings here all the time. He should wait until everyone's present, not sneak around to be alone with you."

Petra leaned on Lola's arm for comfort and sighed. Suddenly, she was afraid of everything—afraid to turn Agustín down, afraid of losing her job and the car, and afraid of her father dying.

"I don't know, Lola. I heard that he's separated from his wife—that she went back to France. Maybe he's depressed over it. He told me she left him and that she's arrogant and doesn't keep her promises."

"Men say all kinds of things about women, especially when they're trying to impress someone else. Who knows what's true? My ex-husband says things about me that make me look like a witch, when the whole time he's to blame for all our problems."

"He drives like a maniac!" Petra told her, suddenly giggling as she remembered his antics on the freeway. "You should have seen him! But he's so handsome and funny. He likes to joke around. It feels good to be with him. He's got all this power. I know he's rich, but that doesn't mean much to me. I don't expect he would ever marry me. And he gave me the car . . . a gift. He's been good to me that way. He's treated me—"

Lola didn't let her finish. "What about Antonio? He's the one who *does* want to marry you. How will you explain all this to him?"

"I won't explain it to him. He'd never understand. He's from another world. I don't know if I can ever go back to that world. I want to succeed here in Juárez, for me, and for my family too. I want to go back to school, travel . . . learn more English. Antonio's so serious. He wants me to go back to Montenegro and marry him—now! If he could take me back today, he would do it, and we would live in Montenegro for the rest of our lives. I can't do that."

"Have you told him that?"

"No, of course not. It would break his heart."

Petra didn't tell Lola about the massage Agustín had asked for at the restaurant, and she didn't mention how Agustín made fun of her engagement ring.

"Don't tell anyone else about your meeting with him on Saturday. We don't want el veijerio to know. Can you imagine what they'll say? They'll have something else to hate you for."

"I can't even confide in my mother. She'll tell my father, and I know he'll get mad. He's already worried about my job here, and he hates Gustavo Rios. He didn't want me to accept the car."

There were tears in Petra's eyes. In her mind, she saw her father's face wasted with illness, his eyes searching her face, loving her—still trying to be a father to her, give her good advice, take care of her.

"Call me as soon as you get back on Saturday from this secret meeting. No matter what time it is. Promise you'll call me!"

"I'll call you."

They stood up together and made their way back into la maquiladora, their shoulders touching gently as they walked.

On Saturday morning, *El Diario*'s headlines told of the death of another young woman whose body had been found in an empty lot in the middle of the city, tortured, raped, with one breast bitten off, and with evidence that her body had been electrocuted. The young woman was positively identified as a seventeen-year-old girl who had worked for New World Industries, a maquiladora owned by U.S. investors. She was from a poor colonia, La Independencia, and she had been missing for over a month before she was found half buried under a pile of trash.

The woman's name was Anita Barbara Ozuna, and her photo in *El Diario* showed the smiling face of a beautiful young woman. Her parents were interviewed and stated they had been threatened by the police every time they asked questions about their daughter's disappearance. They were told to take down posters they had hung up on street corners with their daughter's photo, asking for anyone who would know her whereabouts. The police said they had interrogated some of the girl's friends and found out that she often went out at night without her parent's permission. When her parents asked for the names of friends they had interrogated, the police refused to give any, stating that the investigation was not complete and they could provide no further information.

On television, the girl's mother appeared, weeping, next to her husband, stating that someone was being protected—los intocables, she said, people so powerful and rich no one could stop them. Her daughter had fallen into their hands. Her daughter was a hardworking girl and had plans to attend a university. She wasn't the type of girl to get involved in clubs and to stay out late at night. The governor of Chihuahua was deaf to her cries, the woman said, but God would avenge her daughter's death—that was her prayer.

Evita kept her word and came by on Saturday morning with Mayela and Harry Hughes. Mayela was overjoyed to see Petra and her family again. Flor invited them in and explained that Estevan was in the hospital undergoing more tests. She greeted Evita and el Americano courteously, even though she worried el Americano was Evita's client, and that Evita was no better than the woman they had seen her walking with in el Centro. There were rumors that Evita had run away with one of her mother's boyfriends, and thinking of Brisa and all the drinking she did, Flor suspected there might be some truth to it.

She embraced Mayela tenderly, as if she was her own child, telling her she was growing up and that as soon as her mother got back to Chitlitipin, her sister, Susana, would let her know. Mayela sat by Ester in a large armchair, and the girls laughed because they were almost the same size, even though Mayela was four years older than Ester.

Harry greeted the family in his best Spanish, "Buenos días, y mucho gusto de conocerte."

Abuela Teodora and Flor felt better when they heard Harry's greeting, discounting the strange way the Spanish words sounded to them. They nodded their heads and said he was learning Spanish, yes, he was doing just fine.

"No es presumido," Abuela Teodora said, smiling. She was glad Harry didn't put on airs, acting like other Americans she had seen who looked at Mexicans with disdain.

Harry sat next to Evita, holding her hand attentively and obviously glad to be with her.

"Petra can drive Mayela back to Montenegro after her mother returns," Flor told Evita. "She has a new car. Tell them, Petra, about the car."

Petra bit her lower lip and clasped her hands tightly. "Well, someone from la maquiladora, one of the owners, found out that we were having trouble getting my father to his treatments at the hospital, so he gave me a car—as a gift. You know, he's rich and doesn't need it."

She looked around at everyone and was relieved when they laughed out loud to think of someone being so rich they could give a car away. Flor said she wished they could all be that rich. While they were still laughing, someone knocked at the door, and Abuela Teodora rose to answer it. It was Denise, Ester's friend from next door, with her mother, Cruz. Cruz rushed in with *El Diario* in her hand, the front page open for them to see. She seemed frantic as she showed Flor the headlines announcing the death of another girl, Anita Barbara Ozuna.

"Look! Another death! I tell you that no woman is safe in Juárez!"

Everyone stood up and crowded around the newspaper. It was then that Cruz noticed they had company and began to apologize for intruding on them. She was embarrassed for not noticing there was an American man in the house.

"No, don't apologize," Flor said. "What you have to say is important for all of us. These are matters of life and death, and in Juárez it's death that seems to be winning over life."

Evita looked closely at the photo of the young woman and gasped. She put one hand over her mouth, and with her other hand grabbed Harry's arm for support.

"Qué? What is it?" Flor and Petra were staring at Evita's pale face, her eyes opened wide.

"I've seen her . . . I—" Then she stopped herself. It was the beautiful girl at the private party who stood next to el Junior in the exquisite white gown. She remembered the man's hair—golden red in the room's red glow—and the girl next to him looking helplessly at Evita. Instantly, Evita invented a lie.

"She worked in los mercados on Saturdays, where my mother and I sold merchandise." Harry put his arm around Evita and sat with her on the couch.

"Don't worry," he said in his broken Spanish. "They'll find out who did it."

"No," Petra told him in English. "The police have not been able to tell us who's murdering the girls. They cover things up. They protect themselves . . . it's very hard for us."

Flor and Abuela Teodora agreed with Cruz that not a single second should be spent on the streets by any of them, unless they were accompanied by family, and especially by a man they knew. A silence fell over everyone, and Abuela Teodora reminded them that it was Lent, a time of prayer and sacrifice. Next week, she said, was la Semana Santa, the holiest week in the whole year.

"God came on earth to bear the sufferings and sins of mankind," Abuela Teodora said, "and he will help Anita Barbara's family bear their suffering. I'll light a candle for her, pobrecita, and for her parents, and someday God will right the great wrong done to her. Her death is not in vain." Abuela Teodora sighed and blessed herself with the sign of the cross.

Flor called el Instituto to get permission to have Mayela stay with them for the night. She told Señora Juana del Pilar that Petra would drive her back on Sunday, and it wouldn't be a problem.

"I'll be attending a meeting this afternoon at la maquiladora," Petra told Evita, "and won't be able to spend time with you as we planned. But there will be other times, and now that we both know Mayela we can plan to bring her here to visit."

Harry told Evita that maybe Ester could join them with Mayela, and they would take them to la Plaza and to a movie. Both girls were worried after hearing of the death of Anita Barbara Ozuna, and Ester looked at her mother and Petra and said she'd rather stay home and visit with Mayela.

Evita seemed distracted, her eyes huge and mournful. She looked at everyone as if she was seeing right through them and told Harry she needed to go back home. Then she wrote down the phone number of the flower shop where she worked and told Petra to keep her number in case of an emergency. The next day, Evita would remember this one act as the wisest thing she did that day.

Petra explained to her mother that she'd take her to see her father in the morning, as she didn't know how long the meeting at la maquiladora would last.

"I didn't know there was a meeting today," Flor said.

"Well, just a few people . . . a small business meeting."

"With whom?"

"A few people from the office—uh, Vina and Gustavo Rios. I'm not sure who else. Oh, I think Señor Miramontes will be there too."

"It must be important then," Flor said as she prepared to wash dishes at the kitchen sink.

"What does he look like?" Abuela Teodora asked. "This rich man who gives away cars."

"I don't know—ask Petra," Flor said. "He's too important to show his face on the floor where we work—only at the meetings."

Abuela Teodora and Flor noticed Petra's face turn red. They exchanged surprised looks.

"Well, look at her!" Flor said. "You'd think we had asked her to describe God!"

Then Abuela Teodora's eyes narrowed, and she said sternly, "Antonio was right, Petra; you better keep that ring on your finger."

Just then the phone rang. Flor answered it and said it was Luis Ledezma. She was ready to hand her daughter the phone when Petra said, "Not now. Tell him I'll call him after the meeting."

Luis's call troubled Petra, making her feel as if she should cancel her meeting with Agustín. But she had no idea how to reach Agustín to cancel the meeting. If she canceled, she would have to go to la maquiladora and tell him in person, and she knew he would be angry at her for going back on her word. Meanwhile, her mother explained to Luis that Petra would call him later.

Petra showered and washed her hair, combing it out carefully and letting it fall to her shoulders the way Agustín said he liked it. She put on her makeup sparingly as Ester and Mayela watched. She joked with Ester and Mayela, trying to make Ester's fears go away.

"I'll be back soon—it's only a short meeting," Petra said to her, briefly reaching for her hand. "Hmm? Do I have your permission to go?" She smiled at Ester until her sister's dimples showed and Mayela was laughing as well.

"Mayela will give you a painting lesson while I'm gone."

"I can do that," Mayela said, and held onto Ester's hand, comforting her.

Petra put on a bright blue outfit, with matching shoes and a purse, remembering Agustín said he liked bright colors on her. The skirt was tight around her hips, silky, and tapered to fit her perfectly. She wore a black jersey under the jacket that buttoned at her waist, and she applied fresh smelling cream on her wrists and behind her ears. She let Ester spray perfume on her, sweet vanilla, and the fragrance melted into her skin and rose warm and exhilarating all around her.

She looked at herself in the mirror and smiled, sure Agustín would like what he saw. Petra imagined Agustín's wife to be beautiful and sophisticated. She was a French woman, after all, proud and haughty. He hadn't said a word about her since the time he had told her she was gone to France and had broken all her promises to him. It was as if she didn't exist anymore. Suddenly, Petra felt ashamed of herself for thinking of another woman's husband as if he was her date.

Abuela Teodora walked into the room and told Petra she looked beautiful. But what kind of a meeting was it? Was she trying to impress a man? Petra put her arm around Abuela Teodora and felt the old woman's bony shoulders.

"No, I don't want to impress anyone. It's only a short meeting. I should be back very soon."

"You should dress up like this when Antonio comes to see you on Easter Sunday."

Petra thought about Antonio's visit next weekend. He was coming in with Tío Alvaro from Montenegro. She swished her hair around her shoulders, trying to shake off the thought of having to explain to him about the car and about her meeting with Agustín.

"Of course, abuelita. I know he'll love it."

As if to ward off bad luck, Abuela Teodora blessed Petra, making the sign of the cross on her forehead. Petra felt the blessing and remembered there hadn't been time in her busy schedule to sing to the morning with Abuela Teodora as they had done in Montenegro. She bent down and tenderly kissed Abuela Teodora's cheek.

He was waiting for her in the parking lot, dressed in a gray business suit, with a bright blue shirt and a black tie. "We match," he said when he saw her bright blue outfit.

Petra was expecting to walk into la maquiladora with him. But he said: "The meeting's not in la maquiladora. It's in a restaurant, one of my favorites. I hope you won't mind."

Petra relaxed, thinking they would be sitting with others close by.

"You can leave your car in the parking lot. Barriga will take care of it until we get back." Petra looked toward the guard station and didn't see Barriga around. "He's around here somewhere, and we'll be back soon," Agustín said. He opened the door of the Jaguar for her with a flourish. Petra adjusted her skirt around her legs, tucking her feet under the seat. She braced herself for what she knew would be a wild ride.

"You look ravishing," Agustín said, taking his seat behind the wheel. "Deveras, you should be a model—that would be the perfect job for you."

"I've never modeled in my life! I wouldn't be good at it."

"You're a fast learner, and your looks would be enough—that's the way it is. Beauty sells."

He put on his Ray-Bans and looked glamorous, with every strand of his red hair in place. It made Petra want to reach over and embrace him. Looking at him, she temporarily forgot how terrified she was of his driving.

Petra wanted to ask Agustín about his wife. Was she back from France? And would they get back together again? As she was ready to open her mouth, he accelerated the car at top speed and started telling her about a restaurant he said was close to where he lived in la Villa de las Rosas. He told her they'd have an early dinner while holding their own private business meeting. Petra's hands turned cold when she heard him say "private business meeting." Instinctively, she put her right hand over the engagement ring Antonio had given her.

"You're not nervous again, are you?" Agustín reached over and put his hand on her arm. "I brought some information in my briefcase," he said, motioning with his hand to the backseat.

"I think you'll be interested. It'll mean a promotion for you. Nice. I'll make sure you get to the top, like a shooting star." He laughed out loud. "Like a shooting star—nice!"

"Gracias. I'm in your debt. But I don't want you to go to all this trouble for me. Really, I'm happy working with Gustavo Rios. I've been learning so much."

Petra thought of Gustavo Rios and how she could barely stand to be around him. Compared to Agustín, Gustavo was no more than a lecherous weak old man who wanted to take advantage of any time he could find alone with her. Agustín was powerful and would stop at nothing to get what he wanted. She could rescue herself from Gustavo Rios, but if Agustín pressed her, she knew she wouldn't win.

The restaurant, el Arco Iris, was set behind manicured hedges, trees, and flowers. They followed a circular driveway to get in, and as they stopped at the entrance, an employee ran up to the driver's side to open Agustín's door. As soon as Agustín stepped out, the man raced to Petra's side to open the door for her, then hurried back to the driver's seat to drive the car away. They walked in, arm in arm, through the huge double doors adorned with a stained-glass rainbow, opened for them by two waiters. Petra looked back into the parking lot and noticed the security man who worked for Agustín's family standing at his car, the dark brown sedan with the black top. He was casually dressed, with dark glasses and a baseball cap on his head. Anyone who looked at him would think he was on his way to a baseball game. She could also see the outline of a second man sitting in the passenger side.

The restaurant was dimly lit, plush and elegant. A waiter with a white shirt, black bow tie, and matching pants immediately approached them. He didn't look directly at Petra, concentrating on talking to Agustín.

"Buenas tardes, Señor Miramontes. Would you like to sit at your table or at the bar?"

"At my table."

As they passed a few people sitting in the dining area, Petra heard music playing in another room: stringed instruments—guitars, violins. They walked across a red-tiled patio with a fountain set in the center and into another section of the restaurant, richly decorated and set with only a few tables.

As they sat at his private table, Agustín ordered wine for them.

"Do you have chocolate-covered strawberries?" he asked the waiter. When the man looked at him puzzled, he smiled at Petra.

"Here we go again," Agustín said. "It's an American dessert," he said in English.

The waiter didn't know any English and stood with a linen cloth draped over his arm, wondering what to do.

Already, Petra was worried Agustín would get impatient with him and make him get the strawberries, no matter what. She was relieved when he told the waiter to forget it and just bring a dessert tray.

In his briefcase Agustín had papers, notes, and information he had gathered from people who worked at Western Electronics. He wanted her to look over the information and see how they could make up a training booklet for the new employees in Buenos Aires.

"I'd like you to take the lead on this, be the one who supervises all the training. Would you be willing to do this?"

He handed her a few papers that had notes scribbled on them and a chart showing the structure of the training sessions, six weeks in all. She'd have to be there for the whole training session and live in Buenos Aires, he said. He would go with her, to set things up, and introduce her to the executives of the company. Petra looked over the notes and wondered why this wasn't being handled through Gustavo Rios or another supervisor. It seemed like something that could be taken care of by those already doing training sessions in other cities. She had seen training booklets while looking through information in Gustavo Rios's office, and the notes Agustín showed her seemed to be incomplete, with many pieces of information missing. She didn't say anything to him, only told him it looked as if it would work. He was pleased with her answer, and said he had known she would approve of his plan. Then he leaned toward her across the table and took her hand in his.

"I knew you would be the one who could move forward with this training."

For the first time Petra stared intently into his eyes—brown, with flecks of green, she couldn't decide on the color. His hand was smooth and warm over hers. He took away the notes and put them into his brief-case as if they weren't important anymore.

"Your eyes are beautiful," he said softly. "Gray. I've never seen that color—so different."

"And yours are green, hazel, I can't make up my mind. More beauti-ful, I would say."

"It's the French in me, and my hair—I don't like the red." He ran his fingers restlessly through his hair.

"No! I can't believe you said that. It's perfect." She stopped short of telling him she thought he was perfect and noticed a look in his eyes, the same look she had seen in Antonio's when he had told her he wanted to escape with her to Montenegro. Nervously she looked away, hoping he'd let her look through the paperwork again to distract him from paying attention to her. She wanted to keep their meeting formal and business-like. The memory of Anita Barbara Ozuna's beautiful face surfaced in her mind. She wondered who would do such a brutal thing to someone so beautiful.

"Did you see *El Diario* this morning?" she asked.

"I don't read *El Diario*," he said, obviously irritated. He let her hand go and sat up stiffly in his chair. "I fight with its reporters all the time. They're always trying to make my family look like a bunch of mafiosos—malvados. Lies, that's all anyone can expect from them."

"The story on the front page this morning was of a girl—Anita Barbara Ozuna. She was brutally murdered. I don't know how anyone could murder someone like that! What reason would they have for com-mitting such a crime?" Petra shuddered and instinctively ran her hands up and down her arms as if she was freezing. "Who would do this?" she asked, "and why haven't the police been able to find the murderers?"

Agustín didn't answer her questions. He got up and excused himself, saying he had to make a phone call. He stepped out into a nearby patio. Petra saw him on the phone listening intently to someone on the other line. After a few minutes he walked back to the table, taking up the conversation where he had left off. It was as if Petra had never mentioned Anita Barbara Ozuna.

"Well, now that you understand about the training sessions, I think we can enjoy our dinner."

Petra was already worried because the training sessions were six weeks long. She wanted to tell him that leaving home for six weeks was impossible for her because of her father's illness.

Before she could say anything, the waiter came back with a bottle of white wine for Agustín to approve of and a silver tray with the restaurant's desserts, beautifully displayed.

"All of them," Agustín said. "And bring them now."

"Perdón, señor?" the waiter asked. "All of them?"

"Is there a problem?" Agustín shifted impatiently in his chair.

The waiter sensed Agustín's anger. "No, señor, no problem at all!"

"We'll eat what we want," he said to Petra, ignoring the waiter.

Petra was amazed at the food served to them: fish with a rich creamy sauce and a gourmet plate of filet mignon, with a salad mixed with asparagus, chipotles, and white cheese. The desserts were fruit tarts, flan dripping with rich dark syrup, crescents with a sweet fig-nut filling, and petits fours in various designs and flavors. Petra watched Agustín take a bite of one dessert, leave it, and turn to something else. He wasn't easily satisfied and told her he had tasted better. Flavors, rich and sticky sweet, melted on Petra's tongue as she sampled the desserts; she didn't think she had ever tasted anything so delicious. She was tempted to take the entire tray home to share with her family but was afraid to ask. She was sure the desserts were something Agustín was used to eating.

After their dinner, Petra was relieved to hear Agustín say he had to leave, as he was expecting a call from his associates overseas. He said he had spent months in Europe over the years helping set up businesses for his family, and sometimes he wanted to stay there. But Mexico was his home, and he would always come back. He told her he'd take her back to her car, but before they left he requested a song from the quartet playing at the restaurant. Petra could see them, four men in fancy outfits, set up on a stage in the next room. He requested "Gema," an old love song—it was his mother's favorite.

The sun was casting an orange glow on the distant horizon by the time Agustín drove Petra back to her car. She was surprised they had taken so long at the restaurant and was glad she'd be back in time to take her mother to visit with her father in the hospital. She remembered that Mayela was staying the night at her house. She'd be able to spend some time with her, maybe have her draw a sketch of her and Ester. La Niñita Frida—Petra could hardly believe the success Mayela now had as an artist. She smiled to think of how Mayela had come back into her life through her cousin Evita. She thought about Evita and the look on her face when she saw the photo of Anita Barbara Ozuna in the newspaper. Evita seemed secretive to Petra, as if she was hiding something deep inside her heart—something she showed to no one, certainly not to the American soldier she was dating. She resolved to call Evita at the flower shop, then realized she had left Evita's phone number at the house.

Petra felt lightheaded from the wine, relaxed and with a sense that maybe she was wasting her time feeling threatened by Agustín. He was spending money on her and treating her like a queen. Members of the cartels were ruthless men who committed murders, rapes, and tortures and controlled the police and government officials. In spite of all Luis had told her about Agustín, Petra couldn't believe he was a member of a cartel, much less of a group of mafiosos or drug traficantes. She was getting used to him, to his crazy driving, and to the way he reached for her and put his arm around her, leaving one hand casually looped over the steering wheel. Before they got back to la maquiladora, Agustín rested his hand briefly on Petra's thigh, and she felt his big warm palm through her skirt.

At the guard station stood Barriga, waving them into the parking lot. This time, Agustín didn't bother to put the window down and talk to him. He stopped the Jaguar next to the white Honda and kissed Petra on the cheek before she got out of the car, then gazed passionately into her eyes.

"I'm sorry the night has to end so early. I wanted it to go on forever. Wouldn't you?"

"Yes . . . that would be nice." She was tempted to lean toward him and kiss him on the mouth, but resisted the temptation and smiled, pressing her face close to his.

"I'll call you," he said, his voice full and sensual in her ear. "Before you know it, we'll be together again."

Petra got into the Honda and watched the dark brown sedan with the two men inside trail Agustín home. She sighed in relief and began to feel giddy from the wonderful time she had spent with Agustín. She passed by the guard station and saw Barriga standing inside staring blankly ahead. She raised her hand to wave, but decided not to, as he always pretended he hadn't seen her. She drove faster than usual, imitating Agustín's style, and wondered what Antonio would say if he had seen her in Agustín's car. Maybe he would fight with Agustín, or yell at her, take his engagement ring off her finger. Petra saw Antonio's serious face in her mind, and her feelings became chaotic. She wanted him to come back to her and live in Juárez, get a job, learn English, stay with her, and build a life in the city. In the next thought, she wanted him to stay in Montenegro and live the rest of his days on his ranch, far away from her, as she didn't believe he'd ever understand her. He wouldn't be able to accept her success, her trips to Buenos Aires and the business meetings in El Paso. She was already dreading his visit on Easter Sunday.

As she was thinking of Antonio, Petra noticed the dark brown sedan with the black top in her rearview mirror. She knew it was Agustín's security man and wondered why he was following her. She saw the car loop through traffic to get to her car. At a stoplight, the sedan stopped next to her car, and the driver rolled down his window and signaled for her to do the same.

"El señor," he said. "El Señor Miramontes Guzmán would like to speak to you before you go home. He forgot to tell you something and would like you to go back to la maquiladora."

"Can he wait until tomorrow? Or call me on the phone later tonight?"

The man looked at her, his bushy eyebrows coming together on his forehead. He pushed his cap back on his head. He wasn't wearing his dark glasses, and Petra could see that his left eye had suffered a blow. He was wearing a glass eye, hazy and discolored.

"You have to come with me, señorita," he said firmly. "It won't take long."

Petra hesitated and thought of stepping on the gas pedal and speeding away. She noticed a hard look on the man's face, his one good eye pointed at her, unblinking. Then a second car approached behind hers, and she saw that there was nothing left for her to do but follow the man back to la maquiladora.

35

Barriga was in the parking lot, ready to shut the gate and start security for the night when Petra drove in with the dark brown sedan trailing her. He waved both cars in and left the gate open. As Petra parked the Honda and opened her door, she was surprised to see Vina Salcido driving out of la maquiladora in her gray Toyota. She waved to her, and Vina waved back. Vina rarely worked on a Saturday, and Petra wondered if she was working on a special project with Gustavo Rios, or if Agustín had called her in. Agustín's security man got out of his car.

"El Señor Miramontes is waiting for you," he said gruffly. "You'll ride in my car now."

"Where is el Señor Miramontes?"

"Waiting for you. I'll take you to where he is."

Petra felt herself trembling and looked around to see if anybody was watching them. There were only a few cars in the parking lot belonging to the cleaning crew. Barriga had disappeared from the guard station and was nowhere to be seen. Petra stood perfectly still as the cool night breeze blew through her hair. Her shoes felt stuck to the pavement, and nausea rose from her stomach. Everything she had been warned about was happening to her.

The man pulled out a cigarette from his shirt pocket, lit it up, and watched her, squinting with his good eye. "Do you know Vina Salcido?"

"Yes, I just saw her drive away."

"She'll be there, so you won't be alone. El Señor Miramontes would like to talk to both of you."

When Petra heard him say that Vina would also be there, she relaxed and thought maybe Vina had forgotten to mention to her that she had a meeting on Saturday with Agustín, or maybe she hadn't expected that Agustín would invite her as well. That was Vina, always being suspicious and jealous of her. Maybe this would teach her a lesson—she was just as important to Agustín as Vina was.

She got into the dark brown sedan without another word. There was another man sitting quietly in the backseat. He was young, dark, and bent over, as if he were ready to spring at her. The car smelled of cigarette smoke mixed with greasy hair oil and a man's sweat. The dark young man sat back and said nothing. The driver passed a cigarette to him, and the young man lit it up and started smoking, blowing the smoke into the back of Petra's head.

By the time they arrived in el distrito Villa de las Rosas, night had fallen and street lights were on, glowing dimly in the dark. Petra glimpsed the front of the house, with its marble stone steps leading to a huge double door. She could make out the outline of hedges, rose bushes, and an immense lawn.

The car circled to the back, and Petra noticed the entire length of the property was surrounded by a high block wall with barbed wire looped over the top. The car stopped at an ornate wrought-iron gate, and motion lights blinked on as the gate opened automatically for them. The enormous grounds looked like a park with tall trees and sloping hills spread out into the distance. At the entrance was a guard station, with a man standing outside wearing a gun at his hip. The dark sedan slowed down, coming to a stop in front of the man. Anxiously, Petra looked around for Vina Salcido's gray Toyota in the darkness but didn't see it anywhere. As the car came to a stop, the young man in the backseat got out and opened her door. He was skinny, his eyes closely set, his nose sticking out of his face like a vulture's misshapen beak. His dark hair was streaked back with hair oil, making his hard face appear to be chiseled in granite. When he told Petra to get out of the car, his voice was low and gruff, as if he was speaking to her from behind his hand, purposely muffling his voice. Petra caught the fragrance of roses and gardenias in the air and noticed vines covering the entire back wall of the house, blocking out windows and climbing up to the rooftop.

"Come with me," the young man ordered her. Then he looked at the man who was driving. "I'll take this cargo inside," he said, grabbing Petra by the wrist and digging his fingers deep into her flesh.

"You don't have to hurt me!" she said, alarmed at how tightly he was holding her wrist. He laughed as if it was all a big joke.

"Órale, Cucuy," the driver said. "Don't get anxious. There'll be some for everybody."

All three men laughed. Petra stumbled forward, ready to fall on the ground as she realized she was in the clutches of el Cucuy, the ruthless leader of Los Rebeldes.

"So, you know me!" he said, laughing and sinking his fingers deeper into her flesh.

"Vina! Vina! Are you here?" Petra shouted, wildly searching in the dark for Vina's car.

"Callate! Are you crazy? Shut up!" el Cucuy yelled. "You're just like your brother, that little puto, who isn't even a man!" El Cucuy put up his fist as if he would strike her, then in the distance she heard Agustín's voice.

"Don't you dare touch her! She's my guest!"

Petra ran toward Agustín's voice, rushing into his arms. She felt his clothing, smooth and silky, as he embraced her. She was shaking in fear, and he soothed her, telling her to calm down.

"My security people can get a little carried away, and sometimes they get a little violent," he said. He yelled at el Cucuy to stay back, then called over the driver of the sedan.

"Hilo, take this man away and teach him some manners. He has to learn how to control himself around a lady. Is he crazy?"

"Vámonos!" Hilo said, laughing with el Cucuy, and they disappeared into the darkness.

"Where's Vina?" Petra asked Agustín, her voice breaking. "I saw her leaving the parking lot at la maquiladora."

"Oh, she should be here shortly. I told her to take her time. I have some business to discuss with both of you. But first, I'd like you to do me a favor. Would you do that for me?"

"Yes, I will . . . but first, I have to go home! My family will be worried . . . you see, they're expecting me back by now!" Petra felt her teeth chattering as she struggled to speak.

"Of course they are, and you will get home—that I guarantee you."

He took her hand and led her to the house and into a large room lit by Tiffany lamps with red bulbs. The room was elegant, with French doors adorning one side of the room and a huge circular bar in the center. On one side of the enormous room Petra saw a small stage.

"For my performers," he said.

They walked through the French doors and into a private room with overstuffed couches, chairs, and an ornate fireplace. The room, dimly lit by two chandeliers, smelled of polished wood.

"Sit here," he said, leading her to one of the couches. "Estás en tu casa. You're welcome here. Vina should be along any minute."

Petra wanted to ask about his wife. Maybe she was already back from France and this very moment asleep in another part of the house. He must love her—even if only a little. She wanted to bring him back to reality, as if the memory of his wife could reach out and save her.

"And your wife . . ." she said softly, afraid of offending him.

He glared at her. "That shouldn't matter to you!"

Petra noticed he was wearing what looked like silk pajamas, with slippers on his feet. Her heart raced as she realized he was dressed to go to bed. He walked to a table and picked up a box, white with a big shiny bow at the top.

"A present," he said. "For you. This is the favor I'd like to ask of you—and, of course, there can be no excuses. Remember I said I wanted to prove myself to you. Well, this is how I'll do it."

Petra's eyes filled with tears as she began to understand that there would be no escape for her and that Vina Salcido was not coming. Vina had been part of the plan to bring her, without incident, to Agustín's house. She must open the present and do whatever Agustín told her to do. She was ready to beg him to let her go when he grabbed her chin in one hand, twisted her face up to his, and kissed her hard on the mouth. She broke away from him, wincing in pain.

"You don't like it? But you were ready to kiss me before you got out of my car today. Remember? Oh, you were ready to give it to me then! That's when I decided to bring you here. Since you're so interested in kissing me, I'm making it easy for you. But never mind, si no quieres. You've made your choice, and maybe later you'll feel like kissing me. Open it!" he said, putting the box in her hands.

Petra nervously untied the satin bow and fumbled taking off the lid. Inside was a dress wrapped in fine white tissue paper. Agustín's eyes lit up when he saw the dress. He tore the gift box from her hands and threw it across the room. He held the dress up, and Petra saw that it was an elaborate gown, white, covered with tiny pearls and rhinestones. The neckline was an intricate lace design, and the back of the dress was made to dip to the middle of a woman's back. On the hem were embroidered white lilies with long golden stems. Petra had never seen such a beautiful dress and stared at it in silence.

"Touch it," Agustín commanded her. "French lace at its best! I want you to wear it for me. It was my grandmother's, then my mother's, and now my wife's, after her, my next wife, and who knows how many after that! It's an evening dress, something you would wear at your engagement party—if you had ever had one." He laughed out loud.

"Every time I see it, I think of virgins, waiting for their first man to climb into bed with them—hot, hot women, wanting to do it over and over again." His face turned bright red, and he stared at her. Petra saw in his eyes a look of pure evil, and she went pale as she looked from Agustín to the dress.

"Afraid, Petra? But why? Of wearing a beautiful dress? Here, this woman will help you."

Petra looked up and saw a woman walk into the room. At first, she thought it might be Vina, as the woman was short and round. Maybe she was wrong about Vina, and she really would be there to help her escape Agustín. A sense of hope rushed over her.

"Still thinking about Vina!" Agustín said, watching her face. "Another whore! Well, she did one thing right, she helped me get you here tonight— something about not wanting me to kill her father, as if I would need to kill him! He'll drink himself to death before I can get to him. But I owe her, yes, I do, and I'll repay her—not the way she wants but the way I want!" Agustín motioned impatiently to the woman. "Get her dressed!" he yelled.

Silently, the woman began to take off Petra's bright blue jacket, but Petra pushed her away, crying, saying she didn't want to take her clothes off. Agustín sat down in one of the armchairs and threatened in a booming voice.

"You let her put the dress on you, or I'll call in el Cucuy and he can do it for you! Which would you prefer?"

Petra didn't answer him, but stood still for the woman to undress her in front of Agustín. He sat with one hand on his crotch as he watched. The woman took off all of Petra's clothes, as well as her underwear.

"You won't need anything," Agustín said to her, reaching into his pants and exposing himself to her.

"Just this," he said, laughing, "just this," and he held his member in his hands.

The whole time the woman was silent and seemed to be following directions like a wooden puppet. The dress was a perfect fit, outlining Petra's figure, simply and sensually.

"I knew it!" he cried, obviously happy about the way she looked. "I knew it would come alive again. Anita Barbara didn't look as good as you do! Her tits weren't as big as yours . . . but yours—I can hardly wait!"

When Petra heard Anita Barbara's name, her knees weakened and she began to fall. Agustín grabbed her arm.

"That scared, are you? And you're the one who wanted to talk to me about what you read in the newspaper. One less whore in the world!"

He led her roughly to a gilt mirror and told her to look at herself. "See," he said. "Even Antonio would just love the way you look—especially, him!" He laughed and held up her hand with the engagement ring.

"Can you imagine what he gave you? A cheap ring you get out of candy machines!"

Fear swept over Petra as she heard Agustín say Antonio's name. He knew about him. And Petra now realized that Agustín probably knew about her entire family. How could she have been such a fool to think he didn't know?

"And look over here." He pulled on her hair and spun her around to face a fireplace with an elaborate mantelpiece. Over the mantelpiece was a fancy coat of arms with his family name etched in silver and gold: CORTES MIRAMONTES GUZMAN.

"He was my grandfather, el conquistador himself. Who knows which one of his bastard sons I am! Do you like it? I'm a conqueror—there's nothing you can do but submit, again and again and again!" He yanked her hair as hard as he could, and Petra screamed in pain, feeling blood oozing from her scalp. He shook strands of her hair off his hand, as if it meant nothing to him.

"Bring us something to drink," he told the woman ". . . and the dessert, don't forget the dessert."

He started a tape player, and music began to play. Petra stood frozen, her body heavy, as if she was walking under water. Her head ached, and the spot where Agustín had yanked out her hair burned with pain. The woman returned, carrying a silver tray with a bottle of wine and a dish of chocolate-covered strawberries.

"Your favorite! See how nice I am? I think of everything!"

He poured a glass of wine for her and invited her to sit, pulling her down hard on the couch.

"Drink . . . and eat, but don't get the dress dirty. I know how you people are from los ranchos—those little villages where you live like animals. Brutos, dejados, you've lived covered in filth and dirt all your life. What do you know about elegance. What? Answer me, Petra! What do you know about elegance?"

"Nothing."

"Exactly. And why should someone who knows nothing about elegance be allowed to live? Why?"

He forced Petra to drink the wine, which was sweet, with a bitter taste that clung to her tongue. He said he'd sweeten it up with a strawberry and forced one into her mouth, making her gag as he forced it down her throat. Before she was finished trying to chew it, tears streaming down her face, he forced another one in her mouth and more wine. Dark liquid ran down the sides of her mouth, and she reached for something to wipe it. He only laughed uncontrollably and grabbed a napkin, roughly cleaning her mouth with it and slapping her in the face, "to teach you how to eat with manners."

The song he requested at the restaurant, "Gema," started to play, and he took her in his arms and began to dance with her, tenderly, embracing her close. Petra became dizzy from all the turns.

"Por favor, Agustín. I'm begging you to let me go," she whispered in his ear. "I won't tell anyone . . . I promise, no one will know . . . my father . . . you said you knew what it's like to have a father who's sick."

"I hated my father!" he yelled in a voice that made Petra cringe. He raised his hand and hit her in the face full force, knocking her to the floor. "How dare you talk to me about my father!"

For a few seconds everything went dark for Petra. When she opened her eyes, the chandelier seemed to be moving on its own. In her mind she saw images of her mother's face, her father's, Abuela Teodora's, and Ester's tiny frightened face, worried for her. They would know—something would be done. People would look for her. She could count on Luis, Antonio, Evita, and Evita's American boyfriend. She remembered she had promised her friend, Lola Sesma, to call her as soon as she got home. Lola would know. She'd call the police. Then she shuddered, knowing the police would not look for her. Petra knew now that her father had been right about Gustavo Rios. Everything was a setup, even the car, to get her into Agustín's power. And Vina Salcido? Her betrayer.

The memory of her father came to Petra as she lay on the floor. But it was as if she was staring at him through a hazy glass window. His face was an ugly skull with eyes stuck in deep dark sockets. He was dying, his heart breaking for her. She heard Agustín far away, as if his voice was an echo in her head. In the back of her mind, she realized she had been given something—a drug to make her body feel as if she was dead and destroy her thinking. Even when Agustín got close to her and began to touch her, running his hands over her body, Petra was unable to move a muscle to stop him. His voice was high pitched, like a cartoon character, and she wanted to laugh at it.

Then his voice turned shrill, a hideous howl, as he shrieked in her face that she wasn't worthy to wear the Miramontes dress, and he should have known better than to waste his time putting it on her. A whore like her would know nothing about such elegance, he said. He called the woman back in and told her to undress Petra, as he didn't want to tear the dress off of her and end up spoiling it.

Once the dress was removed and Petra lay naked on the floor, he said: "Now, I'll prove myself to you." He stood over her, enraged, breathing wildly, his eyes narrowed to menacing slits. Then he pounced on her, a vicious animal unleashing itself on its prey.

At nine o'clock that evening, Flor was sitting on the couch desperately watching for Petra. Every time she saw headlights turn the corner of the street, she was on her feet. Even if the meeting had taken longer, it should have ended by now. Her heart raced as she called Western Electronics over and over, hoping someone would pick up the phone. She was trying to remain calm for the sake of Abuela Teodora, Ester, and Mayela. By ten thirty, Flor was ready to take a taxi to la maquiladora to find out if anyone had seen Petra. Maybe the security guard, Barriga, could give her some information. Ester was already crying, wringing her hands, clinging to Mayela for comfort. Abuela Teodora had lit a candle and had her prayer book in her hand, mumbling chants, whispering prayers.

Flor placed a call to her sister, Susana, in Montenegro, calling twice before Susana answered. She tried to remain calm, but as soon as she heard her sister's voice, she broke into tears. Abuela Teodora had to take the phone from her and talk to Susana, telling her Petra wasn't home and everyone was worried. She told Susana to tell Antonio and Alvaro what had happened and that all of them should come to Juárez as quickly as possible.

"God brought us to Juárez to kill us! One by one—that's what He wants to do!" Flor wailed. "We'll all join him on Good Friday; maybe that will satisfy Him!"

Abuela Teodora hung up the phone and turned her attention to Flor. She rushed to the kitchen sink and soaked a towel with warm water for Flor's neck and forehead. She told Mayela to go next door and get Cruz to bring over some rubbing alcohol for Flor, who seemed about to faint.

In a few minutes, Cruz rushed in still wearing her nightgown, with Mayela at her side and a bottle of rubbing alcohol in her hands. Her eyes were huge and frightened. She began to rub Flor's wrists and the back of her neck, and put the bottle under her nose for her to smell.

When the phone rang, Flor grabbed it before anyone else could reach it. It was Lola, asking if Petra was home yet.

"No!" Flor shouted in despair. "She's not home yet! Do you know where she is? We have to do something. I'm going to la maquiladora right now, break the door down if I have to!"

Lola said she knew one of the ladies who cleaned la maquiladora at night, and she'd call her house to see if she knew anything about a meeting that was to be held there on a Saturday night.

"Maybe Petra had to go to El Paso, and they had trouble crossing back into Juárez," Lola told Flor, trying to make sense of Petra's disappearance and at the same time comfort her mother.

"She would have called me, or you, to tell us if she was coming home this late. She knows how things are on the streets. We didn't go visit her father tonight—he knows nothing about this. I don't think he can take it. He's been very ill, not responding to his treatments. Petra would never do this! She would have called us by now!"

"What about Antonio? Wasn't he coming into town?"

"Not until next Sunday, on Easter. He doesn't have a phone, but I called my sister, Susana, and told her to tell him."

Lola told Flor she'd get a neighbor to stay with her children and be at her house as quickly as she could. Flor called the police station and said she wanted to make a report that her daughter was missing. She was aware that she sounded hysterical and that her teeth were chattering as if she was freezing to death. Abuela Teodora was sitting at the kitchen table with Cruz, Mayela, and Ester. Abuela Teodora hugged Ester with one arm and held her prayer book in the other. She stared blankly into la veladora's shining flame, intently whispering her prayers as Ester leaned on her shoulder in tears while holding onto Mayela's hand. Ester was living out her nightmare, and there was no comforting her.

The policeman on the phone told Flor he couldn't send an officer to her house. Her daughter had not been gone for twenty-four hours, and they couldn't start their investigation until then.

"Cálmese, señora," he said flatly. "You will accomplish more with patience—and don't rush the information at me. I can't write that fast." He listened to Flor telling him Petra's name and her address in Nuevo Leon.

"Ah, la colonia Nuevo Leon," he said, as if he would expect trouble from there. "Dónde—where was your daughter going tonight?"

"A meeting with some people at la maquiladora Western Electronics. We both work there."

"A meeting on a Saturday? With whom?"

"Just a few people, and she said it wouldn't take long. It was this afternoon. She should have been home a long time ago!" Flor's voice broke.

"Again, calm yourself!" the officer said impatiently. "How do you expect me to get information if you're stopping to cry every few seconds? Why didn't you go to the meeting with your daughter? You said you work there, too."

"She works in the office. Her boss is Gustavo Rios, and she's in training for an office job. I work on the assembly line; I don't do the same kind of work she does. I don't have to go to the meetings she goes to."

"Did you call la maquiladora?"

"Yes, but nobody answers the phone." Flor started to cry again.

"Señora, por favor! It's Saturday as you know, and most maquiladoras close on the weekend, so this must have been a special meeting. What was your daughter wearing?"

"A blue skirt and jacket, high heels, and a purse to match. She's beautiful, my daughter . . . she's—"

"It sounds like she was going out dancing! Does she go out to clubs? Lots of girls from las maquiladoras go to clubs. Some of them lead double lives, señora. During the day they work, and at night they go to parties and run off with men. Does your daughter have a boyfriend?"

"Sí . . . but he's not here. He's in Montenegro." Anger rose in Flor as she listened to the officer accuse her daughter of living a double life.

"That's what you think, señora. He may be right here in Juárez with your daughter. I've seen these cases many times. Young lovers, ya sabes, they look for ways to meet one another.

"No!" Flor shouted. "My daughter would never do that."

"Many mothers have said the same thing—and their daughters have fooled them. Does your daughter have friends at la maquiladora?"

"One friend. She's on her way here."

"Question her. She may have the answer to your daughter's disappearance. You're ready to have a heart attack, and it may be for nothing."

"And she has a car—a new car she's driving." Flor described the Honda for the officer.

"A new car? I thought you said she worked at la maquiladora. How did she get a new car?"

"It was a gift."

"Now, señora, this is what I'm talking about. A gift, I imagine from a man? Hmm . . . what did I tell you?"

Flor closed her eyes and tried hard not to scream at the police officer.

"And who is this man who gave your daughter a *new* car! I can hardly believe a man would do that for nothing . . . Forgive me if I sound vulgar . . . but I'm speaking the truth."

"El Señor Agustín Miramontes Guzmán. He offered her the car because my husband's ill, and he wanted to help us."

There was silence on the other end of the line after she mentioned Agustín's name. Flor heard the officer breathing hard into the phone, then clearing his throat.

"Did you hear me?" Flor shouted. "Did you hear me? My daughter's gone, and you had better find her!"

"Don't threaten me, señora!" the man said in anger. "It's not my fault your daughter leads a double life and has your family fooled. She may turn up in the next few days with her boyfriend—or maybe she'll hide out and live with him for years before she returns. In any case . . ."

Flor banged the receiver down and stood with her knees shaking. Ester and Mayela ran to her, and she held them close. There was knocking at the door, and Flor rushed to open it, thinking it might be Petra coming home. It was Lola Sesma, standing in the dark, looking like a ghost.

Early Sunday morning, Evita got a call at the flower shop. Flor found the phone number Evita had written for Petra the day before. She was crying, telling Evita that Petra had disappeared.

"We called the police! They've done nothing to help us. They tell us she hasn't been gone long enough. They've accused her of being a prostitute! We must reach Luis Ledezma! Do you have his number?"

"Yes, I have it. I'll call him."

"He'll help us. He knows these streets, and he loves her . . ."

Stunned, Evita dropped the phone. She remembered how she had felt when the policeman had assaulted her, and the fear was there again, a burning sensation in her throat that threatened to choke the life out of her.

Evita saw Anita Barbara Ozuna's face in her mind—the white dress she was wearing, the way she looked at her helplessly at the private party, and el Junior standing next to her, pulling her along as if she was a puppet on a string. She thought of Cristal and wondered if she knew who the man was with the red hair, so handsome and everyone making way for him. But Cristal wouldn't tell her. Evita was sure of it.

She picked up the phone again and asked to speak to Mayela. In a moment she heard Mayela's solemn voice greeting her.

"The woman, Mayela . . . the woman who gave you the photo—who is she?"

"The woman?" Mayela seemed confused.

"The woman in the beautiful dress whose photo you had at el Instituto . . . you were painting her picture."

"She's a rich lady. We went to see her at her house. She lives in el distrito Villa de Las Rosas. Her name's Gabriela LaFarge. She said she was from France, but her husband's from Mexico."

"Did you see her husband? Was he there when you visited?"

"No."

Evita's voice was shaky. Mayela was afraid she wasn't saying something right; maybe she was making more trouble for Petra.

"I'm sorry . . . I don't know anything more. Maybe la doctora at el Instituto or Señora Juana del Pilar. Someone should know more!"

Evita told her not to worry and asked her to call Flor back to the phone.

"Señora, who gave Petra her car?"

"He's one of the owners of la maquiladora—his name is Agustín Miramontes Guzmán. It was a gift, to help us now that my husband's been so sick. I've never seen him." She looked desperately at Lola and asked her if she had ever seen him. Lola shook her head. "Her friend Lola's here, and she says she's never seen him either. We don't know him, only his name."

Evita wanted to tell her she had seen him, but only said she'd call Luis Ledezma. He would know people who might be able to help them . . . and she'd call her American boyfriend to see what he could do. Americans sometimes found solutions to problems when all else had failed. Evita hung up the phone knowing who had abducted Petra.

36 Evita called Luis Ledezma's house just as he finished his cup of coffee and was ready to leave for his second job, working part-time as a driver for a furniture store. He had given up burying chemicals in the desert for the Americans and now ran his hand leisurely over his face, glad his skin was showing signs of health. Evita's words instantly banished all other thoughts and his sense of weariness. Her panicked voice over the phone cried in despair, "Petra's disappeared!"

Luis hung up the phone and drove through the narrow city streets in his pickup truck like a madman, cursing Juárez. He stopped where he saw men gathered to ask if anyone had seen his brother, Chano. The men were dressed in old work clothes, smoking cigarettes, some of them hungover from drinking until the early hours of the morning. They looked at him closely. Was it an emergency? What had happened? Was it another fight between Luis and his brother? They didn't want anything to do with it. Luis wanted to tell them about Petra, but couldn't make himself say her name. He told them he was looking for his brother. He couldn't mention Agustín's name—they would say he was crazy. What did he want? To end up dead? Just the name, Miramontes Guzmán, could mean that somebody would look for you, los muertos no hablan, the code of the cartels—dead men don't talk. Luis gripped the steering wheel, his fingers white, trembling. He had to get his hands on Chano, around his neck, make him tell him where Petra was. If anybody knew, it was Chano. Chano knew Hilo, the Miramontes driver, Agustín's bodyguard. Chano had been used by los Miramontes before, until he got so hooked on drugs he was useless—not even worth a bullet. Luis reached under the seat of his truck with his right hand and felt for the small handgun he used for protection against thieves—and now was reserving for his brother.

Evita called Harry's aunt and uncle in El Paso. She didn't know their last name—Harry had never told her. A man answered, Harry's uncle, Al. Evita asked for Dominica in Spanish, and he responded in good Spanish. She was glad he didn't ask her who she was, as she didn't know how she would explain herself to him. Would she say el Cadet's girlfriend? Or una amiga de Harry Hughes? She was conscious that she couldn't pronounce Harry's name correctly in English. Every time Harry heard her say his name, he smiled and told her it sounded OK to him.

When Dominica got on the phone, Evita told her she must get a message to el Cadet at the base as soon as possible.

"De parte de quien?" Dominica wanted to know who she was, although Evita realized she probably already knew. She said she was Evita Reynosa from Juárez, a friend of el Cadet's.

"Oh, sí, he told me about you. I'm very glad to meet you, even if it is over the phone."

"Es una cosa de emergencia. An emergency. Something he has to know now. It's about one of my friends. He knows who she is."

"Is she hurt? Has there been an accident?"

Evita hesitated, not knowing how much to tell Dominica. How could she explain Petra's disappearance and Anita Barbara's death? All she said was gracias for giving him her message, and please tell him to come to Juárez as quickly as possible. She thought of Harry getting the news, his worried face, and how hard he'd try to get back to Juárez. She missed him, his big body next to hers as they walked down the street, one of his hands covering both of hers. He was gentle with her, something Evita wasn't used to from a man. Somehow he saw her pain, and he told her in his broken Spanish: "Don't run away from me. I won't hurt you."

It was Monday, April 1, the beginning of Holy Week, and the day was cloudy, dark. Flor hadn't slept since Petra had disappeared. Her eyes were red from crying and her mind confused. She couldn't figure out what day it was, or how much time had passed since she had last seen her daughter. It seemed like forever. She had already spoken to Gustavo Rios, though she couldn't remember what she had said to him. She may have screamed at him, because she remembered he hung up on her. She wanted to go to la maquiladora and set fire to it. Make everybody come out all at once so she could look at each one, face to face, and get them to confess: Amapola Nieto and her veijerio, and Humberto Ornelas's whore of a wife, Bridget—how they hated her daughter! If she found out they had anything to do with Petra's disappearance, then they'd see who she really was! Desgraciadas, envidiosas! They couldn't bear it that Petra was beautiful, that she was favored. She'd never go back to Western Electronics, she told Abuela Teodora; she'd rather die. Abuela Teodora heard her mumbling insanely, making plans to get back at all of them, all those who hated her daughter.

"Ya," Abuela Teodora said to her, stroking her hair with her bony fingers. "You'll make yourself sick, and you won't be able to do anything for Petra. You have to sleep. Sleep, mija, sleep." She sat on the couch and cradled Flor in her arms, while Flor held onto the phone. Ester rested on a blanket at her mother's feet.

Mayela sat in an armchair, exhausted, her head drooped over her arm, sleeping heavily. Flor had called el Instituto, telling Señora Juana del Pilar that Petra had not returned home, and now la directora was on her way to pick up Mayela. As she drove through the streets of Nuevo Leon, Señora Juana del Pilar was happy about her decision to fire Narciso Odin. He had argued with her about allowing Mayela to leave with Petra.

That was the last time he would meddle in the child's affairs. She knew Mayela would be pleased that the old Huichol was gone.

A police car arrived at Flor's house, and an officer knocked on the door and said he was investigating the disappearance of Petra de la Rosa. Flor burst into tears and couldn't stop her body from shaking when she saw the officer. Ester ran to Abuela Teodora and hid in the old lady's arms. The officer stepped into the house boldly, determined to take control of the situation. He was short, with graying hair. Brusque and businesslike, he began questioning Flor.

"Tears won't help you at this time, señora. You must calm yourself, so we can start the investigation."

Flor wondered if he was the same officer who had told her over the phone that her daughter led a double life and had probably run off with her boyfriend. Flor explained to the officer everything she knew, trying to control her tears so she could finish talking to him. She mentioned Gustavo Rios and Agustín Miramontes Guzmán, but the man ignored both names, writing a couple of things down on a small notepad. He told Flor they would call the police in Montenegro and ask them to go to the house of Antonio Manriquez, Petra's boyfriend, as she might be there with him.

"No!" Flor shouted. "I already spoke to my sister in Montenegro. She's not there!"

The officer's face turned red with anger. "You listen to me! I've investigated these cases before. Girls lie. Their boyfriends lie. The girls get pregnant and want to hide and worry their families to death. Your daughter could at this very moment be at her boyfriend's house."

Flor was ready to attack the officer when she saw Luis Ledezma standing at the door. She hadn't noticed that the door was open and a crowd of neighbors had gathered outside. Flor ran to Luis, grabbing his hands, crying, and saw in his eyes the agony she felt. Luis's eyes narrowed when he saw the police officer. He wasn't intimidated by him and stared at him coldly.

"You have what you want, I suppose, and now you can leave," he said flatly.

"One more thing—I need her photo."

"What for—to add to your collection?"

The police officer's hand went to his gun, and Luis walked up to him with his chest puffed up.

"Do it," he said.

The police officer looked around at the women and Ester crying, and at the knot of neighbors growing larger every minute. "I should arrest you, but I've got too much to do right now. Don't think it won't happen, señor. Before long, you'll find yourself in jail. I can assure you of that."

"You'll rot there before I do," Luis said.

Abuela Teodora gave the police officer a photo of Petra. She was humble and spoke softly. Her voice touched all of them like a healing balm.

"I beg you to find her, por favor! Que Dios le bendiga. May God bless you for helping us." The officer stared at the photo in his hand, then turned on his heel and left without another word.

Hilo had everything prepared the way Agustín liked it. The room was dark and red, and the bed was ready. The camera scanned the room, making it impossible for Petra to hide. So far things had worked in their favor. The woman had been easy to lure. Vina Salcido was jealous of Petra for the promotion promised her, and besides that, her father had run into problems with the board of trustees of Western Electronics. With her father's life hanging in the balance, it was easy to convince Vina to assist them.

Hilo stared at Petra lying on the bed naked, his one eye straining. As a child Hilo had seen everything bright and sharp. He threaded his grandmother's needle with the finest thread, el hilo, in different colors, and was nicknamed "Hilo" for his skill. His grandmother was an amazing seamstress, and Hilo was her assistant. But Hilo's grandfather told him that sewing was women's work, and he was un joto, gay, for doing it. One day, in anger, his grandfather hit Hilo in the face while he was threading a needle, and the needle got stuck in one of his eyes. It was a miracle the needle had been removed from his eye, but still, Hilo had lost his vision. Eventually, a glass eye was made for him to make it appear as though he still had an eye, but the eye didn't fit well and had turned hazy, making it seem as if Hilo's eyes were two different colors.

Hilo stared at Petra lustfully. He couldn't touch her until Agustín gave him permission. She was the most beautiful of all the women Agustín had brought here, to this place hidden in his own house where he took pleasure in making women submit to him over and over again. El conquistador, he told them, the bastard child of Cortés. He violated them as often as he liked, cursed them, relieved himself on them, and forced electrical wires deep into their bodies, sending electrical currents to destroy their wombs, where he said were conceived the most despicable forms of life, clots of blood that must be destroyed. And Hilo recorded it all, his one good eye pressed up to the camera lens. He made a video that he played over and over again for Agustín and his friends, who sat and watched in the darkness, commenting on the most brutal parts, moaning with pleasure, and devouring the scenes with howls and shrieks that made Hilo feel as if he had descended into Hell.

El Cucuy couldn't be trusted with the filming. He got too excited about cutting up the women's bodies. He wanted to see blood and guts, gouge out their eyes, cut off their ears, their breasts, their arms and legs, split them open, and carve out their hearts. He would hold their hearts, still pumping, in his hand, then lift them over his head as if they were trophies. He wanted to wear their skin like the priests of the ancient god of war, Huitzilopochtli, who donned their victims' skin and danced exuberant, feasting on their blood.

In the end, after Agustín's appetite was appeased, he'd turn Petra over to Hilo and to el Cucuy. Hilo was patient. A woman like Petra would have never given him a second look. Yet, when he picked the women up, listless in his arms, held them in a blanket, walking out of the dark red room with them, the women thought he was saving them. They clung to him, begging to be rescued—if they could still speak. He liked it that they begged him for mercy.

Every day was the same for Petra. The same dark red room, Agustín's voice in her head, and pain, intense and alive in her body. Pain penetrated her. Every opening in her body was bloody and aching. There were bright lights that went on and off and hurt her eyes, blinding her. Her legs were held apart and extended, as if she was flying. Often she could feel chains on her legs, her throat, her wrists. There was blood issuing from her body, and more blood and fluids she tasted in her mouth. At times a rag was stuck deep into her throat, and her mouth filled with a taste so bitter she wanted to vomit but couldn't. Then there was darkness until the rag was pulled out of her mouth.

The woman came in silently. She felt her washing her, the water warm on her body. She cleaned away her feces, her urine. The woman gave her something bitter to drink, pressed fruit into her mouth. Petra had forgotten her body, had left it behind, watching it curiously from the headboard and from a window high up on the wall. From the window, sometimes, she saw a ray of sunlight on the floor and was mesmerized by its beauty. Then it vanished, and she was alone again. She saw her mother as if in a dream, kissing her forehead, and her father, his face now a hideous skull, and Abuela Teodora, her tiny face pleading. Ester's face appeared to her ghostly and frightened, while Nico watched her silently, angry. Antonio showed up, one finger pointed at her, accusing her for being unfaithful, hating her for what she had become, and then Luis Ledezma appeared like a soft white light at her right side, whispering to her. She couldn't understand what he was saying, although she strained to hear. She thought maybe he was giving her instructions on how to get out of the dark red room. He would tell her if he could. If anybody would help her, she knew it would be him. He loved her, of that she was sure. Petra formed a silent prayer, a cry that came from a secret place in her heart. *Help me, Luis, if you love me . . . help me now!*

She had a dream over and over again, a nightmare of el tsahuat-san, the huge serpent with seven heads that roamed the mountains of Montenegro looking for prey. Thunderbolts chased it, making sharp ragged waves of electricity appear in the sky. She heard a whistling sound, and when the serpent fell, lakes of blood were formed. The hideous heads of el tsahuatsan all bore the face of Agustín Miramontes Guzmán.

When Petra felt Agustín's body over hers, inflicting new pain, his howls and shrieks in her ears, she became like one of the crouching figures on the mountains of Montenegro and danced silent and exuberant within herself. Sometimes she climbed up to the dark chandelier and perched there, hidden among its shiny globes. And when he told her she would submit, and submit and submit, Petra resisted and became el Río Gris, fighting the pride and arrogance of the ancient conquistador. She became, once more, el mestizo rising, and she lived for another day.

One day, the woman whispered to Petra: "Give up. He wants your soul. You must surrender." She heard a man's voice tell the woman to shut up and realized the woman was being watched. Petra heard the woman's words, but didn't know how to surrender, except by not breathing. She left her body crouching high up on the dark chandelier to think about what she should do. One of her ankles was broken and her collar bone. Her left eye was swollen and shut tight, her nose was misshapen and bloody. Agustín owned her body but not her soul, never her soul! It was then she decided she would not breathe; she would make her heart stop in her body.

37 Harry got permission to leave Fort Bliss on Holy Thursday. He had been taking on every dirty job he could think of, working all sides, to make himself look good. He wanted a special leave so he could spend several days in Juárez. His aunt Dominica had called and told him that Evita was asking him to return to Juárez as soon as possible.

The sergeant wrote out Harry's pass in his office and told him he better watch himself—he looked like he was bewitched.

"These Mexican women only want one thing—to get an American to marry them, so they can come to the United States," he told Harry. "You're a fool to step into a trap like this, and you'll live to regret it."

Privately, the sergeant called Evita "Harry's Mexican whore," but to Harry's face, he called her his "girl in Juárez."

"You've got four days in Juárez, so take it easy. Go to church. Don't they have churches out there? Isn't this the night of the Last Supper. They believe all that—and more. Yeah, I can imagine what supper you'll be going to." He threw the weekend pass at Harry in disgust.

Then, without realizing the impact of his words, he said, "And, Harry, I don't want no international incident. Stay the hell out of trouble if you know what's good for you. Now, get out of here!"

Estevan knew his daughter was gone before Flor told him. For days he had felt sorrow like a fire burning unmercifully inside him. Flor walked into his hospital room leaning on her brother, Alvaro, with Antonio at her side. Susana was there, too, crying, holding onto Abuela Teodora's arm and hugging Ester as they walked in behind Flor. Alvaro and Antonio had driven all night without stopping. Alvaro, his eyes swollen and red from weeping, begged Flor to forgive him for bringing them to Juárez. Flor held Alvaro in her arms and told him it wasn't his fault. She had wanted to come as well—there was no other hope for Estevan.

Estevan saw their weary faces and his wife's terrible agony. He saw Abuela Teodora's eyes distant, filled with fear, and Ester, thin, pale, and shaking. Ester's nightmares had come true. He looked closely at all of them and saw in their eyes the truth: his daughter had joined las desaparecidas. She had disappeared, and perhaps she would never be found again. Estevan closed his eyes and let the disease in his body have its way. He let it shoot into his heart, like a silver bullet, and within hours it put his body into a deep coma.

Rita Canchola, a reporter from *El Diario*, came to the house to talk to Flor. She had been assigned the case of Petra's disappearance, along with three other stories she had to complete that day. She was pressed for time, and yet, feeling Flor's terrible agony, she listened attentively. She told Flor that the police officer who had started the investigation had told her that so far they had information from a security guard at Western Electronics, a man named José Barriga, who said he had seen Petra leave in a taxi on the day of her disappearance, driven by a man named Santigo Jiménez, also known as "Ponce." Ponce was a driver for women who worked for el Club Exotica. It was now rumored that Petra may have been a dancer at the club, leading a double life. The investigator mentioned that the car, a white Honda given to Petra by Agustín Miramontes Guzmán, could not be found. It was assumed that Ponce, or someone else who might have known Petra, was now in possession of the car.

Flor was sitting at the kitchen table with Alvaro and Antonio, listening to the reporter. She shook her head at everything the young woman said.

"It's not true! That's all a pack of lies! My daughter went to la maquiladora to meet with Señor Miramontes Guzmán and others and never came home. Gustavo Rios should know something about it. He's the one who got us the jobs in la maquiladora."

"We've questioned him. He says he knows nothing about Petra's disappearance, and certainly not about a meeting on a Saturday. And we questioned a woman, Vina Salcido, who worked next to your daughter in the same office. She was on her way to Buenos Aires to work in la maquiladora there and told us she knows nothing about it. She said the last time she saw Petra was on Friday afternoon when they left work to go home. As far as she knows, there was no meeting planned for Saturday."

"What about asking Miramontes Guzmán? If anyone should be questioned, it should be him! He must know what happened to Petra. Question him!"

Alvaro stood up, angry at all the reporter was saying.

"This is all a fabrication of the police. It's just like them to bend the truth to suit themselves and protect the guilty. It's rumored Miramontes Guzmán heads one of the most powerful cartels in Juárez, and my niece may now be in his power. Am I correct?"

Rita Canchola nodded her head and sighed deeply. "But there's no proof," she said. She didn't tell Alvaro that her editors at *El Diario* would now have to decide what they would say about the abduction. They couldn't accuse Miramontes Guzmán without serious consequences. One of their editors might end up assassinated. It had happened before.

"Do you know Amapola Nieto?" the reporter asked Flor.

"Yes, I know Amapola!"

"She said your daughter got into trouble the minute she started working at Western Electronics."

Flor's face reddened with anger at all el veijerio, the gossips, who had accused her daughter and made up lies, saying she was having affairs with men at la maquiladora.

"Amapola hated my daughter—don't you see? Petra's beautiful and intelligent. She's everything Amapola and all those ugly hags will never be." Flor put her head down on the table, crying, and Susana ran to her side.

"You know how women can be," Susana said. "Envious, hateful, and full of revenge when they think they're being set aside for someone else."

Antonio's face was sullen, gaunt. He looked at the reporter. "We were engaged to be married. We have to find her. She's everything I live for." He thought of Humberto Ornelas and what the gossips at la maquiladora were saying about Petra. He remembered the party in El Paso he had told her not to attend, but she had gone anyway. He was angry with her before he left for Montenegro and had tried to make up by writing her a love letter. But she had never responded. Now he wondered if there had been another man in Petra's life.

Antonio put his head in his hands. His shoulders trembled as he tried to hold back tears. In his mind Antonio saw Petra's beautiful face, her slender hands, his ring on her finger, and the way she had of smiling at him, sensually, honestly. She had belonged to him since they were children in Montenegro. He had never loved another woman—only Petra. Now he had fallen into a deep chasm without her.

Rita Canchola's eyes filled with tears. There was a part of her that wanted to place a call to Mexico City, talk to el Presidente himself, and ask him how he could stand by and watch innocent women being murdered and not send help. Rita Canchola knew that las mordidas, the money used to silence police and government officials, meant they would not be able to find out the truth about Petra's disappearance. She put her hand gently on Flor's shoulder.

"I'll do all I can," she said.

Agustín was having breakfast alone, reading through three newspapers, tearing them up as he read. Scraps of the papers landed at his feet and under the table. Hilo watched him from a distance, and when he saw him look up, he walked in and stood before him in silence.

"What?" Agustín asked.

"There's an American soldier asking questions about the woman." Hilo had been instructed never to use anyone's name. Names didn't matter to Agustín. He considered women his property and less than animals.

"Que no chinguen conmigo!" Agustín shouted at the top of his lungs. "Does this idiota think he's got something better because his ass is white? Is he ready to screw with us? I can have whatever whore I want! They can't do anything about it!"

Hilo stepped aside. He knew Agustín's temper. Agustín jumped up from the chair and with one hand knocked everything off the breakfast table. Plates, a coffeepot, food, everything landed on the floor. One of the women servants stood at the door but wouldn't come in until Agustín was gone. She knew there might be other things he wanted to destroy, and his rampage might extend to other rooms as well. Later, she'd clean everything up.

Agustín headed down the hall, cursing at the American soldier, making death threats against him. His angry outburst didn't fool Hilo. He knew Agustín was nervous about the American and didn't want the U.S. Army on his trail, but he didn't want to let Petra go either. He had her where he wanted her—totally surrendered, something he would never have from his wife, Gabriela LaFarge.

Harry attended Good Friday services with Evita at la Catedral and thought about the sergeant telling him, in a mocking tone, to go to church. The sergeant wouldn't believe him if he told him he had really gone to church. The services were solemn. The saints were all draped in black cloth, and there were hundreds of candles lit. Harry wasn't Catholic, so he sat on the bench and held Evita as she cried through the entire service. He watched the priests lie prostrate on the floor to honor the memory of Christ on the cross. People lined up along the middle aisle to kiss the feet of Christ on a big wooden cross at the altar.

When everyone had gone, Licha, the cleaning lady, came up to Evita. She called her Elena and asked why she was crying.

"I'm sad because Christ was murdered," she said.

Licha smiled and looked from Evita to the American soldier and wondered if Evita wasn't crying because el Americano was ready to dump her for someone else. She still thought Evita should have gone to el Instituto, where she could have attended school and would have avoided the hard life on the streets of Juárez.

After Licha left, Evita told Harry she had to talk to him about something very important. They went to a small restaurant, where Harry found a table for them in a corner of the place. Speaking slowly in Spanish, Evita told him that Petra had been kidnapped by Agustín Miramontes Guzmán, who was connected to one of the most powerful cartels in all of Juárez.

"How do you know this?" he asked her.

Evita lowered her head and suddenly looked pale and weary. "I saw him once when I was on the streets—I know it was him. He was with the girl I saw in the newspaper—you remember, Anita Barbara Ozuna. Mayela met his wife at her home, in el distrito Villa de las Rosas. I know this because his wife gave Mayela a photo of herself in the same dress Anita Barbara was wearing the night I saw her with him. That's what made me realize who he was. If it wasn't for that photo, I wouldn't know the truth. Please do something for Petra—whatever you can do—por favor, Haree!" Evita burst into tears and would not be comforted until Harry told her he would do all he could.

That night Harry called the *El Paso Times* and talked to one of the reporters. He told them he was an American soldier but couldn't say much more about himself than that. He wanted to report knowledge he had of the recent disappearance of a woman from Juárez, Petra de la Rosa. A reliable source had told him that a person associated with a drug cartel, Miramontes Guzmán, was responsible for her disappearance. Harry knew that what he was doing could cost him his life, but when he looked at the fear in Evita's eyes, he knew if he didn't do something, Petra might turn up dead like the girl in the newspaper.

In the morning, a reporter from the *El Paso Times* called Fort Bliss looking for the soldier who had called in with information on the Miramontes Guzmán cartel. By Easter Sunday, the MPs were looking for Harry in Juárez. They found him and had orders to escort him back to the base. When Harry arrived, the sergeant had his paperwork ready—he had been transferred to a military base in Georgia.

"Didn't I tell you, asshole, not to start no international incident? What an idiot!"

The sergeant was almost foaming at the mouth cursing Harry. He threw the transfer papers in his face and told him he wasn't gonna start no World War Three with the goddamn cartels from Juárez—not on his watch.

It was the phone call from his tío, Beltran, in Mexico City that convinced Agustín to let Petra go.

"Un incidente, a small affair is going on," his tío said. "And you will do something to make it all go away?" His uncle put it to Agustín as a question, but it was a demand—something that could not go unheeded.

"Are you listening?"

Agustín knew that if he didn't answer, Beltran would wait in stony silence until he did. "Listening," he said.

"We have un Americano, a common soldier, who's talked to someone from the *El Paso Times* and says he has information related to a cartel that operates in Juárez and is involved in the abduction of women."

There was an edge in Beltran's voice that Agustín had learned to dread—like his father's voice, an edge that drove him into fits of madness.

"Are you listening?"

"Listening."

"And Gabriela, your wife? So far away in France. I had my wife call her this morning and tell her how very sorry you are for all that's happened between the two of you and how much you miss her. You do miss her, don't you?"

Beltran waited in silence. In his mind, Agustín could see his tío's fat face, his eyes with the huge drooping lids looking into the distance as if he were watching the world go by, patiently, serenely.

Agustín told his tío what he wanted to hear. "Sí, of course."

"Excellent. And she's pregnant with your first baby—wonderful stuff for the newspapers and la tele. You know how they love us! Gabriela misses you. So I told her you'd be on your way to France tonight. As a matter of fact, I've already purchased your ticket. So you see, your marriage is saved until you decide otherwise. Do you understand?"

"I understand." Agustín knew Petra must come to an end. He would leave for France in a few hours, obeying Beltran's instructions. He was enraged at the American soldier who was making trouble for him, a nobody he could kill with his bare hands. He consoled himself by remembering he had videos of Petra and could watch them whenever he wanted.

That night, Agustín celebrated Petra's surrender by inviting two close friends, confidantes, who watched him as he tortured her with electrical currents that burned her insides but stopped short of killing her. One of the men was elderly, with graying hair and slanted eyes. The second was an American man, tall, imposing.

"What do you think, Arnold?" Agustín asked the American in perfect English.

"I'm surprised she's still alive!"

"I told her she'd be a shooting star—and well, these are the results!"

"It would be interesting," said the man with the slanted eyes, "to see if she could light up a room with all the electricity you've charged her with." And the three burst into laughter.

A man stood at the back of the room. Agustín told his two friends that Gustavo Rios couldn't take it.

"There he is!" he said, pointing to him, "A coward!" The men stared at him. "Sorry, Gustavo. I know you wanted her for yourself in Buenos Aires, but I just couldn't resist the temptation." Gustavo only turned away in disgust.

Hilo had sewn Petra's engagement ring into her left nipple, and said he was marrying her off to all of them. And to think she had never been invited to her own wedding, he added with a smirk.

Agustín called in Hilo to take Petra's body out. He didn't want her to die in his house. He hated to touch a dead body—so cold and clammy.

Petra watched them from her perch on the chandelier and saw beyond the walls of the house and out into the world where the sun still shone, and where marvelous birds of all colors roosted in the ancient ahuehuete trees and sang, joyfully, to the morning.

Close to midnight, a cleaning woman at Western Electronics found the body of Gustavo Rios behind his desk, lying in a pool of blood. Police were called and determined that Gustavo Rios had shot himself through the mouth. They told reporters they had proof that Gustavo Rios had been in love with Petra de la Rosa and had led her into the circle of acquaintances at el Club Exotica that had caused her disappearance and possibly her death.

Nico sat in a dark alley shivering, every bone in his body aching. He had heard the news about his sister. He had seen Petra's photo in *El Diario* and read his mother's plea for information related to her disappearance. Nico had never been so sick in his life. He had stopped doing the drugs that were tearing his body apart and was suffering intensely from withdrawal—la malilla. And now his heart was broken for his sister. He felt as if he was already in a grave. Nico stood up unsteadily, having decided to track down one of Los Trinquetes for drugs, when he saw Luis Ledezma's pickup truck speeding down the dark alley. He jumped at the truck as it looped into the alley across the street and climbed into the back. Instantly, Luis stepped on the brakes, and Nico flew out into the street. Luis was quickly over him with a gun.

"It's me . . . don't shoot! It's Nico!"

Luis lifted Nico up with one hand by the collar of his shirt. "Un idiota is what you are! Are you crazy, jumping into my truck like that!"

Luis's eyes were wild, but when he looked into Nico's eyes, he saw eyes just as wild and sick with la malilla—the shaking and fever of withdrawal from drugs. He looked at him with pity. Nico was still a child, and how it would break Petra's heart to see him in this condition.

"Chano—I'm looking for Chano," Luis said.

"I know where he is!"

Luis grabbed Nico and put him in the front seat. Nico directed him through dark streets to an empty lot, where a pile of rocks with wooden planks set on top formed a haphazard wall. Behind it all, sitting in a stupor, was Chano. Luis dove at his brother, and they scrambled in the dirt.

"You'll pay for this!" Luis shouted. He pointed his gun at Chano's head. "Tell me where she is, porque a mi me vale madre! I'll kill you! I have nothing to lose!"

Chano knew Luis would kill him. It didn't matter to him, except that deep in his mind came the image of his mother, wailing because Chano had been killed by his own brother. He tried to stand up, swayed, and fell to the ground. Between Nico and Luis, they lifted Chano up and threw him into the front seat.

"Las Lomas de Poleo," he said.

"Where in las Lomas—where? North, south, in el centro?" Luis was desperate. Las Lomas was a huge area that could take him a day or more to cover.

"I'll show you."

Petra sensed someone lifting her up, holding her in a blanket, taking her away. With her one good eye, she saw an outline that looked like Hilo. Petra knew Hilo was taking her out to kill her. The image of her father's face appeared, and she remembered his words, *If I die in Juárez, bury me in Montenegro.* Now she understood the urgency of his words and whispered them. Hilo bent down to listen.

"She's telling me she loves me," he said, laughing. "I knew it!"

"What about me?" another voice said. And Petra saw the hideous blur of el Cucuy as he pressed close to her. "You stink," he said. "All whores do."

Petra began to pray, telling God to take her as quickly as He could. She prayed without words as an unbelievable calm came over her. A light, bright and luminous, descended on her, and she saw a beautiful figure, an angel, who touched her gently and made her breathing go quiet. She felt a flutter in her chest, her heart barely beating.

Hilo threw her into the trunk of the Honda. It had been decided that they would get rid of the car along with Petra's body. Hilo drove the Honda slowly to las Lomas de Poleo. El Cucuy followed him in the dark brown sedan. It was a moonless night, the air heavy with the smell of a noxious odor. El Cucuy had his knife at his side. Now he could do with her whatever he wanted. As he saw it, they had garbage to dump in las Lomas, and the job would be done before the night was over.

They arrived and chose a spot that led to a huge ditch and a ledge where they could hide her car. It was a place where el Cucuy had hidden bodies before—even the body of his own sister. No one searched that far. Hilo opened the trunk and got Petra out. He put his ear up to her breast and told el Cucuy that she was dead and he wouldn't touch a corpse. He was disappointed; he should have raped her before he took her out of the house.

El Cucuy grabbed the blanket with Petra's body and threw it roughly on the ground. He got his knife out of its sheath and started cutting her, making a slit under her ribs. Hilo yelled at him, telling him they had company. In the distance he saw a truck, its headlights blinking wildly, turning into las Lomas. It could be a setup—Agustín himself, sending other men to kill them to prove his innocence. Without a word, Hilo and el Cucuy got into the brown sedan and drove away without turning on the car's headlights.

It took them another hour of searching, as Chano said he couldn't remember if it was this far or closer. By the time they reached the spot, it was dawn and the sun was rising over the horizon. It was el domingo de Pascua, Easter Sunday, in las Lomas de Poleo. The gray light illuminated the desolate sand, and the silence of the desert buzzed in Luis's ears. He looked up at the sky thinking he heard birds calling, but no birds appeared. He heard something but couldn't grasp what it was. He moved closer to the sound and heard a human voice gasping for breath but still singing. He didn't recognize the words. He moved closer to a ledge that led to a rocky ditch and saw the white Honda. Next to it, naked and lying on the ground in the shape of a cross, was Petra.

With her one good eye, Petra saw the morning light approaching, and she heard Abuela Teodora's voice in her ear whispering, *Sing, Petra, sing to the morning.* Abuela Teodora put her hand tenderly on Petra's shoulder, and they walked out together to the mountains of Montenegro. The crouching figures were ablaze with the rising sun, and they sang the ancient song:

Iwéra rega chukú kéti Ono
Mápu tamí mo nesériga ináro sinibísi rawé
Ga'lá kaníliga bela ta semáribo
Si'néame ka o'mána wichimoba eperéame
Népi iwérali bela ta ásibo
Kéti ono mápu tamí neséroga ináro ne

Né ga'lá kaníliga bela ta narepabo
Uchécho bilé rawé mápu kéti Onó nijí
Ga'lá semá rega bela ta semáripo
Uchécho bilé rawé najata je'ná wichimobachi
Népi ga'lá iwérali bela ko nijísibo
Si'néame ka mápu ikí ta eperé je'ná kawírali

Uchécho bilé rawé bela ko ju
Mápu rega machiboo uchécho si'nú ra'íchali
Uchécho bilé rawé bela ko ju
Mápu ne chapiméa uchécho si'nú 'nátali
Népi iwéraga bela 'nalína ru
Uchúpa ale tamojé si'néame pagótami

Echiregá bela ne nimí wikaráme ru
Mápu mo tamí nesériga chukú sinibísi rawé
Echiregá bela ne nimí iwérali ásima ru
Mápu ketási mo sewéka inárima siníbisi rawé
Népi iwériga bela mo nesérima ru
Mápu ikí uchúchali a'lí ko mo alewá aale

*   *   *

Be strong father sun,
you who daily care for us.
Those who live on earth are living well.
We continue giving strength to our father,
who fills our days with energy and light.

With great joy we salute our father
with one more day of life.
We are living well following one more day on earth
as you light our way.

One more day to learn new words,
one more day to think new thoughts,
giving you strength you in turn
give energy to your brothers.

Thus I will sing
to you who daily care for me.
Thus will I give you strength
so you will not be discouraged.
With all your strength
care for those you have created
and given the breath of life.

Luis picked Petra up gently in the blanket and with Nico beside him carried her back to his truck. They were sobbing as the sun rose into the sky over las Lomas de Poleo and Petra stopped singing. An enormous sigh hung in the air, growing louder as Petra reached up and gently touched Luis Ledezma's face.

38 Rita Canchola made her way to the hospital as Agustín's plane took off for France. She had been called by Tío Alvaro, who had promised to keep in touch with any news of Petra. As she approached the hospital entrance, Rita's throat tightened, knowing all she would have to face—the agony of the family and Petra's condition—the destruction she knew had been inflicted on her body. There was no telling if she was even still alive. Rita quickened her step, almost running, then realized she didn't know what room Petra was in. The hospital seemed deserted on Easter Sunday, and there was no one stationed at the front desk. She spun around in a circle, uncertain where to go.

In the distance she saw a man approaching, tall, imposing.

"Rita?"

"Sí!"

He took huge strides toward her, and she knew it was Tío Alvaro.

"This way," he said, putting his arm through hers. He led her up a stairway and into a hallway where patients were treated for trauma, hanging onto threads of life. Nurses made the rounds in a rhythmic motion that made it seem as if they were doves, their white uniforms fluttering everywhere.

Behind one of the doors lay Petra. Nearby, holding onto one another, were Flor, Abuela Teodora, Susana, Antonio, Luis, and Nico.

Tío Alvaro looked from one to another.

"What news?" he asked.

Rita held her breath as she heard one of the nurses say, "She's fighting for her life. She's strong. She was found in time and God willing . . ." Her voice trailed off as she walked into Petra's room.

"Dios quiera," Abuela Teodora repeated, and she chanted prayers under her breath, holding tight to Flor's hand.

There was nothing more to say. Rita asked the family no questions as she embraced each one, feeling as if she were part of them. She sat down next to Luis on a couch and listened to him tell her how he and Nico had discovered Petra in las Lomas de Poleo, singing as Abuela Teodora had taught her to do.

Las Lomas, she thought, the sinister desert, the bodies hidden in shallow graves, the mummified faces she had seen in photographs. Rita closed her eyes and sighed. She should leave now, let someone else write up the story. Last year one of the reporters had been assassinated, writing on something much less important than what she was now facing. She looked at the clock and knew that her boss was now at his desk at *El Diario*. He was always there—there were no holidays for him. She excused herself and went to the phone at a nearby desk and dialed his number.

"Petra de la Rosa's alive. I'll write up her story for you."

There was silence on the other end. Then finally he said, "I'll print it."

It took three weeks for Petra to get strong enough to be released from the hospital. By then Antonio had gone back, broken-hearted, to Montenegro. He had visited her once, twice, then could not see her again. His pain was too great, a dark ulcer that ate him up from the inside.

"Don't think about it," Abuela Teodora told Petra. "Ni lo pienses. Ya, God will heal. It will take time, but God always heals."

They had buried her father in Montenegro, Flor told Petra, just as he had asked to be if he died in Juárez.

"In peace," she added, smiling. "We buried him in peace. He lived long enough to know you had been found."

Epilogue: Mujeres Unidas de Juárez

Ten years after the abduction of Petra de la Rosa, Rita Canchola found herself once again assigned to her case, this time as a special reporter for a television station airing news of the Juárez murders from Mexico City. Before boarding her flight to Juárez, she made one last call on her cell phone, telling her live-in maid not to forget to give her three-year-old daughter, Dulce, a dose of her cough medicine before bedtime. Her husband, Felipe Ontiveros, was off on a trip of his own, as an architect for a busy corporation in Acapulco. Thankfully, he would be returning before she did, as Dulce didn't like them to be gone for very long. Rita was glad her husband wasn't at home when she flew out, as the news of her assignment had come as a surprise for both of them. That morning, Felipe had been in Acapulco and unable to return to try to stop her.

"I don't want you to go," he had said firmly over the phone. "That door was shut long ago. Why open it again?"

"Because the murders are still going on! You know that, Felipe. This is the crime of the century—and we can't ignore the victims and their families. How can we live in peace if we do? This must all come to an end!"

"You're putting yourself in danger again, Rita. You're married now; we have Dulce—"

Rita broke in. "That why I'm going, Felipe. For Dulce. She'll grow up and have to face fear, and I don't ever want her to run. If we stand together, we'll become stronger; if we do nothing, we become weaker. I want her to be as brave as Petra de la Rosa. Just like that. Facing a firing squad if she has to and not running, and best of all, living to tell about it!"

As she leaned back in her seat on the plane, Rita remembered the night she had been accosted by the Miramontes bodyguard, Hilo, whose real name was Benito Salas, and the monstrous figure of el Cucuy. They had blindfolded her and driven her to an unknown location, marching her to a ditch they said they had dug for her if she talked. Her days were numbered, they had told her, if she did the story related to Agustín Miramontes Guzmán. If Rita could have looked into the future that dark night, she would have seen that Agustín would be the one to suffer an assassination in France, and the hideous young man, el Cucuy, would be killed in prison a few years later. The only one to survive that night would be herself and Hilo, and no one knew if he was dead or alive.

Rita had believed herself among the dead when she felt the cold hard barrel of a gun against her head and heard el Cucuy's raspy laughter. They had left her there after giving her a beating—not enough to kill her, but enough to make her understand that it was nothing for them to kill her. Finally, Rita had crawled up the ditch and made her way back to the road, seeking help from a family who, mercifully, was driving down the desolate road to take their sick child to a hospital.

She still remembered the agony of Petra's family the night she had interviewed them in la colonia Nuevo Leon. Petra's mother, grandmother, her fiancé Antonio, her uncle Alvaro and aunt Susana, Petra's friend, Lola, her little sister, Ester—all of them frightened, their sorrow reaching for her, threatening to submerge her in its eerie depths. And later, she had faced the tormented faces of Evita, Luis, Mayela, and Petra's brother, Nico. She had spoken to the American soldier, Harry Hughes, by phone months later, after discovering that it was his efforts that had stopped the Miramontes cartel. Later, she had learned from Petra that if it had not been for Luis Ledezma, she would have never been rescued in time, and without Abuela Teodora and her gift of song the whole story would have been forgotten as yet another brutal murder of a young woman in Juárez.

It had all seemed unreal to Rita, the night of Petra's abduction, as if seen through a mirror in a house of horrors, dark and distorted. Everything had been distorted for Rita in those days. Her life was out of control. Night turned into day for her, day into night, and she lost track of time, working up to fourteen hours a day on news stories she could never hope to complete. She was working as hard and fast as she could, chasing nightmares down the streets of Juárez. At night in her dreams, she seemed to hear the cries of mothers weeping for their daughters. Often, there were photographers at her side, documenting the gruesome evidence of bodies disfigured beyond recognition and mummified faces she had to learn to forget. She ran from one story to the next, without any time to do her own mourning for the deaths she was encountering. At times, she had been days ahead of the police, often discovering clear evidence as to who had committed the crimes and having to put up with botched police investigations, sealed with silence by mordidas that filled the palms of corrupt police officials who had lost their souls to the devil. She was only a reporter, she was told, nothing more. Her testimony could be discounted by the police. She had a role to play, one step in Hell and one step in a sanity she had created for herself, a world where she lived with one hope—that someday it would all end: the pain, the darkness, the memory of so many wounded hearts.

And now, the organization Mujeres Unidas de Juárez was honoring their foundress, Petra de la Rosa Ledezma, with festivities, dignitaries, celebrities, and world news coverage. It would happen. Joy would yet come to chase the darkness away, and Rita Canchola was determined not to miss it.

"Rita! Over here!" It was Petra, calling to her from across the crowded room of people looking for seats. Flashbulbs were exploding everywhere, and a TV camera stood in the center aisle. People were lined up to shake Petra's hand and give her an embrace. Behind her was displayed a banner in bright colors embroidered with an emerald butterfly and the words: MUJERES UNIDAS DE JUÁREZ.

And underneath the name were words that Rita didn't understand, written in Rarámuri, the language of the Tarahumaras.

> Iwéra rega chukú kéti Ono
> Mápu tamí mo nesériga ináro sinibísi rawé
> Ga'lá kaníliga bela ta semáribo

Si'néame ka o'mána wichimoba eperéame
Népi iwérali bela ta ásibo
Kéti ono mápu tamí neséroga ináro ne

Né ga'lá kaníliga bela ta narepabo
Uchécho bilé rawé mápu kéti Onó nijí
Ga'lá semá rega bela ta semáripo
Uchécho bilé rawé najata je'ná wichimobachi
Népi ga'lá iwérali bela ko nijísibo
Si'néame ka mápu ikí ta eperé je'ná kawírali

Uchécho bilé rawé bela ko ju
Mápu rega machiboo uchécho si'nú ra'íchali
Uchécho bilé rawé bela ko ju
Mápu ne chapiméa uchécho si'nú 'nátali
Népi iwéraga bela 'nalína ru
Uchúpa ale tamojé si'néame pagótami

Echiregá bela ne nimí wikaráme ru
Mápu mo tamí nesériga chukú sinibísi rawé
Echiregá bela ne nimí iwérali ásima ru
Mápu ketási mo sewéka inárima siníbisi rawé
Népi iwériga bela mo nesérima ru
Mápu ikí uchúchali a'lí ko mo alewá aale

Rita walked up to Petra, who was standing next to her husband, Luis Ledezma. She had seen Petra's photo when she had first organized the group of women from both sides of the border into an alliance of courageous followers who took to the streets of Juárez determined to help in any way they could to end the murders. Petra was tall, slim, dressed in a bright pink outfit, her hand resting lightly on a walking cane. There was a light around her, Rita thought, suddenly wishing she had one of her favorite photographers with her, someone who could capture Petra's radiance.

"This is my husband, you remember Luis? And my cousin Evita and her husband, Harry Hughes, over there." Petra pointed to a couple, a petite and well-dressed woman next to a tall American. "And over there, my Tía Susana and my Tío Alvaro. Alvaro's already eating—just like my tío! He's been the one to hold us all together. As you know we lost Abuela Teodora two years ago. The song she taught me is there!" she said, pointing to the words written in Rarámuri. "The words saved my life, you know. And that little emerald butterfly, it has special meaning for Evita."

"Yes, I remember what Luis told me about the song," Rita said.

"Ay, mi abuela, so precious to me! She lies beside mi papi, in Montenegro. There's room for us all. We all want to be buried next to one another." There were tears in Petra's eyes.

"And all these people!" Rita said, looking around in amazement. "And you—you look like an angel!"

A photographer stepped up to Petra. "May I take your picture with your friend?"

Petra smiled broadly, pulling Luis into the picture, and a beautiful young girl. "Ester!" Petra said. "And Nico! Hurry! Come and have your picture taken." Nico came up, tall and handsome, and stood next to Luis.

"Lola—my friend—you remember her? She's the director of our women's shelter. We now have two shelters in Juárez and have plans to extend to three more cities this year. There she is, talking to some reporters." Rita saw a woman dressed in a business suit speaking to several reporters. Lola heard Petra's voice and turned. "One picture!" Petra called to her. "Hurry!"

"Mamá, por favor, come—Rita's here!" Petra said. Flor walked up and embraced Rita, who felt Flor's tears on her cheek and remembered her face, a mask of agony, so many years ago.

"Mayela!" Petra called to a young Indian girl dressed in a bright blue dress, her hair up in braids, "Ven, we need to take your picture!"

"Evita, Harry!" Petra and Luis said at the same time. Everyone laughed, and Luis kissed Petra's cheek. Evita pulled Harry's hand as she stood next to Petra; Harry stood behind everyone, conscious of his height.

"We're ready!" Petra said, and they all smiled as the photographer snapped the picture.

One of the television reporters approached Petra. "Senator Garcia is here," he said, speaking into a handheld microphone, "and representatives from everywhere, including the Governors of Chihuahua, Texas, New Mexico, California, and Arizona. Senator Garcia says he has arranged for a Senate committee in Washington DC to hear testimony from your organization on the murders still being committed in Juárez. Do you have a comment?"

For a moment Rita Canchola felt like taking out her notepad and writing down what Petra had to say. Then she hesitated, knowing that whatever Petra had to say, she had already said with her heart.

About the Author

Stella Pope Duarte was born and raised in la Sonorita Barrio in South Phoenix. She started her literary career in 1995 after she had a dream in which her deceased father related to her that her destiny was to become a writer. She is the recipient of two creative writing fellowships from the Arizona Commission on the Arts, for *Fragile Night* (Bilingual Review Press, 1997), a collection of short stories, and her novel *Let Their Spirits Dance* (HarperCollins, 2002). A graduate of Arizona State University, Ms. Duarte has taught extensively in elementary through university classroom settings. Her work has won awards and honors nationwide, and she is recognized as a dedicated advocate for human rights. In 2004 she received the Barbara Deming Memorial Fund Award for an excerpt from *If I Die in Juárez*. Ms. Duarte is a highly sought-after inspirational speaker for audiences of all ages on topics related to her work, as well as on issues related to women's rights, culture, diversity, Chicano/Latino history, and storytelling.

Library of Congress Cataloging-in-Publication Data

Duarte, Stella Pope.
  If I die in Juárez / Stella Pope Duarte.
    p. cm. – (Camino del sol)
  ISBN 978-0-8165-2667-3 (pbk. : alk. paper)
    1. Poor women—Fiction.   2. Women—Mexico—
Fiction.   3. Women—Crimes against—Mexico—
Ciudad Juárez—Fiction.   4. Murder—Mexico—Ciudad
Juárez—Fiction.   5. Ciudad Juárez (Mexico)—Fiction.
I. Title.
PS3554.U236I38   2008
813'.54—dc22   2007026134